Cold As Ice

WILDER WOLVES
BOOK ONE

LAUREA MATTHEWS

Cover Design: Books and Moods, www.booksandmoods.com
Character Artwork: Bruna Garret
Copy Edit: April Editorial, www.april-editorial.com
Proofreading: Bonnie Macleod, www.editsbybonnie.com

This is a work of fiction, created without the use of AI technology. Any names, characters, places, or incidents are products of the author's imagination and used in a fictitious manner. Any resemblance to actual people, places, or events is purely coincidental or fictional.

First Edition

ISBN: 979-8-9985032-2-1

Also by Laurea Matthews

The Bad at Love duology

Little Do You Know

Almost

The Reckless Love series

Chasing After You

Before You

For anyone who has been through hell and back, but still believes in their happy ever after.
And if you aren't quite there yet, I'll believe in one for you.

Author's Note

I could not be more proud of this book, but I also recognize it includes heavy topics that can be difficult to read. *Cold As Ice* is first and foremost a love story, but it does focus on the healing of two imperfect individuals who have experienced trauma at the hands of people they believed loved them. If you do not wish to read through the content warnings, you may skip to the first chapter of *Cold As Ice*.

A lot of love and care went into writing this story to give Jack and Alondra the happy ending they deserve, and I hope you'll agree.

This book does contain scenes that include on-page scenes of domestic violence and discussions around previous experiences in an abusive relationship. Additionally, *Cold As Ice* includes mentions and flashback scenes of Jack's childhood where he witnessed his mother in an abusive relationship with his father.

If you or a loved one are experiencing abuse, please visit https://www.thehotline.org/ or reach out to the national hotline for help: *1-800-799-7233*.

CHAPTER 1

Alondra

"HE'S STARING AT YOU!" Macy yelps, grabbing onto my arm, causing me to jump.

"Macy, seriously?" I ask, looking at her in disbelief. *What the hell is she talking about?*

"That guy over there," she says, pointing to a booth in the back, making it glaringly obvious that we've seen the guy with light brown hair and striking pale eyes. Even from all the way over here, I can tell he's handsome. Yet, for some reason, he looks familiar, but I can't put my finger on where I know him from.

His mouth curves at the corners, promising that everything about him is trouble I don't need in my life. I look away, rolling my eyes as I order another beer. "He's staring at you, hot stuff. You should go talk to him," I suggest, as the bartender slides me another bottle, and I push the lime all the way through the top of the opening. Lime makes everything better, but anything is better than standing here sober while my cousin and best friend attempt to get over her *now* ex-boyfriend.

Realistically, they'll be back together within a few days, but my hope is this time the breakup might stick. There's definitely a reason everyone says the best way to get over someone is to get under somebody else, and while I wouldn't normally push her directly into the arms of another guy, anyone would be better than the pretentious prick she's been stuck in this endless cycle with.

Maybe I recognize him from class, but if he's the guy I'm thinking of, he's usually flocked by girls. Right now, sitting at a table surrounded by guys, he doesn't look quite as intimidating.

Macy scoffs, her shoulders slumping as I glance in her direction. "As if. Why don't *you* go talk to him?"

"Because I don't *want* to. Tonight is about you." I'm nowhere near ready to put myself out there again—I'm not sure if I ever will be. I think Bradley might have permanently broken the part of me that is capable of trusting another person.

I think Bradley might have broken me.

She rolls her dark eyes, framed by lashes I would kill for. "Al, it's also about getting you out of your comfort zone, and let's be realistic, he's out of my league. You should go over there. It's been almost a year since . . . you know? Maybe it's time to get back in the saddle," Macy suggests, and I take a long drink of my beer.

Yeah. I do know, but I'm not ready to have this conversation. I figured it was only a matter of time until she pressed the issue, but it's not happening tonight.

"Thanks, but no thanks," I say, trying not to let it sour my entire mood. I reach forward to twirl one of her strawberry waves, succeeding in making her smile. "Macy, you're hot as hell, and any guy would be lucky to have you, especially one who looks like him. Chad's a fucking loser who never deserved you in the first place."

"I'm definitely looking at him," she muses, ignoring my comment about Chad. He's the source of a lot of our arguments, and every time Macy convinces me to give him another chance, he shows exactly why I shouldn't.

Macy has always struggled with her body image, and while she used to be quick to point out the things she saw as flaws, the therapist she saw in high school helped her fall in love with herself instead of constantly comparing herself to others. She eats healthily and exercises regularly, and while there are ups and downs, she seems to be doing at loving herself. Until Chad, anyway. There are more than a couple of reasons I hate him, but the biggest one of all is the way he makes her second guess herself. Also, who names their kid Chad? It's almost like his parents were asking for him to grow up and be an asshole with that name.

I follow her gaze to the table where the guy is still watching us, and I grimace before turning back around to wait until I have the bartender's attention again.

"Can I get two shots of vodka?" I ask once she looks my way, hoping a little liquid courage will do us both some good.

She nods, quickly pouring the shots as the music grows a little louder from someone in the back messing with the juke-box. "Thanks," I say, smiling warmly at her.

"I should be thanking you. The guy at the end over there is refusing to get the hint I'm not interested because I keep serving him drinks," she says, tilting her head in the direction of a guy who has the nerve to look more self-absorbed than the one at the table.

"Does he not realize it's your job to pour the drinks?" Macy asks, a small dose of laughter slipping from her.

The bartender chuckles, sliding the shots in front of us. "Probably not. Men like to think the world revolves around them."

Macy and I clink the tiny glasses together, but when I tilt my head back to down the shot in one go, she nudges me, causing some of the clear liquid to spill into my mouth before I'm ready.

"He's coming over here!" The liquor burns as it hits the back of my throat, and I sputter, coughing to clear it as she has the nerve to look at me confused when it's her fucking fault I'm choking in the first place. "What's wrong with you?" she whispers, just as a tall guy leans against the empty spot on the counter behind her.

I cough, blinking back the tears forming in my eyes. *I'm going to murder Macy, and I won't even feel an ounce of guilt over it.*

"You okay?" he asks, tilting his head at me, and I hate seeing how much prettier he is up close.

"Perfect," I answer, my voice a rasp as I clear it one more time. "Do you need something?"

"Can I buy y'all a drink?" he asks, his voice slow and smooth, oozing confidence with the added lilt of a subtle Southern accent, and Macy melts.

"No, thanks," I say at the same time Macy nods.

She glares at me. "Al, be nice," she scolds.

Fine. I paste the sweetest smile I can on my face, batting my lashes at him. "No, thank you."

He has the nerve to laugh, his smile brightening his entire face. "Well, Al, that was much nicer. What are y'all having?"

"Vodka soda," Macy says, and I sigh. *I suppose it won't matter. I already have a half-full one sitting in front of me.*

"Ultra with a lime."

He runs a hand through his short chestnut hair, and I ignore the way the simple movement causes his bicep to flex, making my stomach flutter despite all the reasons my brain is reminding me why it shouldn't matter how nice his arms are.

Pretty boys aren't worth the price my heart has already paid in heartbreak and everything else the façade of love has cost me.

I learned my lesson. Keep my head down, focus on class, and avoid my dad and his players as much as humanly possible. So far, I've succeeded at all of the above.

The bartender's smile appears to be amused as her gaze

bounces from me to Macy to whatever the hell this guy's name is. I'm not sure I feel bad about the guy at the end of the bar anymore as she takes the order. *Just kidding, I do, but I think she'd take pity on me now instead of finding this funny.*

"I haven't seen two ladies as pretty as y'all around here in a long time," he says, and I down the other shot of vodka since Macy still has yet to take it. I grimace, but the burn is much needed to get through this conversation.

"Al is looking to get out of her comfort zone and back in the saddle. I heard from a friend in class that Twin City is the bar to be at, so here we are," Macy says, offering me up on a silver platter.

I snap my jaw shut, wondering if she realizes just how easy it would be for me to shove her off the barstools we're perched on.

His light eyes, which I can now identify as a pale blue, shift to me, interest flaring as he cocks his head to the side. "Is that right?"

I'm going to kill her.

Macy must be forgetting that her room is across the hall from mine, and I could smother her with a pillow while she sleeps peacefully.

I don't bother responding, instead choosing to take a sip of my drink. The warmth of the first shot and the beer I already had are causing a fuzzy feeling in my body. The second shot hasn't hit me yet, but there's no way I'm going to finish both bottles in front of me. I need to be done drinking before I make any stupid decisions.

"I'm going to the bathroom. You'll keep an eye on her, won't you?" Macy asks him, before giving me a smile, sealing her fate.

She's dead to me. I'm actually going to kill her. Tonight was about finding someone for her to hook up with, not me.

"Cross my heart and hope to die."

Macy slides off the stool, disappearing just as I'm tempted to bang my head on the counter.

"You can go back to your buddies. I'm not interested," I say, hoping it comes across as venomous as I intend.

Instead, he slides into the now-empty seat, and the sheer mass of his body should intimidate me, but my radar isn't going off. If anything, I'm tempted to appreciate the way his dark shirt hugs him in all the right places. I haven't been interested in anyone in a long time, and I definitely don't want to be interested in him.

Angling toward me, he smiles, teasing at a dimple on one side, making me curious if there's one to match on the other. "I'm Jack. What does Al stand for?"

"Well, Jack, I'm afraid that information is classified."

He laughs, the other dimple making an appearance as I try *really* hard not to stare at the strong column of his neck or the dusting of stubble covering his jaw. "Allie?" he guesses, studying me for a reaction as I tap my fingers on the neck of the cold bottle. I raise my eyebrows at him, and he shakes his head. "Alex?"

I shrug, not planning on telling him my actual name, and Jack shifts closer to me, making my head spin. *Seriously, what the hell is he still doing over here with me?*

"Alex, I think you're beautiful."

A short laugh escapes me as I drag my finger over the condensation on the glass. "Does that line normally work for you?"

He chuckles, shaking his head, allowing me to catch a glimpse of silver around his neck before it disappears beneath the collar of his shirt.

"Usually, but lucky for you, I'm a fan of the coy act too."

"It's not coy if I'm actually not interested," I point out, but I'm entertained at the very least by this entire encounter. Or maybe I'm lying to myself because I don't want to want him.

Jack leans forward, and I find myself angling toward him

as well, waiting to hear what comes from him next. *It's definitely the alcohol talking now.* "Darlin', you're making me look bad in front of my friends," he teases, and I laugh, hating that I'm enjoying this—*even just a little bit.*

"Boo hoo."

His dimple winks at me as he smiles, lowering his voice. "My buddies will never let me hear the end of it if I walk away from you without a kiss, but I have a feeling your friend won't let you leave either unless she thinks something happened between us. So, what do you say to getting out of your comfort zone and saving me from public humiliation?"

As much as I don't want to admit Jack's probably right, I'm afraid he is. I know if I really want to put my foot down, Macy and I would leave in a heartbeat, but at the very least, I don't think I'd hate kissing Jack. My body is reacting to him more than it has to anyone in a long time, and kissing Jack doesn't mean trusting him.

There are a hundred reasons why I shouldn't kiss him, but maybe I don't want to think for once. I can blame this on the alcohol tomorrow.

"One shot, buddy. Do your worst," I say as he steps off the stool to tower over me. I pull my lower lip into my mouth, trying not to gasp when Jack lifts his hand to tuck some of my long, dark hair out of my face.

His blue eyes drop to my mouth, and his touch skates along the back of my neck, angling my head up to meet him. "I wasn't pulling a line on you when I said you're beautiful."

"Sorry if I don't exactly believe yo—" Jack silences me by slanting his mouth over mine, and my eyes flutter shut while I lean into him. I'm highly aware of how his fingertips are gently holding my head as Jack's lips move unhurried against mine.

I rest my hand on his chest, feeling the warmth of his skin through the soft material of his shirt as Jack sweeps his tongue over my bottom lip. I open my mouth, letting his tongue explore further as I respond by curling my fingers into his shirt, tugging him closer.

He rumbles a delicious sound from the back of his throat, and it's a great kiss. Maybe better than great, but it's over before I can decide, as Jack pulls away a few moments later. "How was my worst?" he asks, oozing confidence, but I don't miss the way his voice wobbles, telling me he enjoyed the kiss as much as I did.

I look at my hand, still gripping his shirt, making a show of removing it to wipe my mouth on the back of my hand, as if it's enough to erase the electric feeling of our kiss. "Solid three."

"You're killing me, Alex." Jack's head tips back as a laugh escapes him, his handsome features crinkling with joy, and I can't help the smile that forms on my face.

"Sorry, Jack. Maybe you'll do better with the next poor girl you solicit at the bar to keep your friends from making fun of you."

His thumb gently strokes the back of my neck, sending shivers down my spine, but Jack catches me by surprise when he leans in to graze his lips over mine once more. "Can I get your number? Maybe I can convince you I can do better than a three." His head dips again, and his breath tickles my ear as Jack's deep voice tempts me. *"In all areas."*

Yeah, I have no doubt. I'm afraid to let myself wonder if this is what kissing Jack feels like, then how much better would everything else be with him compared to my previous experiences? Yet, it's also a stark reminder of how different I am, because I have no business entertaining this idea.

"My number's reserved for men who earn at least a seven, which makes this a one-time thing."

He shakes his head, taking a step back as if somehow understanding the thoughts running through my mind. "Guess it makes me selfish to say I hope I'll see ya again, Al."

"Don't hold your breath," I joke, and he walks back to his friends, his shoulders shaking with more laughter.

My phone ringing at full blast pulls me out of my dreamless sleep, and I fumble for it blindly in the dark room. It slips out of my grasp, clattering to the floor.

"Alondra, answer your fucking phone before my head explodes," Macy groans from her spot in the bed next to me.

"Maybe you should have slept in your bed," I groan when I finally grasp where it fell. "Hello?" I answer, my head beginning to throb.

"Good morning to you too," my dad says, and I wipe my eyes with my hand, sitting up. My blackout curtains are working a little too well.

"What time is it?"

He sighs, his disappointment clear, which is exactly what I need this morning. "Eight. I need you to stop by my office this morning," he says, and I bite back my groan. I have no interest in going to his office.

"Seriously? I have plans with—"

"It's not optional, Al." Great, he's using his coach tone with me, and when he's like this, it's not worth arguing.

"I'll be there in an hour."

"The team will be in at nine thirty, but we should be done by then."

"Got it." I hang up quickly, and the sound of Macy's snoring fills the room again. *I wish I could fall asleep that fast.* I lie there for a moment, recalling how Jack's lips felt against mine. Completely sober, I know what a bad idea it was kissing him, but I also can't deny it was an amazing kiss. Far better than the three I told him it was.

But sober me remembers where I recognize him from, and it's the class we have together.

Jack has never noticed me before, so hopefully our brief kiss doesn't change anything.

I drag myself out of bed to shower, regretting the shots more than I did last night as I wash in the dark, going through the motions of muscle memory. I wince when I have to flip them on, but I'm glad I did because the raccoon eyes I'm rocking from not taking the five minutes to remove my makeup last night are horrendous. The best I can muster right now is semi-presentable, and I hope Dad can't tell I'm hungover. It's like a sixth sense for him after all the years he's been coaching at Wilder University, he always seems to know when I've been drinking.

I falter as I enter the building where I used to spend every day, but by the time I reach Dad's office, I've composed myself. He's already sitting at his desk, flipping through his prized playbook, but he at least smiles when he sees me. "I feel like this is the first time I've seen you in weeks."

Because it is. I'm surprised he noticed with how busy I'm sure he's been with pre-season games.

I shrug, offering him a small smile as I sit in the chair on the other side of his desk. "I've been busy with class. Macy and her boyfriend broke up again, so we've been nursing her broken heart."

He raises an eyebrow at me, and I probably shouldn't have said anything, but my hangover is giving me looser lips than normal. "Have you been going to parties?"

"Of course. Every single night, *and* I get shit-faced at all of them," I reply, my voice dripping with sarcasm, and Dad's face is priceless.

"Al—"

"I'm joking, Dad. You don't need to lecture me like I'm one of your players," I reply, playing with the cuff of my sweater.

He frowns, and I know I shouldn't have said it. Dad will never admit he puts them over me, but there's no denying the truth. I can't act entirely innocent, though. Bradley took advantage of the cracks in my relationship with him and turned them into chasms. "You're not one of my players. You're my daughter."

Funny. Where was he during my last skating competition, then?

"What am I here for?" I ask, the smile falling from my face.

Dad rubs his face, and I wonder if pretending everything is fine is as exhausting for him as it is for me. "I wanted to hear how things are going. Are you liking classes?"

The hair on the back of my neck stands up because I can feel the direction this conversation is going to take. He's going to ask if I've reconsidered skating. I have a voicemail on my phone from my old coach asking the same question.

"I've got friends. Classes are fine. I'm fine," I reply, feeling my headache start to rear its ugly head.

"Coach Presley called me the other day and asked if you were still keeping up with your training? He's held your spot for you in case you've changed your mind."

I cross my arms over my chest as I sink lower into the chair, looking away. The thought of stepping on the ice is unbearable. It's not like I haven't tried. "I quit skating. I haven't stepped on the ice sinc—" I'm interrupted by the sound of guys laughing in the locker room right outside the office, and I take that as my cue to leave, standing up from the seat.

If anything, I love hockey, but I wish it didn't take my dad away from me. I started figure skating as a way to get his attention after Mom wouldn't let me try hockey, but I stuck with it once I fell in love with the feeling of being on the ice. It always felt like I was flying, and there wasn't a better feeling. In my world of colorful chaos, I was disciplined the moment I stepped on the ice, waking up and spending countless hours training to be the best.

I wanted to prove to my dad that even though I wasn't

playing hockey, I could still be good enough to make him proud.

I know hockey is his job, but I'm his daughter. I would have thought it meant something, but he still missed more competitions than he made it to. The moments when Dad was there made up for all the ones he wasn't, but I can't help wondering sometimes how different everything might have turned out if he'd been at the competition when I quit.

I haven't been able to bring myself to step on the ice since then, but I still keep my skates under my bed to make it easy when I sneak out in the middle of the night. It feels a little pointless, considering I haven't done anything other than stare at the beautiful, glassy ice every time I mustered the courage this past summer to use the copy of my dad's key to get into the arena. I'd sit there for hours, paralyzed by the memories of the last time I skated.

Dad's asked countless times before now, wanting to know why I quit, but I can't explain. I don't know how to make him understand why I accepted a love that left bruises where they wouldn't be seen. Why I put up with it for as long as I did, at the cost of nearly everything, including myself.

But that was last year.

This year is a blank slate, ready to be painted with a kaleidoscope of colors I hope to find in myself again.

I just haven't found a way to skate again.

"Alondra, we're not done here."

I roll my eyes and pull my braid over my shoulder. "Your team is here, so I think we are, Dad."

I retreat before he can say anything else, but I collide with a large figure in the doorway. "Woah, don't think I've seen someone run out of Coach's office this fast since Baxter had to tell the team we were bag skating." Strong hands grip my shoulders, steadying me as everything within me tenses, moving in slow motion when I look up to make eye contact with Jack. "Alex?" he asks, his eyes widening.

Oh fuck. Jack is a fucking hockey player?

"Schultz, get your hands off my daughter," Dad warns, a surprising bite to his tone, and I step back as Jack's handsome face pales. His hands fall quickly to his sides as he looks over my head to my dad.

Schultz? As in Jack *Schultz*?

There's a reason behind my rule against hockey players, and it's for my own self-preservation.

"Alex is your daughter?" he asks, and I try to shake my head, internally begging him to shut up.

He has no idea how bad this is, but he won't be the one in trouble. He's the golden boy who can't do anything wrong in my father's eyes, whereas I'm his greatest disappointment for quitting the one thing that held value to him for no apparent reason.

"Last I checked, I didn't have a daughter named Alex, but I do have one named Alondra. I'm sorry, how do you know each other, and why do you think her name is Alex?" Dad asks, and Jack looks down at me, his eyes widening with what I can only assume is panic, because I feel the exact same way.

The *last* thing I need is for Jack to tell my dad I met him at a bar.

"Um, we're in Comp II English together, and I'm tutoring him. He assumed my name was Alex because I go by Al," I blurt out, but the only way this works is if Jack doesn't correct me. I tutored in high school, so it makes it believable.

"She's tutoring you?" Dad asks, and I look up at Jack, hoping he can snap out of it.

He clamps his jaw shut, nodding. "Yeah. We've been meeting every Tuesday and Thursday night to go over what we learned in class the day before," he replies, and I'm so relieved I think I might cry. Jack might think I'm insane, especially if he has no reason to need a tutor, but I'm not ready for the lecture I'd get if Dad thinks I'm distracting any of his players, let alone Jack Schultz.

"Exactly. That's all it is. Tutoring," I reassure my dad, glancing over my shoulder.

He fixes a serious gaze on me, his eyebrows knit together. "Al, I hope you're taking this seriously. Our chances at making the Frozen Four drop significantly if Schultz is academically ineligible."

"She is—we both are," Jack interrupts, which is better than anything I would've said.

This is my very definition of hell.

CHAPTER 2

Jack

ALONDRA.

I can't stop thinking about how the beautiful girl I couldn't stop staring at on Friday night has the prettiest name, but she's Coach B's daughter.

I'm so fucked if he finds out I kissed her.

My best friend, Dylan, knocks my shoulder, jarring me from my thoughts. "Man, what is with you today? Get your head out of the clouds before Coach B notices," he says, and I shake my head, adjusting my grip on the stick.

"Nothing, I'm fine," I mumble, but I couldn't feel less like myself.

What the fuck happened in Coach B's office again?

Alex is actually Alondra, but Alondra is Coach B's daughter, which makes her so extremely off-limits that it's not even funny. I then lied to him in his office about his daughter tutoring me, but the truth is I am struggling in Comp II. I should care more about how, if my barely-there C drops to a D, I'll be academically ineligible.

Dylan and I set up next to Nate, running a simple two versus one puck protection drill as I focus on the ice beneath my skates and keeping the puck away from Nate while working seamlessly with Dylan.

I lose myself to the familiar feeling, a sense of calm washing over me to help settle the unease in my mind.

Hockey is the one thing that's always made sense to me.

On the ice is the one place I was good enough for everyone but Momma. She's only ever cared if I'm happy—well, and that I get my degree. It's the only thing she's asked of me, and I can't tell her no. Not after everything she's gone through and sacrificed for me.

I've never been the smartest kid in the room. No matter how hard I try, or how long I spend studying, or even how many times I proofread an assignment before turning it in, it's never good enough. Unfortunately, my average grades reflect it. After getting drafted by the Carolina Dolphins in the first round, I wanted to sign my contract right away, but Momma begged me to get my degree first since I'd already signed my National Letter of Intent to Wilder University after Coach Brown offered me a scholarship in my junior year of high school. It was the only way Momma could afford to send me after putting pennies together to help me play in the first place, and she was right when she said I had a lot to learn from Coach Brown.

He played a few seasons in the NHL before multiple back-to-back concussions on the ice forced him into early retire-ment, but he's had one hell of a run since taking over as the head coach for the Wilder Wolves. Coach B has sent more players to play professional hockey after leaving college than anyone else, and I can already see the difference in my abili-ties after the past two seasons.

Momma's always told me there's different types of smart, and my dyslexia doesn't define me unless I let it. I've done tutoring and joined study groups, but this goddamn English class is going to be the death of me. I already failed it once, and if I fail again this semester, I'll be ineligible for not making progress toward my degree. With our schedule slowly growing more intense the closer we get to season, I haven't been able to attend as many of the groups as I'd like, and unfortunately the graduate teaching assistant, Maggie, is too busy trying to flirt with me to be of any actual help. The last thing I need is someone accusing me of trading sexual favors for grades when I'm already struggling to keep my head above water.

My head is still spinning after practice, trying to decide if I should confess everything to Coach B, but I keep seeing the look on Alondra's face before she blurted out that she was tutoring me. I'm not sure it's worth trying to decipher the meaning behind it when I'm the idiot who fell for a fake name from a girl with a pretty smile at the bar.

"Schultz, you good?" Coop asks, lifting a blond eyebrow in my direction as I finish pulling my shirt on.

"Yeah, why?" I ask, pulling my team-issued jacket out of my stall.

"You're a little out of it today," he says, and thankfully, Dylan's too busy arguing with Nate over what football team they think is going to win the Super Bowl to listen.

"Just a lot on my mind. I have an essay for my Comp II class I need to work on, and I think I have like three words written so far," I say, because it's the truth, even if it's not the whole truth. I can't exactly blurt out in the middle of the locker room I kissed Coach B's daughter last night at the bar and it's messing with me. I look away to grab my keys and wallet, shoving them into my pockets to grab my phone next. "Think Ellie would help me again?" I ask, and Coop shrugs.

"I'm her brother, not her babysitter. You'll have to ask her."

I snort, shaking my head at my roommate, who also happens to be the best damn goalie I've ever played with. "I was just asking if you thought she'd say yes or if she said anything along the lines of *I'm never helping Jack again* to you."

I feel bad for asking the question because Ellie's my friend, and she has a heart of gold, but everyone has their limit of how many times they can sit for hours helping me with something they can do without a second thought.

It sucks that Alondra wasn't actually being serious earlier, but it probably wouldn't be a good idea.

"Well, I doubt she will, but if she says no, I'll help you instead," he says, which makes me feel a little better. "Just let me know what she says."

"Thanks, Coop," I say, just as Dylan yelps after not moving out of the way to miss the towel Nate snaps in his direction.

"What the fuck, Baxter! You know Coach banned that shit from the locker room," Dylan says, pulling his briefs up, glaring at Nate.

"I was tired of staring at your ass. It doesn't take that long to get dressed," Nate says, tugging his hoodie over his head.

"It's a great ass, you should be thanking me." Dylan scoffs, flipping Nate off as I shake my head. I've seen Dylan's ass more times than I can count over the last two years that it doesn't even faze me anymore.

"Jones, put some damn clothes on," Coach Brown interjects, causing all of our heads to snap his direction. I swallow the lump of fear forming in my throat, averting my gaze because I feel so damn guilty about lying to him. The sound of his office door shutting echoes off the walls, and the chatter is slow to pick up afterward.

"What the hell crawled up his ass this morning?" Nate asks, grabbing his things.

"No idea, but do you think he'd prefer his name tattooed on my right or left cheek? I want to get on his good side, and what better way than to have his name on me permanently?" Dylan jokes, and Coop shakes his head.

"For fuck's sake I hope you're kidding," he says under his breath.

Knowing Dylan, there's a very real chance he's not, but getting a tattoo is a bit further than his normal ideas tend to go.

"Schultz, you were in Coach's office before practice, right? He say anything to you?" Nate asks, and I shake my head.

"Nope," I say, keeping my answer vague because I haven't quite figured out what the hell I'm going to do with what I learned in his office.

"What if we take a little break?" Ellie suggests, and I could definitely use one, but I feel bad she's wasting her Saturday afternoon helping me. I called her on my way home from practice, and Ellie said she had some free time today, which works in my favor because I need all the help I can get sorting through the research database to find my sources. Even with using the text-to-speech feature on my computer, I still have to scan through dozens of articles to find enough sources and then flip through them to see if they even work for my assignment.

It's a nightmare from start to finish, and my only hope is I pass the class this time around. I don't have a different option.

"I'm good," I say, but the way my leg is bouncing from my restlessness tells a different story. "Let's keep going."

"Jack, it's fine to take five minutes. Honestly, I need to pee so please don't make me take your computer into the bathroom with me," she says, standing up, leveling me with a look identical to one I normally get from her brother.

"Fine, I'll take a break," I agree, sighing as I push the computer away from me. Ellie's right, it'll probably help.

"Thank you because that's disgusting, and I really didn't want to do it," she says, laughing as she walks away.

I glance around her apartment instead, taking in the subtle

decorations, but it's the sheer number of blankets on the couch and chair that confuses me. *Why on earth does anyone need this many blankets? I'm not even sure we have one in our living room.*

My curiosity gets the better of me, and I reach for the purple fuzzy one on the couch, and the second my fingertips brush over the soft material to pick it up, I think I understand. *This might be the softest blanket I've ever felt.* I wonder where Ellie got this because Christmas is coming up, and I need a present for Momma. Hell, I might even buy one to keep on our couch at the house.

The lock on the front door flips, opening a moment later as I spin around, still holding the blanket when Alondra walks through the entry, rifling through her bag. "Elli—" Her eyes lift, widening at the sight of me as she chokes. *Oh fuck. Of course Alondra is one of Ellie's roommates. Why would it be anyone else?* First, she's Coach's daughter, and now she's living with Coop's sister? "What the hell are you doing here? Are you stalking me?" she asks, crossing her arms over her chest, taking a step back.

"What?" I ask, a laugh of disbelief slipping from me. "You think I'm stalking you?"

"You're literally standing in my living room, holding my blanket. What else should I think?"

"Sorry, I set a timer because I didn't think you'd actually take a few minutes if I came right back . . ." Ellie trails off, her gaze bouncing from me to Alondra. "Al? I thought you were going to be gone until tonight?"

"Macy's ex called her, begging for forgiveness, and I . . . I'm sorry, what is he doing here?" Alondra asks, and hell, I must have a death wish, but I smile at her.

"I asked Ellie for help with an assignment. Where did you get this blanket?" I ask, holding it up as Alondra scoffs.

"Why *do* you have my blanket?"

Ellie whistles, causing both of us to wince as she captures

our full attention. "I'm sorry, I feel like I'm missing something. You guys know each other?"

"Jack hit on me in a bar last night," Alondra says, tilting her chin up in what feels like a challenge, and my blood instantly heats at the reminder of what it felt like to kiss her. But I can't forget she's Coach's daughter.

Ellie's head whips to face me, her blonde hair flying around her. "You hit on my roommate? What the hell, Jack? I actually like her, and I don't need you scaring her away with your dick," she says, waving her arm at me like this is my fault.

I don't love the insinuation there, but it's not my fault her last roommate fell for Coop after they hooked up, and he might be even more emotionally unavailable than I am.

"I didn't know she was your roommate or my coach's daughter when I went up to her last night." I watch Alondra to see if I was right not to confess everything to Coach B or if I should add it to the list of mistakes I've made in the last twenty-four hours.

"You're what?" Ellie asks, and Alondra straightens. I think her eye might even be twitching.

"Okay, look, I'm sorry. I know I wasn't supposed to be home, but I'm exhausted and my head is killing me. Short version is Jack came up to me at a bar last night and told me his friends would make fun of him if he had to walk away without a kiss, so I took pity on him, but it was awful. I figured out who he was after I ran into him while trying to escape my dad's office, and yes, he's the head coach of the hockey team, but it's not something either of us advertises. Can we be done now with whatever this is?"

"Actually, if it was so awful, you would have given me a one instead of rating our kiss a three," I point out, unable to resist the grin tugging at my lips.

"A three out of ten isn't good, Jack," Alondra says, fixing me with a stare that would probably scare the shit out of me if she were taller, but she barely reached my shoulders earlier. I like how feisty she is. Fuck, what is wrong with me? I shouldn't *like* anything about her.

"In baseball, it's a .300 batting average, which is pretty good," I say, stuffing my hands into the pockets of my sweatpants.

Ellie drags her hands over her face, groaning. "This is a nightmare."

Actually, this is so much better than finding sources for my paper, which is my definition of a nightmare.

"By academic standards, it's the equivalent of filling in your name on the ACT." Alondra presses her hand to her temple, wincing slightly. "Stay, or go, I really don't have it in me to care right now, but I'm going to lie down," she says, slipping off her shoes. I raise my eyebrows in surprise when she walks toward me instead of the direction Ellie came from, holding out her hand.

"You gonna ask me to lie down with you? I make a pretty decent pillow," I tease, and her pink lips twist into a frown.

"Not a chance, but I do want my blanket."

I hand it to her, chuckling under my breath. "Would you tell me where you got it if I said I want to get my momma one for Christmas?" I ask, catching a whiff of strawberries from her. *She's Coach B's daughter. Forget it, Jack.*

Alondra's eyebrows knit together as she looks up at me. "Maybe," she says, taking it and walking away.

"We'll be quiet," Ellie promises, her tone sweet, but the glare in my direction after it leaves her mouth tells a different story. "No," she says, pointing her finger at me.

"What?"

"Don't what me. You know exactly what I'm telling you no for."

"I wasn't doing anything," I say, and Ellie hits my bicep with the back of her hand.

"No," she repeats. "I mean it, Jack. Don't fuck with Alondra."

I put my hands up in surrender. "Do you think I have a death wish? Al's my coach's daughter, and he can make my life a living hell if he wants to."

Ellie crosses her arms over her chest, skepticism written all over her face. "Maybe I'd believe you if you hadn't just offered to let her use you as a pillow. I don't think you know how to not flirt with a girl."

It stings a little, but I mask it with a smile. "I don't flirt with you or Sara." Sara is Ellie's best friend who loves to cause pure chaos to get her and Ellie in enough trouble to keep all of our blood pressure higher than it should be.

"I'm Coop's sister. He'd murder you if you did, and Sara's gay, so she's immune to your charm," she points out, and I reach forward to ruffle her hair, trying to stoke a reaction as I wink at her.

Ellie rolls her eyes and pushes my hand away. "Just leave Al alone, okay? She doesn't like hockey players, which makes her the perfect roommate after Willow."

"And I thought it was just me she didn't like," I say, moving back toward my computer sitting on the counter.

"Well, it sounds like it might also be you she doesn't like," Ellie says, laughing as she follows behind. My head is already spinning at the thought of trying to focus on finding my sources for this paper, especially now that I know Alondra is just down the hall with that damn fuzzy blanket of hers.

CHAPTER 3

Alondra

THE LAST PLACE I expected to feel a spark of color in my world of gray was with Jack Schultz, of all people, but I especially didn't think I'd find him standing in my apartment holding my blanket.

My head was throbbing, but the second I stepped in front of him to get my blanket, I couldn't focus on anything else but the stupid, intoxicating smell of cinnamon from him. Instead of taking a nap, I ended up tossing and turning the entire time until I was certain he was gone.

I felt awful when Ellie wouldn't stop apologizing for letting him come over because it's her apartment, too. I was in rare form, jarred from the meeting with my father and running into Jack in his office. Usually I can be more civil than *Stay or go, I don't have it in me to care.*

Since then, I've spent the last few days trying to grapple with the fact that Jack from the bar is the same guy as Jack Schultz, the future of professional hockey. A lot of things are making more sense about our class together, but I feel like an idiot for not piecing it together Friday night.

I should have known who Jack was before he came up to Macy and me at the bar.

I've kept up with the Wilder Wolves hockey team for longer than I care to admit, and I'm embarrassed to say how many of the players' stats I know off the top of my head. I am my father's daughter after all, but at the same time, I pay more attention to the stats and not the pictures of the players, which, unfortunately, led to my downfall in not recognizing Jack.

Nothing he wore or said gave any indication that he was one of my dad's players, let alone his prized player.

I've never forgotten how excited Dad was after coming home from his trip to Texas where he signed Jack. He raved about the center, already predicting him as a first-round pick in the draft, and he wasn't wrong. Dad's not big on compliments, but the way he talked about Jack's skating and puck handling ability made me sick with envy.

I know for a fact if my dad finds out how I actually met Jack, I'd be the one in trouble for distracting him, not the other way around. It's better for everyone involved if he thinks Jack only knows me because he thinks I'm his tutor.

A quick glance around the auditorium tells me that Jack isn't here yet, or, if he is, I can't see him. I slide into my usual seat next to my friend Keri in one of the upper rows.

"Hey," I greet, and her short hair swishes as she snaps to look at me from her phone.

"You will never believe what my roommate did . . ." Keri trails off, her dark eyes widening as she looks behind me.

"What did Taylor do?" I ask, waiting for her to continue, but whatever is behind me has captured her full attention. "What are you looking . . . at?" I falter at the sight of Jack in the seat next to me, his full lips curled into a knowing smile, his dimple peeking at me as he bumps my leg with his backpack.

Oh, kill me now, please.

"Hey, Alondra. Funny seeing you here," he muses as he reclines in the seat, making himself comfortable.

I clamp my jaw shut, and turn away, putting my back to him as Keri watches the interaction with blatant curiosity.

"Um, why is Jack Schultz sitting next to you?"

"Because he doesn't know what to do with himself when women don't fall at his feet." So much for being civil with him. Oops.

"You know I can hear you, right?"

Jack changing seats in the class is a big deal—*whether he meant it to be or not*—and I can feel the weight of everyone's stares in our direction. This is attention I don't want.

"Go away, Jack. Your groupies miss you, and we can continue not knowing the other exists," I say, leaving Keri's question unanswered.

"I need to talk to you, and if you're going to continue being a ghost, then we'll just have to talk now."

"How can I be a ghost if you know where I live?" I ask, turning around to face him. He doesn't look like he has a care in the world right now, and while it might have been attractive at the bar, right now, it only frustrates me. All Jack is showing me right now is he's used to the world revolving around him, and he doesn't care what anyone else thinks.

I see someone pointing at us out of the corner of my eye, and I wish the professor would start class already.

"I was trying to respect your space, but I've been looking for you everywhere else trying to track you down so we can talk," he says, his blue eyes staring intently at me.

I sigh, twisting the end of a dark curl around my finger as I find the willpower to look away. I might want nothing to do with him, but there's a reason his bedpost is rumored to have so many notches in it, and I bet his baby blue eyes combined with his dimples are the culprit. "There's nothing for us to talk about."

"What do you want to talk to her about?" Keri asks, and I look at her, giving her a silent shake of my head.

"I can think of a couple things. Off the top of my head, you never told me where you got the blanket from, and I'd like to know why you told me your name was Alex?" he asks, pulling the writing tablet down to rest his arm on it.

"Can you please go away?" I ask, avoiding his questions despite the fact his mention of my goddamn blanket makes me want to smile.

Jack shakes his head, his mouth tilting into a smirk. "Sorry, darlin', you're stuck with me now since Coach thinks you're my tutor."

"You're tutoring him?" Keri interrupts, and I'm losing hope she'll help me get rid of him.

"Yes," Jack answers, but I'm quick to correct him.

"No."

I watch in horror as Keri melts like chocolate in the warm sun on a hot summer day, and I just know he's flashing his dimples at her. One glance in his direction proves me right— those goddamn dimples.

"Sorry, I didn't catch your name. I'm Jack, and Al's my tutor, but I promise I rate her higher than she rates me," he teases, and even though Keri has no idea what he's getting at, I do.

"I would have rated you higher than a two if you deserved it," I protest, grumbling under my breath as a chuckle escapes him.

"The way you're dropping your rating makes me think you need to give me a second chance to do better," he teases, and I roll my eyes. Of course, the one day my professor is late has to be today of all days.

"I'm Keri. Do you deserve a second chance for whatever it is she rated you poorly on?" Keri asks, engaging in his antics, and it's tempting to pull down my own writing tablet for the sole purpose of banging my head on it.

"No, because he also has a problem with listening. Jack, I

think your fan club misses you," I say, angling my head in the direction of the girls seated where he normally is. If looks could kill, Keri and I would already be dead.

"They'll survive," he says, shrugging, and I'm relieved when my professor finally shows, setting her things down.

"I'm not a tutor, so if you actually need the help, find someone else," I say, pulling my things out of my bag, but our professor starts speaking before Jack can respond.

I do my best to focus on everything Professor Rayburn says, but it's hard to when Jack's leg hasn't stopped bouncing since she started. I feel bad for being surprised that Jack takes notes, but every time she changes screens, he swears quietly under his breath, his eyebrows furrowed in deep concentration.

I know it's wrong to make assumptions, but maybe I judged him too quickly. Too bad every time I start to feel bad about wanting nothing to do with him, he opens his mouth and I lose my cool.

The second our professor is done, I'm putting everything in my bag to dart around Jack, but all he has to do is stretch out, making it impossible for me to get past him unless I want to straddle his waist. To be clear, I don't want to.

"Where do you think you're going, Al? We haven't had a chance to chat," he says, smirking at my eagerness to leave.

"I didn't think we had anything to talk about, and I have to meet Macy," I say, frowning at him.

"Perfect, I'll walk with you," he says, an easy smile forming as he stands up, leaving me to follow behind.

Seriously? What could he possibly want to talk about so badly?

My only problem with using Macy as an excuse is we don't actually have plans to meet since she's in a lab all morning. I only said it because I thought if Jack knew I had somewhere to be, he'd leave me alone—not act as my personal escort.

"Perfect," I say, the single word dripping with more sarcasm than I thought possible. "Bye, Keri, see you Wednesday."

She offers me a traitorous smile and a thumbs up before I walk down the stairs with Jack following closely behind. There's a slight chill outside, and I'm glad I wore a sweater today. It feels like sweaters are all my wardrobe consists of, but we're approaching the descent into the unforgiving temperatures of winter.

If I'd been able to transfer to Texas Tech, I wouldn't have to worry about whether my backpack can fit over all the layers I'm going to have to start wearing eventually.

Fucking Minnesota and their stupid snow.

Before Jack can say anything, some guys across the hallway call his name. The girl with them tilts her head, watching me, and I wish I had a hoodie on to pull over my head and hide. I mean, seriously? He's a jock who can simultaneously skate and shoot a puck. Not a god or anything incredibly special. He's just . . . Jack, I guess.

I continue walking, hoping they'll capture his attention long enough for me to ditch him. Except the sound of his heavy footsteps catching up to me tells me it didn't work.

"Are we just going to continue wandering aimlessly, or are we actually meeting up with your friend?" he asks after another five minutes of walking silently. I have no interest in hashing this out with him.

"What makes you think I'm not meeting up with Macy?" I ask, turning my head to look at Jack, noting the way the sun makes the lighter shades of brown in his hair stand out. Hell, he was attractive in bar lighting, but in actual daylight, his features are much more noticeable. I roll my eyes when his mouth tilts into a smirk, almost like he knows I'm involuntarily checking him out.

Is that even something you can do? It's not like I'm staring at his ass.

"Why do you call me darlin'?" I blurt out before he can respond to my previous one with a witty remark.

"Does it bother you, *darlin'*?"

Yes, but I'm not going to admit this to him. "Doesn't bother me, but I'm sure it'd bother my dad if he hears it." I direct a cheeky smile his way, and his expression shifts to become guarded.

"Why didn't you say your dad was my coach? I never would have . . ." Jack trails off, rubbing the back of his neck.

"Solicited me so your friends didn't make fun of you?" I scoff, adjusting my backpack on my shoulders. "Obviously, I didn't know he was your coach."

"Seriously?" His blue eyes scan my face, and if I were him, I'd probably be skeptical too. It's not like I told Jack my real name either. "Not to sound like a jerk or anything, but I'm pretty well known around campus. How do I know you didn't actually know, or are you trying to get me in trouble with your dad?"

"Why the hell would I try to get you in trouble with my dad? I'm pretty sure I've asked you to go away multiple times, and you've ignored me every time," I point out, growing defensive because Jack is the one who approached me at the bar—not the other way around.

"I don't know. Did we hook up last year at a party, and you're pissed I didn't call you?"

My jaw drops. "You didn't seriously just say that." Hockey star or not, he's acting like a narcissistic dick. I think civility has gone way out the window at this point.

Jack at least looks a little embarrassed. "Look, I'm sorry. I'm just having a hard time believing this is one big coincidence."

"You came up to me. You claimed your friends would tease you, and I wasn't exactly sober. It seemed like a good idea at the time. Let me get this straight: I didn't pursue you, and if I'd known you were one of my dad's players, I wouldn't have let you within ten feet of me," I snap, and Jack closes his eyes, inhaling a sharp breath.

"Why didn't you say who your dad was?" he asks, somehow still not understanding I didn't intentionally hide it from him.

"Are you fucking kidding me? Have you taken too many hits to the head or something? Do you go up to random people in a bar who are hitting on you and tell them about your dad?"

Jack's face changes, and if I didn't know better, I'd think I hit a sore spot. "No, I don't," he answers, his voice rough.

"Exactly, so why should the same be expected of me?" I ask him point-blank and Jack shifts, looking different from his cocky self in our previous encounters.

"Al, you're right. I'm sorry," he says, but he doesn't stop there, continuing to dig his own grave. "Can you blame me, though? You're my coach's daughter, which makes you extremely off-limits."

Again, if he thinks I'm so off-limits, why is he still walking with me? The funniest part is how wrong Jack has it. If Dad finds out, my ass is the one in trouble, not his. "Just forget about it, okay? You're not going to be the one in troubl—"

He shakes his head, interrupting me. "I really don't feel like getting my ass handed to me by my coach because you run to daddy after I eventually hurt your feelings."

"Oh my god, what part of this are you not getting? If he finds out, it won't be you in trouble, it'll be me. So please just stop going on about how much trouble you'll be in, and listen to what I'm saying," I snap, crossing my arms over my chest as I turn to face him. Jack has nothing to worry about.

His eyebrows knit in concern, and he drags a hand through his hair, causing some of the chestnut locks to flop into his face. "What do you mean you'll be in trouble?"

I can't do this. It's too much and we shouldn't even be having this conversation since he's so worried about being caught with me.

I back away, offering a small smile in surrender. "I really didn't know who you were. It was just a kiss, and I'm not going to rat you out to my dad. I'll see you around, Jack."

CHAPTER 4

Alondra

"I CAN'T BELIEVE you never watched this show before," Ellie says, throwing popcorn into her mouth, distracting me from the medical drama she introduced me to a few days after we moved in together. We've since gone through three seasons, with plenty more to go, and I'm hooked.

"Be quiet, you're talking through the whole episode," I whisper, reaching for my own handful of popcorn.

After Rose told us she was transferring to the same college as her boyfriend, Macy and I entered the portal for university housing to be paired with a random third roommate. We went into it knowing we might not like our new roommate, and it didn't sound like a bad idea. Thankfully, Ellie is so easy to get along with, I couldn't help but like her, even after learning her brother is one of my dad's players.

Coop's nice, but he doesn't say much whenever he pops by, which is kind of a relief, but the best part is there's zero recognition in any of our exchanges. I shouldn't expect anything less, though. I guarantee my father has not once gone to practice and told a bunch of young men overflowing with testosterone about his daughter named Alondra. It's hard to pretend it doesn't hurt, even after all the years I've had to get used to it.

God, I should have known who Jack was, especially with him being Dad's star player and all. It's finally biting me in the ass for not looking at their pictures because I've always cared more about their stats and the way they move on the ice. It's a rare occasion when I give in to my genetic predisposition to love hockey by actually watching a game, but I don't care to look at their pictures since it doesn't matter to me what they look like.

"I'm not talking through the whole episode," she retorts, pulling me from my thoughts, and I feel a piece of popcorn hit my cheek.

Grabbing the remote, I pause the television to turn toward Ellie. "Did you just throw popcorn at my face?"

She smiles and shrugs. "Whoops, I guess I missed my mouth."

I pick up the piece and toss it back at Ellie, causing laughter to bubble from her. "Oops," I say, holding my own laugh back.

"Just unpause the show. I think they're about to bang in an on-call room," Ellie says, grabbing more popcorn from the bowl. I roll my eyes, hitting play, immediately getting sucked into the world playing on the screen.

Ellie was right—the doctors did bang in an on-call room.

"I honestly can't imagine wanting someone so badly, I'd fuck them at my place of employment," I say, shaking my head as I adjust the purple blanket keeping me warm. Unfortunately, the blanket also reminds me of Jack and his annoying persistence in wanting to know where I got this one from.

I should be relieved Jack didn't continue following me after class, but I haven't been able to put one part of the whole exchange out of my mind.

Does he actually need a tutor?

On the other hand, I can't believe he asked me if we hooked up last year because he couldn't remember. If that doesn't tell me I was right not to give him my number at the bar while letting him believe my name was Alex, I don't know what would.

"I can't say it's something I would do either, especially in a hospital knowing there's sick and dying people around you, but I think if it were the right person, maybe it'd be different?" Ellie ponders out loud, pulling her bright blonde hair back.

"I guess. At least they had enough common sense to lock the door behind them."

"Only because they didn't a few episodes ago, and her ex-boyfriend walked in on them," Ellie says, securing her hair up with a ponytail. "Have you ever had anyone walk in on you during sex?"

"Nope," I answer, trying to keep the details vague like everything else I've shared when Ellie asks about my past dating experiences. I don't want to talk about Bradley in the slightest.

She tilts her head, wrinkling her nose as her eyebrows knit together. "Just nope?" she asks, and I roll the soft fabric of the blanket between my fingertips, trying to focus on the feeling instead of remembering what it was like to be used by Bradley.

"Yep," I say, my stomach souring, but I try to maintain the lightness of the room.

Ellie chews her lower lip, her eyes scanning over my face while I fight the urge to turn away. "I haven't been walked in on, but I definitely saw more of Coop than I've ever cared to when he and a girl forgot to lock his door at one of the parties they threw at their house last year. I don't think I was able to look him in the eyes for two weeks after," she says, continuing on like I didn't make things awkward a moment ago by clamming up.

I cover my mouth with my hand in shock. "Why would you go into your brother's room during a party? That's just asking for trouble," I say, and she groans, dragging her hands over her face.

"I know. Literally not even at the worst part of the story yet. He was with my roommate at the time, and Willow was a nightmare to live with afterward. Poor girl thought because she sucked his dick once, it meant they were supposed to be together, and she never stopped talking about him after that. I love my brother, and I'm aware of his flaws—emotional intimacy being one of his biggest ones. Coop stupidly believed Willow when she hit on him at that party, asking to fool around, and couldn't see she was obsessed with him. To be fair, I didn't see it either until after."

"Holy shit, Ellie," I say, understanding why she made it clear the first time we met how it was better I wanted nothing to do with hockey players. Ellie had made a couple of comments in passing over the last three months, but it wasn't enough for me to piece it all together. I have plenty of my own shit I don't want to talk about, so how would it be fair for me to ask the same of her?

"Still not to the crazy part yet," she says, grimacing. "Willow had asked me to grab her laptop for her since my next class was in the building next to hers, and I found some photographs of Coop and me, where she had cut me out of the pictures and taped herself into a wedding scrapbook."

"What the fuck?"

Her old roommate sounds insane. Who does something like that?

"So, honestly, you hating hockey players is the best thing to ever happen to me after that experience. I made Coop fix the lock on my bedroom door that was broken in case she decided to ever use those scissors for something other than pictures, but it was a long six weeks after that," she says, shuddering, and I can't even blame her.

"I'm so sorry," I say, trying to sound sympathetic, but in reality, I start laughing instead. "Okay, shit," I say, stumbling over my words as I try to stop. "I don't mean to laugh, but . . ."

Ellie crosses her legs and begins laughing too. "No, it's okay. It's funny now, but my brother is not allowed to ever come near any of my friends with his dick ever again."

"Valid," I say, reaching for my emotional support water bottle always nearby to take a drink. "Want to watch another episode?" I ask, exchanging the water bottle for the remote, and she beams.

"I am always looking for an excuse to avoid doing my homework. Do we need more snacks?" Ellie asks, holding up our mostly empty bowl of popcorn.

"Sure. I also have a bottle of wine in the fridge if you want to open it?" I ask, but Ellie stands before I can.

"You don't have to ask me twice," she says, walking toward the kitchen.

I pull my phone out, scrolling through a few notifications, and I roll my eyes when I see there's a request from Jack to send me a direct message. He's persistent, I'll give him that.

"I think this is the dinner of champions," Ellie jokes over the sound of the popcorn kernels popping in the microwave.

I turn my phone off, deciding against reading the message from Jack when there's a knock at the door. "Are you expecting anyone?" I ask, but Ellie looks confused too, taking her phone out of her pocket to check.

"Oh, I think it's Coop. He sent me a text earlier asking if I was home, and I never responded," she says, shooting an apologetic smile in my direction. "Is it okay if I see what he wants?"

"Go for it," I say because I really don't mind her brother. He's a little intimidating at first because of his height and the way he carries himself, but despite being a man of few words, he's nice—for a hockey player, that is.

"Door's open," Ellie calls out, opening the microwave at the same time my phone chimes with a text from Macy, and I'm distracted when the door opens. "What are you doing?" she asks, and I jerk my head up, my mouth falling open in surprise at the sight of Jack shutting the door behind him, his backpack slung over his shoulder.

"Heard you say 'door's open,' implying it was fine to come in," he says, his mouth tilting into a smile before his gaze lands on me. "Hey, darlin'."

"Don't call me that," I say, frowning immediately.

His smile widens, a dimple peeking out. "Does it bother you?"

"Why are you here?" I say, ignoring the question. Is he really standing in our apartment *again*?

Jack takes off his backpack and takes a seat at the counter. "It's Tuesday. Pretty sure we have a tutoring session," Jack says, taking his time to enunciate every word as if I don't understand.

Ellie's eyebrows skyrocket, giving me a bewildered look, but I don't have any clue what's going on. I thought we covered this yesterday after class.

"There is no tutoring, Jack. I literally only said it to save my ass with my dad. Pick any of the other girls fawning over you in Comp II, I'm sure you'll be fine," I say, and he sighs, rubbing the back of his neck.

"I'm not fine," he argues, and even if he's not, isn't there anyone else Jack can go to for help?

"Look, if this is some type of punishment you're trying to subject me to because of how I rated our kiss, it was better than a three," I admit, causing Jack's smile to slip for a moment, and his posture straightens.

"Forget it, this was a bad idea," he says, shaking his head, and I'm wondering if maybe I've misjudged the cocky hockey player. "I didn't come here to make out with you. I actually do need help with Comp II, but you're right, why would I ask you when I have everyone else falling over my feet?" Jack says, a hint of bitterness bleeding into his rich voice.

Ellie gives me a pleading look as Jack grabs his bag, and her puppy dog eyes are a lethal weapon.

"I'm sorry," I blurt out, caving to her silent request. Jack appears skeptical as he freezes his movements, and I realize I have to say more than an apology. "You don't have to go."

"Is that an invitation to stay? Because if it is, it might be the least enthusiastic one I've ever gotten."

I cross my arms over my chest, and Ellie clears her throat. "Jack, please do yourself a favor and stop talking before Al changes her mind," she says, taking the popcorn out of the microwave to shake the bag.

"Hey, Ellie," he says, pulling his laptop out of his bag. "Is it cool if I borrow your roommate for a bit?" he asks, flashing a smile in her direction.

"As long as you remember what we talked about last time, okay?"

What did they talk about last time? You know what, it doesn't even matter.

"Yes, ma'am," Jack replies smartly, offering her a little salute.

Shit, I want to know what they talked about.

Ellie looks at me, raising her eyebrows in question. "Do I need to supervise or can you be nice?"

"I can be nice," I protest, feeling my cheeks flame bright red. At least, I think I can.

She sticks her tongue out at me, putting the wine back in the fridge. "Sure, well while you try to be nice, I'm going to go eat this popcorn in my room. Jack, give us a heads up before showing up next time."

"You got it, little Coop," he says, and Ellie rolls her eyes, giving me a thumbs up before disappearing into her room. "So you like the sexy doctor show?" Jack asks, a smirk forming, and my head snaps toward the television, where the screen is paused on the show's intro featuring a shirtless man with a stethoscope around his neck.

"I thought Ellie warned you to stop talking before I change my mind?" I ask, reluctant to stand up from the couch.

"I'm just making conversation. It was on your screen, and if doctors are your thing, I'm not going to judge you," he drawls, continuing to talk, and I take a deep breath, reminding myself I'm playing nice.

"Please don't call me that," I say, giving him the fakest smile I can muster. "So you need help with Comp II?" I ask, picking a neutral question instead of continuing to go back and forth with him.

I slide onto the stool next to his, shifting away because his size is overwhelming. Biting my cheek, I glance over at him, noting how the tips of his ears turn a bright red and the color of his cheeks tint. "Yeah, um, I have dyslexia, and I do my best to keep up, but I get . . . overwhelmed, I guess? It takes me a long time to work through the assignments, but finding sources for the essays before even trying to write the papers is . . ." Jack trails off, shrugging his broad shoulders.

Holy fuck, I'm the worst human alive.

"Do you have any accommodations?" I ask, struggling to speak because I'm so fucking embarrassed by how quick I was to dismiss him when he was genuinely asking for help. I know there was no way for me to know about his learning disability, but it makes sense why Ellie was helping him the other night.

"I get audio recordings of the lectures, and I'm supposed to get extra time on assignments. Since we do a lot of peer review, it's hard to explain why mine isn't done unless I want to share why, so I try to hit the same deadlines as everyone else, but it's not going so great for me," he explains, opening his laptop. "I failed the class last year, but it's a requirement to graduate, so I had to retake it this semester."

"I'll talk to our professor and see if we can be partnered the rest of the semester for any peer assignments," I say, and his blue eyes slide to meet mine, widening for a moment. I'm a little surprised I'm offering to be stuck with him for the rest of the semester, but everyone has the right to an education. It's not his fault that his brain works differently from others. "We'll meet Tuesdays and Thursdays to work through the material from class, but if you need help with something outside of that, let me know and we'll find time to meet."

"Thanks," Jack says, and I exhale, wiping my palms on my thighs.

"Don't mention it," I say, twisting my curls back to tie them up off my neck. "I tutored in high school, so I might be a little rusty, but you have to tell me if I'm going too fast or you need a break." When he doesn't say anything, I look up at him, only to find his gaze trailing over the exposed slope of my neck. "No funny business, okay? This is just tutoring," I say, swallowing the lump forming in my throat, tucking my hands into the sleeves of my sweatshirt.

He flashes a cheeky smile. "Is friends on the table?"

"Nope."

Jack chuckles, scratching the back of his neck. "We'll see about that. I think you want to be my friend, but you're afraid you can't handle it."

"You think I can't handle all the glares from everyone who are desperate to get close to you? Please, Jack, give me some credit." I snort, reaching over to pull his laptop closer to me, wanting to maintain the space between us.

"Then why can't we be friends?"

Because you're my dad's star player, and a walking representation of sex on a stick?

I raise an eyebrow, wondering if he really needs me to answer this question. "Do you even have any friends who are girls?" I ask, skimming over the screen to see where he's at with our current project. The number of tabs he has open on his browser makes my eye twitch.

"Ellie," he says, sounding awfully smug.

"She's your roommate's sister. I don't think Ellie counts."

"I think she counts, but it's cool if you don't want to be friends right now. I'll wear you down at some point."

I bite back my smile because he has no idea I'm as hard-headed as my dad. Maybe I should refer him to someone who is actually qualified to be his tutor and has experience with learning disabilities, but it sounds like he really does need the help.

Agreeing to be his tutor is one thing, but becoming his friend would break my rule against having anything to do with hockey players.

"Walk me through what your paper is over, and we can start on some of the material on our midterm exam," I say, redirecting the conversation back to why he's here.

For the record, Jack and I are *not* friends.

CHAPTER 5

Jack

My energy is spent by the time I walk into the house I share with my teammates, and my brain is swirling with everything Alondra and I covered in our second tutoring session. She helped me sort through all the open tabs of potential sources by reading the abstracts to determine whether they would support my argument, and we created a brief outline to help me get started on each section of the paper. We also worked on reviewing sections of what our midterm covered.

Dylan is on the couch, his flavor of the week straddling his lap as they make out, and I shut the door louder than necessary. Their heads separate, but Dylan doesn't look phased, and the girl doesn't climb off his lap.

"Get a room," I say, shaking my head as I drop my bag on the ground.

"This is a room," Dylan replies, snorting, and I roll my eyes, moving into the kitchen to find Coop with headphones on as he cleans the dishes in the sink. The aroma from dinner still lingers in the air, and my stomach rumbles with the hope that there are leftovers.

Opening the fridge, I'm relieved to spot the container on

the top shelf labeled with my name on the sticky note attached to it.

"You're lucky there's enough chicken stir fry left for you. I thought Dylan was going to square up with Nate over the last serving," Coop says, and I turn around, grinning.

"Have I told you that you're my favorite?"

"Whatever," he says, rolling his eyes. I grab a fork out of the drawer, diving straight in without even bothering to warm it up first. "Are they still on the couch?"

I nod, too busy chewing the mouthful of rice and vegetables. I didn't realize how hungry I was until now, too distracted by the effort it took to keep my focus on my paper at Alondra's. "Dude, this is fucking awesome," I say, taking a moment to breathe.

"It was better hot," Coop says, drying the pan in his hands, and I lean against the counter.

"What do you know about Ellie's roommate, Alondra?" I ask, curiosity getting the better of me.

Coop laughs under his breath. "Ellie will murder you if you go anywhere near her. She barely lets me come over when she's home."

"That's because her last roommate was obsessed with you," I say, taking another bite as Coop levels me with an unamused expression.

"Fuck off, Willow wasn't my fault. Don't say you want to hook up with no strings attached, then start cutting out pictures of me for a wedding scrapbook," he says, shuddering, and I can't blame him because I'm just glad that shit hasn't happened to me. "Alondra's been nice the few times I've been around. I've never met the other one, but Ellie said they're quiet and clean. Ellie seems to like them, though. My sister would eat me alive if I said she's pretty, but I'm not blind either."

Nice and quiet aren't exactly how I'd describe Alondra.

She's not just pretty—she's beautiful. It really wasn't a line I used on her Friday night.

I swallow the food in my mouth, clearing my throat. "She's the girl I kissed at the bar Friday," I admit, and his eyebrows raise. "I didn't know she was Ellie's roommate, or that she's Coach Brown's daughter."

This time, Coop's jaw unhinges, and he laughs. "His daughter?"

"Yeah," I say, scratching my jaw, and Coop walks toward the living room.

"Dylan, say bye to Sally and get your ass in here," I hear him say just after I take another bite of the dinner I'm inhaling, making me choke.

Coop walks back in, shaking his head at me while tears stream from the corners of my eyes as I cough, trying to swallow the food in my mouth. Dylan's scowling, and if I could laugh, I would. "Couldn't you have told me what the hell is going on without making Sandy leave?" he grumbles, giving Coop a look of irritation.

"Tell Romeo," Coop says, crossing his arms over his chest.

I cough once more, but my voice is raspy. "Wow, Coop. Thanks for asking if I'm okay first after I almost died," I say, setting down my dinner on the counter. "The girl I kissed Friday night is Ellie's roommate and Coach B's daughter."

Dylan scoffs, rolling his eyes. "Very funny. Coach B doesn't have a daughter, and Eleanor made it clear we're not to even be in the same room as her roommate. Did you really have to make Sandy leave?"

"Al's also tutoring me for my Comp II class," I continue, choosing not to look at either of them.

"You're not joking?" Dylan asks, and I wish I was. "Holy shit, you kissed Coach's daughter? What the hell were you thinking?"

"Probably the same thing you were thinking when you and Sandy decided to camp out on the couch in the living room instead of going upstairs to your bedroom," I say, and Coop's silence tempts me into looking at him, but I can't tell what he's thinking. "Obviously I didn't know she was Coach's kid when I went up to Al at Twin City."

"But you knew who she was when she became your tutor?" Coop rumbles, asking the right question, and I sigh. "Why didn't you tell me things were that bad with your class? I would have helped you, and so would Ellie," he continues, and I know they would have helped me, but it's not their job.

"Alondra might be Coach's daughter, but she's smart, and she's in my class with me. She already got our professor to agree to let us work together so I can use my accommodations the way they're meant to be used." I'm aware that I was letting my pride get in the way of using them before, but I've had enough people over the years tell me their perceptions of dyslexia, and it always ends up with them either looking at me or treating me differently.

"You're a fucking idiot for having Alondra tutor you because you can't keep your dick in your pants," Dylan says. I would try to deny it if I hadn't struggled to focus on what Al was saying tonight because I was too busy staring at her full lips, remembering how it felt to kiss them. At one point, she leaned over, and all I could focus on was the smell of strawberries that flooded my senses, and it was intoxicating.

"It's a bad idea, Jack," Coop echoes, and I tug a hand through my hair.

"She has no interest in anything other than a tutor and a . . . tutoree relationship. Fuck, whatever you want to call it. She wants nothing to do with me."

"And what do you want to do with her?" Dylan asks, and I wish I knew.

The simple answer would be that I'd love to find out what she's like in bed, but unfortunately for me, even if Alondra were interested in me, she's off-limits.

"I want to pass this stupid class," I say, walking past him toward the living room to flop on the couch.

Aside from this class determining my eligibility with the team, if I don't pass it, I won't graduate. I refuse to disappoint Momma when it's the one thing she's asked of me after everything.

I'm aware Alondra is my best bet at making it through this course, but I've never had to work this hard to get someone to like me. She begrudgingly gave me her number before I left, making me swear I wouldn't use it for anything other than changes in my tutoring schedule. But it's a good thing I wasn't a scout.

I found Alondra on social media, but her accounts are private, and I doubt she'd accept a request from me. I did end up tracking down the other roommate's account through Ellie's, and thankfully, Macy didn't ignore my direct message asking how Al takes her coffee so I could bring a cup for her yesterday.

I barely got a smile from her.

I can't figure Alondra out, and it's equally as frustrating as it is intriguing.

A part of me enjoys the fact that she isn't fawning over me like most of the girls I meet, because as much as I don't want to admit it, I'm not the best at platonic relationships with women. I'm afraid that option might already be out of the question for us, though, considering I can't seem to push our kiss out of my mind.

She's stubborn, insisting it was only a three, but the way her breathing hitched tonight whenever my arm brushed against hers, tells a different story. It makes me think our kiss felt the same way for her as it did for me, even if I can't quite figure out how it makes me feel.

I had every intention of leaving her alone after finding out that Alondra is Ellie's roommate and Coach's daughter, but then I walked into class and saw her sitting with her friend.

Before I knew what I was doing, I found myself taking the open seat next to her.

Sure, an explanation for why she lied about her name would be nice, but I can't fault her for not telling me exactly who her father is. It's not like I openly share that information myself.

I wish I knew what it was about her that's gotten under my skin.

First, I asked for her number at the bar, something I *never* do. Then, I practically had to beg her to tutor me.

What I really don't understand is why Alondra thinks she'll be in trouble if Coach B finds out about the kiss. She's his daughter, and I'm just one of his players, but my fear of failing Comp II again outweighs my fear of Coach B for the time being.

A pillow lands on my face, pulling me from my thoughts. Dylan's laughter echoes off the walls, and I throw it back at him. "What the hell did you do that for?"

"Because I've been talking to you, but you're in la-la land thinking about your tutor," he jests, and I flip him off.

"Wrong. I was thinking about your mom," I retort, just as the front door opens, and Nate walks in.

"Whose mom are we talking about?" he asks without skipping a beat.

"Dylan's."

He raises an eyebrow, kicking off his shoes. "Why? Yours is hotter," Nate says, and I wish I hadn't thrown the pillow back at Dylan already, so I could throw it at him instead.

"Really? That's my mom, Baxter."

My mom had me right after her eighteenth birthday, and I'm used to her being the youngest of my friends' mothers, but it's weird hearing my friends talk about her, even if I'm the one who opened the door by making a comment about Dylan's mom.

Nate puts his hands up in self-defense when Coop walks

into the living room, and I try to gauge exactly how upset he is with me right now. Unfortunately for me, Coop can be like a brick wall when he wants to be.

"Don't mind Jack. He's stressed because Coach's daughter is his tutor, and he kissed her at Twin City last Friday night," Dylan says, and I flip him off. He has no room to talk when I've seen how he looks at Coop's sister, but that's one of those things I pretend not to see, especially because he seems determined to use every other girl on campus to fuck Ellie out of his system without actually touching her.

"No fucking way," Nate says, laughing, and I'm about done with everyone finding my situation hilarious.

"You guys are annoying," I say, crossing my arms over my chest as I lean back into the cushions.

"Find new friends then," Coop suggests, and Dylan chuckles.

"He shouldn't have a problem with that. Everyone wants to be Jack's friend," he says, and Nate snorts.

"Depends on what your definition of friend is, Dylan. Girls want Jack as their boyfriend or fuck buddy, not their friend."

As much as I deny it, he's not wrong. It should be flattering, but it gets old being seen as a piece of meat. Probably also doesn't help that I play into it all the time because it's easier than trying to convince everyone that I'm more than a one-trick pony.

No wonder Alondra seemed so sure I didn't have any girl friends.

The conversation shifts away from me when Nate asks Dylan about a class they're in together, before hockey eventually takes over.

I call it a night after a while, and Dylan follows suit, his footsteps loud behind as we make our way up the stairs. I'm about to open my door at the end of the hall when he clears his throat, catching my attention.

"Do you think having Alondra as your tutor is actually going to help?"

I'm surprised by how serious he looks, since Dylan is usually the first one to make light of a situation, but I can't blame him for being worried about this.

"I don't think it'll hurt."

Dylan still appears skeptical, and I don't know how to fix it. "Just be careful, Jack."

I feign confidence, grinning at him so he can't see the turmoil in my head. "When am I not?"

Unfortunately, we both know the answer: *never*.

Being the first one on the ice in the morning is my favorite part of the day. I'm extra early to morning skate today, and I could hear Dylan snoring through his door when I walked by his room half an hour ago.

I slept like shit last night, but if I went back to sleep after waking up, I'd be dead on my feet for the rest of the day. The rink's always been the one place where I can clear my head, and if it was an option to never leave the ice, I wouldn't. It's my safe place and always has been.

All the other shit fades into background noise the second my skates hit the smooth surface, reflecting the overhead lights like glass. After a few laps, the only thing I'm aware of is the slicing sounds of the sharp blades as I pick up speed.

There's something intoxicating about hockey for me— once I started, I never wanted to do anything else.

I lose myself in the mindlessness of my warm up routine before retrieving my stick and bucket of pucks from where I left them on our bench, setting up near the goal to work on my wrist and snap shots. With our season kicking off next week, I need to be at my best, proving that the team and

Coach B did the right thing by putting their faith in me as team captain.

Losing in the Frozen Four last year was devastating, but I'm proud of the work everyone put in during the offseason. We're down a couple of great players this season, but I'm just glad Coop hasn't signed his entry-level contract with the Washington Eagles yet. With him protecting the net, we should be set for a repeat season, only this time, a different outcome. Everyone wants to win this year.

Our schedule is intense, balancing classes, team study halls, practices, weights, and anything else Coach decides we need to do, but everyone is throwing themselves headfirst into it.

None more than me.

Despite what my roommates suspect, pursuing Alondra as anything more than a friend is a distraction I don't need or want. If I can convince her to give me a chance, I do want to be her friend. Al doesn't put up with my shit, and I like how she doesn't beat around the bush, getting straight to the point.

If only I could figure out how to ignore my attraction to her, but maybe this is why I don't have girls in my life who are just friends. Maybe I'm the problem.

I just need to get Alondra out of my head because nothing can ever happen between us. She's made it crystal clear she isn't interested, regardless of her physical reactions around me. Hell, maybe I'm imagining half of it to justify my thoughts.

Besides, even if she weren't Ellie's roommate or Coach B's daughter, Al seems like the kind of girl who needs a relationship, not a hookup without strings attached. Unfortunately, the only thing I can promise is a fun time. It's hard to consider anything more when you don't believe in love.

I won't make promises I can't keep because I've had too many of the ones made to me broken, each lie smashing the pieces of my heart I imagine were supposed to belong to someone else, until became impossible to put them back together.

I shake my head to clear my thoughts, taking my frustration out on the puck and sending it flying into the back corner of the net.

Again.

And again.

And again.

CHAPTER 6

Alondra

I'M NOT sure it's physically possible for me to walk any slower, but I can't stall forever. The neon glowing sign of Twin City is up ahead, sealing my fate for the evening.

Macy wouldn't take no for an answer after I tried to get out of going out tonight, especially after she said we were going to Twin City and her loser boyfriend would be joining us.

I changed into a pair of jeans, but I refused to take off my fuzzy sweater, picking comfort and warmth over the skimpy top Macy wanted me to wear.

It's probably wishful thinking, but I'm hoping Jack and his buddies have decided to go somewhere else tonight, sparing me the agony of spending more time with him.

I grumble under my breath, kicking a loose pebble with the toe of my shoe. I want to be at home instead of shivering while cold air seeps through my layers after the significant drop in temperature since the sun went down hours ago. I tucked my hands into my sleeves at the beginning of our hike to the bars, but my fingertips are beginning to go numb.

Of course, we just *had* to go to the scene of the crime I

committed only a week ago, even if it feels like it's been way longer than seven days.

In my head, I'm throwing knives at the back of Chad's head, trying not to gag when he opens the door for her and she melts, giving him one of her beaming smiles that feels like a direct ray of sunlight. I've learned the more I tell Macy how much he sucks, the less likely she is to listen to me about it.

I mumble a quiet thanks to Chad when he holds it for me, and the heat welcomes me like a warm hug, thawing my fingers immediately upon entry.

I do not want to be here.

The bar is just as loud tonight, and the smell of alcohol and sweat is strong. I expect Macy to make a move toward the bar, but instead, she makes a beeline for the loudest table. It only takes me half a second to recognize Jack, and now I'm wondering what else Macy didn't tell me about tonight.

Scanning the rest of the table, I'm relieved to see Ellie, and it makes me feel better she looks as confused to see us walking toward them as I am. At least she wasn't in on whatever this setup is.

Jack stands up, hugging Macy, and my jaw drops. *When the hell did they become friends?*

Macy says something to him before turning around, hooking her arm with mine to pull me toward the bar. "Maybe we should get you a drink before we go sit down," she says, and I would call that an understatement.

"Maybe we should just order a bottle of vodka, and you can pour it down a beer bong for me before we go sit down," I retort, and her eyes widen.

"I don't think hanging out with Jack and his friends for one night is going to kill you, but that absolutely would."

"They're hockey players, Mace," I argue, and at least this time she has the decency to appear like she feels bad.

"I know, but I ran into Jack this morning before your class together when he was getting you coffee, and he invited us out tonight to prove to you he's worth being friends with," she says, and I sigh, twisting one of my curls. *She's a sucker.*

"Fine, forget the bottle, but I'm not paying for my rum and coke," I say, and she smiles.

"I'm proud of you, babe," Macy says, and I try not to think about how Jack's eyes lit up earlier when I smiled at him after he handed me the cup of coffee.

"If you're proud of me, then make it a double please."

Thankfully, the bartender makes mine first, and I take a long sip, trying to prepare myself, but I have a feeling this won't be as terrible as I'm hoping it will be. Maybe that's what I'm most afraid of—seeing my dad's players as people instead of something he's picked over me, time and time again.

It's easier to hate them when I think of them as assholes and playboys, but Jack is doing everything possible to prove me wrong.

The table is lively and roaring with laughter as we approach, and Jack smiles, his goddamn dimple winking at me. "Hey, Al," he greets, "happy you made it."

I smile back faintly—it's hard not to when he smiles like that. "Didn't have much of a choice, but I think you knew that since you didn't say anything in class," I say, adding a smile so he knows my claws are retracted.

"I think what she means to say is thanks for the invite," Macy adds, giving me a look as everyone shifts around to make room in the circular booth.

"That's what I heard," Jack says, winking at me, and Ellie rolls her eyes, patting the seat next to her.

"Ignore him," she says, and I feel my face start to burn from the number of eyes staring at me.

"You're the tutor?" the guy sitting next to Jack asks, peering at me.

"You're a hockey player?" I counter, tilting my head back at him. He laughs, flashing me a pretty smile.

"Feel free to ignore Dylan too," Ellie says, and I stir my drink with the straw before taking another sip.

"Hey, Coop," I say, giving Ellie's brother a smile, and he tips his beer at me in return. The guy to his right is the sucker stuck in a conversation with Chad, and I feel a little bad for him because I've always thought conversations with Chad were as interesting as talking to a wall. But to each their own.

"Sara, have you met Al?" Jack asks, motioning to Ellie's best friend on his other side.

"Dude, I hate to break it to you, but you, Dylan, and Nate are the only ones who haven't met her," Sara says, giving me a warm smile. I usually see her once a week or so whenever she comes over to hang out with Ellie.

Jack's jaw drops, and the way he turns to look at Ellie causes laughter to spill from me. The only way I can describe his expression right now is utter betrayal, and I think it's hilarious.

"Sara has met Alondra too? Do you just hate me or something?" he asks, and Ellie laughs too.

"No, I don't hate you, Jack," she says, taking a drink.

Jack's mouth tilts into a smile, and his eyes slide to meet mine. "See, Al? I told you I have platonic friends who are girls. Ellie and Sara count."

"So you haven't asked either of them for a kiss to save your ego with your buddies?" I ask, giving him the sweetest smile I can.

His blue eyes flash, and Dylan snorts. "That's how you got her to kiss you? Damn, Schultz. You're losing your touch," he says, shaking his head at his captain.

"It worked, didn't it?" I can't help laughing because it did. I smile back at Jack, surprising both of us, and as much as I don't want to admit it, maybe he isn't so bad.

"Did I miss something? I thought you hated hockey players, and now you're kissing them in bars, Alondra?" Chad asks, chiming in, and Macy quickly elbows him, but it's too late. The question is already hanging in the open while we're surrounded by hockey players.

I stir my drink, biting back my immediate response. I wouldn't have even been here if it weren't for him breaking up with Macy, only to ask her to get back together less than a week later. Jack raises an eyebrow at me, waiting for an explanation, but I don't have one—or at least, not one I want to share in front of four of my father's players.

"How do you hate hockey when your dad coaches?" Dylan asks, and I shrug, stalling by taking a drink of my rum with a splash of Coke.

"I don't hate hockey," I answer, and Ellie bumps my knee under the table with hers.

"Well, I think it's boring, and my brother plays, so I'm not sure why it matters," Ellie says, and Jack gives me a smile before taking a swig of the water in front of him.

"Good enough for me. I appreciate honesty more than a dick trying to put someone down in front of others," Jack responds to Chad, his eyes never leaving mine. He just won himself some major points in my book.

Out of the corner of my vision, I see Chad stiffen. "We're going to the bar. Does anyone need anything to drink?" he asks, but I think there's a good chance he'll spit in every glass after that.

"I would like if you went away and never came back," I mumble under my breath. Ellie's quiet laughter next to me tells me I wasn't quiet enough. Macy's face shifts into a silent plea, begging me to be nice to Chad. "I'm good, thanks."

Everyone else shakes their heads before we reshuffle to let them out.

"I thought they broke up?" Jack asks, watching them walk away.

"It changes by the week," I say, sipping my drink.

"He's a dick." The guy who was stuck talking with Chad says, and Coop grimaces.

"Took you that long to figure out? Chaz talked over her ten times in the first three minutes of them sitting," he says, and I can honestly say I think Coop might be my favorite at the table.

"I was being nice—something you might want to try every once in a while," he says, rolling his eyes before offering me a smile. "I'm Nate. I think I owe you a drink for helping Cap with his class." He exudes charisma, drawing me in with his easy smile and honey eyes. That makes him Nate Baxter, leader in the Wolves' penalties last season, but the man sitting in front of me is very different from the "tough guy" persona he presents on the ice.

"Or I can get her one myself, Baxter." Jack's voice is a low rumble, drawing my attention back to him. I bite back a laugh because he might as well be a dog lifting his leg on a tree, claiming it as his.

Too bad for him, I have no intention of being pissed on anytime soon.

Coop rolls his eyes, taking a drink of his beer when a grunt slips from Jack.

"Why did you kick me?" he asks, narrowing his pretty eyes at Ellie, and she scoffs.

"Do you even have to ask? Did you take a hit to the head at practice today or something?"

Jack sputters and I shake my head, turning to talk to Ellie's brother instead. "Coop, you're left-handed, aren't you?" I ask, and he tilts his head.

"Yeah?" he answers, and suddenly his difference in saves from the right and left sides of the goal makes sense.

"You should work on drills to strengthen your right side. If I'm remembering correctly, most of the shots that snuck past you last season were on that side of the goal," I say, taking a long drink of my rum and Coke, a fuzzy feeling beginning to soften the hard edges of my personality.

Coop looks at me like I'm a pig that sprouted wings. "Your dad told me the same thing last month."

A lump forms in my throat at the mention of my dad, and I shrug. "Good," I say, feeling the weight of Jack's stare. I know I started this conversation, but silly me thinking Dad wouldn't be brought up. "You planning to spend less time in the penalty box this season?" I ask, directing the question at Nate while tugging the neck of my sweater.

"Not a chance." Nate grins, and I chuckle, shaking my head. I reach for my drink, taking a long sip, and this isn't as bad as I expected it to be. I'll never admit it to a soul, though.

I comb my fingers through my curls, lifting them off the back of my neck. It seemed like a great idea when facing the chill outside on the walk over, but now this bar is beginning to feel more like a sauna. Maybe I'll get lucky and Macy and Chad will want to leave soon, giving me an excuse to leave with them.

Ellie's leg bumps mine, and she smiles at me. "I'm glad you're here. Saves me and Sara from being the only ones getting glared at by all the puck bunnies."

"You're not making me want to stay," I say, taking another drink and look around the crowded bar. Sure enough, there's more than a few people staring at our table.

"What if I said Jack drove, which means we don't have to walk back to the apartment from here?" Ellie suggests, and it does sound better than walking back in the dark. "He also usually takes Sara and me to get food before dropping us off," she continues, and I think I can stick it out a little longer.

Still, it feels more like I've been thrown to the wolves—literally.

CHAPTER 7

Alondra

WITHIN TEN MINUTES, everything went to shit. When Macy and Chad were at the bar, a girl approached that Chad had been messaging during their short break. Except, they'd continued messaging after he and Macy got back together.

There were text messages from just an hour before we got to the bar, in which where he told the girl he would come see her later. Once she spotted him with Macy, it was game over.

Hoes before bros.

Macy ordered a round of shots after her very public breakup, and friends don't let friends do breakup shots alone so I took them with her. Ellie felt bad and roped Coop, Nate, and Dylan into also taking a shot, but Sara and Jack stayed sober.

Ellie and I continue taking shots with Macy after the guys switch back to their beers, and I'm a giggling mess as Macy moans about what a terrible lay Chad was. I'm hopeful that after coming face to face with another girl Chad planned on messing around with, this will be the last time they break up.

"He didn't deserve you," I say, and she grabs the last shot from the middle of the table, throwing it back with ease.

"He didn't deserve me," she repeats, and Ellie gasps, covering her mouth with her hands.

"Isn't the best way to get over someone to get under someone else?" she asks, and Sara laughs, shaking her head.

"I'm all for living in the moment, but maybe not tonight."

Macy grins, and I think I agree with Sara. "El, last time we tried that mentality, I ended up kissing Jack," I say, giggling as I point to the hockey captain sitting across from me. The corners of his mouth tip up into a smile. I feel my face heat as my gaze drops to stare at his pink lips, and I wonder if he'd kiss me again?

"I didn't say you needed to end up under someone else," Ellie says, grabbing onto my arm, pulling my attention away from Jack.

"She does," Macy adds, and I turn too fast to look at her, my vision spinning for a moment.

"I do not! This is not gang up on Alondra night," I protest, beyond mortified we're talking about this.

"I volunteer as tribute if you're looking for someone," Dylan adds, winking at me, and I can't deny he's handsome. All four of them are, but there's something inviting about Dylan, with his warm brown skin and dark eyes. Maybe it has something to do with his personality, but if I'm going to break my rule about hockey players, I'm afraid the spot is already taken—whether I want to admit it or not.

"You're against my rule," I say, a short laugh sputtering from me. I look at each of the annoyingly attractive men sitting at the table with us, shaking my head. "All of you are."

"What rule?" Nate asks, tilting his head to the side.

"We need more shots," I say, switching gears, and Ellie beams, sliding out for me to climb out.

"Get another round of lemon ones," she says, giving me a thumbs up, and I laugh as Coop drags a hand over his face.

I'm halfway to the bar when I realize Jack is following

behind me. I turn to look at him, and my feet trip over each other, sending me straight into his firm chest.

Holy buckets.

His large hands land on my waist, helping to steady me, but I don't take my hands off him. Instead, I reach up to where the silver chain is peeking out from underneath his shirt, and his chest hitches. "Hi," I say, laughing as I look up at his dreadfully handsome face.

He's been quiet tonight, and I'm not sure what it means. Normally I'm begging him to be quiet, but this hurts my head.

"Where are you going?" he asks, and I tilt my head—*or maybe everything else tilts*—because I thought I made it clear where I was going.

"To the bar for more shots?" I say, twisting the chain between my fingers, warm from his body heat. "What's this for?"

Jack's face softens, and I think I'm imagining the concern swimming in his crystal eyes. "Don't you think you've had enough, darlin'?" he asks, but I can't think because his hands are on me, and all I can think about is how it'd feel to have them all over me instead.

"No," I say, another laugh slipping from me, and his lips tease the ghost of a smile.

"Alondra," he says, his hand closing around mine to pull it from his necklace, and I feel my stomach drop.

Oh my god. What am I doing? He's one of Dad's players, and I'm his tutor. That's all this can be.

I shake my head, stepping back from him, feeling the room spin as the music grows louder, pounding through my head. "Go back to the table, I'm fine, Jack." Someone walking by bumps into me, and I grab the barstool next to me for stability. His eyebrows knit as he looks at me, frowning, and before he can say anything, I realize I'm nervous because of Jack. What the fuck is going on with me? "I need to pee," I squeak out, retreating toward the bathroom to hide, hoping he won't follow me.

I do actually have to use the bathroom, and thankfully, it's not too busy for a Saturday night. After washing my hands, I take a few deep breaths, trying to untangle the chaos in my head, which is worse than a pair of neglected headphones.

I shouldn't want anything to do with Jack, but I'm starting to feel like my old self again—the one I said goodbye to.

Fuck, pull it together.

I'm drunk. That's all this is. I don't actually want him to kiss or touch me, and I don't want to know whatever shitty meaning lies behind his stupid necklace.

Jack isn't your friend—he's a hockey player, and not just any player, he's Dad's *star* hockey player.

But Jack is . . . stubborn, hot, and a great kisser. He makes me feel something, even if I shouldn't.

Two girls stumble into the bathroom, jolting me from my silent conversation with myself, and I slide past them, exiting the bathroom. I move toward the bar, and I feel like my life flashes before my eyes at the sight of the guy I've successfully avoided for the last nine months.

My feet stop of their own accord, and I'm frozen, caught in a replay of all the horrible moments with Bradley right up until the moment he left me lying broken on the ground at the bottom of his front steps in the freezing cold like I was no better than a broken doll he was tired of playing with.

I'm not even sure if I'm breathing, my throat constricting to the point I'm choking on the air intended to keep me alive.

Al, move before he sees you.

Bradley's hunched over the pool table in the corner of the bar with some of his friends. His back is to me, so there's no way I've been spotted, but even the close proximity of being in the same room as him sobers me.

And then I make eye contact with Jack after he spins

around with two waters in his hands, a smile transforming his face.

My shock and horror must not show on my face because he walks in my direction, extending a water to me. "You should drink this. It'll help make you feel less shitty in the morning," he says, and I blink, staring at it.

I shouldn't be here. I *knew* tonight was a bad idea.

"Al?"

I blink again, looking up at Jack who is beginning to look at me in a way that makes my blood pound in my ears.

"I need to go," I say, unable to help from taking another glance to make sure his back is still to me. *Move, Alondra.*

Jack looks in the same direction I did, but unlike me, he's noticeable in a crowded room, and it's enough to kick me into gear.

I move through the crowd of people, desperate to get out of here. My phone vibrates in my back pocket, and I can't even bring myself to care that I left my roommate and my best friend at the table. The chill hits me the moment I walk out the front door, but the first breath of cold air feels more like inhaling shards of glass, and I try not to disappear into the nightmare I've already escaped.

My head spins from the shots like I'm on a merry-go-round unable to stop, moving faster and faster and leaving me no choice but to hold on.

While my mind has cleared, my body hasn't received the same memo, and my foot slips on one of the stairs, causing me to lurch forward. An arm hooks around my waist, catching me before I can fall face first into the pavement, and I don't have to look to know it's Jack.

"Who are you running from?" he asks, his voice somehow breaking through all the noise in my head.

"No one," I say, giving myself a moment to regain my balance before moving again.

Bradley is no one, and I force another breath into my lungs.

"Al, you've taken enough shots to knock out a horse. You're drunk, and it's cold as hell out here. Let's go back inside," he says when I remove his hands from me.

"You don't tell me what to do," I say, because I can't go back in there. I can't be the smallest version of myself again, and Bradley has a way of making me feel microscopic.

"Alondra," Jack says, his footsteps following me.

"Go away, Jack."

He scoffs, and I trip on a crack, except this time I catch myself without his help. "For fuck's sake, will you just slow down and tell me what's going on before you get hurt?"

I wrap my arms around myself, trying to conserve my body heat, but it's colder now than it was when we first got to Twin City. "Jack, go back inside. We're not friends—you don't need to follow me to make sure I'm okay."

"Why are we not friends again?" he asks, appearing unfazed by the temperature despite only wearing a short sleeve and jeans.

"Because you're you!" I shout, throwing my hands out in frustration.

"I'm me?" Jack has the nerve to look hurt when I've been nothing but honest about wanting nothing to do with him from the moment I learned who he was.

I have no desire to have the conversation regarding my daddy issues or my complex relationship history with him ever, but especially not now.

"Jack, it's nothing personal, but I don't want to be friends with you. I've done the whole 'hang with the jocks' before, and I can't make myself small enough again for your ego to fill a room. I'll tutor you, but that's all you'll get from me. Tonight was a mistake."

He doesn't have a chance to say anything before my

stomach rolls, and I'm bent over into the bushes, vomiting. I'm too busy losing all of my pride to protest when he pulls my hair gently out of my face, and I only feel worse because I wish he wasn't so damn nice to me, especially when I just insulted him.

I wipe my mouth on the sleeve of my sweater, feeling more disgusting than I ever have before. Jack hooks an arm around my waist, helping me up, and I'm afraid to look him in the eye.

"C'mon, Al. Let's get you back home," he says, and it's the tenderness in his touch that causes a flicker of doubt in my resolve to not let Jack anywhere near my heart. It's already been broken more times than I can count, and I'm not sure it's possible to rebound from another one, but it seems inevitable where Jack is concerned.

The next morning, I wake up with a pounding headache, feeling like the biggest bitch in the world as the events of last night replay in my mind. Jack drove me home and helped me to bed without a single complaint.

A wave of nausea rolls in my stomach when I remember what caused me to flee the bar in the first place.

I knew at some point I would run into Bradley, but I was naive to think I'd be unaffected. Unfortunately, thinking you're prepared and *actually* being prepared are two different things.

I was *not* prepared is an understatement.

My phone vibrates on the nightstand, and I unplug it, seeing dozens of texts from Macy and Ellie—some legible, but most a random collection of letters put together. The most recent one is from Jack, reminding me to take the pain meds and drink the water he left on my nightstand.

Today is a day I'm pulling the covers over my head to hide from the world when I should be hiding from myself.

Am I being too mean to Jack?

Absolutely.

Am I afraid of becoming friends with Jack?

Yes.

Should I become friends with Jack?

Potentially.

I groan, twisting to shove my face into my pillow. I need to make things right with him by trying to explain my apprehension.

Jack isn't the same as Bradley, and it was unfair of me to take my fear for one out on the other.

ALONDRA

Can we talk?

JACK

at the rink

u said plenty last night

I feel sick to my stomach, and not because of how many shots I did. We were having fun last night before I saw Bradley. I was being a flirty drunk, but Jack did nothing wrong—I did.

I pull myself from the safety my bed promises to shower. I unfortunately have to stop mid-shower to puke again. I'm moving slowly, but I'm awake, even if I wish I were still sleeping. Then I could pretend I wasn't a huge bitch to Jack last night.

Pure stubbornness is how I find myself walking into the rink, and finding Jack is easy. I question my sanity for a moment, but it's crazy what a guilty conscience will make you do. Each step toward the ice feels like a death march, but I get closer to the ice than I have on any of the mornings I've snuck into the arena with the intention of skating.

Stopping at the clear paneling, I watch as Jack sends shot after shot into different areas of the net with frightening accuracy. He's really good. The Carolina Dolphins will be lucky to have him. He looks larger than life out there with the added height from the skates, but he took care of me last night with the utmost gentleness.

Jack doesn't spot me until he's fishing the pucks out of the net, and his facial expression becomes guarded. When he's done collecting them all, he glides to the exit, moving past me without a second glance as he takes off his gloves and sits on the bench next to his things to unlace his skates. I cross my arms over my chest, trying to figure out where to begin.

He sighs, grabbing the bench, looking at the ground. "Al, I heard you loud and clear last night. You don't want to be friends."

My guilt already felt like a knife had stabbed me, but the resignation in his normally upbeat demeanor twists it. "I was drunk, but it's not an excuse. I-I'm sorry."

"It wasn't just last night," he says, turning up to look at me, and Jack's unwavering stare makes me want to hide. It's like Jack's looking right through me.

I chew the inside of my cheek and shuffle closer to sit next to him, my nose wrinkling slightly from the smell coming from his gloves. I'm not really in a position to complain about it, though.

"It's not about you," I say, being deliberate with every word, but there's no beating around this bush. "Chad was trying to be an ass last night when he said that I hate hockey players, but he wasn't wrong. It doesn't really have anything to do with the players, but more so with my dad's priorities and where I fit into them."

I cross my arms over my chest as if it's enough to protect me here. I feel a longing in my heart to put on my skates and try skating today, but the thought of facing my fear makes my lungs constrict.

"My dad has always put his players over me. It didn't matter what I did or how hard I tried, they were always more important than me. I've spent years trying to make him love me the same way he loves his players. I really am sorry. I've been holding it against you because it's effortless for you to get his time and attention, and that's not fair."

"Oh," Jack says, exhaling a long breath. I turn in his direction, confused by what *Oh* is supposed to mean.

"Oh?"

He dips his chin in a nod. "Oh," he repeats.

What is happening?

"Jack?"

He rolls his shoulders, and I watch as Jack's hand drifts to his chest, his finger running over the length of the necklace. "I'm sorry he makes you feel like we're more important to him, but for what it's worth, I think Coach does love you. He might just have a hard time showing it."

I don't argue with him because a small part of me is desperate enough to hope Jack's right.

I push my pride aside, extending my hand. "Friends?"

Jack smiles, the corners of his eyes softening. "I'd prefer a kiss actually," he teases, and I think my rudeness has been forgiven.

I chuckle, dropping my hand after returning his smile with one of my own.

"Not happening, but nice try."

"Can't blame a guy for trying." He shrugs, and I roll my eyes, hoping my face isn't bright red.

"Guess I can't. Thank you for taking care of me last night. I wouldn't have blamed you if you'd let me walk off on my own."

"You could have told me I was the worst person in the world, and I still would have taken care of you. Friends don't let friends walk away drunk. I wasn't going to leave without knowing you were safe."

I can tell by his expression he's serious. "I thought we just became friends?" I ask, trying to lighten the mood.

Jack shakes his head. "Darlin', I've been your friend, even if you weren't mine," he says, and it's so brutally honest, it renders me speechless. "Are you feeling better?" he asks, and I twist my damp curls around my finger.

"The spins hit me again this morning, but I should be good," I say, leaving out the part where it was in the middle of my shower.

He laughs, the sound resonating through me. "I'm shocked you had anything left in you to throw up."

My cheeks flush because last night really wasn't my finest moment. "Me too."

I catch the way his eyebrows narrow and his lips purse before the uncertainty melts from his handsome face. Am I allowed to think he's hot? I'd have to be blind not to be aware of his attractiveness, and it's not like it's something he doesn't already know.

"What?" I ask, and Jack raises an eyebrow, flashing a crooked smile.

"What?"

"You made a face. What is it?" I ask, wondering if this is something I should be asking.

"Who were you running from last night?" he asks, and the question lingers in the silence of the empty rink.

"Nobody," I answer, swallowing the lump forming in my throat as I look away, recalling the ghost of my former self who didn't know what it felt like to lose the thing she loved most.

Maybe she's still there, flying across the ice, and I just have to find her again.

CHAPTER 8

Jack

"AL," I whisper, trying to get her attention, but the lecture hall is so quiet I can hear the clacking of the keys on Alondra's computer next to me as she takes notes. I should be taking my notes, but I can't sit still anymore.

She sighs, pursing her pretty pink lips, which I'm trying not to stare at because I've just convinced her to be my friend. The last thing I need is for her to catch me thinking about kissing her. Al brushed me off earlier when I asked if she needed to borrow one of my extra jerseys for our game on Friday night, but I think it was pushing it too far to ask her to go.

I don't actually have anything to ask her, but the more she ignores me, the more I know I'm getting under her skin. I lean in, catching a whiff of strawberries, and it makes me want to bury my nose in her curls.

They suit her—perfectly unbound and messy, matching Alondra's fiery temper. I never know what's going to come out of her mouth, and I'm drawn to the chaos.

"Alondra," I whisper, and the corner of her lip tugs, and I know she can hear me. "Al, stop ignoring me."

God, I should be paying attention because our midterm is

next week, and with hockey in full swing, I know my schedule is insane. My brain is overwhelmed by the thought of what will happen if I don't pass, and it's stressing me out to the point where I can't even try to focus on piecing everything together.

Keri chuckles on the other side of Al, and I smile. "Hey," I whisper, and Alondra huffs, but still doesn't look at me. "Darlin'," I drawl, and my smile grows when she shifts in her seat.

Al turns, her hazel eyes narrowing as she frowns. "Shut up, please," she whispers, but while trying to get her attention, I inadvertently attracted the attention of our GTA, Maggie, as well.

"I'm sorry, am I boring you?" she asks from the front of the auditorium, and every head in the room turns in our direction.

It's tempting to blurt out yes, but it won't help the situation.

I clear my throat since Alondra's rendered speechless next to me, trying to maintain my casual demeanor instead of letting Maggie think she's winning by embarrassing me in front of everyone. "Sorry, I was asking Al a quick question about something you said a few minutes ago," I say, leaning back in the small seat.

"Next time, raise your hand, or see me after class," Maggie says, crossing her arms over her chest, and Al's scowl deepens.

Yeah, won't be doing that.

I didn't want to tell Al that part of the reason my grade slipped so much is was that I stopped attending the study group Maggie leads and her office hours when I realized she was going to spend the whole time trying to flirt with me instead of listening to or answering any of my questions. I'd rather fail than have anyone accuse me of passing because they think I'm fucking the GTA for extra credit.

The next few minutes pass painfully slowly, and I don't

miss Alondra glancing at me. If I had just sat here and left Al alone, I could've avoided pissing her off again. Why can't I just leave the fucking hornet's nest alone?

Al still hasn't said anything when she follows me down the stairs on our way out of class. I'm forced to turn around when Maggie calls my name.

Staying to talk to her is the last thing I want to do right now, but it's my own damn fault. I roll my shoulders, trying to get rid of some of the tension, but I don't think I'll be able to relax until I'm out of the building. "I'll meet you outside?" I ask Al, but I doubt she'll be here by the time Maggie is done with whatever she wants to talk to me about.

Alondra glances at Maggie, her expression resembling the one Coach Brown gets when he's pissed off about our performance. "What does she want?" Al asks, seeing right through all the bullshit, and I don't know if I want to know what she's thinking right now.

"It's fine, don't worry about it," I reassure her, pushing a smile onto my face.

Al appears skeptical when she turns away, walking through the doors.

The rest of the auditorium has cleared out as Maggie gathers her things, her eyes following me as I walk toward the desk, feeling slightly nauseous. "Are you feeling prepared for the midterm exam next week? I haven't seen you at any of the study groups recently," she says, leaning against the desk behind her, and I shrug.

"I have a great tutor. I'll be ready," I answer, shoving my hands in my pockets.

Maggie's mouth flattens, and she twirls a lock of her blonde hair around her finger. "If you needed a tutor, you could have asked me," she says, but the way her eyes trail down me like I'm a piece of meat makes my skin crawl. Contrary to what everyone believes, I don't drop my pants at the first sight of a willing girl.

"I'm okay, but thank you," I say, glancing over my shoulder, hoping Al hasn't made it too far for me to catch her. "I'm go—"

"What was your question?" Maggie asks, tilting her head, tapping her nails on the top of the desk.

"What?"

"The one you needed to ask your *tutor*, disrupting the whole class," she says, and I try not to laugh. I'm not sure whispering to Al was disruptive, but the way Maggie called us out in front of everyone certainly was, not to mention unprofessional.

"You know, I can't remember. Guess it wasn't that important," I say, forcing a sheepish smile. "Sorry, but I've gotta get to hockey," I lie, knowing she has no idea what our schedule is.

"If you think of the question, you know where to find me to get the answer," she says, pushing off the desk to step closer to me, and I adjust the straps of my backpack on my shoulders.

"Great, thanks," I say, turning and walking away before she can try to sink her claws into me.

I breathe a short sigh of relief once I step through the door, but I'm shocked to see Alondra leaning against the nearby wall. When I told her I'd meet her outside, I didn't actually expect her to wait, but to say she's irritated would be putting it mildly.

"You waited?" I ask, walking up to her, and she glares at me, smacking my chest with the back of her hand. "Ow, what was that for?" I rub the spot, but it didn't actually hurt.

"Stop acting like that hurt. I think you bruised my hand with your pecs of steel or whatever you implanted in your chest. Why do you look surprised I waited?" Alondra asks, looking up at me, and in just a few moments, she's erased the oily feeling clinging to my skin.

"Pecs of steel?" She makes it so easy to smile and laugh,

but her frown has the opposite effect I think she intended it to have. "You're cute when you frown," I say, laughter bubbling from me again when Al's jaw drops and she hits me again.

"You're my friend, you can't call me cute," she says, crossing her arms over her chest and turning to walk away from me.

A few long strides are all it takes for me to catch up, and I open the door for her. She stops, almost like she's going to argue with me about how I can't hold a damn door for her because we're friends.

"Sorry, darlin', if I didn't want to be just your friend, I'd sure as shit try harder than just holding a door for you. And if I told you I call all my friends cute, what then?" I ask, messing with her. I don't think I've ever called anyone cute in my life.

She rolls her eyes, walking through the door. "Has anyone ever told you how annoying you are?" Al grumbles, and after I fall into step beside her again, I sling my arm over her shoulder. It feels like a victory when she doesn't immediately slip away. "What did she want?" she asks, and I wish she hadn't.

"To know why I haven't been going to the class study group," I say, leaving it at that. "You want a ride back?"

"Sure, thanks," Alondra says, and I squint, adjusting to the brightness of the sun.

"Can we move up our tutoring tomorrow? Coach scheduled a team meeting for when we'd normally meet to get it in before our game Friday."

"Sure," Al says, and her sudden agreeableness is suspicious. I glance down at her, trying to figure out where the hell my feisty girl has gone.

Her lower lip is tucked between her teeth as she chews on it, and I'm not sure she's hearing anything I said past asking if she wanted a ride.

"Dylan's going to get a tattoo on his ass of your dad's name. Which do you think is better: left or right?"

"Left," she answers, and I swallow the laugh back, wondering how much I can get away with before she notices.

"Maybe I'll get a matching one on my right cheek of your name," I continue, unable to help chuckling. The idea of getting someone's fucking name tattooed on my ass is so preposterous I can't believe Dylan is even joking about it.

"What?" Al asks, tipping her head up, a confused expression forming on her face.

"You just told me which ass cheek Dylan should get a tattoo of your dad's name on," I say, my chest shaking with silent laughter, and a choked sound escapes her.

"Did you just say which ass cheek?" she asks, sputtering.

"I want to say he's joking, but I've been proven wrong before."

I know I should move my arm from her shoulders, but it seems like more work than it's worth when I'll just take it off once we reach my truck in a minute.

Alondra laughs next to me, and I know I'll happily make a fool of myself if it makes her laugh again.

CHAPTER 9

Alondra

My hands are steady despite my heart hammering in my chest as I pull the laces tight on my skates, the muscle memory coming back to me like I never stopped.

Dad mentioned last night how he gave the team the morning off to rest before their first game tonight, but even then I didn't want to risk someone walking in on me, so here I am at five o'clock in the morning, staring at the ice again.

I take a few steps closer to the crystal-clear ice, free of any imperfections, but I falter once I reach the gate, and now my hands are shaking as I take off the skate guards, and my side aches from the memory of the last time I skated.

It isn't real, I remind myself, trying to shake the nerves.

I pull the edges of my long sleeves over my hands, fisting the soft fabric as my breathing quickens.

God, I'm nervous, and there's no reason to be.

Jack was nervous during tutoring yesterday, but he's trying, which is more than I can say. I've spent nine months staring at the thing I love most, too afraid of someone who doesn't have the power to inflict any more pain on me to do a damn thing. It's been a year since I skated, but I didn't let myself even look at the ice while I was still with Bradley.

I reach forward to grab the top of the boards, and I don't give myself a chance to second guess it, forcing my feet onto the slick surface.

"I did it," I whisper, feeling tears well up in my eyes, and I let them fall.

I push off the ice, gliding forward as the cool air stings my cheeks. Tension I didn't even realize I was still carrying seems to melt away as I relax, losing myself in the moment.

I know I can never be who I once was—the innocence of not knowing what it felt like for someone I love to lay a hand on me is gone—but this feels like one step closer to finding myself again.

I've been going through the motions, purely existing because I had to and not because I wanted to.

Right now, I don't want to go through the motions. I want to be unpredictable like a kite dancing in the wind, free of any responsibilities tying it down.

I spin. I laugh. I smile.

I spread my arms out to pretend I'm an airplane when I follow the wide curves of the rink.

I skate.

Minnesota might not be where I wanted to stay, but maybe it's where I need to be. I'll never admit it to my parents, though. All I'd hear is an *I told you so.*

I pick up speed until I feel like I'm flying. The flyaways that have escaped from my braid are fluttering around my face, but I feel alive. Eyeing the exact spot where I want to land, I use my speed and toe pick to propel myself into the air and spin twice to see if I can still land a double toe. I used to spend hours working on my jumps to execute them flawlessly when I was competing, both on ice and off ice.

Except it's been a while.

I haven't kept up with the proper training to get the height I need to complete both turns, and I land hard, busting my ass on the ice. I'm quick to push myself up again, continuing to try despite falling repeatedly. It's comical how out of shape I am, but my face hurts from smiling.

I go again and again, the scraping sound of my blades on the ice is music to my ears, and I've finally escaped the black hole I've been trapped in, letting me feel everything.

My whole body aches, but I don't regret a single moment, only wishing I'd worked up the courage sooner to come out here. Turning, I move to skate back toward the exit when I notice a lone figure watching me next to where I've left my things.

My smile drops in an instant, and I can only imagine how many questions are running through the hockey captain's head. I was so lost in feeling like my old self again that I have no idea how long he's been standing there.

His gaze is intense and unwavering as I brush past him, quickly dropping into a seat to pull my skates off and wipe the blades off before covering them with soakers.

Jack's presence is hard to ignore as he looms over me, and I hold my breath.

"Darlin', where did you learn to skate like that?" he asks, his voice rough, and I avoid meeting his gaze.

"I don't skate."

He scoffs, the sound echoing off the walls of the otherwise silent arena. "Oh, so you were possessed by some magical demon who gets off on the adrenaline rush of skating?"

My lips press into a flat line. No one was supposed to see me here. Not even Jack.

"What are you even doing here?" I ask, finally lifting my head. "You have a game tonight. My dad said he cancelled morning skate for the team and that no one was supposed to be here."

"Shouldn't I be asking you that question?" Jack retaliates, and I glare at him, but it's not his fault I haven't skated in nearly a year. "I'm working with an underclassman on drills per your dad's request, and he wanted to get in a quick session this morning before our game tonight."

I grab my bag and stand up, forcing Jack to move back to give me space. I feel off-balance now, and Mom always used to say I'm more graceful on ice than on land.

Jack's voice softens, and he shakes his head. "*Dammit. Please, will you just talk to me?*"

I know it's because I'm scared and feeling vulnerable right now that I lash out at him instead of communicating with him like a normal person, knowing I'll regret it later. "Why should I?" I ask, tucking the stray curls that have fallen out of my braid behind my ear. "I know literally nothing about you! It goes both ways, *buddy.*"

Jack was taller than me to begin with, but add the skates, and he really is larger than life. I feel like I'm at a disadvantage for having already taken mine off. He chews on his bottom lip, pulling it into his mouth before tugging a hand through his hair. I've started to notice Jack does that a lot, and I wonder if it's a nervous tic for him.

"You asked me last week if I tell people about my dad, and it's not on my list of conversation starters, but when he does come up, I tell people he's dead because he might as well be. He's in prison, and I hope he stays there for as long as fucking possible after the hell he put me and my momma through," Jack says, and his chest might as well be cracked wide open because I can feel every bit of the raw emotion pouring from him. Jack's mouth parts like he's surprised to have said it, but I don't ask any questions. I step forward without thinking to wrap my arms around him, catching him by surprise as it dawns on me that we might have more in common than either of us would have guessed.

His arms are slow to close around me, but I don't miss the quiet sigh of relief Jack lets out. I don't know how long we stand there, but a reminder of where we are is enough for me to untangle myself from him, stepping back.

He's staring at me in a way that I can't tell what he's thinking, and this feels like a bigger moment than it should be.

"How was my worst?" I ask, trying to lighten the air.

Jack chuckles, shaking his head at me, but the question does make him smile. "Shut up, I'm not answering that."

The tension of being caught on the ice slips away from me, but whoever Jack is waiting on could show up any minute, and I need to get out of here.

"Why not? I think my hug was a ten out of ten," I argue.

"Solid four."

My jaw drops because there's no way, and I push his stupidly muscular chest in retaliation. "Liar," I say, calling Jack on his bullshit and his smile widens.

"Oh, cry me a river. You gave my kiss a three."

A snort slips from me, causing Jack to laugh again. "For as graceful as you were out there, that was the complete opposite," he says, and my cheeks flush.

"It happens sometimes." I shrug, maintaining my smile, but the high of skating is starting to fade, and I glance toward the doors where I'm sure his buddy is going to come out any second. "You didn't see me out here, okay?"

"I'll keep your secret for a kiss," Jack teases, and I roll my eyes.

I kiss my hand, reaching up to press my palm to his cheek, trying not to let my hand linger for more than a few seconds. Jack's cheek is smooth, and he must have shaved this morning, but his skin is warm and the chill is settling into my hands. "There you go," I say, clearing my throat as I pull back. "That's what a real kiss is like."

"Your hands are cold."

I stick my tongue out at him, tucking them into the sleeves of my shirt. "You're the one who wanted a kiss. You didn't specify what kind." I turn away from him to grab my bag, pulling it up over my shoulder to carry it back to my car.

"Hey?"

"Yeah?"

Jack hesitates as I look back at him. "About my dad . . . I don't . . ." He rubs the back of his neck, his cheeks tinted red.

He wants to know if I'm going to keep his secret.

"Don't worry about it, Jack. We've all got our shit. My lips are sealed."

His throat bobs as he swallows, dipping his chin in a nod. "Thanks. If you want to stash your bag somewhere for when you're definitely *not* skating, I can put on top of my stall for safekeeping. Beats lugging them around campus."

I hesitate, but I end up pulling the strap off my shoulder to hand it to him. "I don't skate," I repeat.

"Got it. You don't skate."

The clang of a door opening and shutting catches my attention, causing me to back away so quickly I almost trip over my own feet. "Schultz, you're not going to make me puke before our game tonight, right?"

"Depends on how many shots you miss," he calls back, setting my bag next to his stuff. "Thanks for dropping off my notes, Al. You're a lifesaver." Jack winks at me, and I sigh in relief, realizing he's giving me an excuse to be seen here, even if his teammate doesn't know who I am.

Correction: *Jack is a lifesaver.*

I make my escape, but I'm stopped in my tracks when I think the guy who shows up recognizes me, his head tilting as he looks me up and down. He squints, but I don't stick around to find out if he figures it out.

Instead, I try to focus on clinging to the euphoric feeling of gliding across the ice again—it's been a year too long without it.

CHAPTER 10

Jack

I'VE SPENT the last week asking myself why the hell, out of all the things I could have told Alondra at the rink, the first thing that came out of my mouth was my dad being in prison. I could have said anything else.

I could've said I hate ketchup and mayo by themselves, but mix them together? I'll dip anything in it.

I had braces for four years as a teenager.

Sometimes when I'm walking around campus on my way to class or to the team's study hall, I'll put my earbuds in with no music playing so that people don't talk to me.

Or I've never had a girlfriend because I don't believe in love.

But I didn't say any of that.

I willingly told Alondra the one thing I never tell people the truth about. My roommates know, but they're family to me. I'm not actually sure what Ellie knows and what she doesn't, and quite frankly, I don't give a shit so I've never cared to ask. She's been a good friend to me.

Fuck, the last thing I expected that morning when I walked into the barn was to see Alondra doing fucking jumps and skating with the biggest smile on her face. I had no idea she skated, let alone like that.

I'm trying not to see Coach B differently after what she told me, but it's hard. I've looked up to him for years, even considering him to be the closest thing I have to a father figure. He might be a hard-ass most of the time, but I know he's always had my best interests at heart.

Now? Every time he praises one of us or checks in to make sure I'm doing okay, I wonder if he does the same with Al. It's not my place at all, but I keep picturing the look on her face when she came to the rink two weeks ago to apologize. She looked like she'd rather swallow a handful of nails instead of tell me their relationship sucks, but Al did it because she wanted me to believe her apology.

I tip my head back, keeping the soap out of my eyes while the water from the showerhead hits all the right spots on my sore muscles. I forgot how sore my body is during the first few weeks, but we started our season going against some of the harder teams in our conference. Nate's doing his best to protect us out there, but he can't protect both me and Coop at the same time, and other teams know it.

Fuck.

Why did I tell her about my dad?

Most of the guys have already cleared out of the locker room by the time I'm done rinsing off, since Coach wanted to talk to me after practice about my thoughts on the team so far this season. He wants this as badly as we do.

He hesitated before asking how tutoring was going, and I tried to be as vague as possible, knowing how his relationship with Alondra is, but he's still my coach. There's a fine line to walk here.

I feel like I'm fraying at the edges while I wait for our midterm to be graded, but I keep reminding myself that if I scored poorly, I can do test corrections.

At least Coach B didn't ask me how she's doing. I'm not sure what I would have said if he had.

After getting dressed, Alondra's bag tucked on the top shelf of my stall taunts me. She had me set it out a few days ago for her, and it took everything in me not to get here early to watch her not skate. Al can deny it all she wants, but clearly she's just as much of a junkie for ice time as the rest of us, but I've been trying to respect the boundary she set.

I'm pretty much failing at trying to get her out of my head, and I don't know what to do about it.

Johnny asked about her after she left, but I shut it down fast by explaining Al's my tutor, and he didn't say anything else.

My dark sweater is warm, but I still pull my team jacket over it to keep out some of the chill on my walk to the library where I'm supposed to be meeting Al. I should have borrowed Nate's blow-dryer because the towel I used to dry my hair didn't do much, but I'm already running late. The last thing I want to do is piss Alondra off by making her think I don't respect her time. The wind is brutal today, and pretty soon I'll have to start taking the underground tunnels between buildings when there's too much snow to clear all the sidewalks, but it makes me feel claustrophobic.

I replay the voice memo she sent me yesterday, listening for where she said she'd be sitting before recording a quick one back to her. "Sorry, running late, but I should be there in a few. See you soon," I say, picking up my pace as the wind bites at my face.

I've never been more happy to be at the library than when I step through the doors and make my way toward the second floor where Al said she'd be.

Something in my chest settles when I see her sitting at a table in the back with two coffees in front of her, and I slide into the chair opposite her.

"For me? You shouldn't have," I say, shrugging out of my jacket to wrap my hands around the warm cup.

"It's just coffee, don't make a big deal about it," Alondra says, twisting a long dark curl around her finger, but her hazel eyes are twinkling today. Goddamn, sometimes it's really hard to pretend she's not beautiful. "How was practice?"

It catches me by surprise she's asking about hockey, since any time I broach the topic of her coming to a game, Al can't run in the other direction fast enough. "We had off-ice conditioning today," I say, and she grimaces.

"Gross. I've started going to the gym in the mornings and my ass is paying for it," Alondra says, taking a sip of her coffee.

She makes it too easy to flirt with her.

"You need some help with massaging it? I've been told my hands are pretty magical, darlin'." I smirk at Al, and she rolls her eyes, tempting me to ask her if she wants them to get stuck in the back of her head.

"Dylan's already volunteered, so yours aren't needed," she replies, tipping her pretty pink lips into a smile, and mine drops.

When did Dylan run into Al? Why didn't he say anything?

"I wouldn't let Dylan's hands touch me with a ten-foot pole, but your loss," I say, trying to let it roll off my back as I take a sip of my coffee. It helps warm me from the inside out, especially when I taste the sweetness of the caramel and the notes of vanilla in it. *She remembered my coffee order.*

A laugh sputters from Al, and she crosses her arms over her chest. "You say it like you're any better?" Alondra scolds, and I lean back in my chair.

"I'm happy to confirm I always wrap it before I tap it," I say, but I know Dylan does too. His family is loaded, and his parents have told him on more than one occasion that they're not ready for grandchildren. Regardless of how much he gets around, he's careful.

Unfortunately for me, I've been getting pretty familiar with my hand. I haven't been interested in anyone for a couple of weeks now, and my roommates haven't failed to notice either.

"Good for you," she says, but I don't feel any better thinking about Dylan putting his hands all over Alondra's ass.

"I'm just saying be careful." I take another sip of my coffee, and Alondra rolls her eyes again. "You know if you keep doing that, they're gonna get stuck in the back of your head," I say, and she rolls them again to prove a point.

"Then stop saying stupid shit if you don't want me to roll them," she retorts, tapping her purple nails on the table, and my traitorous mind imagines what they would feel like clawing at my back and what they would look like wrapped around my cock. *Shit, maybe I can't just be friends with a girl.*

"I didn't say anything stupid. I told you to be careful if you're going to mess around with Dylan," I say, trying not to vomit as I do. I can be attracted to her and be her friend.

"It was stupid because I'm not going to mess around with Dylan. I said he offered to give me a massage which is literally no different from what you offered to do. So can we agree what you said was stupid, or do I need to roll my eyes again?" Alondra asks, raising an eyebrow at me.

"It is different," I say, but I honestly don't know how it is.

"Shut up and drink your bougie coffee."

My jaw falls open because Alondra never ceases to surprise me. "You know, you're kind of bossy." I laugh under my breath, watching as Alondra plays with a curl.

"I think you like it, or maybe you'd stop picking fights with me," Alondra says, and she's not wrong. Fighting with Al feels like foreplay, but it's wrong because it can't happen. Fuck, it feels good, though.

I take a sip of my *bougie* coffee, looking around the large room. "So, what are we doing in the library? I thought campus was supposed to be closed today?" I ask, moving to a much safer topic because I'm honestly not sure I trust what I'm thinking to not come out of my mouth.

I'd bet if I were to go around and count, there's only a handful of people in the building, including us.

"The library really never closes, but I think they have a skeleton crew today if anyone needs help. I like to come here for a change of scenery," she says, and I tap the sides of my cup, setting it down to look back at Alondra. Her pale cheeks flush a bright red, and she tucks some of her long curls behind her ear before closing her laptop most of the way. "Sorry, I probably should have just asked you to meet me at the coffee shop or something. This was dumb," she rambles, and sure, the library isn't first on my list of places to go, but if it's on hers, I'll add it to mine.

"Al, I don't care where we hang out. I'm sorry my schedule has been kind of crazy this past week, but I want to hear how yours went," I say, losing the flirty swagger from before. "Are Macy and Charzard still broken up?" I ask, purposefully messing up his name to make Al laugh.

She wrinkles her nose in disgust, a scoff leaving her. "I think so, but Chad has a way of worming his way back in and getting Macy to take him back like a parasite. You wouldn't believe how many nights we've spent drinking after a breakup only for them to get back together while I'm nursing my hangover the next morning. I know he didn't cheat on her this time, but he has before and she's still taken him back, so I really don't know. Macy likes to ignore me when it comes to Chad."

"I don't see the point in relationships, but I guess that's just me," I say, taking a long drink of my coffee. "It seems like a miserable cycle to be caught in."

"Not all relationships are as toxic as theirs," Alondra says, pulling my attention back to her. When I'm with her, it's hard to look away for too long, even if that's not something a friend should think about another friend.

Maybe I'm just torturing myself by asking this question because Alondra seems like the kind of person who needs to be in a relationship to be intimate with someone, but I'm curious about how her answer compares to mine. "Have you had a good relationship?"

Her entire body stills, and I watch as she builds her walls again, brick by brick, right before my eyes. "Yes and no," she says slowly, and it causes the hair on the back of my neck to stand up.

No? What is that supposed to mean?

Is her ex the reason she ran from Twin City?

"Who?" I ask, the question rumbling from my chest before I can stop it. I know I'm jumping to conclusions, but she looked like she'd seen a ghost, and I haven't forgotten what Alondra said about making herself small, either.

Alondra looks away, her jaw clenching. "I don't think Chad and Macy are right for each other, but I'm not sure I'm ready to give up on my hope that there's someone out there for everyone," she says, avoiding the question. If I ask again, she's going to run. Alondra's always running from me, and I want her to stay. "What about you?" Alondra asks, turning it around on me.

"Me?"

She twists her hair around her finger again. "I don't see anyone else sitting by us, so yeah, you."

"I've never had a relationship," I answer, and finally, I've surprised her.

"Ever?"

I shake my head. "No, what's the point? I don't believe in love, and I'm not interested in tying myself to someone."

"The point is, you'll have someone there for you unconditionally. Someone who will accept you as you are and support you no matter what," she says, and I admire her answer. I really do, but it's not that easy.

"Sure, it sounds simple enough, but I'm sorry. I don't believe there's a perfect person out there for everyone. It always ends," I explain.

"Who knew you were such a cynic about love?" she muses, her fingers resuming their tapping.

I haven't seen anyone even move in this place since I sat down. Are we the only ones here?

"I'm not a cynic, I'm a realist." Fuck, I mean after seeing my dad wail on my mom my entire childhood until he got locked up, I don't think I ever stood a shot in hell at believing in relationships. I try so hard to make sure I'm completely different from him in every way, but the fact of it is, I am his son. The apple doesn't fall far from the tree, and I'm not interested in finding out if I'm anything like him.

Ergo, no relationships.

"So you're telling me you've only ever hooked up with people without any of the attachment?"

"I spend too much time at the rink to bother trying to have a relationship, even if I wanted one—which I don't. Sex is just sex," I say, dragging a hand through my hair before stretching, my muscles protesting.

"I'm going to find you a girlfriend," she says, her lips curling into a distracting smile.

"Sure, Al. Whatever you say." I laugh, brushing her off. It's probably a mistake to ask, but I need to know if I'm creating shit in my head that doesn't really exist. "Why did you need to leave Twin City?"

Her gaze averts from mine, staring instead at the coffee cup in front of her. "Drop it, please."

Fuck, I should have left it alone. "Al—"

"Jack, don't ask me about that. It doesn't matter," she snaps, and I put my hands up in self-defense.

"You don't need to bite my head off. I was going to apologize since you clearly don't want to tell me about it."

Meanwhile, I've spilled my deepest secret to her last week like it wasn't a big deal. This is great. My new friend won't open up to me at all, yet I can't seem to keep my mouth shut around her.

Her shoulders slump, and she drags her hands over her face, peeking at me through them. "I'm sorry, I just don't want to talk about that."

"Don't worry about it. I shouldn't have asked," I say, smiling at her in reassurance, but for the life of me, I can't figure her out. Al's moods are all over the fucking place. One minute, she's smiling and laughing with me. The next, she's shutting down, and I'm on the other side of the wall she puts up.

And even now, I'm the sucker who still wants to know everything about Alondra.

"So Johnny asked me if you were seeing anyone the other day," Coop says, holding the door for me on our way out of the training facility as I take a long drink of my water, causing me to choke when it goes down the wrong pipe.

It takes a moment for me to clear my throat, my eyes watering as I bend over, coughing.

"Why the fuck would he ask that?" I croak out, looking at Coop who is watching me with an amused look.

"Said he saw you with some girl at the barn, and I thought he was messing with me because there's no way you'd risk Coach killing you to bring a girl there. Then Johnny said he saw you with her again around campus."

Fuck, I thought Johnny was smart enough to keep his mouth shut about seeing her at the rink, but my friendship with Alondra isn't a secret.

"What'd you tell him?" I ask, and he shakes his head.

"I said Alondra's your tutor, and you don't do girlfriends. Am I wrong?" Coop asks, shoving his hands in his pockets.

"I don't do girlfriends," I repeat, because my stance on relationships hasn't changed.

Coop shakes his head, walking in the direction of the parking lot, leaving me to follow him.

"Al didn't think anyone would be there," I say, catching up to him. I'm tall at six three, but Coop is massive, standing at six five, and freakishly agile for his size.

"Have you forgotten her dad is our coach?" he asks, and I know I'm playing with fire by getting close to her.

"No." Coop's eyes slide to meet mine, and they say everything he isn't. "I haven't forgotten, Cooper. I didn't know she was going to be there because it was the morning of our first game, and Johnny wanted to work on his backhand shots. Hell, I didn't even know she could skate."

"Now you're being stupid. Coach's kid knows her shit, and you didn't think she'd know how to skate?"

Yeah, it was a stupid assumption on my part to think she wouldn't, but it's not my place to share what her relationship with her dad is like. If we hadn't shown up early to practice that day, I'm not sure I ever would've known Alondra is his daughter. Hell, I'd probably still be calling her Alex.

"Schultz!" a voice calls out behind us, and I swivel to look back. I don't know his name, but he looks familiar enough that I can place him as a football player.

"You know him?" Coop asks, and the closer he gets, the more I'm sure I don't.

"No idea. You go ahead, I'll meet you at my pickup," I say, pulling the keys from my pocket and tossing them to him. Coop tips his head up in acknowledgement at the guy, walking off as I get a better look at him. "Hey, man. All good?"

I'm not a small guy by any means, and he's built like a

freaking freight train, which makes me think he's a line-backer, but I don't think we've ever spoken.

"Bradley Smith," he says, flashing a quick smile. "I'm friends with Johnny."

I'm sorry, what am I supposed to say to that?

"And I'm friends with Seth," I say, dropping the quarter-back's name, but it doesn't seem to faze him.

"I heard my girl's tutoring you, and I'd hate for you to get the wrong idea."

His girl? I set my shoulders back, clenching my jaw to keep from asking who the hell he thinks he is.

"I think you might be the one with the wrong idea, *buddy*. Al doesn't belong to anyone, but good luck to you if you think she does because she hasn't mentioned you at all. I think I'll stick with what I'm doing. Seems to be working out for me," I say, forcing an easy smile on my face when really, I feel like I'm wound so tightly, the slightest move and I'll deto-nate. What the hell is Johnny doing being friends with this guy?

His dark eyes narrow, but he doesn't scare me. It does cross my mind that maybe I shouldn't have told Coop to go on ahead without me.

"She likes to play hard to get, but maybe you heard me wrong—stay away from her," Bradley warns, checking my shoulder with his.

The goosebumps on my arms linger long after the encounter, and my number of questions for Alondra has increased tremendously.

CHAPTER 11

Alondra

"I'M SORRY, YOU'RE WHAT?" Ellie asks, gaping at me from the beanbag she's camped out on, while Macy refills our wine glasses in the kitchen.

"Finding Jack a girlfriend. Do you have any pictures of him you think I should add to his profile?" I ask through a fit of giggles at her reaction. The account I made for Jack is open on my phone, but I'm struggling to pick what pictures scream *boyfriend material* instead of *fuckboy vibes.*

Ellie grins as Macy walks back into the living room balancing the cheap wine in her hands. "I told her it was a bad idea, but she's hell-bent on this plan."

"Oh, he's going to kill you, but I'm totally for this." Ellie snorts, pulling her phone out.

"Jack said it was fine!"

Macy shakes her head, and I roll my eyes, regretting telling her about the conversation in the first place. "No, tell her exactly what he said."

"Fine. It was more so along the lines of 'Sure, whatever you want,' but if he didn't want me to do it, he should have told me no," I argue, but I did consider the idea he didn't think I'd actually do it.

Ellie sends me a few pictures, and we arrange them in a specific order, starting strong with a gold mine from his mom's post on social media for his first day of school photo this year. It highlights his dimples and makes him look more sweet than sexy, and I ignore the little flutter my heart does upon realizing he took the photo to make his mom happy. Ellie suggested following it up with a picture of Jack and his mom from a game she came to see last season, sliding in that he plays hockey and he's a momma's boy. Maybe he wasn't giving me a hard time by asking where my blanket was from.

"I feel like a shirtless picture sends the wrong vibes," I say, hesitating on the picture Macy strategically cropped from a trip he took this summer with his roommates.

Ellie shakes her head. "I disagree. I think if someone's made it to the third picture, the shirtless picture could tip the scales in his favor if someone is trying to decide whether he's worth a swipe or not."

"Okay, shirtless picture it is," I say, adding it in, and then we end with a picture of him and his friends in the booth at Twin City.

Based on pictures alone, it's a solid profile, but a bio can make it or break it.

"What do you think? Something hockey or Texas related?" I ask, taking a sip of my wine, tossing the phone to Ellie.

"Can I just say one more time I think this is a terrible idea?" Macy chimes in, and Ellie shushes her.

"Don't take away my entertainment. This is good practice for me because I'll probably have to do this for Coop, considering he has the emotional depth of a toddler," Ellie says, and I snort.

"Maybe Texas? I feel like there's way more material." Macy shakes her head, taking a drink from her glass. "What about *I'm looking for the yee to my haw*?"

"How about *save a horse, ride a hockey player*?" I suggest

through a fit of giggles. Ellie gasps and covers her mouth, and our laughter is so loud it's echoing off our apartment walls.

Once she settles down enough to take a breath, she unfortunately brings up a very good point. "I feel like we need to change it to *save a horse, date a hockey player* instead," Ellie says, and Macy nods her head, using the hand holding her wine glass to point in Ellie's direction, almost toasting her.

"Ride a hockey player might send the wrong message if you're wanting someone to be girlfriend material and not just someone for him to hook up with and forget about."

It makes sense, but it's definitely less funny that way, and I stand by it. "Okay, fine, you're probably right about that," I agree, typing it in, and I hesitate before posting it. "So like, how bad of an idea is this?" I ask, finally considering Macy might be right.

"I think you need to drink more wine and accept however Jack reacts to this is a future Alondra problem," she says, and I tip mine back, drinking a large portion of my glass before making Jack's profile live.

It takes about three minutes of us struggling to all look at the phone at the same time before I realize we can stream my phone screen to the television. "You know him the best out of us," I say to Ellie, my gaze sliding to meet hers. "What's his type?"

"Blondes, so I say we pick out some brunettes. I mean, if you want to keep things temporary, you go for what you don't like, right?" she suggests, and I'm absolutely dumbfounded by the logic. One look at Macy tells me she is also stunned by the logic, but in a way, it makes sense?

Why would you pick out someone you like if you don't plan on them sticking around for long?

"I can't argue with that," I say, and I'm tempted to ask Macy if she and Chad are talking again or not, but I'm afraid to bring it up because I don't want to upset her.

Another bottle of wine later, and way more no's than yes's, we get our first message before we send any out.

"Oh, I think Jack will like she messaged first, but *hey* is a little bland," Ellie says, making a face, and Macy sets her glass on the coffee table, wrapping a blanket around her shoulders.

"Seriously? Out of everything you could possibly open up with, she just says *hey*?" Macy asks.

"Maybe she's just shy?" I say, trying to give her a chance before writing her off. I click on Gina's profile, and I think she seems sweet. She likes the outdoors and puzzles, and she's really pretty, from her dark hair and eyes to her bronze skin. I type howdy back, sending it before anyone can tell me not to.

"Wait, I want to message the next girl," Ellie says, motioning for me to hand her the phone.

She scrolls through the matches we already have, clicking on one of our early ones—a girl named Veronica with the straightest hair and teeth I've ever seen. Ellie grins, tapping a Lightning McQueen GIF, following it up with, *Are you lightning? Because I'm trying to make you my McQueen.*

I burst into laughter, nearly spilling my wine all over my hand as it sloshes against the side of the glass with my sudden movement. "Oh shit. This is perfect. I love it," I say, my face hurting from smiling.

"I feel like you're really the only one of us who can confirm how Jack hits on a girl, so is this the kind of sappy shit he says?" Ellie asks, and I feel my cheeks flush at the reminder.

"Yes, this is very on brand for Jack."

"Dibs on next. I know exactly what to use," Macy chimes in, already laughing and holding her side.

She chooses a girl named Ava for our next attempt.

JACK

did it hurt?

AVA

What?

I cover my mouth with my hand, trying not to let the wine go to my head, but I'm afraid I'm past that point already. Ellie's cheeks are already flushed, her blue eyes shining as she smiles. Macy giggles, getting into this as much as me and Ellie, despite her reservations at first.

JACK

When you fell from heaven?

I roar with laughter, and she shoots me a smile. "It's not like it's something he wouldn't say. Shit, he was flirting up a storm with you the night we met him."

We message a few other girls some cheesy lines, but ultimately end up narrowing it down to three finalists for the evening. Our responses start to take much more thought and concentration as we end up opening another bottle, filling our glasses again, but in our defense, we're not going anywhere tonight, and there are three of us.

At some point, I end up texting Jack at the same time as I'm messaging to one of his girls, while Ellie is explaining her brother's lack of emotional availability and everything with Willow.

ALONDRA

what r u up to tmrw?

JACK

depends

ALONDRA

on?

My phone starts to ring with an incoming call from Jack. I shouldn't be surprised that he's calling me, because we rarely exchange texts. He mentioned in passing that voice memos are less time consuming and that it's easier for him to make sense of everything, but I couldn't send him a voice memo without Macy and Ellie knowing everything I say.

"Why is Jack calling you?" Ellie asks, her eyes widening.

I panic and toss the phone at her. "You answer it! I can't talk to him right now, he's flirting with this chick!"

Macy giggles, looking up at me from where she's now sitting on the floor. "No. *You're* flirting with this girl and pretending to be Jack."

Ellie shakes her head, taking a long breath and answers, "What's up, pup?" *Pup? Is she crazy?*

I don't hear whatever his response is, but I can see her brain trying to work. "No, we're fine. Sara isn't here," she says, rolling her eyes. curling up into the corner of the couch. "Shhh, don't tell Coop. We're literally fine, it's girls' night."

Her eyes widen as she turns toward me, motioning frantically at the television. What is that supposed to mean? "I don't like you," Ellie says, her voice somehow lacking the panic written all over her face.

She hangs up and groans before standing up. "They're on their way here. Turn the TV off, quick!"

Oh shit, their townhouse is just down the block.

"*They?* Which ones?"

"Jack said Coop and Nate are out tonight, but he and Dylan are bored so they want to come check on us."

Ellie makes a move for the remote in front of Macy and almost takes a nosedive into the coffee table, easily losing her balance.

"They're coming like here? Right now?" I ask, and she nods, pressing a hand to her stomach.

"Literally any second. I think they might already have been on their way because of whatever you said to Jack. What did you say to him?"

"I asked him what he was doing tomorrow?" I say, and she turns off the television to hide the evidence. There's a knock on our front door, and I get up, only a little steadier on my feet than Ellie is at the moment, but at least I don't face plant on my way to the door, opening it to find Jack and Dylan staring at me.

Jack raises an eyebrow as he looks at me, and I can't help but laugh knowing what we've done all night. I turn to smile at Ellie, who grins almost like she can read my mind, but when I look at Macy, I notice that somehow, amid the chaos of the last few minutes, she's managed to fall asleep and is out cold on the arm of the couch.

"Y'all okay?" Jack asks, making the first move to enter.

"Why wouldn't we be?" I ask, giving him a smile, setting a goal for myself to walk back to the couch without tripping.

Ellie levels the guys with a look I didn't think she had in her. I feel like it's rare to even see Ellie without a smile on her face, let alone one of annoyance. "See? We're fine. You didn't need to come check on us."

Jack crosses his arms, and it's really not my fault my eyes go straight to his biceps. *Wow.* Gina, Veronica, or Ava are really going to reap the benefits of his hard work and dedication to hockey.

"What were you guys doing?" he asks, and I smile cheekily at him.

"It's girls' night."

"Damn, I thought girls' night meant pillow fights in your underwear?" Dylan says, looking around the room.

"Sorry to disappoint, but it's only wine and movies," Ellie says, and he chuckles.

"How can you watch movies if the TV isn't on?" Jack asks, taking a seat on one of our barstools. I think he's suspicious, but why? We look perfectly innocent, and besides, he gave me permission—*kinda.*

"It finished right before you got here," I say, yawning and Ellie nods in agreement.

"Yep, so feel free to leave now."

"Why don't you want us here?" Dylan asks, kicking off his shoes, making it apparent he's not planning on leaving.

"Cause we're tired and about to go to bed," I say, and Jack starts to smile when I point my finger at him. "That was not an invite, Jack."

He puts his hands up in defense. "Darlin', I didn't even say anything," he says, chuckling, not realizing that both Dylan's and Ellie's heads snap in his direction.

"*Darlin'*? You call Coach B's daughter *darlin'*?" Dylan asks, his voice raising comically in pitch.

"Are you serious?" Ellie asks, her jaw dropping.

"I've told him not to call me that." I cross my arms over my chest, feeling smug.

He rolls his eyes, dragging a hand through his hair, flexing his arm in the process. "It's just a pet name. It doesn't mean anything," he says, seeming unfazed by their reactions.

Ellie stands up, opening her mouth, but quickly closes it as she sways, her face going white as a sheet.

"Oh shit," Dylan swears, moving for her faster than I can. "Bathroom?" he asks, looking at me, and I point down the hall.

"She has her own bathroom in her room," I say, and Dylan quickly ushers her that direction. I grimace as the door shuts behind them, grabbing the blanket draped over the back of the couch to cover Macy with it. She'll probably wake up in the middle of the night to move to her room, but I don't want her to get cold.

I stand, waiting to see if the room starts spinning, but so far, there's only the happy, warm feeling that comes with being drunk. "Do I need to worry about you getting sick?" Jack asks as I reach for my half-full glass of wine and Ellie's empty one to put them in the sink.

"The room isn't spinning," I say, walking past him, but when I turn around to grab the empty bottles and Macy's glass. Jack is right behind me, having already gotten them. "Thanks, you didn't have to help."

"C'mon, you look tired. Let's get you to bed," he says, and while it's already what I was planning on doing, the fact that Jack is telling me to makes me not want to go to bed.

"What if I don't want to?" I ask, staring up at him defiantly.

"Al."

"*Jack.*"

He pinches the bridge of his nose, closing his pretty blue eyes. "You're gonna give me a headache. Let's go."

"You're not the boss of me," I argue, but I don't even know why I'm fighting with him.

"Are you going to throw up?"

I blink, confused why he's asking again. "I already told you no, I'm not going to throw up." I realize why when he bends down and lifts me over his shoulder as if I weigh nothing. "Oh my god. Jack!"

He laughs, his grip tightening on the back of my thighs. "What?"

"You can't just pick me up and throw me over your shoulder like a freaking caveman," I protest, and a part of me wishes I was on the verge of throwing up so I could vomit on him. I guess the muscles in his arms serve a purpose beyond just making him look good.

"You know, you don't have to argue with me all the time," Jack says, opening the door to my room. "Is this going to be a regular thing? Me taking care of you when you're drunk?"

I reach down, pinching his butt, and he barks out a laugh. "I didn't ask you to come over and check on us."

"No, but you should be thanking me because now Dylan is helping Ellie instead of you," he says, setting me gently on the bed.

"What about Macy?" I ask, and Jack shrugs.

"I think she's fine on the couch."

I frown, crossing my arms over my chest. "That's rude."

"How is it rude?" he asks, reaching to turn on my lamp, filling the room with a soft glow.

"Because you're in here taking care of me, Dylan's taking care of Ellie, and no one is taking care of Macy. Why aren't you taking care of Macy?"

The corners of Jack's mouth tilt up in a smile. "If you'd stop finding reasons to fight with me, I'd tell you how I'm going to step out of the room to get you water and check on Macy who looked pretty damn peaceful on the couch, so you can get changed into pajamas."

Goddamn, how is he so nice? "You were going to check on Macy?" I ask, reaching up to pull my hair out of the clip it's in, my curls spilling down.

"Yeah," he says, like it's the most obvious thing in the world.

"Do you like her?" I ask, my mouth apparently lacking a filter, and despite the fact I spent all night with Ellie and Macy on the hunt for a girlfriend for Jack, I don't want him to like Macy. I don't know why because Jack is once again proving to me what a nice guy he is, and Macy deserves a nice guy, but I don't want it to be him.

"Al, I'm not interested in Macy," he says, and I nod, adjusting to sit in a crisscross position.

"Right," I drawl, mimicking his accent. "You're not interested in anyone. Maybe you just haven't found the yee to your haw." I yawn again, and Jack laughs, shaking his head at me.

"I think you had too much wine to drink."

"I didn't have *that* much. Besides, do you really have room to judge, *Mr. Hockey Star*? I'm sure you've had your fair share of nights partying."

Jack shakes his head, scratching his jaw. "Nope. I don't drink. I go mostly to keep an eye on everyone, but I'm sober the entire time."

"Cause of your dad?" The words slip out before I can even try to keep them in, and I gasp, covering my mouth with my hand. "I'm sorry," I whisper, noting how he tenses at the mention of his dad, and I'm ready to hide under the covers now for the rest of my life. I blame the wine.

"It's okay, Al. Yeah, I don't drink cause of my dad," Jack says, and I feel worse than awful. "I'll give you a sec to get changed. Do you need anything else?"

"No. Thank you, though," I say, dragging my hand over my face, hearing the soft click of my door closing behind him.

I get my shirt and bra off with no problem, pulling an oversized T-shirt over my head, but my leggings bunch around my knees, causing me to lose my balance and land on the floor in a heap. I sigh, staring at the ceiling for a moment, admitting defeat.

Jack's not going to be upset about the dating app, right? At the most, he gets a girlfriend, and at the least, he suffers through a date. Maybe he'll even come out of it with a really good story.

There's a soft knock on my door before it opens. "Why are you on the floor?" he asks, holding my water bottle in his hands.

"I got stuck taking off my pants," I admit, and he offers me a hand, pulling me into a standing position so I can move toward the bed again, sitting on the edge.

"You should drink some water," he says, handing it to me, but I'm glad I haven't taken a drink yet because he lowers himself to his knees, and I'm honestly not sure if I'm breathing or not when he takes my ankle, taking his time to pull the fabric down my calf.

His fingertips brush over the sensitive skin on the back of my knee, and my whole body feels like it's been plugged into an outlet, electricity sending sparks through me. His hands are huge, and I'm suddenly very aware of the ache beginning to grow in me. Is there a chance I might not be as broken as I think I am if my body is reacting like this to Jack? I didn't think it was possible after all the ways it was used against me, but if this is what it feels like to come back to life, it feels like a step in the right direction.

I shift on the bed, trying to ignore the pressure building, but it only causes his eyes to travel up to meet mine. "Al?"

"Yeah?" I ask, my voice breathless while my mind pictures Jack on his knees in front of me for an entirely different reason. I really shouldn't, and maybe that's the reason it feels so damn good.

His hands are warm as they make the final move to pull them off, his eyes never leaving mine until he grabs the shorts I had pulled out and set on the bed before falling on the ground. "You okay?" he asks, looking at me through his dark lashes. I wonder what it would feel like to have Jack touch me everywhere if an innocent touch from a beautiful man on his knees is enough to have me panting over him like a dog in heat.

I don't trust myself to speak, so I nod, and Jack pulls his lower lip into his mouth as he helps me into the shorts, my breath catching as his touch dances higher up my thighs.

It's nice to have someone else take care of me.

I rest my hands on his broad shoulders, standing up as his hands pull the shorts up underneath the fabric of my long shirt. His touch is respectful, skating back down over the curve of my hips, and damn it, I don't want him to be respectful right now.

Jack is slow to rise into a standing position, and who knew that having someone dress you could be such an intimate experience? I certainly didn't, but I would give anything to read his mind to know what Jack's thinking as his baby blue gaze dances over my face, and his throat bobs when he swallows.

I turn away, grabbing my water bottle off my nightstand to take a drink, but my pulse isn't slowing.

He clears his throat, and I hope I'm imagining the tension in the room. "I should check on Dylan and Ellie, and you should get some sleep," Jack says, his voice a low rumble like thunder during a summer storm.

It feels wrong for some reason, pulling the sheets back and letting him walk away, despite knowing it's the right move. Two weeks ago, I didn't want to call Jack my friend or be in the same room with him, but tonight, I don't want him to leave. It's the alcohol talking, and there's a chance I'll regret it tomorrow, but the worst he can say is no.

"Wait," I say, sitting down. Jack looks back at me and I don't want him to go. "Will you stay?"

"Sure," he says after a moment, walking around to the other side of my bed to lie next to me as I try not to focus on how at ease I feel having him here. "You want to tell me what y'all really did tonight?"

I roll to face him, a nervous laugh escaping me. "What makes you think we didn't have a wine and movie night?"

"Your face just now." Jack chuckles, his lips curling up into a smile.

"It was movies and wine for girls' night," I repeat, batting my lashes at him.

"If that's the story you're sticking to."

I face away from him, pulling the blankets up. "Yes, because that's what we did."

"C'mere," he says, giving me a brief warning before he pulls me against him. The weight of his arm draped over my side is a comfort I should protest. Except, much like the desired effect of a weighted blanket, I find it hard to keep my eyes open.

"You're warm," I mumble.

"You're drunk. Close your eyes, Alondra," Jack says.

This time, when my eyes shut, I don't open them until I wake the next morning in my bed alone, wondering how much of last night I imagined and what was real.

CHAPTER 12
Alondra

MACY SHIVERS IN HER COAT, pulling it tighter around herself. "It's so fucking cold here," she moans, and I have to agree with her.

"It's seventy-eight in Texas today." I looked this morning to torture myself when I saw the temperature for Minnesota. The sun is shining, but the wind is brutal, cutting through every material designed to keep it out, chilling you to the bone.

"I say we pack our shit up and go there."

"Right now?" I ask, laughing at the absurd idea.

"Of course. We both have cars—let's run away."

"Does this mean you're done with Chad?" I ask, and Macy's smile fades into a grimace.

"I'm done with him this time. Sorry you have to keep picking up the pieces every time we break up," she says, and I bump her with my shoulder.

"I didn't mean it like that. Besides, I have no room to be upset after all of your help when things ended with Bradley." Macy gives me a sympathetic smile.

I know she's my cousin, but I couldn't ask for a better best friend.

By the time we'd decided to move so Bradley didn't know where we lived, it was impossible to find a two bedroom since Rose wasn't going to live with us again, but Macy didn't complain once. I really should just shut my mouth about Chad, but I wish she knew she deserved better than him.

"Al, that was different, and you know it."

I force out a short laugh. It was different, and it also wasn't. "I guess," I mumble, shoving my hands into my pockets.

"Have you told Jack you've been planning dates for him?" she asks, and I stuff my hands in my pockets.

"Not yet, but the girls seem nice enough."

Macy snorts, chuckling under her breath. "It's kinda weird that you're doing this. I know you said he would be cool with it, but are you sure he even wants a girlfriend?"

It is weird to be picking out potential girlfriends for him when I'm trying to make sense of why he makes me feel things nobody else has for the last nine and a half months. I don't want to be his girlfriend, but I'm not sure I know how to be his friend either.

"I guess I'll find out when I tell him." I'm avoiding telling Jack until the last possible moment because I don't think he knows I was serious, and I'm a little worried this might be the thing that pushes his golden retriever puppy energy over the edge.

"How's tutoring going?"

"Really well, actually. We're waiting to get scores back on our midterms." I'm hoping he passed. I don't want to see the defeat on his face if he scores badly. He worked so hard to do well on it.

The wind blows again, and I try to shrink further into my winter coat I've already had to break out, but I have no doubt everyone will be risking hypothermia next week for their Halloween costumes.

Macy shivers again, and I swear, our parking lot is too

damn far away from the buildings on this campus. "I'm glad you decided to help him. He seems like a nice guy."

He is a nice guy. I spent all last night during our tutoring session trying not to remember how sexy it was to have him dress me while we worked on some of his homework for a different class. We're friends, and friends don't look at friends like that.

"Jack's pretty great."

"Do you think you could see him as more than a friend?" she asks, and I'm quick to shake my head. I knew it was only a matter of time until someone asked me.

"I know he's not Bradley, it's just . . . being friends with him is one thing. Anything more is a boundary I'm not sure I should ever cross with Jack," I admit, sighing. Maybe if everything hadn't gone down the way it did, I'd consider it, but I can't. It doesn't matter that he makes me feel light and vibrant instead of the box of black, white, and gray I've been locked inside.

Macy falls silent, then she bumps me back just before there's a loud whoop behind us. I turn in surprise to see Jack running at a full sprint towards us. *Speak of the devil.* He's managed to attract the attention of everyone else walking as well.

Jack has a wide smile on his face and doesn't slow down until he skids to a stop right before me, his arms wrapping around me as he spins me, backpack and all.

"Jack! What the hell are you doing?" I shriek, holding onto him.

I'm laughing when he sets me down on the ground. "I got my grade back," he says, sounding only a little out of breath, but his eyes are sparkling.

"And?"

I'm assuming it's good news based on his mood. How long was he running around? Was Jack just going to keep going until he found me?

"I got a fucking eighty-one!"

The smile on his face is brilliant and contagious.

"Jack, that's great. I knew you could do it," I say, my smile growing from the pure joy radiating from him.

His arms fold around me, pulling me into another hug, and then I'm swung again, laughter slipping from both of us. "It's not great, it's a miracle," Jack says, and I hate that he's been made to feel like he's less than because of his dyslexia.

Macy is laughing at us once I'm back on solid ground, and I adjust the straps of my backpack on my shoulders from where they've slid out of place. "That's Al—a miracle maker."

"Celebrate with me tonight," he blurts out, and I'm not sure I could say no even if I wanted to.

"Is that a question?" I tease, and his cheeks pink.

"No."

"What kind of celebration?" I ask, anticipating it not to be Twin City now that I know he doesn't drink. Jack reminds me of an onion, having to peel back each layer back to learn more about what lies beneath the pretty exterior.

Jack's dimples are out in full force, his eyes crinkled with happiness. It makes my pulse race. "It's a surprise. Dress warm and comfortable. I have to go to practice, but I'll pick you up at eight."

"What do you have planned?" I feel like I should be worried, but I'm not.

"You're not the only one allowed to have secrets." He winks before letting go of me. I shake my head at Jack, watching him walk away for a moment before turning back to Macy.

"Yeah, you don't stand a fucking chance of staying just friends with Jack," she muses, before another gust of wind sends her long hair into her face.

She's wrong. That's not how it is between us. I roll my eyes and brush off her comment, but the smile on my face lingers.

"What's the plan?" I ask, climbing into Jack's truck, smiling at the sound of the radio humming in the background with a country station playing. It's older and worn, but I like that it isn't flashy and new. The inside is clean, and it's clear he takes care of it, but it's simply another one of those layers to peel back.

"You'll see," he says, shifting gears while I get buckled.

"Am I dressed warm enough for whatever it is you have planned?" I ask, causing him to peek in my direction. I went with a thick sweater, a pair of leggings, fuzzy socks, and a pair of Birkenstock clogs. I held out for the longest time on getting them before I finally cracked and asked for a pair last Christmas. I practically live in them once the temperature starts to drop.

Jack glances at me and nods. "Yeah, you should be good."

Where could he possibly be taking me? The things I know about Jack tell me he's a nice guy I feel safe alone with—which is honestly enough for me—but there's a lot of gaps in what I don't know, and I have no clue where he'd take me to celebrate his score. "What are some things you like to do in your free time?" I ask, turning in my seat to watch him as the glow of the dash and the passing streetlights cast shadows over the edges of his face.

He chuckles under his breath. "I'm not telling you where we're going. You'll find out in a few minutes."

"Rude." I stick my tongue out at him. "I was asking because I want to get to know my friend better."

"My whole world revolves around hockey. I don't have a whole lot of time to do other things, so I guess it's a good thing hockey is what I like to do when I have free time," he says, and I understand because I used to spend every spare second either on the ice or thinking about skating.

"What about during the summers?" I ask, pushing further because there's got to be something more.

Jack sighs, tapping the steering wheel as he shifts gears with ease. "I work in manual labor in the summer, but I spend the rest of my time with my momma."

"Oh, like construction?" I ask, trying to picture Jack on a construction site, and he shakes his head.

"Not really," he answers vaguely, and now I'm even more curious.

"So like what then?"

"I'm from Amarillo, which is cattle country, and once I turned fourteen, the guy that lives in the house next to ours helped me get a job off the books during the summers at the ranch he works at."

My jaw drops, and my imagination runs wild. *Oh my fucking god.*

I was right.

Save a horse, ride a goddamn hockey player instead.

I wonder if he wears a cowboy hat and assless chaps? Boots? Oh great, now I'm picturing Jack in assless chaps, and I *really don't* need an excuse to think about his ass.

"Al, you're gonna catch flies if you leave your mouth open any longer," Jack jokes, and I can't stop staring.

"Are you serious? So you know how to ride a horse?" I ask, trying to picture it, and he laughs at me.

"That's what you want to know?"

Don't ask him about the chaps. "I mean, yeah?"

"Yes, I know how to ride a horse," he says, his smile growing.

This changes the game. "Do you have any pictures?" I ask, and he snorts.

"Of me riding a horse?"

"Or like petting one, but I think it'd be pretty cool if you had one with a baby horse," I think out loud, imagining how many more matches his already popular dating profile would get if he had a picture with a baby horse.

"A foal, and I don't know if I have any pictures because I'm usually focusing on my job, not posing for pictures," he says, a hoarse laugh escaping him, and it does sound a little ridiculous to imagine him doing an impromptu photoshoot when he's supposed to be working. "Does this have something to do with what y'all were up to the other night?"

"I already told you what we did," I say, because technically, I did tell him in the library I would find him a girlfriend. It's not my fault he didn't think I was serious.

After Macy's comment earlier about how she thinks I don't stand a chance of being just friends with Jack, it's motivated me even more to find him a girlfriend, to prove that it's not like that between us.

"I don't believe you were only drinking wine and watching movies," Jack says, and I roll my eyes.

"Sounds like a you problem if you didn't believe me," I say, but my stomach sinks when he pulls into the parking lot for the arena. "Jack, what are we doing here?"

He parks, turning off the engine, and my heart stutters. I really hoped he had dropped this when he hadn't mentioned it.

"Seriously, why are we here?" I repeat, and he unbuckles, turning to face me.

"Al, we're here to not skate," he says, giving me a warm smile. "You'll have fun, I promise."

It's a miracle the parking lot is empty. There's a reason I only come here in the middle of the night or before the ass crack of dawn. I don't talk to any of my old teammates because what are you supposed to say after quitting something so abruptly and not having any answers for the questions they ask? Sorry? My abusive ex-boyfriend told me how pathetic I was for thinking if I won enough medals, it'd be enough for my dad to finally love me, and when I argued with him, he punched me so hard in my ribs I couldn't breathe so I had to drop out of the competition? How he begged me to forgive him at the same time he promised to never do it again, because he was so afraid of losing me?

But Jack isn't Bradley.

Maybe that's why I argue with him all the time. My brain is trying to prove to myself it doesn't matter how far I push Jack, he won't lay even a finger on me.

With Jack, I can fight with him all I want, and he'll still lift me over his shoulder to carry me to my bedroom before helping me get dressed in my pajamas.

I swallow my nerves, unbuckling my seatbelt. I cross my arms over my chest as I walk around to meet him in front of the truck, trying to quell the uneasy feeling in the pit of my stomach. Skating by myself when no one else knows I'm here is one thing, but knowingly skating with someone else is completely different.

No. I can't do this.

My feet are rooted in place.

"No." The words are hoarse as they come out my mouth. "I told you I don't skate."

"I looked you up," Jack says, turning to look at me. "You were good. You were really good. The forums said you were on track to compete at the U.S. Figure Skating Championships before you quit out of nowhere."

I close my eyes, and I don't know what to say. Who I was then and who I am now are completely different people.

"Is this because of your dad?" he asks, his voice quiet and low.

I bite my lip so hard, I wouldn't be surprised if it started to bleed. It's about him, but it's so much more at the same time. It's about how I craved acceptance and love from my father while leaving myself vulnerable for Bradley to swoop in, stealing every piece of me until I became an unrecognizable husk.

"Jack, I can't."

"Al, you can't let him stop you from doing the things you love." He's right in front of me, but I keep my eyes shut, even after the scent of cinnamon floods my senses, because I know that if I look at him, I'll cave. "Do what makes *you* happy."

I count backward from ten in my head, willing myself to go in with him. *Ten, nine, eight, seven, six, five, four, three, two, one.* My anxiety lingers, beating a silent drum in my stomach, but I can still breathe.

"We don't have to skate long," Jack promises, his smooth voice tempting me to open my eyes. "Please, Al? If you won't do it for yourself, then do it for me."

I choke on my laugh, shaking my head. "Do it for you?" I ask, amazed by his brazenness.

His dimples are showing as he looks down at me. "Yeah. We're here to celebrate."

"You drive a hard bargain," I say, nodding my head, following him into the building.

I lean against the wall outside of the locker room, waiting while he retrieves our skates. When Jack steps through the doors a moment later, his smile widens. My fingers are itching to take my bag from him, but another part of me is afraid.

"What?" I ask, and the corners of his eyes crinkle.

"You're still here," he says, and I cross my arms over my chest, exhaling a shaky breath.

"Still here," I say, giving him the best smile I can muster right now.

It feels like Jack's staring into my soul right now, and it doesn't matter how many walls I try to put up, he's doing a damn good job of tearing them all down. "Al, you don't have to do this if you don't want to," Jack says, and I'd believe him if he didn't look like a kicked puppy while he said it, especially after the pep talk he gave to get me in the building.

"This is what you wanted to do, so as your friend, we're

going to not skate," I say, marching toward the doors leading to the arena. My stubbornness helps me take them from him, but after tightening the laces, I falter when I pull the edge of my socks over them.

"What if I can't do it?" I ask, glancing over at him.

Jack's kind eyes find mine, and he reaches over to place his hand on top of mine.

"Then we just sit here, and we don't skate."

His hand is large and callused, but his touch is gentle, thawing the fear freezing me in place.

Jack is slow to stand, making the first move to step onto the polished ice, and I let muscle memory take over, gripping the boards as I try to decide if I'm actually going to take the final step to willingly skate in front of someone else.

And I dive straight into the deep end, trying not to feel like I've been stripped naked and shoved into a crowded room.

After a quick lap, I feel myself loosening up, and the tension seeps from my body. Jack skates over to me, an easy smile on his face that I do my best to return.

"Wanna race?" he asks, his lips quirking into a smirk, and I snort.

"And get my ass kicked? No thanks."

"C'mon, you know you want to," Jack says, turning to skate backward in front of me at a leisurely pace.

"Do I? You already got me out here, so can't you just be happy with that accomplishment?" I ask, wondering what he would say if he knew how many mornings I've spent sitting in the bleachers trying to make myself come out here.

"Are you having fun?" Jack asks, stuffing his hands into the pockets of his hoodie.

I can't even try to lie to give him a hard time. I feel my smile grow before I nod because I am having fun.

"I want to hear you say it. You were right, Jack. I'm having so much fun because you're so fun and the sexiest guy ever," he says, attempting to mimic me.

Laughter sputters from me, and I gape at him. "I hope that isn't you pretending to be me because it's not something I would say."

Jack's deep laugh seems to echo with mine off the plexi-glass. "I bet you can't beat me," he challenges, changing how he's framing his idea. What's even more annoying is it's working.

I push him, catching him by surprise as I quickly take off for the other side of the rink. I'm almost to the goal lines when Jack blows past me, beating me to the boards.

"You cheated," he says, and I roll my eyes.

"You still beat me."

I'm fast on skates, but he consistently works out and is one of the fastest players in the division, if not the fastest. It's honestly kind of a miracle he hasn't decided to leave Wilder early to sign with the Dolphins.

"Did you want me to let you win?" Jack asks, smirking at me in the most infuriating way.

"Just a reminder, but you don't 'let' me do anything." I roll my eyes, flipping him off as I take off again.

At some point, Jack hooks his phone up to the speakers, and I'm stunned when my favorite song starts playing through them. I give Jack a questioning look where he skates next to me, and the only thing he says is that Ellie told him I liked this song.

I've lost track of time, just trying to enjoy being in this moment. I don't attempt any jumps, wanting to spend more time in the gym to rebuild the body strength I lost.

"Thank you," Jack says, pulling my attention to him. I'm glad I'm wearing my skates as well, because without them, I wouldn't reach his shoulder anymore. "I meant it when I said I wouldn't have passed the midterm without your help. You didn't have to, but you are, and I really appreciate it."

"You didn't really give me much of a choice, but your persistence is one of your best and most annoying qualities," I joke, trying to keep the air light because I don't want Jack to look at me the same way Macy does when she thinks I'm not looking.

The tips of his ears turn red, and Jack rubs the back of his neck. "I could see on your face while you were skating that you loved it out here like I do. I don't know what happened to make you quit, but I thought that maybe tonight would help you . . . I don't know." Jack sucks in a sharp breath. "I wanted to help."

My heart jumps to my throat at the sincerity in his voice. If I didn't know better about Jack's stance on relationships, I'd almost go far enough to wonder if this were actually a date—except I know it's not, and I don't want it to be.

I am enjoying spending time with Jack, though.

"It's complicated, but you're right, I do love it out here. I just can't go back to who I was before . . ." I trail off, my thoughts becoming a muddled mess. The pop music playing in the background feels out of place with the memories weighing me down.

"Before what?" he prods, his voice gentle, and for the second time tonight, Jack reaches for my hand.

For a brief moment, I let him, before pulling away. "Nothing. Before nothing."

Before Bradley.

Before everything.

I turn away from Jack, but he catches my arm, trying to stop me.

It feels like an unavoidable car crash, experiencing that moment when everything happens in slow motion, like in an old film. Each second a frame of time before it all happens at the speed of light, sending me straight into fight or flight mode as my anxiety spikes through the fucking room.

How I'm feeling must be reflecting on my face or something, because Jack's eyes widen in blatant confusion, and he drops my arm.

It doesn't matter, though. It's too late, and my mind is struggling to differentiate between the two men while panic is coursing through my veins.

I'm here with Jack. I'm not with Bradley. Jack didn't mean anything by it because he isn't Bradley.

"Al? Fuck, what did I do? How can I help?" he asks, this time keeping his hands to himself.

I shake my head, trying to reason with myself, but my brain isn't thinking logically right now.

Jack *isn't* Bradley. I repeat it to myself over and over, trying to pull myself together.

"I'm sorry," he says. "I'm so sorry. Tell me what to do, please."

Jack isn't Bradley.

I count backward from ten again, feeling my heart rate slow down, and I shake my head. "It's okay. I'm okay," I force the words out, and Jack's whole face is knit with concern.

I'm fine. *I'm safe.* It's okay.

Ten, nine, eight, seven, six, five, four, three, two, one.

The repetition of counting down from ten always helps. It's something my brain can make sense of when everything else is moving too fast.

"I didn't—I'm sorry. I shouldn't have grabbed your wrist," Jack says, apologizing again. His eyes roam over my face to see if I really am fine, but the truth is I'm not. If I were, I wouldn't be losing my shit over Jack catching my arm.

"It's not your fault," I say, trying—and failing—to smile at him because it wasn't. I have plenty of issues, and unfortunately, grabbing my arm triggered some of them. I don't know how to explain this away, and based on his facial expression, I don't think I can.

Jack drags a hand over his stubble, exhaling. "Was—did your dad . . ." Jack trails off, struggling to get the words out.

"Dad never touched me." I clasp my hands in front of me, trying not to twist them as I kick to keep my head above water. "Sometimes that happens. Um, I count in my head to calm myself, but I have some shit I haven't dealt with yet. It's just . . . hard."

"But Coach B . . ." Jack trails off, his jaw clenching as if the idea of my dad hurting me causes him to feel physical pain.

"Never, I promise," I reassure him, and he nods, but I'm desperate to know what's running through his head.

There's an awkward silence between us, the sound of the music echoing to fill the gaps, and I wish I could rewind us back to fifteen minutes ago.

I move closer and lace my fingers through Jack's. His eyes flicker to meet mine, and the apprehension lurking in the crystal coloring shakes me to my core. It feels like I'm staring into a looking glass, seeing everything I've tried so hard to hide reflected on Jack's face.

"I'm okay. I trust you," I whisper, trying not to let the words scare me into running as fast as I can in the other direction. "I wouldn't be here with you if I didn't."

It's terrible because it's true.

I don't trust easily, but somehow, like a parasite, Jack has infiltrated all of my defenses with his easy smile and the kindness he's shown me. I know I haven't known him long, but despite every verbal sparring match we've had, Jack's taken everything I've thrown at him without so much as raising his voice. In fact, I yelled at him outside of Twin City, yet he still drove me home and took care of me to make sure I was okay.

I don't like being someone who looks for the worst in people.

Maybe believing that if someone shows you who they are, you should believe them can also apply to recognizing when someone isn't a shitty human.

I don't think Jack is a shitty human.

Jack is sweet like honey, but I can only hope it's not a trap designed to lure me in before going in for the kill.

"I'm sorry if I pushed too far to get you out here with me. I just wanted you to have fun . . . with me," Jack says.

"You didn't push me." I squeeze his hand, trying to reassure him in the best way I know how. "Wanna race?"

"Even if I kick your ass?"

I laugh, shaking my head despite knowing he could probably beat me in his sleep. I haven't spent enough time at the gym yet and am trying to rebuild my endurance. "I'd like to see you try." Jack holds on to me, his grip unwavering.

It occurs to me that maybe I need Jack in my life, and the reason I fought against his friendship is that it's terrifying to rely on other people. But maybe, *just maybe*, Jack might need me too.

CHAPTER 13

Alondra

"You signed me up for a dating app?" Jack asks from his end of the kitchen counter where we're studying, while Coop makes dinner. Coop's head turns in our direction, his eyes wide.

My mouth opens, but I can't make any words come out. *Oh, shit.* Is he mad? I can't tell.

"Al?"

"I plead the fifth," I squeak, grabbing my phone to run to the bathroom on the first floor, getting enough of a head start on Jack, he doesn't catch me before I shut the door. I twist the lock, hugging my phone to my chest as the handle rattles.

"Alondra!"

I cover my mouth to hide my laugh, calling Ellie. She made a beeline for their hot tub out back after we got here, claiming they don't use it enough, and it's going to waste. Dylan was quick to follow her out there after flipping off Jack who asked him if he had something better to do than perv on Coop's sister. He's lucky Coop hadn't come downstairs yet to start making dinner, but I sure got a kick out of it.

"Did you change your mind about coming out here with me? The water feels amazing, and I brought an extra suit for you," she says, and a laugh slips out when the door handle jiggles again.

"Al, unlock the door," Jack says, and I shake my head, even though he can't see me.

"He knows."

"Oh fuck," she swears, gasping. "Is Jack mad?"

I hear Dylan in the background ask what Jack would be mad about, and I sit on the closed toilet lid.

"Unsure. I ran to the bathroom before I could find out," I say, and Jack knocks on the door. "Jack, are you mad?" I ask, trying not to laugh.

"What do you think?" he asks, his voice dripping with sarcasm. *Oops, Macy was right.*

"I'm coming to rescue you," Ellie says, but I'm not quite sure how she's going to do that when Jack has probably already figured out that she did it with me.

"Is Ellie in on this with you?" he asks through the door, and I lower my voice.

"Save yourself, he knows you're involved," I say, looking around for any escape saving me from having to open the door for him.

"I bet you could fit through the window?" she suggests, and I look at the window barely big enough for me to squeeze through. Actually, I doubt I could make it. My hips are deceiving with how low set they are, and I'm not getting stuck halfway out a window.

"I'm not climbing out the window to avoid Jack!"

Jack knocks again on the door. "You know I can hear you, right? You don't have to hide in the bathroom, or climb out the fucking window."

I sigh, glancing skeptically at the door. I know I have to face him eventually, but how long can I actually stay in here? Maybe Coop would be willing to pass me a plate of whatever he's making downstairs for dinner. "Gotta go, Ellie."

"It's been nice living with you," she says before hanging

up, and you'd think we were saying goodbye for the last time.

"Open the door, Al."

"Why should I?" I counter, but I still flip the lock on the door, slowly cracking it open to reveal Jack standing on the other side with his arms crossed over his chest. He's not quite scowling, but there is zero chance of his dimple winking at me right now.

"I'm not mad," Jack says, and I laugh because the expression on his face says he is.

"I don't believe you."

He snorts, and I feel like a little kid who got caught with their hand in the cookie jar. "Why would I be mad at you for making me an online dating profile you didn't tell me about?" he says, and despite everything, the alarms that Bradley always set off in my head are silent.

"Jack, you sound kind of mad," I say, and he grumbles something under his breath.

"Why?"

I roll my eyes because we had a whole ass conversation about this. "Why else do you think? I told you I was going to find you a girlfriend."

"I told you I didn't want one," Jack retorts, and I shake my head.

"Actually, you said *'Sure, whatever you want,'* so technically, you didn't say no," I say, mimicking his deeper voice.

He frowns, and it's so damn tempting to tell him it takes more effort to frown than to smile. "I don't sound like that, and I was being sarcastic because I didn't think you were serious."

"You shouldn't be such a cynic about love," I suggest, and he drags a hand over his face.

"Dating apps are not where you find love. They're where people go to find fuck buddies, which is exactly why I got a text from some chick who wanted to know why I didn't reply to her message," he says, and I have to admit, this is a scenario I hadn't considered. I open the door the rest of the way, fully prepared to argue my case.

"Not everyone on dating apps is there to find a fuck buddy. Maybe they have social anxiety, or they're intimidated by your fan club. We picked out some really nice girls, and I think that if you give them a chance, you'll learn I'm right." I tilt my head, trying to read his body language. "How mad are you?"

Jack sighs, but I think I'm starting to win him over on the idea.

"I'm not mad, but I wish you asked first," he says, shaking his head. "So how many girls am I talking to?"

"A few," I answer, keeping it vague on purpose. Ellie and I agreed we shouldn't tell him how every single girl we swiped right on ended up matching with him, because it would inflate his ego to dangerous levels.

"Dinner's ready," Coop calls from down the hall, and Jack holds his phone out to me.

"Sign me in on the app so I can figure out what kind of damage control I need to do."

I download the app and try to remember the password while I follow Jack the kitchen. Ellie's sitting at the counter with her blonde hair piled on her head, and the tie of her teal swimsuit hanging out of the top of her shirt. Honestly, I think she had the right idea coming over to use their hot tub.

Nate's getting out plates and silverware when Dylan shuts the back door behind him.

"Hey, Jack," she says, giving him a hesitant smile, and Jack snorts.

"So, Eleanor, how much of this are you responsible for?" he asks, and I pass the phone to him. It's tempting to hide in the bathroom again once he starts scrolling.

"Um, I plead the fifth?" Ellie says, and I cough to hide my laugh.

"What did I miss?" Nate asks, the corners of his mouth turning upward.

"The girls signed Jack up for a dating app without him knowing," Dylan says, and Nate's smile turns into a grin as he gives us both a thumbs up.

"Is it a good idea for you to live together?" Coop asks, and I carefully take my seat from earlier, packing up our things since I have a feeling we won't be studying after Jack reads through everything.

"Well, you stuck your dick in my last roommate, and Al's not cutting out pictures of any of you to use in a scrapbook of your future wedding, so I'd say it's a good idea," Ellie says, flashing a sweet smile at her brother.

Coop's neck flushes a bright crimson, and he doesn't say anything else.

"Save a horse, date a hockey player instead? Who came up with this shit?" Jack scoffs, and I snicker as Dylan and Coop roar with laughter.

"It would have been better if you had a picture of you riding a horse," I add, and his mouth parts as he looks at me.

"That's why you wanted a picture of me with a horse?"

"That's an option?" Ellie chimes in, and Jack looks back down at the screen.

"This is fucking awesome," Dylan says, moving to help Coop by getting plates and forks out for everyone. I'm impressed they're capable of making actual meals, considering Bradley and his roommates lived off premade dinners. My stomach rumbles as Coop turns off the burners, and I'll be happy if it tastes even half as good as it smells.

Between Ellie, Macy, and me, we're decent at cooking, but I'm excited for any meal I didn't have to make myself.

"*Will you be the yee to my haw?* Are you fucking kidding me?" Jack drops the phone on the table, pinching the bridge of his nose, and I do feel a little bad, but not bad enough to take any of it back. Dylan makes a move for the phone, grabbing it before Jack can react.

In my defense, Macy was responsible for that one.

"While the execution is flawless, you didn't need to sign him up for a dating app. Jack gets harassed more than the rest of us by puck bunnies when we go anywhere other than Twin City," Nate says, and I roll my eyes.

"You're proving our point exactly. We were trying to find him someone he could date, not just hook up with," I say, and Dylan's smile is wide as he scrolls on the phone.

"This is gold. Schultz, did you see how many matches you have?" he says, shaking his head before reading a few of them out loud. *"If I could rearrange the alphabet, I'd put 'U' and 'I' together. If you were words on a page, you'd be fine print. Do you have a name, or can I call you mine?* I can't believe any of these worked for you guys," Dylan says, and maybe we took it a little far with some of the messages, but they did work.

"I think my ears are bleeding." Jack groans, getting up to grab a plate.

Coop chuckles, his face transformed into a rare smile. "That might be some of the corniest shit I've ever heard. What the fuck have you two been up to?"

"Three," I correct, and Jack shoots me an annoyed look. "Macy was in on it too."

"Remind me to use you guys as wingwomen in the future," Nate says, and I stay in my seat, waiting for them to get their dinners first.

"Maybe we could start a matchmaking business," Ellie ponders out loud, and considering what a success Jack's profile was, I think it's something we'd be good at.

"What should we name it?" I ask, going along with it as Jack slides a plate made up with steaming vegetables and chicken on top of white rice in front of me on the counter. "I was going to get a plate after you all sat down?"

"Yeah, well now you don't have to get up. It's just a plate

of food," Jack says, grabbing another plate to get back in the makeshift line to get his own, and I'm floored. Why would he make me a plate before making one for himself?

Ellie clears her throat and looks as confused as I do. I lift my shoulders in a shrug, the gears in my head turning faster than I can sort through the thoughts.

"Sign me up as your first official customer," Nate says, and I'm wondering if I'm making a bigger deal in my head about the plate in front of me.

"Baxter, don't encourage them," Coop says, and Jack nods his agreement.

"Yeah, this isn't funny," Jack chimes in, and I roll my eyes because of course he would say that. He doesn't believe in love.

"Maybe if you were open to the idea of girls being more than just something you can fuck, then I wouldn't have had to take drastic measures," I tease, picking up my fork to take a bite.

"I don't just see them as playthings. Give me more credit than that," Jack says, making his plate while Dylan hops up to sit on the counter. Coop shakes his head, leaning against the counter while holding his plate. "I'm perfectly content with the way things are. I have y'all for the emotional crap," he says, this time setting the plate in his hands in front of Ellie.

Okay, so it wasn't weird he made one for me. I'm definitely overthinking this.

"Thanks," Ellie says, smiling at him.

"I'm not good with the emotional shit, so don't come to me," Coop says, taking a bite, and I use my fork to spear a piece of broccoli. The seasoning and teriyaki sauce are the perfect touch, and I'm glad Jack gave me a bigger portion than I would have served for myself.

"Wow, Coop. You're such a great friend," Ellie says, scoffing.

"At least I didn't sign my friend up to date half the women at Wilder," he throws back, and she points at me.

"It was Al's idea!"

"Way to throw me under the bus." I snort, and Jack takes the seat next to me again, finally sitting down to eat. "Technically, we weren't signing you up to date all of them. The goal was to find you a girlfriend, and I think you're overreacting."

"I don't want a girlfriend."

"Yeah, Jack. Go on a few dates," Nate says, and I glare at him because teasing Jack about this is not going to make him any more likely to go.

"No."

"Please," I say, aware this is one of the weirdest conversations I've ever had, trying to get a hockey player to go on a few dates with vetted girls. Everyone deserves love.

"No," Jack says, and Dylan snorts.

I smile at him, nudging his thigh with my knee under the counter. "I'll rock paper scissors you for it."

"Rock paper scissors? Are we five?" he asks, raising an eyebrow.

"Didn't we do rock paper scissors to decide who got the master bedroom?" Nate says, and Ellie shushes him.

"Are you afraid you'll lose?" I taunt, and his posture straightens. I have no problem using his competitiveness against him, just as he does to me.

"Yeah, Jackie," Ellie adds, egging him on.

"Do I get to set you up on a date if I win?" Jack bargains, the challenge hanging in the air.

"Uh, no," I say, scoffing. This is about Jack, and it has nothing to do with me.

He tilts his head, his bright eyes trailing over my face as if he's looking for something. "Because you're already dating someone?"

What?

I reel back, caught off guard by the question, and I'm

aware that all other chatter in the room has ceased, with everyone's attention on me.

Why would Jack ask me that?

"You have a boyfriend?" Dylan asks, his voice strained.

"No, she doesn't," Ellie says, coming to my rescue as I scramble for an explanation that makes sense without raising more questions.

"I don't have a boyfriend, but I said no because I have no interest in seeing anyone." Where is this coming from?

Jack's smile doesn't meet his eyes, and it's so unlike him, I'm not sure I like the sudden change. "How is that any different from me not wanting a girlfriend?"

The energy in the room has shifted from what started as fun and games to something that causes the hair on the back of my neck to stand up. I swallow the lump forming in my throat. "It just is. Pick something else," I say, and I set down my fork.

Someone say something please. This is so fucking awkward right now.

I look at Jack, wishing I could ask what's going through his mind right now to have made him ask me that, but I can't.

"What if you went to our games this weekend?" Nate suggests, and while I'm not a fan of this idea either, it's better than going on a date with someone.

"Wait, I like this idea. Then I'll have someone else besides Sara to sit with who isn't talking about fucking my brother and his friends," Ellie says, but my palms feel sweaty. "Sorry, Al, I know you don't want to go, but I feel like it's a pretty good middle ground to wager?"

I look at Jack at the same time his gaze flits to meet mine, and Jack's eyes soften, and this time, he bumps my knee with his. "What do you say, Al?" he asks, his voice quieter than before. "Rock paper scissors?"

I take a breath, trying to let the uncomfortable moment

slide off my shoulder. "Deal," I say, because there's no way I'll lose.

Except I do, and my jaw drops as his hand covers mine for a moment because paper beats rock.

Oh my god, I lost?

"Paper beats rock, but don't worry, I have a spare jersey you can borrow for the game," Jack says, taking another bite of his dinner, and I'm not sure what the fuck just happened.

"I'm not wearing your jersey," I say, huffing. Who picks paper? I mean, seriously? I feel like everyone always goes with rock or scissors.

"You can wear mine," Nate and Dylan both offer at the same time, and Ellie scoffs.

"Or we could be happy she's going?"

Jack leans in, distracting me from the spinning in my head. "Just a tip, Macy told me you tend to rely on rock paper scissors for diplomatic problems, and that you lean toward rock."

I gasp, my jaw hitting the floor. "You cheated."

"I didn't cheat, but I used my resources to beat you at your own game."

Macy's going to regret giving me her spare key when I use it to smother her with her own pillow.

"I don't like you," I say, frowning at Jack as his phone rings on the counter next to Dylan.

"Whatever you say," Jack says, his dimple peeking out before he inhales another bite of dinner.

"Dude, it's your mom. Can I answer?" Dylan asks, and Jack nods, trying to swallow.

"Momma Schultz!" Dylan greets, and a gentle laugh filters through the line as Jack coughs, choking on his food.

"Maybe you should take smaller bites," I suggest.

"Hi, Dylan. How's my boy?" she asks, her accent thicker than Jack's.

"He's choking on his food right now, but other than that,

he's driving me crazy like usual," Dylan says, while Coop rolls his eyes.

"Dude, that's cold," Nate says, shaking his head before rinsing his plate in the sink when Jack finally stops choking. "As entertaining as this shit is, I have homework to go back to."

"Both of you can fuck off," Jack croaks, and I'm trying to figure out if I should be concerned about Jack or highly entertained by the relationship the guys seem to have with his mom. Nate laughs as he makes his way toward the stairs, disappearing.

"Maybe he needs to try smaller bites when he eats, and then he wouldn't choke. Tell Jack I said to be nice or none of the cookies I send in the next package will be for him," she says, and Jack stands up so fast, his barstool falls backward as he makes a move for where Dylan's standing.

"Give me that," Jack says, reaching for the phone.

"No, I'm not done talking to her," he argues, and Coop moves out of the way as Dylan holds the phone out of Jack's reach, using his position on the counter to his advantage.

"Dylan, she's my mom," Jack complains, and I look at Ellie, trying to figure out this new piece of the puzzle, but she's watching them with a smile.

There's a sharp whistle, and both of them freeze. "Boys! What on earth are you two squabbling about? It's hurting my ears," Jack's mom scolds, and Dylan sighs, lowering the phone to where they can both talk into it.

"Sorry, Momma," Jack mumbles, and I clap my hand over my mouth to keep my laughter from spilling out. I never thought I'd see two grown men grappling over a phone like this.

"Is Coach Brown not working y'all hard enough at practice that you somehow still have energy to bicker like children?"

"Momma, you brought the cookies into it, and Dylan's

lying. I'm not driving him crazy." If looks could kill, Dylan would be six-feet-under.

"I think you'll survive without cookies for a month."

Ellie leans over to whisper to me. "They get like this when she calls, but the cookies are totally worth fighting over. They're the best I've ever had, and none of them are willing to share."

"Really?" I ask, trying not to be jealous of Jack for having a parent who loved him because the only thing I ever got from mine was a lack of praise and the occasional home cooked meal.

"Oh yeah, his mom is seriously the best. I feel bad she only gets to see a couple of games in person a year because she can't take the time off work, but she loves to watch Jack play. You'll literally never meet a nicer woman than her," she says just as Jack asks her when she's visiting.

"I'm hoping the weekend after Halloween if everything works out. How are practices going? Are you still helping out with that underclassman?" she asks, and he smiles, leaning against the counter.

"They're going good. Yeah, I'm still helping him. Richards has potential, but he needs to fine-tune his skills," he says, and Coop makes a face, and if I had to guess, I'd say he isn't the biggest fan of the underclassman. I'm not sure there are many people Coop actually likes, but I don't think Johnny is one of them.

"Is everything okay? You sound—"

"One sec, Momma," Jack says, grabbing the phone from Dylan to take it off speaker. "I'll be back in a minute," he says, excusing himself as he walks off, probably heading upstairs toward his room.

"What do you think that's about?" Ellie asks her brother, who shrugs. I pick up my fork again, taking another bite.

"Maybe it has to do with the guy who came up to Jack on our way back from the trainers a few weeks back. I think Jack said he was friends with Johnny or something, but he was pissed off when he caught up to me at the truck," Coop says, setting his plate down.

"Oh shit, was that the same night he didn't come out of his room?" Dylan asks, and Ellie frowns.

"Well did you ask him about it?" she asks, and Coop looks at her like she's sprouted a magical horn from her forehead.

I'm more curious to know when this happened because aside from being stressed about the midterm, Jack hasn't seemed off at all to me.

"If he wanted to talk about it, then he would have said something."

"You're telling me he didn't leave his room at all, and you never asked him about it?" I ask, and Dylan chuckles.

"No. We're not like you. We don't need to talk about our feelings until we're blue in the face," he says, and sometimes it's easy to forget how simple-minded men are.

"You're all idiots." Ellie snorts, and I think I'm inclined to agree with her. "Do you at least know the name of the guy?"

"No clue. I didn't stay to hear his name, but he was fucking huge."

Goosebumps prickle across my arms as it dawns on me that it could have been Bradley, but there's no way. What reason would he have to go up to Jack?

Ellie holds a finger up, chewing her food. "You didn't ask Jack what his name was?"

"No, but if you really want to know, you can," Dylan says, sharing a look I don't understand with Coop.

I stay silent as the pit in my stomach grows, forcing myself to continue eating as they switch topics to the games this weekend while we wait for Jack to come back down.

CHAPTER 14

Jack

I GLANCE over my shoulder to make sure no one has followed me as I step into my room. "Sorry, Momma. I don't want to talk about this in front of the others," I say, trying to shake the look on Alondra's face after I asked if she didn't want to be set up with someone because she already has a boyfriend.

Fuck, I feel guilty for even having said it out loud.

It's like I erased every bit of progress I've made with her over the past few weeks.

It's not that I believed Bradley, but he got under my skin, and it just fucking slipped out. I should've been more careful.

"Talk about what?" Momma's calm voice asks, and I drag a hand over my jaw, trying to sort through what I suspect with the tiny scraps of evidence that support it.

It feels like trying to put a piece of paper back together after it's gone through the shredder, except there are a hundred other pieces to sort through to find the right ones before taping it together.

"It's about Alondra. I just . . . I have a bad feeling," I admit, sitting on the edge of my bed.

"What kind of bad feeling?" she prods gently, and I hope

to God I'm wrong about this. I need to be wrong about this. "Jack?"

"I don't want to be right, but I think someone is—or was—hurting her," I say, and the thought of someone laying a hand on her makes my stomach turn. I care about Alondra—more than I ever expected to.

I hold my breath, waiting for her to say something. "Honey, that's a very serious thing to suggest," Momma says, but it's the only thing that makes sense, as much as I don't want it to.

"I know, and I thought maybe I was imagining it. I want to be wrong, but then we were skating earlier this week, and Al was avoiding a question I asked. She's always running from me, and I caught her arm to stop her. The way she looked at me . . ." I pause, recalling the awful moment when I just wanted Alondra to tell me what was going through her head. "She was afraid of me. I didn't mean to scare her, but Alondra looked at me like she expected me to hurt her."

"Jack," Momma says, softly, and I know I'm running out of time before someone comes looking for me.

"I just wanted her to stop running from me," I admit, reaching up to untuck the silver chain from where it always lies beneath my shirt to twist the small figure skate pendant between my fingertips. "She said it had nothing to do with Coach—actually, she insisted it didn't, and I believe her. Alondra's admitted she's had a bad relationship before, but she wouldn't say anything else about it."

"I don't know. Has she explicitly said someone hurt her?"

"No, but Johnny Richards, the sophomore I'm helping, walked in on Alondra and me talking at the rink, and he asked some questions about her, which I played off. Next thing I know, this football player who's friends with Johnny tracked me down and threatened me to stay away from her because she's his. Momma, she's a person, not a fucking toy.

Alondra doesn't belong to anyone, but especially not that asshole," I say, my temper slipping for a moment.

"Hey, take a breath. It sounds like you really care about her, but I can't tell you what to do other than to do your best to be there for Alondra, and make sure she knows she can come to you for help if she needs it."

I inhale a ragged breath, but this conversation has opened up old wounds I've never taken the time to deal with. "I'm sorry, I shouldn't have swore," I mumble, tucking the pendant back under my shirt, the weight a comfort.

"Jack, I'm so proud of you and the man you're becoming, but please, don't do anything rash," Momma warns, and I feel a pang of homesickness so deep that it aches like a rattle in my bones.

"Yes, ma'am," I agree quietly.

"She's lucky to have a friend like you," she says, and I swallow the acid forming in my mouth.

I'm the lucky one.

I probably should have called first, but it seems like the universe is determined to make it impossible for me to have a chance to talk to Alondra so I can apologize. We definitely need to talk about the whole dating app thing, but first, I need to apologize for the way I asked if she was seeing anyone. Unfortunately, Alondra left with Ellie a few minutes after I went back downstairs last night and I didn't get a chance.

Then Sara called me, asking if I'd come get her from the bars, but she turned out to be way more messed up than I thought, so I spent the rest of the night playing babysitter to make sure she was okay.

To make matters worse, our professor cancelled our class today, taking away my guaranteed time with Al. My voice memo I sent earlier went unanswered, which is fine, but I want to check on her.

I knock on Alondra's apartment door, stuffing my hands in my pockets to keep them warm while I wait for her to answer, but Macy answers instead. "What the hell is on your face?" I ask, confused by the green shit she has smeared everywhere.

"What's on yours?" she retorts without skipping a beat.

"Who is it?" I hear Alondra ask from inside, and Macy opens the door wider, motioning for me to come in. I spot Al instantly on the couch, wrapped up in my favorite purple blanket, and her face is identical to Macy's. She sits up, tilting her head. "Oh, hey, Jack. Are you looking for Ellie? She's not here," Al says, and I smile, unable to take her seriously right now.

"Sorry, just wanted to see if you were busy. I should have texted first before coming over," I say, noting the movie paused on the television and the array of snacks in front of them.

"We're kind of having a spa night," she says, reaching up to play with one of the twin braids her curls are trapped in, bouncing her gaze between me and Macy.

"You're welcome to stay if you want, but you have to put some of this shit on your face too," Macy says, offering me a smile.

"No, it's okay. You guys are busy," I say, but honestly, I do want to stay.

I like being her friend, even if it means getting whatever the fuck is on their faces smeared on mine. Fuck, Al has me wrapped around her finger, and she doesn't even realize it. There's something about her that draws me in, trapping me in her orbit, but I can never act on my physical attraction to her.

Alondra deserves better than a one-night stand from me, and that's all I have to offer.

"Sorry, you're stuck now, so take your shoes off. We have

enough for a third because Ellie ditched us to study at the library for a test tomorrow." Macy hooks her arm with mine, giving me just enough time to kick off my sneakers, before pulling me toward the couch next to Alondra. I look in her direction, expecting her to tell me to leave, but instead, she's smiling at me. I guess that means I'm staying.

"Just don't put too much of whatever that is on my face, okay?"

"You might want to take your sweatshirt off," Al suggests, and I'm just happy she isn't telling me to leave. Unlike Alondra, I'm capable of following directions without arguing, and I pull it over my head. "Macy, can you grab a headband?"

"What do you need that for?" I ask, staying still as Al uses it to carefully push all of my hair out of my face, and I can only imagine what I look like right now.

"Do you want avocado and cucumber in your hair?"

"I'm not sure I really want it on my face," I tease, hoping it makes her laugh.

"You'll thank us after," Macy says.

When she leans in to smooth the cold paste on my cheeks, I take full advantage of the opportunity to memorize the finer details of her face.

Alondra's eyes are a deceiving shade of gold that appears brown in most lighting, but looking closely, I can see the green ring inside the iris, made more prominent by the green mixture on her face. Her dark eyebrows are knit in concentration, and her touch is gentle. Alondra's pink lips quirk upward into a hint of a smile, and I can't look away, remembering how it felt to have them pressed against mine.

I wonder if she ever thinks about our kiss?

It took everything in me not to steal a second one from her that night, and I think Alondra would have let me.

"I know I'm pretty, but you're staring," she says, her voice soft as she traces the slope of my nose.

"You're beautiful. Of course I'm staring," I say, distracted when she sinks her white teeth into her lower lip in an attempt to hide her smile.

"Sorry to break it to you, but I'm developing an immunity to your charm."

My smile grows wider. "So you admit you find me charming?"

A pillow hits my arm, and I turn to find Macy frowning at me. "Stop flirting with Alondra," she scolds, and even if I were flirting, Macy and Ellie could be awarded with trophies for being the world's best cock block a guy could ask for.

I shouldn't be thinking about kissing Alondra.

"I'm not flirting. If I was, you'd know." I smirk at Macy, and she sticks her tongue out at me.

"You know you're not as hot with avocado on your face."

I press a hand to my chest, groaning. "You just broke my fragile ego. I think my heart is failing. Quick! Give me CPR," I joke, causing Alondra's hazel eyes to sparkle as a laugh slips from her.

"Shut up," Alondra says.

"Make me."

This time, her eyes land on my mouth, and I really need to stop thinking about how her fingers curled into my shirt, pulling me closer.

I wink at her, leaning back to rest against the couch cushions, hoping to calm the racing of my heart. "So what happens at spa night? Karaoke? Naked pillow fights? The saddest romance movies ever made?" I ask, trying not to think about how her leg is pressed up against mine.

"You and Dylan do know we wouldn't get naked to have a pillow fight, right? Nor do we actually have pillow fights."

Obviously, but can't a guy dream a little?

"Darlin', you're killing my fantasy," I complain, and Alondra tries to push me, but unfortunately for her, she lacks the muscle necessary to make any impact.

"Can you move? You take up so much room."

"It's because I'm so big," I say, fully aware I sound like a conceited ass, but if you got it, flaunt it.

Fuck, maybe I shouldn't take advice from Dylan.

Macy bursts into laughter, doubling over as she holds her stomach. "Oh, you're funny."

"Are you and Chadwick back together?" I ask, batting my eyelashes at her innocently.

She sputters, and I feel like an ass for a moment until she laughs, shaking her head at me.

"Don't be mean," Al scolds, pushing me again.

"I'm literally sitting here with gunk on my face and a headband. Pretty sure I'm allowed to make comments about how big my dick is without getting laughed at, but I'm sorry, Macy. It was a low blow."

"Just like I'm sorry for this," she says, pointing her phone at me, and I realize the grave mistake I've made. Next thing I know, my phone is going off with a chime of alerts, but the thought of trying to look at all the messages while keeping up with the conversation sounds mentally exhausting, so I don't even bother reaching for it.

I know my friends well enough to know they're going to get a kick out of that photo.

"Lots of big dick talk from his highness over here," Alondra reads out loud, and I'm not even sure I care they're making fun of me because of how goddamn dazzling her smile is. *Dazzling?* What the hell is wrong with me? I'm not sure I've ever used that word in my fucking life. "Sorry, Jack. I'm with Macy on this one," she says, shifting in her spot.

"Go ahead, it's okay to laugh. I'm secure enough in my masculinity and my manhood to take it," I say, and then Al rotates, draping her legs and simultaneously the purple fuzzy blanket over my thighs, making herself comfortable. I, on the other hand, am trying to keep my shit together because I'm spinning out in my head, realizing Al didn't have to read Macy's text out loud.

"Macy, can you please press play on the movie so I don't have to listen to princess here talk about his dick anymore?"

Shit, maybe I should have just moved over when she asked because my brain is malfunctioning while trying to figure out what to do with my hands. I've tried really hard since the day we went skating to be careful, letting Al make the first move when it comes to touching her because she's not mine to reach for. But Alondra was the one who put her legs on my lap, so I have to assume it means she's okay with me touching her.

I thought spa night was supposed to be relaxing, but instead, I'm overthinking every little thing.

I rest my hands on her shins, and she doesn't budge, helping some of the coiled tension in my body melt away as I let myself get sucked into the movie.

"How cute. If I didn't sit here with Al and Ellie last week and help them with your dating profile, I'd say you guys look like a domesticated couple doing your face masks and sitting on the couch together," Macy coos, and at the mention of the dating profile, I manage to laugh, but the truth is there's a heavy dose of fear coursing through my veins.

"Right, you were in on that too," I muse, trying to ignore my dad's voice ringing in my ears as Al pulls away, standing up.

The apple doesn't fall far from the tree, Jack. You're going to be just like me.

"Instead of refusing to go on a single date, you should be thanking us. We worked hard to find the right girl for you," Alondra says, and I feel off-balance, like I'm standing on a rowboat, rocking back and forth in the middle of the ocean with nowhere to go.

"Sorry you wasted your time," I say, and Macy stands too.

"They're all really nice and pretty. You're missing out," she adds, but I disagree.

I don't want someone really nice, and I doubt they would

compare to the feisty brunette I can't seem to stay away from. I'm a glutton for punishment, because I think if I were capable of loving anyone, I would hope it'd be with someone like Alondra.

I hate to admit it, but after washing off my face and using the moisturizer they passed to me, my face is really soft, but it's too much work to do on my own if I were to try another face mask—which I'm not.

I'm not sure how it happens, but at some point, Macy drifts off to sleep during the next movie, and my head ends up on a pillow in Alondra's lap. She's watching the movie, but I'm too busy looking at her to pay attention to it. Her fingers are slowly combing through my hair, and it's a fight to keep my eyes open.

It feels fucking fantastic.

"You know, I'm glad you showed up tonight," Al says, breaking the silence after my eyes have fallen shut, and I blink quickly, forcing them open.

"You left so fast last night, I wanted to check on you," I murmur, glancing up at her. "I also came to apologize. I shouldn't have asked you if you were seeing anyone in front of my friends."

Alondra's fingers in my hair still and then resume moving through the strands a few beats later. "So you stayed for a spa night?"

A low chuckle rumbles from my chest as I smile, because staying was the easiest decision I made today. "What can I say? I needed a night of relaxation, considering your dad has no problem kicking my ass every morning."

"Poor you."

My throat tightens as my heart spasms in my chest. "Are you okay?"

I don't want to be right. I really don't.

"Why wouldn't I be?" she asks, looking down at me, and I don't think I can ruin tonight by asking her about Bradley.

There's so much left unsaid in her question, and the tightrope I'm standing on sways beneath me.

"You don't have to go to any of the games if you don't want to," I finally say, deciding against telling Alondra about my run-in with Bradley.

She softens, dropping the prickly exterior she wears most of the time. "A deal's a deal, but I'm not wearing your jersey. I should have known Macy would tell you about my inability to choose something other than rock."

"Okay, but if you change your mind, you don't have to go."

I want her to stop running away from me, instead of giving her more reasons to.

"Your mom seems great," she compliments, changing the topic, and my smile grows.

"She is."

"I'm glad you have her."

"Momma asked to meet you while she's here in a couple of weeks. Are you okay with that?"

Her smile brightens. "I'd love that."

I wake up the next morning thanks to my internal alarm surrounded by the familiar smell of strawberries. I shift to fumble for my phone when I realize I'm not in my bed *and* I'm tangled with someone else.

It takes me a moment to realize Alondra's draped over me. I must have fallen asleep here last night.

My head drops back into the cushions, and I relax, despite how fucking tiny the space on this couch is. The only reason my feet aren't hanging off the edge of the couch is because my legs are bent, and I'm curled around Alondra, or maybe she's curled around me. All I know is it's hard to tell where I end and she begins.

I've never stayed with someone long enough to wake up still holding them, but I don't think I hate it. The night she asked me to stay when she was drunk, I selfishly said yes, but I left a few minutes after Al fell asleep to check on Dylan and Ellie. Now, I'm wishing I hadn't because I think I like that she trusts me enough to sleep next to me. It's a good feeling, especially when she's usually on the verge of bolting in the other direction from me.

She's soft, lacking the tension she normally carries, and knowing she's sleeping soundly will make every ache I'll feel in my body later worth it.

Except then Al groans, shifting further into me, and my body is all too keen to react to her ass pressing against my pelvis. I clench my jaw hard enough I'm shocked I haven't cracked a tooth, trying to move backward to create space between our bodies so I can give myself a fighting chance of getting my morning wood to deflate before she wakes up.

Think about how pissed off Coach would be if he knew you woke up with his daughter and a bone—

Alondra moves again, her warm breath tickling my bicep she's using as a pillow, pressing her body against mine, and I'm a fucking goner.

Taking a deep breath doesn't help because I'm *wrecked* by the smell of strawberries overwhelming every semblance of common sense.

Fuck me.

I guess there's worse places to be trapped than on a couch with a pretty girl and a throbbing erection, but usually when I'm in this situation, we're both consenting and conscious.

"Al," I say, deciding the best idea is to try to spin this as a natural reaction to someone rubbing their ass against my pelvis, but there's a better chance of her losing her shit on me.

Alondra doesn't budge, and just as I move to pull my arm out from under her head, my phone begins blaring from where it must have fallen on the ground while we slept. *Fuck, I have practice.*

She tightens her grip, pressing herself further against me, causing a low moan to slip from the back of my throat.

Her entire body tenses, and she lifts her head, looking at me as my alarm continues to shatter the peace. "Jack?" Alondra whispers, her voice thick with sleep, but I'm afraid to move. "What are you still doing here?"

Then Alondra moves to sit up, and I am in agony, biting my lip to keep any more sounds from escaping, but she's practically sitting on my lap now. It's too dark for me to see her face, but she freezes, and embarrassment floods over me.

"Turn the fucking alarm off before I smother you with a fucking pillow, Al," Macy threatens, scaring the shit out of me because I had no idea she was in the same room as us. This is a nightmare. I rest my hands on Alondra's hips, trying to move her off me as she leans to grab the phone, but all I do is cause her to go flying off the couch. She yelps, hitting the floor with a thud.

"Fuck!"

"Shit, are you okay?" I ask, terrified I just hurt her when it's the last thing I ever want to do.

"Fine," she chokes out, tossing the phone at me, but it's pitch black, smacking me straight in my eye.

"Motherfucker," I swear, my hand going up to my eye, and Macy groans again.

Why didn't she turn the alarm off before chucking it at me?

I fumble for the phone, finally silencing it when a door opens and a light flips on. At least now, my eye is the only thing throbbing. "What the hell is going on out here?" Ellie grumbles, and I blink, adjusting to the light.

Macy's hair is a tangled disaster on her head, but the murderous glare she's directing my way is as scary as Coach

Brown's sometimes. Wow, who would have guessed Little Miss Sunshine over there isn't a morning person?

"Sorry, I guess I fell asleep," I apologize, climbing off the couch, and I feel fucking awful when I see Al touching the bump on her forehead from our uncoordinated attempt to separate.

"It's fine," Alondra mumbles, not looking up at me.

Great. We took one step forward last night, and a thousand backward this morning.

"Jack, your eye," Ellie says, staring at me.

My phone rings in my hand, and Macy opens her mouth, but I quickly answer it before she can threaten to smother me with a pillow. I can feel my eye starting to swell, and I'm honestly not sure how I'm going to explain it to Coach.

"Yo, are you already at the barn?" Dylan asks, and I spot my hoodie on the ground and grab it before moving for my shoes and keys by the door.

"No, I'm not there yet."

He laughs, but I don't find anything amusing about this. "Where the hell are you then? Morning skate starts in thirty."

"I know," I reply, my tone harsher than needed. "Can you grab some clothes for me, and I'll meet you at the locker room in ten? I'm at Al's."

"Jack!" Al protests, and it's too early for this. "You shouldn't have told him you were here."

"You got it, Capt. You should check the group chat, though," he suggests, and I'm honestly not sure if I want to look.

Ellie is leaning against the wall, her arms crossed over her chest. "Sorry, Al, they already knew he was here. Dylan was fucking with you." Apparently, I've pissed everyone off this morning. Ellie does not look happy with me, but I have to get to practice before Coach has my head. If you're fifteen minutes early, you're on time, and he's a stickler when it comes to our schedule.

"It's not a big deal. We *accidentally* fell asleep, which makes it a platonic sleepover." I pull my hoodie over my head, slipping into my sneakers. "Sorry," I blurt out again, making my retreat. If I had more time before morning skate starts, I'd probably try to find the right words, but how exactly do you apologize for accidentally staying the night and then waking Al up to my dick stabbing her.

I'm out of breath by the time I arrive at the arena, having sprinted from my truck in the parking lot to make it with enough time to get dressed before we have to be on the ice.

The locker room is filled with chatter, and I duck my head, hoping to avoid questions about my eye for as long as I can, walking straight toward Dylan as he pulls his practice jersey over his pads. He bows dramatically. "Your Highness," he mocks, causing Coop to cough from the stall next to mine.

"Not in the mood," I answer in a clipped tone, and now Coop and Nate turn to face me as Dylan tosses a bag in my direction.

"I would have thought you'd be shooting sunshine out your ass since you looked pretty cozy snuggling with your tutor last night in the picture Ellie sent the group," Dylan continues, ignoring my sourness. "Oh shit, what happened to your eye?"

"Nothing," I say, doing my best to get ready on time.

Just Al having the best fucking aim in the world.

"Did she hit you?" Nate asks, trying—and failing—not to laugh.

"No. We fell asleep on the couch last night, and I woke up to my alarm with morning wood."

Coop chuckles, shaking his head. "What happened to your big dick energy from last night?"

"Fuck off."

"So what? She woke up to it, and punched you?" Dylan asks, doing a terrible job at keeping the shit-eating grin off his face.

I start pulling on my pads, trying not to picture the look on her face when I left. Goddammit. I didn't mean to hurt her this morning.

"No, Macy was asleep on the other couch and is about as chipper in the mornings as a demon from hell. I accidentally threw Al off the couch, so she threw the phone at me, but it was dark so I caught it with my face," I say, grimacing because it sounds even worse saying it out loud. "Al wouldn't even look me in the eye before I left," I mumble, wondering how the fuck I'm going to fix this.

"Any chance she didn't feel it?" Nate asks, and for someone so smart, he sure likes to ask dumb questions.

"I don't know. Is the sky blue? Of course she fucking noticed."

The chorus of laughter in the locker room doesn't make me feel any better.

CHAPTER 15

Alondra

I HAD HOPED the goose egg I earned from falling off the couch yesterday would look better today, but instead, it's turned into an awful blue and purple knot right on my forehead.

Jack cancelled tutoring last night because there was a team dinner my dad let the guys know about last minute, and damn, if I wasn't a little relieved to have a night to collect myself.

I'm fucking mortified I woke up snuggling into Jack. I'm not even sure when I fell asleep, or how I ended up wrapping myself around him, but it's embarrassing.

It's not a big deal he woke up with a boner because it's a perfectly normal human reaction. Doesn't make it any less awkward, though.

All his jokes about size the night before were surprisingly accurate.

I tried to cover up the bruise with makeup, but I can't do much to hide the lump so it feels pointless to even try. I do feel a little better knowing I beat him to class, but Keri gasps, immediately seeing the bruise. "Oh my god, are you okay?"

"I got into a fight with the floor yesterday," I explain, shrugging out of my coat before taking the seat next to her.

"Been there, done that, but I guess I was lucky I didn't end up with one of those," she says, and I fidget with my curls, glancing at the front of the auditorium to see if Jack's here yet.

I don't care he stayed the night, but I am freaking out a little because I didn't think I'd enjoy being held by him so much. I didn't think I was ready to be so comfortable with someone else, but maybe it's my mind's way of telling me I'm ready to move on.

Yes, Jack is more attractive than anyone should be, which makes it even more of a bad idea to enjoy sleeping next to him.

Jack plays hockey, doesn't believe in love, and he's one of Dad's players.

I'm too busy watching the door to pay closer attention to Keri's rant about the drama at her sorority house, but I think it'd be hard to miss Jack walking in. He's wearing the hockey team's jacket, and his jeans are hugging his muscular legs. The closer he gets climbing the stairs to our seats, the more I notice his hair looks like he's been dragging his fingers through it, and he's sporting a black eye that's the twin to the knot on my forehead.

Oh my god, did I do that?

He glances up, and his mouth turns up at the corners into a faint smile, and at least I don't look away, unlike yesterday when I couldn't make eye contact.

"Hey," he greets, and Keri gasps.

"Dude, your eye."

Jack chuckles, leaning back in his seat. "Someone threw my phone at me, and I caught it with my face."

I wince, trying not to stare, but I got him good. I hadn't even realized it because I was so flustered from everything going on, and Macy is a fucking demon in the morning.

"I bet that someone is sorry," I say, and he shrugs.

"It'll be fine in a couple days, and it gives me an excuse to go as Rocky Balboa for Halloween," he says, his smile widening enough for his dimple to make an appearance.

"What were you going to be?"

Jack laughs, shaking his head, but his gaze drifts to my forehead, and the humor fades. "Classified, but I will say it was better my eye was hit than my nose. I'm not sure I could pull off a crooked nose," Jack continues, lifting a hand to brush his fingertips over my bruise, and my heart jumps in my chest. "You okay?" he asks, his eyebrows knitting in concern.

"All good. Just a little clumsy," I say, giving him a smile so he knows we're okay. It was an accident.

"I feel like I'm missing something," Keri says, and Jack drops his hand.

"Nope," he answers, the picture of nonchalance.

"Al?" she asks, and I look at her and shrug.

"I don't think you're missing anything."

She purses her lips, narrowing her eyes at us in scrutiny. "No, there's a weird vibe here—especially with the matching bruises."

My legs are sore from my workout at the gym this morning, but it doesn't stop my leg from bouncing. "You're imagining it," I say, feeling a little bad I'm gaslighting her, but there is a weird vibe and I'm not sure how to explain it to her. I want us to go back to normal. "How was morning skate yesterday?"

"Thanks to Macy sending the face mask photo in the group chat, I've gone from Schultz to Your Highness." He groans, and I can understand why. I notice he doesn't mention the photo Ellie took of us on the couch.

Ellie and Macy went back to sleep after Jack left, but there wasn't a chance in hell I was going back to sleep, so I went to the gym and worked on my core and upper body strength.

"What picture? Stop talking about vague shit I don't know anything about. It's rude," Keri complains, and I whip my phone out, showing her the photo of Jack with his green face and headband on.

Keri's dark eyes widen for a moment, covering her mouth to smother the sound of her laughter since class is about to start. "That's amazing. Seriously, your best look yet, Jack."

"Al," Jack grumbles, and I nudge his arm with my elbow.

"You're the one who said you were secure enough in your manhood you didn't mind," I remind him, but my face still burns because now I don't need to wonder why he was just fine. I felt all his business pressed up against me, and Jack wasn't lying.

"No offense, Keri, but it's bad enough the whole team has seen it. Pretty sure Dylan shared it with Coach because he called me princess last night at our team dinner."

That's hilarious. "Why don't you try channeling your big dick energy again, princess?" I tease, and his neck flushes a scarlet hue, creeping all the way to the tips of his ears.

Jack sticks his tongue out at me like the mature adult he is, but our professor walks in, and the room falls quiet.

Halfway through class, Jack pulls his phone out and I look at him, curiosity getting the better of me because I don't think I've ever seen him pull it out during class.

My phone vibrates a moment later.

JACK

we good?

I send back a thumbs up, and he lets out an audible sigh of relief. I squirm in my seat, trying not to think about how he moaned in my ear yesterday.

It's fine. I'm fine. This doesn't have to be a big deal at all.

It's not anything new to me that I'm attracted to him, so it shouldn't be weird now?

Maybe it's a sign I'm more ready than I thought to put myself back out there. It's been long enough since Bradley.

Jack nudges my leg with his knee, and when I look, there's another text on my screen.

JACK

i'm sorry

I lean over, dropping my voice to a low whisper. "It's fine. Do I need to offer to let you touch my boobs to make it less weird I've felt your dick?"

He coughs, and I bite back a laugh when he looks at me with wide eyes, but I don't miss how his bright gaze flickers down to my chest before looking me in the eyes again. "Don't tempt me with a good time, darlin'," Jack whispers back a moment later, and I roll my eyes.

"Pay attention, pretty boy," I scold, but then Jack smiles at me, and I'm hopeful yesterday isn't the big deal I thought it would be.

"I want to go out this weekend," I say, setting my things down at the table Macy's occupying at the library.

"Go out where?" she asks, looking confused, and I really can't blame her. I hardly ever want to go out, and it's never my idea.

I let out a shaky breath as I slide into the chair. "Like out somewhere. I want to go to a party or a bar, and I want to meet a guy."

"Is this you freaking out because Jack stayed the night?"

I roll my eyes. "He stayed the night, but only because we fell asleep on the couch—*platonically*," I say, adding an extra emphasis on the word platonic because she's already jumping to conclusions. "This isn't because of Jack staying the night. I want to go out because I think after everything with Bradley, I might be ready. I'm not saying I want to find a boyfriend, but would it be so bad if I hooked up with someone?"

Macy blinks, tilting her head. "Al, what exactly are you hoping to gain from this?"

"I don't know. Does it matter?" I ask, tapping my fingers on the table.

I want to know if my body is capable of responding to someone. I need to know if my brain is playing tricks on me because I can't let myself want Jack.

"It's just that it's only been ten months since Bradley. Are you sure you're ready?" she asks, choosing each word with care. "There's no harm in taking more time."

I'm being sensitive. I know I am, but it still hurts.

"So you're allowed to go back and forth with Chad after I don't even know how many times he's played mind games and cheated on you, but I say I might be ready to put myself out there again and—" I take a second to breathe because I'm angry and not thinking rationally. The shock reflected on her face makes me feel guilty because I don't want to hurt my best friend. "Why aren't you supporting me like I've supported you?"

"I am supporting you—" Macy tries to say, but I push my chair back.

"No, you're not. You have no idea what it was like to be in that relationship, and how badly I want to feel like myself again. When it was on your terms, you were more than happy to push me toward kissing Jack. I-I've got to go."

"Al—"

"Whatever, I'll ask Ellie to go with me," I snap, grabbing my things. I'm not sure where I'm going to go, but I don't particularly want to be here right now.

It's too damn cold to wander around campus, so I head in the direction of my apartment. It's a fifteen-minute walk that doesn't feel awful in the fall or spring, but most people drive once the temperature begins to drop. I caught a ride with Ellie this morning, but she's in a lab all afternoon.

I understand why she's worried. A lot of shit went down

with Bradley, and there's still so much Macy doesn't know because I didn't want to see the way she'd look at me.

I'm doing my best to move on, and I know I'm not whole yet, but I think the fact I'm willing to try should say something. I don't want a relationship, but maybe I'd like to have a guy buy me a drink or feel desired? Is there something so wrong with that?

I'm crossing the parking lot when my phone rings with a call from Jack. Of course it's him.

I hesitate before answering because I want to wallow in my feelings, but I don't want him to think I'm still freaked about yesterday morning. He's probably checking to see if I'm going to his game tonight, but a deal is a deal.

"Hello?"

"Hey, what's up?" Jack asks.

"You called me," I remind him.

"Yeah, I guess you're right. I did," he says, and I think I understand, but Jack doesn't deserve my frustration.

"Macy called you, didn't she?" I ask, my tone as bleak and tired as I feel right now. "What'd she tell you?"

I haven't worked up the nerve to ask Jack about the guy who came up to him, too afraid it will open the door to a discussion about Bradley, and I don't want to talk about him with Jack. I like how he doesn't handle me like I'm made of glass.

"Something about you biting her head off, and she's worried, so she asked me to check in with you," Jack says, and I hate that she brought Jack into it.

"I'm fine, but it's nice to know she thinks I need a babysitter."

"You know that's not it. What's wrong?" he asks, but this isn't something he can fix.

I suck in a sharp breath, starting up the stairs. "Nothing. Absolutely fucking nothing."

"*Nothing* has put you in a pissy mood," Jack remarks.

"Maybe I don't want to talk to anyone right now. It's none of your business, Jack. Macy had no right to bother you with this."

"If you tell me what this is, maybe I can help?" he asks, and I'm sure some people might find his tenacity a charming quality, but it's just annoying right now.

I know I'm overreacting, but I want to sulk before I pull myself together for tonight. "I don't want your help." I'm his friend, not a bird with a broken wing for him to rescue with the savior complex I'm beginning to suspect he has.

"I thought we were good?" Jack asks, and I let out an exasperated sigh.

"We *are* good. This has nothing to do with yesterday."

I turn to go down the walkway on my floor as Jack finally brings up his game tonight. I'm so busy listening to him ramble again about how I don't have to go if I don't want to until I'm a few doors down from my apartment, and notice the large figure waiting next to the door.

No. Please tell me this isn't real.

My grip on my phone tightens, and it takes everything in me to keep my voice steady when all I want to do is run in the opposite direction. He's already looking at me, though.

"Dad, I said I'd be there soon. I'm just stopping at my apartment to get changed," I say, loud enough for Bradley to hear.

The grin on his face makes my bravado falter because there are so many ways this could go wrong. He knows where I live. *How?*

I can hear Jack's confusion, but my brain isn't processing anything he's saying. "Hey, Alondra. It's been a while," Bradley teases, stepping closer to me, and I feel like I'm going to vomit.

"No, you don't need to send Jack and Dylan to deliver me. I'm perfectly capable of making it there by myself," I continue, trying to add an extra bite to my tone to make it believable.

"Al, what is going on?" Jack demands, and I grab the pepper spray hanging from my keys.

"I'll see you soon," I say, swallowing the bile creeping up my throat. *Keep it together, Al.*

"Don't hang up—" Jack starts to say, but Bradley knows too much about my relationship with my dad to know I wouldn't stay on the phone with him longer than necessary. I hang up, wishing I could do nothing more than keep him on the phone.

Fuck. I can do this. I'm not his victim anymore.

"What are you doing here?" I ask Bradley, trying to keep my voice devoid of emotion. Bradley wants a reaction.

He seems unfazed, but his cheeks are red from the cold, and I wish I knew how long he's been waiting out here. If I had stayed with Macy, maybe he would have left before I got back. "I was waiting for you." Or Ellie would have found him if she had come home before us. I don't think he'd hurt her, but I know from first-hand experience how fucking convincing he can be of his 'nice guy' routine when he tries.

"Why?" I ask, keeping my hands tucked inside the sleeves of my coat. My phone vibrates in my hand, and there's no doubt in my mind it's Jack. I decline it by using one of the side buttons.

He looks me up and down, and I stand my ground, even as my heart rate quickens in my chest. "I heard you've been screwing around with Jack Schultz. What happened to wanting nothing to do with hockey players?"

I shrug, and as much as I want to look away, I know better than to take my eyes off of him right now. I decline another call, hoping Jack understood what I meant.

"You think your dad will finally love you because you're on your knees for one of his players?" he says crudely, and there's nothing I can say right now to convince him that Jack and I are only friends.

"Why do you care? We're not together," I say, but my hands are sweating as another call comes through.

Bradley looks over me again, and I'm afraid to move a muscle as his face relaxes into a calm smile. "Sorry, angel. We're not over until I say we're over. Stay away from Schultz."

My feet stumble backward like I've been struck, and his words echo in my head.

We're not over until I say we're over.

His smile widens, pleased I've finally given him the reaction he wanted. I'm shaking, and there's no hiding it now. "If I'm not at the rink in ten minutes, my dad is going to send Jack and Dylan to fetch me. Please leave."

I hate that I use the word please, but I just want him to go.

"I haven't seen you at any of my games," he says, ignoring my comment about the guys. Bradley's fucking delusional.

"You need to go," I say, my voice wavering and I feel as small as ever. It's like I'm right back where I was this time last year.

"I miss you, Al."

If I open my mouth, I'm either going to scream or throw up, and I really don't know which one it's going to be, so I clamp my jaw shut. He doesn't miss me. He misses having someone to control.

His hand reaches for my face, brushing his fingertips over the lump on my head. I flinch, and his nostrils flare while his jaw clenches.

"Think about what I said, and stay away from Jack." His dark gaze meets mine as tears well in my eyes and I close them, nodding once. Maybe if I agree with him, Bradley will leave.

When I open my eyes again, Bradley's walking away from me, already halfway to the stairwell. I fumble with my keys, finally finding the right one to unlock the door before shutting and locking it quickly when I'm on the other side in case Bradley changes his mind. I cover my mouth to smother the sound of a sob from breaking loose as my phone clatters to the ground, the vibrations rattling against the vinyl flooring echoing in the silent apartment.

Oh my god, he knows where I live.

My legs give out underneath me, and I sink to the floor like a stone in a pond, all of the terrible memories of Bradley surfacing from the corner of my mind where I've shoved them.

Five minutes with Bradley have undone months of progress, shattering the mosaic of hope I'd put together using the broken pieces of myself left in his wake.

We're not over till I say we're over.

He can't possibly believe that.

I close my eyes, feeling the tears stream down my cheeks as I gasp for air.

You're fine, Al. He didn't touch you—not really. You'll be fine.

Ten, nine, eight, seven, six, five, four, three, two, one.

Fuck free college. This is why I wanted to go to Texas. It would've been a fresh start, and there wouldn't have been a shot in hell of Bradley showing up at my door because he felt threatened by one of my friends.

There's a loud knock on the door, and I scramble to my feet, biting my lip to hold back my sobs because if he hears me, he'll know I lied, and he won't leave peacefully this time. *He came back.* Bradley didn't care I said my dad was waiting for me.

"Al, it's Jack. Are you here?" his familiar voice asks, knocking again.

He came. He really came. I move to unlock the door for Jack, but once I see him, my vision blurs to the point that I can no longer focus on anything. I'm immediately scooped into his strong arms, and I wrap mine around his neck, clinging to him as my tears fall faster.

Jack holds me effortlessly, supporting my weight as he walks us into the apartment while I bury my face in the crook of his neck. "I've got you. It's okay," Jack whispers, and I can't do anything but cry, too damn relieved he's here. "Dylan, lock the door and tell Ellie not to come back here," he instructs, his voice shaking.

I've ruined everything.

"Can you tell me what happened?" Jack asks quietly, and I feel nauseous as the adrenaline fades from my body.

I shake my head, struggling to even know where to begin, so instead, I focus on trying to take a deep breath, inhaling the comforting smell of cinnamon and the feeling of safety that comes with being near Jack.

We're not over until I say we're over.

CHAPTER 16

Alondra

AFTER I'VE FINALLY STARTED to calm down, I peel myself away from Jack, crawling out of his lap to sit next to him on the couch. Dylan is sitting on one of the bar stools, tapping on his phone screen.

"Alondra?" Jack asks when I reach for a tissue to clean up my face.

"Sorry, I think I got snot on your sweatshirt," I mumble, taking my coat off and dumping it on the floor. I'll deal with it later because not hanging up my coat right now is the least of my problems.

"It's fine," he says, turning to face me, but it's not fine. It's really gross, and I feel bad.

"Are you okay?" Dylan asks, and I feel raw and exposed.

I sniffle, looking down at my hands for a moment. "No, but I will be. Thanks for coming—both of you," I clarify, glancing up at them to find Jack staring at me.

"Who did this to you?" he asks, frowning. Jack reaches for my face, and I hate that I flinch instinctively. A new piece of me fractures from the way he's looking at me. I never wanted Jack to look at me like this.

"Who did what?"

Bradley didn't touch me today. He only showed up to remind me I'm not free.

"Your lip is bleeding," Dylan's voice is gentle, and I grab another tissue to press it to my mouth, and sure enough, my lip is bleeding.

I wipe my cheeks and blow my nose again, trying to think of what I did to bust it. "I must have bitten my lip."

"Al, you don't have to lie," Jack says, tugging his hands through his chestnut hair.

"I'm not. I'm *fine*," I say, my voice breaking as I twist the tissue in my hands. "Thanks for coming, but you guys should go. It's all good."

I'm lying. I'm not good, but I have to put myself back together.

A low chuckle slips from Dylan as he shakes his head, crossing his arms over his chest. "You're not fine, and it's not all good. Maybe we can help, but we have to talk about whatever happened to know what to do."

"He left. There's nothing more to it than that," I say, reaching back to twist my hair into a bun, needing to do something with my hands.

"Who left?" Jack asks, and I notice the dark spot on the collar of his sweatshirt where my lip must have bled onto him.

"Does it matter?" I ask, unable to help glancing at Dylan. I don't think I have a choice in the matter of telling Jack, but the way Dylan's looking at me—whether he knows it or not—is why I don't jump to tell people the truth about Bradley. It's the same way Macy looked at me when I told her the truth in the hospital.

Jack follows my gaze to Dylan and wipes his hands on his thighs, offering one to me. I stare at it, blinking before taking it. "Dylan, you good out here for a couple minutes?" he asks, turning to look at his friend while I stand, wobbling on shaky legs.

"Sure," he agrees, and I wish I was standing on solid ground for this conversation. "I'm sorry we didn't get here faster," Dylan says, and I try to smile back, pulling my hand from Jack's to walk toward my room, climbing on the bed as Jack follows behind me.

"It was Bradley, wasn't it?" Jack asks, after shutting the door, confirming my suspicion that it was Bradley who approached him. I've been careful never to mention his name, and while Macy can't keep a secret, she wouldn't have told Jack about this.

"Yeah," I admit, swallowing the acid creeping up my throat. "Bradley was waiting for me to get back."

Jack tenses, bracing his arms on the back of his neck. "Fuck, Alondra. What would you have done if you weren't on the phone with me?"

I don't even want to consider it because I don't know.

I close my eyes, shutting them tightly because I don't think I can look at him when I say this. "We were together for a year and a half. Bradley was sweet and charming, and he made me laugh." It's hard to remember the good when the bad would happen so fast. "The first time he put his hands on me was because I laughed at him. Bradley told me he didn't like the way I spoke about one of my friends at the rink because he was a guy, and he asked me not to talk to him anymore, and I laughed. He shoved me against the wall, and I couldn't believe it. I thought I imagined it, but then it happened again a few weeks later when we got back from hanging out with his friends. Bradley shoved me from behind and told me not to act like such a slut around his friends."

I feel the bed dip next to me, but I can't open my eyes. I can't see him look at me the same way Dylan was in the living room. "He'd beg me for forgiveness, and no matter how sick and twisted it all was . . . I loved him, so I let myself be manipulated. I wanted to be loved so desperately I did whatever he wanted because I thought if I could make him happy, it'd be enough and he'd stop." I feel another tear slide past my defenses, and I reach up, wiping it away. "I was wrong."

I wait for Jack to say something, but I'm terrified of what he's going to say.

I know how stupid I was to become that girl, but everyone thinks it'd be so damn easy to leave until they're in the situation being told no one else will ever love you, especially if even your dad doesn't. Bradley was so good at twisting everything until I was the one apologizing because if I hadn't told him no, then it wouldn't have happened. When I wouldn't apologize, he wouldn't let me leave the room until I forgave him because who would believe me if I told them? It'd be my word against his, and everyone believed he was the perfect and charming guy he led them to believe he was— the type of guy I swore he was at the beginning of our relationship.

I took pictures of the abuse because I think I needed to convince myself it was real, especially when Bradley made it seem impossible to think anyone would believe me.

I would have done anything to make him happy.

Now, it makes me nauseous to even look at the hidden folder of pictures, let alone do something with them. Regardless of the photographic evidence they provide, at the end of the day, I'm not sure they're worth much. It'd still be my word against his.

"He thinks you're his," Jack says slowly.

"I know," I say, finally looking up at him. He's pulled his necklace out from underneath his shirt, twisting the pendant at the end.

We're not over till I say we're over.

"Bradley is why you stopped skating," Jack says, putting the pieces together.

"I know how stupid it sound—" I'm cut off by how fast his head snaps in my direction, his crystal eyes shining like glass. His black eye sticks out like a sore thumb, and I can't believe it was just yesterday we woke up on the couch.

"No, it's not stupid. Don't ever call it that," he says, and being here with Jack—feeling safe and seen and heard—is exactly what gives me the courage to continue.

"The last time I skated before the morning you saw me was a little over a year ago. There was a local competition my coach entered me in to practice my programs, and my short was incredible. I didn't pop a single jump, and I was so excited because my dad was supposed to be there, but then I realized Bradley wasn't smiling. He just tilted his head and looked at me like he was confused before asking me why it wasn't enough for me to have him there. He said it didn't matter how well I did, my dad was never going to put me over hockey and his players." I pause, taking a second to catch my breath, swiping away the tears threatening to fall because it feels silly to shed any more tears over the past. "I tried to argue with him, insisting he was wrong because Dad promised—he *promised* he would be there. Then Bradley punched me in my ribs so hard I couldn't breathe. I knew better than to argue with him, but I still did it anyway, and it was for nothing because he was right. My dad never showed up.

"I think they were just bruised, but I couldn't catch my breath, so I knew I had to drop out of the competition. Bradley was so apologetic afterward, saying if I tried to leave him, he'd hurt himself. I was in pain and afraid of the person who I thought loved me, and I quit that night."

I hate that I quit skating because of Bradley. I hate it more than anything because I loved it, but at the time, I thought I craved the feeling of being loved more.

Jack hasn't let go of the pendant, and I want to ask what it means to him. He exhales a shaky breath, tucking it back under his shirt. "He was wrong, Al. I-I wish I knew what to say, but all I can think about is how fucking wrong he was. I hate him for taking advantage of you, but even more than that . . ." Jack trails off, hanging his head as he grips the comforter in his fists.

"More than that?" I ask, and Jack shakes his head.

"He thinks of you like a possession. I have a very hard time believing he'll let you go easily."

I scoff, hating that I agree. "Bradley doesn't have a choice in the matter. I'm not his. I'm not anyone's property."

Jack leans forward to rest his elbows on his knees. "Does your dad know?"

I never told my parents. The night Bradley and I broke up, he pushed me down the stairs outside his house. I hit my head on the railing, but the way I landed caused my arm to twist underneath me, breaking it along with a few of my ribs. I called Macy, and she came to get me, only when she got there, I was passed out in the snow. She called my parents on the way to the emergency room, and they believed me when I told them I slipped and fell down the stairs because I was upset we'd broken up.

It was icy, so it was believable. They never questioned it.

"No."

"What did he want?" Jack asks.

"For me to stay away from you. I guess he's threatened by you." Way more than just threatened if he was willing to come here to tell me himself. "Why didn't you tell me he tracked you down a few weeks ago?"

"Honestly?" he asks, and I nod. "I was afraid you'd run from me again if I pushed you for answers you weren't ready to give me. Now I'm starting to think I should have listened when you told me to stay away the first time. I don't want to be the reason he's making you feel small and afraid."

I can't blame Jack for being afraid of me running. I shiver, grabbing a pillow to hug to my chest. "I don't care. If it's not you he's threatened by, it'll be someone else. You're my friend, Jack. I like being your friend, but Bradley's influenced enough of my decisions, so I mean it when I say *I don't care.* He doesn't get to control me anymore."

"I'm sorry," he says. "I'm so sorry."

"It's not your fault. I know exactly how Bradley is."

Fuck, Bradley knows where I live.

Jack stands, rolling his shoulders, but I'm not sure there's anything I can do to help relieve the tension coiled in him. "You hung up the phone, Al. Don't ever do that again, okay?" God, I'm so glad he came. I know Jack didn't have to, but he did. "Are you okay?"

"I'm fine. He's gone. Thank you for coming." I quickly check my phone, noting the time. I sniffle, wiping my nose on my sleeve. "Don't you guys have to get ready for your game soon?"

"Fuck," Jack swears, pulling out his phone before looking at me with his intense gaze. A part of me feels relieved that he knows about Bradley, but what I appreciate most is he's not looking at me any differently. "Get your stuff, you're not staying here."

"And go where? Jack, this is where I live."

His face softens, and his hand lifts to rub the top of his shirt, subconsciously finding comfort in whatever meaning lies behind the silver he wears around his neck. "I know you don't want to let him control you, so if it makes you feel better, do it for me. Please, stay at my place. It'd make me feel better about leaving you alone, and Dylan already told Ellie not to come here. We'll figure it all out later."

"I won't hide from him this time," I insist, and maybe it makes me stupid.

Jack moves to kneel in front of me, reaching to pull the pillow out of my hands. "I'm not asking you to hide, Alondra. I'm asking you to give me a little time to figure this all out because I won't be able to focus on hockey tonight if the only thing I can think about is whether you're safe or not."

I grip his hands before he can pull them away to give me

space. "Okay," I whisper, dipping my chin in agreement, and he breathes out a sigh.

"I've got you," Jack says, and I lurch forward without a second thought to wrap my arms around him. He folds me into his chest, resting his head against mine as I relax in the safety of Jack's arms.

"Thank you."

I know I was mad at Macy earlier when I told her she pushed me into kissing Jack, but really, I should be thanking her because who knows where I'd be if she hadn't.

CHAPTER 17

Jack

MY ARMS ACHE, and I can feel the sweat dripping down my back underneath all the layers of gear, but I've never felt more alive.

Hockey often reminds me of a carefully choreographed dance, each player knowing exactly what steps to take from the countless hours spent getting ready for these sixty minutes. Tonight has been a hard-fought battle, but it's not over yet, and I refuse to let this game end in a tie with thirty seconds on the clock. The Michigan Lions are good, but we're better.

The Lions' forward misses the pass, and I make eye contact with Nate before I take off. "Mine!" I call, retrieving the puck as it bounces off the boards. Checking my other shoulder, I spot Dylan filling in the open area between the dots as the other team's forward closes the gap I planned to take behind the net. I pass the puck to him as I wheel behind the net, pushing hard to catch up to my zone. Dylan passes the puck to Shane, the senior right wing on our line, and he uses his body to protect the puck, pivoting to drive behind their net as I find a gap in the Lion's defensive line with both of them trying to focus on the puck and so little time left while their goalie shouts, eying me. Like a well-oiled machine, Shane flicks the puck in my direction as I crash the net, giving me the perfect opportunity to tip it into the goal just before the buzzer sounds.

"Atta boy, Schultz," Shane shouts, shaking my shoulders as he lets out a loud whooping sound that disappears as the crowd roars.

I grin at him, relieved this isn't ending in a fucking tie. "Fucking filthy! You're an animal," Dylan says, hitting me from behind and we meet the rest of our team at the bench as Coach Brown tips his head in approval at the breakaway and scoring opportunity I helped facilitate.

For the first time all night, I let myself think about the girl with dark curls who I hope listened to me for once and is waiting at my house with Ellie and Sara. Thank god we still have another game tomorrow because it means the guys should keep their celebration tonight on the tame side compared to their usual celebrations after a grueling win.

"How does it feel?" Nate asks, clapping me on the back as I unclip my helmet to drop it on the bench while I grab my water bottle, squirting some into my mouth.

"You should know since I thought you were out there with the rest of us." I snort, giving him a side eye because what the fuck is he talking about? A win feels damn good, and this was a much needed one.

He grins, dragging a hand through his dark hair, damp with sweat. "I'm not talking about that. I'm talking about your girl showing up with my name on her back," he says, pointing a gloved hand further up in the stands where I find Ellie, Sara, and Alondra. Sure enough, Alondra's wearing a Wilder Wolves away jersey with the number four on it—Nate's number.

My jaw falls open when she lifts her hand in acknowl-edgement, a faint smirk pulling at her lips, and while I'm happy to see her with her usual spark compared to the way I found her earlier, I'm thrown by how fucking jealous I am.

Nate laughs, and I clamp my jaw shut, forcing a smile, but when her head tips back in a laugh, that's when I know Al's trying to get a rise out of me. If I didn't think it would attract her dad's attention, I'd consider making a scene.

The hustle back to the locker room is a rush, with everyone chimes in about Shane's puck handling and how Coop was a wall in the net. On our way to the tunnel, Coach Brown catches me.

"Schultz, whatever lit the fire under your ass tonight, keep it going," he says, squeezing my shoulder as he glows with pride.

I stare at him for a moment, trying to understand how the man in front of me can be the same one who didn't show up for his daughter at her last skating competition while her boyfriend hit her. I force a smile that feels wrong. "Will do, Coach," I say, and he lets go of me, letting me follow the team into the locker room, but the interaction sobers my mood.

The locker room smells worse than a dead animal, the stench of twenty-five hockey players' gear and sweat casting a fog. I'm quick to strip and jump in the shower, so I can get out of here fast to meet Alondra. "Where are we going tonight to celebrate?" I hear Johnny ask when I walk back to my stall, holding the towel around my waist in place.

He got some playing time during a line change in the second period, and Johnny looked better than he had before I started working with him outside of practice.

Nate looks to me, and I shake my head because I have no plans to go out. As much as I'm sure she's going to try avoiding the conversation, we need to clue our friends in on Bradley and make a plan to keep Al safe.

"We'll celebrate tomorrow night. Maybe we should all take a page out of Schultz's book and spend the night doing our hair with face masks. I think I can do without the black eye, though," Shane suggests, and I snort, rolling my eyes.

"Wanna see how much of a shit I give?" I ask, flipping him off with both hands. Honestly, I keep forgetting I have the damn thing until someone else mentions it.

"If you're going out tonight, don't be fucking stupid. We still have a game tomorrow," Coop reminds everyone.

"Can we come hang at your house?" Johnny asks, pivoting, and I know I'm team captain, but that doesn't mean I want the team at our house tonight. Richards reminds me of an overeager puppy, and I can't for the life of me figure out why he's fucking friends with Bradley.

"No," Coop answers before I can say anything. I need to remember to get him some of that fancy olive oil he likes to use when he cooks as a thank you.

"Why not?" he asks, refusing to drop it.

"Because I don't want to," he says, and Nate chuckles.

"Dude, you and your sister could not be more different," he says, shaking his head when Dylan struts to his stall like a damn peacock flashing his feathers.

"I think I've figured it out," he says, and I'm not sure I want to hear whatever stupid shit is about to come out of his mouth.

"I'll bite. What'd you figure out?" Nate asks, and Coop sighs.

"Well, I was showering and I thought about how instead of getting Coach's name tatted on my ass, I'd rather get Jack's, cause we're bros for life," he says, thumping his chest twice with his fist, and I'm not sure I could make this shit up if I tried.

"Are you fucking kidding me?" Coop asks, and Dylan holds his hands up.

"It gets better, just wait for me to finish," Dylan argues, and I shake my head.

"You know, maybe you should stop. I don't really want to

hear about you thinking about me and Coach while you're in the shower," I say, turning away as I step into my dress pants, pulling them up.

"It sounds weird when you put it like that," Dylan says, and I'm not sure what I did to deserve this.

"Maybe because it is weird?" Nate adds.

"Whatever. Anyway, so I was debating which name and which cheek, but then I realized I have two cheeks so why do I have to pick at all when I could get both and have one on each," he says, and I blink, laughing while I try to figure out if he's being serious. *Oh my god, I think he is.*

Nate snorts as he finishes buttoning up his shirt, giving me a look. "This is who you pick as your best friend?"

"Jones might be an idiot, but at least Al didn't show up wearing his jersey," I say, slipping into my button-up.

Dylan's eyes widen, his smile slipping at the mention of Alondra, and I shake my head, trying to be subtle. There wasn't time before the game to explain everything to Coop and Nate, so we agreed to fill them in after, but first, I need to talk to Alondra.

"You know, you didn't have to come tonight," I say, peeking at Alondra sitting in the passenger seat of my truck.

"We made a deal," Al says, but the deal happened before this afternoon. It happened before I heard the change in her tone, and I felt fear in a way I haven't since I was a kid. I was able to block it out during the game because I needed to, but I'm trying to find a way to not make what happened with Alondra today about me and my shit.

"I know we did, but . . ." I trail off, flexing my grip on the steering wheel.

"Jack," she says, and I look at her again. "I don't want things to be weird."

"Am I making them weird?" I ask, turning the radio down, hating that we're caught in traffic on our way back from the stadium.

"Yes."

I chuckle under my breath. "You didn't even take any time to think about it. What am I doing?"

"For starters, you haven't said anything about what I'm wearing, and instead of thanking me for coming to your game tonight, you're telling me *again* I didn't have to come. You're making it weird," she says, and I'm not quite sure I'm following.

"I thought it was standard practice to not comment on what your friends wear, especially if they're women?" I ask, looking at all the glowing red brake lights in front of us. "Is there a reason you want me to say something about what you're wearing?"

Alondra groans, huffing. "No."

"Darlin', I'm not making things weird, but if you want to pick an argument with me to feel like you're in control, go for it," I say, easing off the clutch to let the truck roll forward a few feet. "Thank you for coming to my game, though," I finish, wishing the line hadn't started to move so I could look at her.

"I'm not trying to pick an argument with you," she protests, but I see her shift in her seat out of the corner of my eye. "Okay, maybe I am, but I want us to be normal. Arguing for us is normal, and I don't want you to treat me differently just because you know about Bradley."

God, I hate hearing his name come out of her mouth. I hate that he hurt her. I hate all of it.

"So you wore Baxter's jersey because you wanted to pick an argument?" I ask, finally acknowledging the elephant in the room, and I turn out of the line, picking a random empty parking spot.

When I turn to look at her, Alondra's smiling.

"So you do know what I'm wearing," she says, looking awfully pleased with herself.

If only she knew how aware I am of her all the time.

"Al, I'm not going to treat you differently. Did you look at me differently after I told you about my dad?" I ask, and Alondra shakes her head. "Then why would I treat you differently?"

She relaxes, and I find myself wanting to reach out to take her hand. "Thanks," Al says, giving me a small smile.

Don't make it weird, Jack.

"Would it make you feel better if I offered to kiss you?" I tease, trying to lighten the mood.

"Can you make it better than a two?" she asks, tilting her head up in a challenge, and if I weren't so damn grateful to see her attitude, I'd be offended. Our kiss was a fucking ten out of ten, and saying it's anything less is a lie. If it makes her feel better, though, she can lie to me because I know the truth.

"Whoa, what happened to the three you gave me?"

Alondra grins and laughs, twisting a long, dark curl around her finger, and I'm utterly entranced. "I guess kissing you really wasn't very memorable. Threes are for winners."

"Oh, shut up. Three out of ten is still for losers, and I promise, I'm not a loser," I say, unbuckling my seatbelt and to face her entirely, despite the small space.

"Prove it," she dares, and I raise an eyebrow, trying to figure out if I heard her right.

It's so tempting to tangle my fingers in Alondra's dark curls and lean in while I decide how I want to kiss her.

All I know is I don't think one kiss would be enough, and it's not fair for me to want that when I can't offer her everything she deserves. Al said herself she believes there's a right person for everyone, and I'm not anyone's right person. I don't know how to be.

The next person she picks should be someone who can make her happy.

Alondra leans closer to me, her glimmering eyes dropping to land on my mouth, but I don't want her to dare me to kiss her because I helped her feel safe earlier.

I didn't want to be right.

I clear my throat, drawing her attention back up. "If I kissed you right now like I think you're asking me to, you'd freak out about us going back to normal even more than you already are," I say, wishing for a moment we were different people so everything weren't so complicated.

"Yeah, probably," Al says, angling herself away from me, and I think I've fucked up more than I would have if I had kissed her just now. "Looks like the traffic has slowed down a bit. We should go back to the house."

"Can I say something first without you hating me for suggesting it?" I blurt out, and Alondra looks down at her lap, avoiding my gaze. Fuck, maybe I shouldn't say anything.

"I guess."

"I know I'm probably overstepping, but I think you should consider telling your dad about Bradley."

I know it's a lot to ask of Alondra, but I want to believe if he knew, he wouldn't let her think she has to earn his love.

"Why? It's over," she says, turning to look out the window. This was a bad idea. I shouldn't have said anything.

"Because I think he might be able to help, but it's just a thought. You don't have to say anything to anyone if you don't want to," I say, trying to salvage the conversation.

She's not alone. I know we haven't been friends for long, but I'm in her corner.

"Please don't tell him," she whispers.

"Al, I wouldn't do that. Trust me, I'm very careful to keep my friendship with you and your dad as my coach separate. It's like church and state—you don't mix them together," I say, and she shifts again in her seat, glancing in my direction.

"Why did you come up to me at the bar?" Alondra asks,

catching me off-guard. I don't know what I expected her to say, but it wasn't this.

"Because I couldn't look away from you, and Dylan noticed I was watching you. You were giving off some very strong fuck off vibes, though, so he dared me to kiss you. I know I didn't have to agree to it, but I liked that you weren't throwing yourself at my friends. Believe it or not, the puck bunnies here are relentless," I explain, being as honest as I can without admitting I noticed Alondra the second she entered the bar with Macy.

I probably would have gone up to her at some point, whether Dylan said anything or not.

Alondra's laugh fills the inside of my truck, and I can't help joining her. "As if you don't eat their attention up," she says, rolling her eyes.

"It gets a little old after a while," I reply, and her eyebrows raise in disbelief.

"Tell that to your fan club then. I'm tired of all the dirty looks I get when I'm with you." Alondra scoffs, but I think she needs to ignore them like I do. Honestly, after a while, you don't even notice it.

"Oh please. Being my friend is totally worth every dirty look you've received," I say, nudging her arm with my elbow. Maybe we do have a shot at being normal again.

"Sure, pretty boy. Keep telling yourself that," she says, laughing so hard she snorts, and I can't help but join in.

CHAPTER 18

Alondra

"I'M ACTUALLY OBSESSED," Sara says, her jaw dropping as she takes in my costume.

"It's not too much?" I ask, looking down. I feel a little ridiculous in the flannel and denim shorts, but it's the cowboy hat and boots that make it obvious. It's not practical in the slightest because who in their right mind would wear shorts when it's forty degrees outside? But I guess that just means I'm not in my right mind.

"Hell no. Girl, if I thought you swung that way, I'd spend my entire night trying to take you home," Sara says, and I think my cheeks might be as red as the cowboy boots on my feet.

"It's perfect. Chef's kiss," Macy says, blowing me a kiss, and I think she might have the most creative costume of us. She's wearing a white apron over a red dress with lipstick kiss marks on it that match her cherry lips and a white head-band. The mixing spoon in Macy's hand really completes the costume.

"She's right. You do look good," Ellie adds, pushing in the last bobby pin, securing her blonde hair up in the high bun.

She slips into the light-up wings, spinning around. "How do I look?"

"Dylan won't be able to keep his tongue in his mouth," I tease, and her whole body flushes a bright red color. Maybe we would have been better off buying those inflatable dinosaur costumes off the Internet. I feel good, and I know I look hot, but what if I actually look stupid?

"Shut up. I don't know what you're talking about," she mumbles, adjusting her wings and the top of her citrus green dress.

"Oh my god, are we still pretending you haven't had a crush on Dylan Jones since freshman year, Tinkerbell?" Sara asks, and I probably shouldn't be laughing because I'm more confused than ever about Jack.

I may or may not be wearing this in my attempt to get him to kiss me to prove that my attraction to him is purely physical.

"And what are you planning on riding tonight?" Ellie asks, raising an eyebrow at me. "Maybe a certain hockey captain, who's been crashing on our couch the last few nights?"

The conversation with Jack's friends and Ellie about Bradley was uncomfortable, but I'm not sure anything would have been worse than Jack shooting me down in his truck after the game last Friday night. I made up with Macy, but I couldn't avoid telling her about Bradley when Jack insisted we all crash at their place that night. I got into a heated argument with Jack because he wanted to give up his bed for us to sleep in, but with another game Saturday, he was reluctant to agree.

I didn't give anyone specifics—just a generalized explanation that the last guy I dated wasn't a great guy, and he showed up at the apartment. I couldn't even look at Dylan during the conversation because he had been with Jack, and obviously there's more to it than what I said, but he didn't call me on my bullshit. Jack suggested later that night I should tell all of them, but I don't want to.

Even with the vague details, all three of them volunteered to give up their room for us to move into temporarily, but we quickly vetoed that idea. I refuse to let Bradley scare me from my safe place, and I love our apartment, so we compromised by agreeing to let them take turns crashing on our couch. I have yet to see them take turns, though, because it's been Jack staying the night every night.

It feels like overkill, especially because Bradley's not stupid enough to show up twice in a week, but it does make me feel better knowing there's someone there who can help if he does.

A laugh sputters from me, and I struggle to find my words. "We're friends," I say, but it feels like a weaker argument every time I have to point it out.

"A friend you wanna make out with," Ellie sings and Macy pours a round of shots. "Look, I know I talk a lot of shit on Willow for trying to get with my brother, but as long as you aren't going to go all stalker chick on Jack, I like the idea of you guys together. He's hot, you're hot, and you guys would make really cute babies, but it also helps that he's not my brother."

"Guys, I'm his tutor and I'm helping him find a girl-friend," I say, taking the shot glass from Macy. There's zero need to be talking about babies.

"Damn, maybe I need to get a tutor," Sara adds, adding the final dusting of glitter to her arms. She's going as a vampire, but all I know is that glitter is going to be a night-mare to get rid of later. "I think you all look hot enough to bang, and I guarantee those boneheads will agree with me. There won't be anyone sleeping on your couch tonight," she jokes, but goddamn, a part of me wants her to be right.

❄

"I fucking love Halloween," Macy says, an extra bounce in her step as we walk up to the guys' booming house, filled with more people than I've ever seen here. It fits the label of what you'd imagine a stereotypical college athlete's house to look like on one of the biggest party nights of the year.

"I bet Coop's head is about to explode. He hates stuff like this," Ellie adds, laughing, a slight wobble to her step from the additional shots she and Sara did with Macy before we left the apartment.

Sometimes I wish I had a sibling so they could be a built-in best friend, and so they could understand what it was like for me growing up because they would've been in the thick of it with me. Or they could have been someone else my parents would've loved more than me, like Macy and her sister, so I guess maybe it's a blessing my parents didn't have any other kids.

"I think he just hates people," Sara adds, and I tug at the bottoms of my shorts as if I were magically able to add an extra few inches of denim to the length. I did one shot for courage, but they look like they're having a much better time after the three shots they took in quick succession.

I know athletes tend to run in the same crowd, but I'm hoping Bradley isn't stupid enough to show up here tonight where the entire hockey team will be, and I think they're more likely to shoot first and ask questions later where their captain is involved.

I shove aside all thoughts of my ex, trying to focus on my mission for tonight, when we enter the chaos of the house I've become very familiar with.

I find Jack in the kitchen on my mission with Macy to find drinks, but I plan on sticking with something light so I can't blame alcohol for my decisions tonight. He wasn't joking about using the black eye to his advantage, and I should be far more worried about how little clothes he's wearing than how short my shorts are.

I've felt his muscles and seen them before in the picture we uploaded to Jack's dating profile, but it's different seeing them in all their glory right before me. His athletic shorts hang low on his hips, and his hands are wrapped in some kind of athletic tape while he holds a water bottle in his hand, but it's his damn dimples I can't look away from.

It feels like time slows down when he laughs, and his eyes land on me as he turns his head.

He doesn't say anything, walking away from the guy he was talking to, stopping in front of me. If it weren't for the look in his crystal eyes, I'd think Jack was mad at me, and I capitalize on the moment. I tip the brim of my hat at Jack, smirking at him. "Howdy, partner."

"You know, I think I'll find the drinks on my own," Macy says, giving me an extra push forward that knocks the smirk right off my face as I stumble into Jack, catching myself by landing with both palms on his hot, muscular abdomen.

Oh my god.

I pull away, and a full laugh bursts from Jack. "If you wanted to touch me, all you had to do was ask," he drawls, leaning in for me to hear him over everything else going on around us. "I like your costume, darlin'."

"I would say I like yours, but you've left very little to the imagination," I say, looking up from his rippled stomach to Jack's ridiculous pecs, realizing his necklace is on full display.

At the bottom of the silver chain hangs a dainty silver pendant in the shape of a figure skate. It's simple, and the metal is worn in some spots, but as much as I want to keep staring at it, I force myself to look up at his stupidly handsome face, marred by the fading green bruise around his eye.

"I think you've given me too much to imagine," Jack mumbles, and I'm pretty sure I wasn't supposed to hear him say that.

"What?" I ask, pretending like I'm not sure what he's implying.

Jack reaches up, twirling one of my curls around his finger, tugging on it gently. "Do you want a drink?" he asks, reaching to adjust the way my hat sits on my head. "I cut a lime earlier and hid it in the back of the fridge if you wanted some."

"You cut a lime up?"

"Yeah. You like to add them to your drinks, but I didn't know what you were wanting to drink tonight, so the least I could do was make sure you have limes," Jack says, his blue eyes twinkling, and I feel off-balance.

Jack knows I like limes in my drinks, so he bought a lime and cut it for me?

"So what are you drinking tonight?" he asks, and I swallow the lump forming in my throat. I'm terrified of wanting to be physically close to someone again, but I think if I were to take the first step, Jack would be the perfect person. He's king of unattached hookups, and just because I'm attracted to him, it doesn't mean I have feelings for Jack.

"Just water," I say, changing my mind from the beer I planned to have because there is zero doubt in my mind that Jack will be hooking up with someone by the end of the night, and I think I want it to be me.

His eyebrows knit, and he tilts his head. "Why don't you want a drink?"

"That's for me to know, and maybe for you to find out," I say, taking a step back. I'm painfully aware of how fast my heart is pounding in my chest, but I like knowing he pays attention to me to know I add limes to all my drinks. I turn to find Ellie, but Jack's fingers brush against mine, stopping me.

He rubs the wrapping on his hands. "Wait," he says, watching me with an intensity that threatens to burn me from the inside out. Jack chuckles, looking me up and down before taking my hand to pull me up the stairs.

"Where are we going?" I ask, laughing under my breath as I try not to trip on people sitting on the stairs to make out while I follow him. I should be looking at the stairs to know where to step, but I can't decide between looking at Jack's back or his firm ass.

"Somewhere I know you can hear me," Jack answers over his shoulder, stopping in the hall at the top of the stairs, and I try not to let the questions rise in my head asking why he thinks love doesn't exist. I know I'm not an expert by any means, but Jack is very clearly capable of loving other people, yet for some reason, he doesn't believe in it.

"Why?"

"He isn't going to show up here tonight, and if he is that stupid, I'm here," Jack says, lowering his voice at the same time he reminds me I can't just be a normal girl at a party on Halloween with a hot guy she's *physically* attracted to. "You don't have to worry about it, so if you want to drink tonight, then you should."

Shit, I really don't want to talk about Bradley tonight. "I'm not worried about him tonight," I say, because I'm not. I know Jack will keep me safe, and if anything, the level of trust I have in him is what worries me.

"Then why aren't you drinking? You don't have to, I just don't want you to worry abou—"

I reach up and cover his mouth with my hand, forcing Jack to stop talking. "Can I talk?" I ask, and Jack licks my hand, causing me to jerk my hand back. "Ew, gross."

"Gross? You're the one who cut me off," he says, and I try not to stare at his necklace. I want to ask if it's from an old girlfriend, but things ended poorly, and that's why he doesn't believe in love. Wait—that doesn't work because he's never been in a relationship before, but what if it was a relationship, and he had no idea? I wouldn't be surprised because men can be very stupid at times.

"Because you haven't let me say anything about why I'm not drinking!"

His face pales immediately, and Jack looks like a deer

caught in the headlights when he glances down at my stomach. "Are you pregnant?"

My jaw drops because, seriously? Did Jack really just ask me that?

"No, I'm not, but never mind. It was a stupid idea." I roll my eyes and push him back a bit so I can escape downstairs, because now I might actually need a drink.

"Alondra," Jack says my name, his hand covering mine on his chest to hold it in place against his warm skin.

"What?" I snap, feeling my cheeks flood with embarrassment. This might be more mortifying than Jack turning me down in his truck.

"I'm sorry, I'll shut up," he says, giving me the best damn puppy dog eyes I might've ever seen. "Why aren't you drinking tonight?"

"Because I want you to kiss me, and I don't want you to think I'm asking because I've been drinking. It doesn't mean anything, but I just . . ." I trail off, feeling my entire face flush. I slump against the wall behind me, needing the added support to get through vocalizing my thoughts.

"You just?" Jack prods, his voice lowering, and his piercing eyes never leave mine. I swear I can feel his heart beating out of his chest from where he has my hand trapped against him. Trapped feels like the wrong word because I could definitely pull it away, but I don't want to, which is a whole different problem.

"I want to be ordinary. I don't want you to be you and I don't want me to be me, and I just want to not think so damn hard about all the reasons why I shouldn't kiss you, because it's so complicated," I ramble, and someone tries to pass behind Jack, forcing him closer to me. I haven't had anything since leaving the apartment, but I feel drunk on the closeness of my proximity to him.

He tips my chin up, and my hat is uncomfortable on my head, making it hard for me to have the right angle to look at him. Jack plucks the hat off my head and rests it on his, and despite it being a prop, it looks a million times better on him.

"Can you say something?" I ask, hyperaware of how my breathing has quickened, and Jack looks as torn as I feel internally, but he doesn't pull away.

His knuckles brush along my jawline, the simple touch feeling like so much more than it is. My mouth parts and his touch skims down the gentle curve of my neck. "Do you know there's a rule about these?" Jack asks, and despite being the one with every intent to catch Jack in my web, the cards have been flipped on me, and I'm enraptured, unable to look away.

I shake my head, not trusting my voice right now as he cups the back of my neck, sliding his fingers into my scalp, and the feeling is *delicious*.

"Wear the hat, ride the cowboy," Jack says, smirking, and now I know I'm not imagining how quickly his heart is beating in his chest because it's matching mine.

"You're wearing my hat," I say, trying not to get my hopes up as I hook my other arm around his neck. This is an awful idea, but we've already kissed once, so what's the worst that can happen?

"Am I?" he asks, his dimple winking at me as the corners of his mouth pull upward while his other hand falls to rest on the curve of my waist. "Well, a rule is a rule, and I'd hate to make you break another one."

I laugh because it sounds so ridiculous. Being here with Jack is definitely the rule I'm breaking, but my laughter dies when he leans in.

"Don't run from me, okay?" he whispers, the words a quiet plea as I rise on my tiptoes, my eyes fluttering shut at the feeling of his breath tickling mine.

There's no running, even if I wanted to. "Let's be ordinary, boring people," I say, and Jack's chuckle is a low rumble.

"I'm not sure we could be ordinary if we tried, but okay,"

he agrees, and I feel the gentle brush of Jack's lips against mine.

It's like testing the waters, but I don't want to dip a toe in. I want to dive in headfirst. I want to be messy and free, and I don't want to *think*.

I pull Jack further down to press my mouth more firmly against his, and it's like a switch flips in him. His mouth is hot and demanding, causing my toes to curl in my boots. I scratch my nails gently on his chest, and Jack angles his head, his nose bumping against mine as he presses me against the wall with the length of his body.

Oh my god.

I'm actually kissing Jack.

I match his every move, reading him like a book I've memorized, or maybe it's the other way around. I can feel the wall behind me vibrating from the bass resonating downstairs, but my only focus is being consumed by Jack.

A moan rises from my throat as Jack's thigh nudges between mine, and I hook my leg around it to feel his hardness press against my lower stomach. I nip at his full lower lip, pulling at the short strands of hair on the back of his head, knocking the hat off.

Jack's hand on my waist slides to grab my ass, his fingers teasing over the fraying edge. I'm surprised by how much more of him I want as his tongue slides into my mouth, a needy sound ripping from him.

This is different from last time because I thought I knew what it felt like to be kissed by Jack, but this moment blows our first one out of the fucking water.

My hips move on their own accord, seeking more friction against Jack's muscular thigh as he wraps my curls around his hand, exposing my neck as his mouth moves, latching onto the sensitive skin of my throat. His fingers slip underneath the denim of my shorts, and a soft moan escapes me when his fingertips dig into my skin. Jack helps guide me against him, the seam of my shorts rubbing against my clit with every movement, sending sparks of pleasure through my body.

I like that he's not treating me like I'm made of broken glass.

"I think ordinary suits us," I say, wishing we were wearing less layers.

God, I can't remember the last time I felt this desperate to be touched by someone. "Didn't think I'd like it so much," he says, chuckling softly, palming my ass through my shorts. I want more of Jack than I should. "Fuck, Al, you're . . ." Jack trails off, kissing me again instead.

I really like kissing Jack.

And then he stops, his breathing labored as he looks at me through dark lashes.

"I'm what?" I ask, trying to calm the chaos Jack's created inside my body.

Jack stops, shaking his head as his thumb sweeps back and forth across the back of my neck. "You're beautiful."

"Don't," I say, feeling a blush crawl up my neck, and I move to untangle myself from him.

"I'm not saying anything that isn't true, but I am stopping to check in with you," he says, his hand sliding to rest on the small of my back instead. "Are you okay, or do you want to run?" Jack asks, looking me over.

Somehow, in the six weeks since we met at Twin City, Jack has infected me with his kindness, and I think I'm better for it.

Hell, two weeks ago, I would have never believed I'd be in this position with Jack, but here I am.

"I think I'm okay," I say, exhaling a soft breath. "This doesn't mean anything, right?" I ask, needing to hear him say it, because the longer we stop to talk about this, the more my brain is tempted to overthink everything. I want to be ordinary for a little longer.

Jack nods, leaning down to kiss the corner of my mouth. "It doesn't change anything," he says, and I'm tempted to ask more, but out of fear of running out of time, I wrap my arms around his neck, kissing him again before he can tell me something different.

He's smooth as he reaches behind my thighs, his bare hands making my whole body hum with electricity as he lifts me in the air to wrap my legs around his waist. "Where are we going?" I mumble against Jack's mouth, and he silences me with another kiss as I'm vaguely aware of him moving for the bedroom at the end of the hall, fumbling with the door handle until it's just us in his room alone, surrounded by the echoing noise of the party below.

"Too many people," he says, flipping on a lamp before taking a seat on his bed, keeping me in his lap. "I don't always mind an audience, but I wanted you to take what you need without getting in your head," Jack says, but I can barely think as he pulls aside the collar of my shirt to kiss my collarbone.

Did he just say he likes to be watched? The idea of someone watching me and Jack in the hallway sends a thrill through me as his talented mouth licks and sucks at my skin. "And what do you think I need?" I ask, shifting in his lap to find the same pressure to apply to my clit. My hands drag over the rippling muscles of his shoulders, his skin hot underneath my touch.

Fuck, I like how it feels to have his mouth on me.

Jack lifts his head to look at me, a playful smirk forming. "Do you trust me?" he asks, and as unbelievable as everything else tonight has been, this might take the cake.

"I do," I say, my voice husky, and Jack's hands squeeze my ass one more time before moving to the front of my shorts.

"Stand up, Alondra."

"Why?" I ask, my heart kicking into overdrive when he unfastens the button and pulls down the zipper.

"Because I think you need to come, and you're going to do it riding my thigh just like you tried to do in the hallway," Jack says, and I rock my hips against his bulge, loving how his jaw flexes. "Now are you going to argue, or are you going to let me feel how wet your pussy is?"

My legs are definitely shaking as I untangle myself, but I sure am glad I picked a pair of lace underwear tonight. I kick off the red boots, to let the denim fall as Jack watches me. "Put the boots back on?" Jack asks, and it makes me laugh, giving me something else to focus on besides how exposed I feel right now.

"You got a thing for boots?" I tease, stepping back into them.

Jack smiles, motioning for me to come back to him. "I've got a thing for seeing you in them apparently." The second I'm within reach, his hands fall on my hips, toying with the lace material. "Goddamn," he mutters, pulling me down to sit on his thigh, the fabric of his shorts having ridden up so I'm seated on his bare thigh, and I bite my lip, trying to hold back another moan at the feeling.

I lean forward to cup his face in my hands, kissing him again as he molds my body like putty, encouraging my hips to move the way I need them to. He groans into my mouth, and I drag my thumb over the stubble lining his jaw, grabbing his shoulder with my other for leverage to rock my hips, feeling the wetness soaking my underwear.

The pressure continues building in my body as Jack's sinful mouth devours me, helping to work me toward the edge as I ride his thigh. I gasp, breaking our kiss, digging my fingertips into his shoulder.

"That's it, darlin'. Use me however you need to," Jack coaxes, encouraging me to continue. "Your pretty pussy is dripping, making such a fucking mess on me," he says, and I never thought dirty talk would be something I was into until now.

"Jack," I say his name, but it sounds more like another moan. My breath is coming out in short pants as I work myself closer to the edge, and almost like Jack can read my mind, he moves his hand to press his thumb on my clit through the lace. "Oh my god." I arch as he swirls slow circles, short-circuiting my brain as I tip over the edge, my body shattering into a hundred little pieces.

He combs his fingers through my hair, peppering little kisses along my brow. "You're beautiful, Alondra," Jack repeats as I try to grasp control of my sensibility again. I didn't think it could be like this with someone. It certainly wasn't like this with Bradley, but it's more than a little relieving to know my body is capable of responding to another person. That the pieces of myself are capable of being whole again with the right person.

"So are you," I say, and he laughs, smiling at me with an ease and a familiarity I'm beginning to crave. I hate how used to Jack I'm getting, especially at night knowing he's on the other side of my door, camping out in our living room in case my crazy ex-boyfriend shows up in the middle of the night.

Stop thinking, Al.

I slide my hands from his neck down his chest, but he catches my wrists, stopping me on my path. "What are you doing?" I ask, just as Jack lifts them, pressing a kiss to my pulse in each one, and it'd be easy to get used to being treated with such care after being shown the opposite of what can happen.

"I'm okay. Let's get you cleaned up," he says, and I look down between us, a hoarse laugh escaping me.

"Yeah, I'm pretty sure there's hard evidence proving you're not okay." *Why doesn't he want me to touch him?*

"It'll get the message soon," he says, helping me up. "This wasn't about both of us. It was about you needing to take back control of that part of your life, and I get it. Happy to help, but I'm okay, really," Jack says, giving me a tight smile.

"Did I do something wrong? Were you not into this?" I ask, trying not to spiral, but it's really hard not to.

Jack brushes a stray curl back behind my ear, his touch gentle and sure. "Al, you were perfect. I'm into this, but I don't want you to feel like you owe me anything. I want to say yes, but I'm really okay."

I let his words digest in my head, and as much as I'm confused, I also understand where Jack's coming from. "And this doesn't change anything?" I ask, needing to hear him say it again.

"Not a single thing," Jack says, and I step away, moving toward the bathroom attached to his room. "We're still best friends."

I raise an eyebrow, wondering when the hell that became our label. "Since when are we besties?"

"You can deny it all you want, Al, but we're totally besties. You should hurry before our friends start to wonder where we've disappeared to," he says, chuckling softly to himself.

I roll my eyes, but he has a point. If we're gone for too long, it will raise all sorts of questions I'm not sure I want to have the answers to.

CHAPTER 19

Alondra

IT'S BEEN a few days since Halloween, and Jack has been true to his word. Things haven't changed between us or become weird, and I'm grateful for it. At the same time, I also haven't been able to stop replaying it in my mind. I thought it was hard to ignore what one kiss with Jack felt like, but now that I know what hooking up with him is like, I'm tempted to know what *everything* feels like.

No one questioned our disappearance at the party, but I guess I was a little too enthusiastic when kissing Jack's neck, and I left a hickey behind. Jack left his mark on me too, but at least my hair was able to hide it for the rest of the night.

I've gotten the hang of how to blend the concealer into my skin to hide it the last few days, and it's fading, just not as fast as I wish it would.

Now I'm just trying to figure out if I can be true to my word because every time I look at Jack, I think about kissing Jack, and then I spiral down a rabbit hole I have no business going down.

I twist my hips, turning my skates to stop quickly on the ice before taking off again, darting around Jack as I pick up speed. "Catch me if you can," I call out over my shoulder, and I catch a glimpse of his smirk before I turn around.

"Al, you could at least make it challenging for me," he says, and the sound of his skates scraping as they push off the ice makes it easy for me to hear how close he's getting. I cut a sharp turn after hearing Jack behind me, and a laugh rumbles from his chest.

I slow down, glancing back at him. "That defeats the purpose of skating together this morning. You're supposed to be taking it easy before your game tonight, and while I can't skate faster than you, I am the better skater because I'm more efficient and controlled than you are."

"Al, I might not be able to do any of the fancy jumps and shit you can, but it doesn't mean you're the better skater."

"Prove it then, pretty boy," I say, scoffing. Whatever. If I were in my prime before I quit skating, I could beat Jack with my eyes closed.

I push off again, but this time, he catches up to me faster than before, and I anticipate him catching me moments before Jack's arms wrap around my waist.

A yelp slips from me, and I grab onto his arms as he laughs, his chest shaking against my back through the thin sweatshirt I'm wearing. "Jack!" I exclaim, spinning in his arms to hit his chest.

"Al!" he mimics, feigning a falsetto voice, and I push out of his grip, laughing.

"That isn't what I sound like."

"That isn't what I sound like."

I roll my eyes and skate backward. "You suck." I wish I could come up with something better on the spot, but my brain feels scrambled from Jack's arms around my waist.

Oh my god, I need to get it together. I do not want to be the clingy girl who can't let a hookup simply be just that.

"You're getting stronger and faster," he compliments, and I feel a spark of happiness rise in me because the grueling hours I'm putting in at the gym are paying off. My jumps are cleaner and my spins smooth with more rotations. Slowly but surely, I'm getting back to what—*and who*—I used to be.

"Just not as fast as you," I retort, shaking my head at Jack.

"You took some time off, but if it makes you feel better, I'm me. No one's faster than me."

If anyone else said it, I'd say they're a cocky son of a bitch, but after watching his last few games, Jack's saying it as a fact. "Can I ask you something?"

Jack chuckles, dragging a hand through his hair. "Sure," he says, flipping around to skate backward next to me.

"Why haven't you signed a contract to go into the league?"

"Honestly, I wanted to sign right after the draft, but my momma begged me to come here first to get my degree. She never went to college, and always said she regretted it, so it's her dream for me. Hockey is mine, but I knew if I went right away, I'd miss out on time on the ice where I could get more experience. Coming here to play for Coach B seemed like the best choice for everyone."

"Why didn't she go?" I ask, letting curiosity get the better of me.

"She fell in love with the wrong guy, and they got pregnant with me the summer before her freshman year," he says, his hands reaching to find his necklace hiding beneath his shirt. The necklace I've been too chicken to ask about because I feel like if Jack wanted to talk about it, then he would. It would make sense, though, if it belonged to his mom. "The only thing she's ever wanted for me was an education. It's the least I can do after everything she has done to make my dream of playing hockey possible."

For a moment, I'm envious of the relationship he has with his mother. I mean, the way Jack talks about her and the person she raised him to be goes to show what kind of person and mother she is.

"I bet she's really proud of you, Jack," I say, trying to let myself feel two things at once because it's possible to be happy for someone for having an incredible parent, and be jealous of the relationship at the same time.

The cool air kisses my cheeks, and I veer away from Jack, swinging into a spin on one foot after shifting to the front of my blade. As I rotate, I tuck my arms in as I pull my free leg across my body, and the world around me becomes a blur.

I feel like myself.

"You're in a good mood today," Jack comments, smiling at me when I slow and tilt my head.

"What's not to be happy about? We're alive and we're free. Am I not allowed to be in a good mood?"

He pushes his hands into the pockets of his sweats. "It's just a good look on you."

I'm not sure what to say to that, so I push off again, skating around the edges of the rink, immensely grateful that I've gotten to a place where I can be on the ice again. Jack is leaning against the boards, watching when I come back around.

"What time does your mom's flight get in today?"

"I'm heading to the airport after Comp II so I can spend some time with her before I have to come back here to warm up," he says, smiling as he moves to step off the ice. "Are you coming to the game tonight?"

I actually had a lot of fun at the game last Friday, sitting with Ellie and Sara, but it was stressful waiting to see if my dad was going to see me.

"Do you want me to go?" I ask, following after him, grabbing my skate guards off the boards to walk toward the bench he's taking a seat on.

Jack chuckles, giving me an odd look. "I do, but I've been trying not to make you feel like you have to go. I know it's complicated for you."

"I mean, it is, but . . ." I trail off, sitting next to him. I'm worried if I go two weekends in a row, I'll be pushing my luck when it comes to my dad seeing me in the stands.

He nudges my arm with his elbow, smiling at me with those damn dimples that make my brain turn into a pile of mush. "Would it help if I told you Momma wants to sit with you during the game? She keeps asking me during our calls if you're going, but once she's here, I'm not going to be able to avoid answering."

"Really?" I ask, reaching down to undo the laces of my skates as Jack does the same.

"Yeah, why wouldn't she want to meet you? You're one of my best friends," he says, his blue eyes sparkling. "Please, Al? Will you come and wear my jersey?" Jack asks, jutting out his bottom lip in a pout, drawing my attention to his very kiss-able lips. *Nope.* I'm not thinking about kissing him, because if I do, then I'll start thinking about other things with him, and that's not fair.

I laugh, shaking my head at him as I pull off my skates. "Jack, you're a grown ass adult. Why are you pouting?"

"Because this pout works on everyone, and I want you to say yes."

"You're ridiculous." I snort, because maybe it worked when he was five years old instead of twenty-one. "I'll go, but I'm not wearing your jersey."

Jack bats his lashes at me. "Please?"

"No, it'll send the wrong message," I retort, taking off the skate guards to dry them with a towel before covering the blades with soakers.

"You're worried wearing my jersey to my game will send the wrong message?" Jack asks, and the amusement in his tone makes me want to stick my tongue out at him.

I'm pretty sure wearing Jack's jersey will be the least of my worries when it comes to sending the wrong message, but it'll make it a little easier for me to pretend I'm fine after hooking up with him if I'm not wearing a jersey drenched in the intoxicating smell of cinnamon for an entire night.

"You really want to argue with me, pretty boy?" I ask, raising an eyebrow at Jack.

"If I didn't know better, I'd say I think you're the one who likes to argue with me. Wearing my jersey doesn't have to mean anything," he says, and I know I'm not imagining his eyes dropping to the lingering mark he left on my neck. We haven't spoken about it once since leaving his room that night, but now I'm wondering if he thinks about it as much as I have.

My god, it'd be so easy to lean over and kiss him.

Jack's gaze is slow to rise again to meet mine, and his full lips part, causing shivers down my spine as I picture how it felt to have them on me.

"I'll think about it," I say, hating the way my voice sounds breathy. I clear my throat, turning away from him to stand up, creating space between us to put my skates in my bag.

"Cool, um, great. I'll bring one to class in case I don't see you this afternoon," Jack says, fumbling over his words for a moment, and it's nice to know I'm not the only one affected by this. "Now as much as I enjoy spending time with you, if you don't want to get caught by your dad, you might wanna get going," he says, and I grab my phone, realizing the time. Shit, it's later than I thought.

I feign a dramatic gasp, trying to make myself act normal, but maybe I'm not even sure what my normal is anymore. "You like spending time with me?"

Jack laughs, wiping his blades with the same towel I used. "Of course I do. You and your sparkling personality. Seriously, though, you should go."

"Are you good with holding on to these still?"

Jack looks at his phone for a moment before setting it down again. "Of course. Is it okay if I ask our equipment manager to sharpen them when he sharpens the teams' this morning?"

"He's not going to tell my dad you threw in some figure skater's skates in with a bunch of hockey skates?" I ask, doubtful, but my skates do need sharpening, and it'd save me the time from taking them to a shop.

"Frank's easily bought with sweets," Jack says.

"If he's okay with it, then that'd be awesome. I appreciate you." I smile at him as I slip into my slides.

"Damn right you do." He winks at me with a goofy smile on his face, and I make my escape before I'm caught red handed by my father.

CHAPTER 20

Jack

THERE'S a knock on my door as I fold my spare away jersey for Alondra, setting it next to my backpack. "Yeah?" I call out, and the hinges creak, swinging open.

"You stayed at the girls' apartment again last night?" Dylan asks, leaning against the frame.

"Yep," I answer, but my lower back pinches when I turn to look at him. After a week of sleeping on their couch, I'm paying for it.

"So what was the point of all of us volunteering to take turns if you were just planning on using it as an excuse to sleep there every night?" he asks, crossing his arms over his chest. I'm not sure what it is that Dylan thinks he knows, but there's nothing to tell.

I mean, fuck, I guess we hooked up on Halloween, but Al was adamant it didn't mean anything, and I promised it wouldn't change anything.

Hasn't stopped me from replaying it in my mind when I fuck my hand, but I'm doing the best I can to keep things as normal as possible.

"Dude, I'm sleeping on their couch, not in Al's bed," I correct, giving my best friend a look.

"Who really gave you that hickey on Halloween?" Dylan asks, and I smirk, giving a half shrug.

"Like I told you, it was some girl who got a little carried away trying to get over her ex," I say, but it feels like my mouth is coated in acid describing what happened with Alondra like that.

She took my fucking breath away when I saw her standing there in her cowgirl costume, and I would've done anything she asked of me. I'm not an idiot, though. After everything that happened with Bradley the weekend before, Al wanted to feel in control, and I was happy to be a willing participant.

"That's funny because I didn't see you with anyone other than Alondra after the girls got there, and you didn't have it before they arrived. The only time you disappeared was at the same time Al did, and you reappeared at the same time."

I didn't plan on anything happening when I took Al upstairs, but I didn't want anyone overhearing us talk about Bradley. I certainly wasn't going to tell her no when Alondra said she wasn't drinking because she knew I wouldn't kiss her if she was. I probably shouldn't have kissed her regardless, because now all I can think about is kissing her, and the way her sweet body felt grinding on me as she chased her orgasm. *Fuck, and the sounds Al made?* I hear them on repeat in my head.

But I can't say any of that, because I promised nothing would change.

"Just drop it, okay?" I snap, losing some of my patience.

"No, I'm not going to drop it because Al's perfect for you, but you're too busy fucking around to see it," Dylan adds, and I want to argue that I'm not fucking around, but it would completely invalidate my bullshit story that it was some random girl. He already doesn't believe it, but until I admit it, Dylan doesn't actually know anything.

"She's my *friend*."

"So you both keep insisting, but nobody is buying it."

"Dylan, I don't know what you want me to say. You don't need to buy that Al and I are friends, but that's all we are," I say, laughing in disbelief. I don't know what's so hard for him to understand about this.

"Are you forgetting how you walked into the class I was in last week out of breath, and pulled me out without saying anything to run the whole way to their apartment? I saw how fucking afraid you were, and I've never seen anything shake you," Dylan says, and I haven't forgotten. It's the reason I've been on their couch every night. The thought of Bradley showing up when I'm not there haunts me. I know Coop, Nate, and Dylan wouldn't let anything happen to them, but until you've lived through it, you don't understand how quickly things can turn bad. "All I'm trying to say is you're not acting like you're just friends."

"If you're implying I'm acting like she's my girlfriend, Alondra's not because I don't do girlfriends." I hold back my comment about how he has feelings for Ellie, and he doesn't look at her like she's just a friend, but it's a low blow I'm not willing to stoop to.

"Are you really telling me you're not attracted to her?"

I shove the jersey into my backpack, tired of this conversation. "Of course I'm attracted to her. She's fucking beautiful, and not just on the outside, but as a person. Al's a beautiful person, and she deserves better than me." It's because I care about her that I believe Alondra should be with someone who can love her with every fiber of their being, after being made to feel like she has to earn love her whole life.

"I think you're an idiot, but if you're not going to ask her to be your girlfriend, then don't do anything besides be her friend. All of us like Al, and would prefer if she stuck around." Dylan scoffs, rolling his eyes. "Actually, I want to say Al couldn't do better than you, but that's for you to figure out, I guess," he says, walking away, his bluntness catching me off guard from his usual easygoing personality. I have to give him credit for having the balls to say it to my face.

I drag my hands over my face, trying to hear everything he said, but honestly, I haven't even considered the idea of dating Alondra. Maybe it makes me the idiot Dylan accused me of, but being someone's boyfriend? It's not an option, and never has been.

I don't know how to be someone's person.

Maybe it was after seeing my sperm donor throw around my momma like she was nothing more than a rag doll for the hundredth time I decided love didn't exist. If loving someone means letting them hurt you over and over again, then I don't want it. Relationships aren't worth the pain they can wreak on a person.

I don't think I'm wrong for what I believe, and I'm not going to apologize for it.

Dylan's never questioned my decision until now.

But . . . the scary thing is that I think if I ever were to change my mind for someone, I could see it being for Al.

My adrenaline is working overtime tonight.

After taking the fastest shower of my life and changing back into my game day suit, I feel like I'm on cloud nine after playing one of my best games ever.

Every line tonight was solid, and Coop was a beast, blocking every shot the Eagles tried to get past him. We gelled, and if this is how we play the rest of the season, I have no doubt we'll make it to the Frozen Four tournament.

What makes it even sweeter is knowing Momma's waiting for me with Alondra.

I spent all of our class earlier thinking about my conversation with Dylan instead of paying attention, but I told Al I couldn't focus because I was anxious for my momma to get here.

I couldn't find Al before the game in the stands, and everything was too chaotic to look for her afterward, so I'm dying to know what jersey she ended up wearing. I know she's here because she sent me a selfie with Ellie and Momma, but the photo didn't let me see what number was on her shirt.

Fuck, I guess I should just be happy she came.

It was a great game, and there's no way she didn't have fun tonight. The energy in the crowd was electric, and I was on fire. I could feel it roaring in my veins every second I spent on the ice tonight.

When I spot Al, my smile grows at the sight of her in my light purple jersey, my number emblazoned on the front and back of the jersey, and I know it doesn't mean anything, but I like seeing her wear it. She's talking with Ellie and my mom, and I don't know how to describe the way it causes my stomach to jump.

Alondra sees me and her smile is . . . radiant. Absolutely *radiant*.

Then she's darting toward me.

I brace myself for impact as she throws herself into my arms. "Jack, you were fucking incredible out there," she says, and the praise means everything coming from her. I wrap my arms tight around her, taking in a deep breath of her strawberry shampoo.

"Thanks for coming," I say, trying to mask the unexpected emotion bleeding into my voice. I know what it means for Al to come to games, knowing her dad is coaching, but she came anyway.

"Good game, pretty boy," Al teases, unraveling herself from me, so my momma can hug me too.

"You were amazing," she says, and I close my eyes, leaning into her embrace. Momma feels like home.

I'm overwhelmed from feeling so many different emotions

right now, I struggle to speak for a few moments. "I love you," I finally say, and Momma squeezes tighter.

"I'm so proud of you."

"Momma S!" Dylan exclaims behind me, and I'm reluctant to let go, but I do.

"You had a great game," she says, patting him on the cheek before hugging him next.

Ellie gives me a brief hug before disappearing to find her brother, and I drape my arm across Al's shoulders. "So you had fun?" I ask her, whispering as I twist a curl around my finger. I've spent too much time thinking about how I wrapped them around my whole hand to kiss her neck.

"I did," Al admits, sighing dramatically.

"You're wearing my jersey," I point out, trying not to sound too happy about it, especially when I'm probably pushing my luck.

She doesn't get a chance to respond before Shane approaches, clapping a hand on my back, and I try not to feel sad when Alondra twists out from under my arm.

Al glances around, and I realize she's probably trying to see if her dad has spotted her. For a moment, I forgot Coach Brown is her dad. I've been so careful to separate church and state. Hockey is church and Al is my state. It's kind of confusing, but it makes sense to me.

"Are you coming to Twin City?" Shane asks, a grin on his face, distracting me. "Hi, Momma Schultz. You picked a good game to see."

"Good to see you, Shane. It was a great game to be at," Momma agrees, giving him a warm smile.

I can't think of anywhere I'd want to be less tonight than in a crowded bar with hockey players celebrating a big win. Normally, we'd have a Saturday game, but this weekend we only had a Friday night game, so I'm sure they're going to be insane. "Sorry, I'm taking Momma out for dinner."

"What about you, Jones?"

"Are Coop and Nate going?"

Shane laughs, running his fingers through his dark flow of hair still damp from showering. "They're both coming, but Coop only said yes after Ellie did. He figured Jack wouldn't be going out tonight, so someone needs to babysit everyone."

Momma turns toward me, and I know what she's going to say before she says it. "You should go out with your friends. It's getting late anyway, and I could go back to the hotel."

"Hel—heck no, I want to celebrate with you," I say, managing to catch myself just in time, but she still lifts an eyebrow at my close call.

"We see Jack too much, please, go with him. Give us a break," Dylan adds, and I roll my eyes, but at least this is better than our conversation this morning.

"And he tried to tell you I was being mean to him. Momma, do you see what I have to deal with?" I ask, but I can't even fight the smile on my face because I'm just so damn glad she's here.

She's too busy talking to Al to hear me. "—coming too, right?" Momma asks, and Al's cheeks flush as she twists a curl. I wonder if she knows how much it distracts me when she does it.

"I really don't want to impose. Jack's been so excited to see you, and I don't want to take any time away from you," Al says, glancing at me. Does she want to go to the bars with everyone else?

"Don't do anything stupid tonight," I say, and Shane chuckles, pulling Dylan with him.

"No promises, Captain," he says, saluting me before they walk away.

"Jack, will you please tell Alondra she's welcome to come to dinner with us?" Momma asks, and my smile widens. I knew she'd love Al once she met her.

"Please come with us. It's not imposing at all if I want you there." I give Alondra my best smile, hoping she'll say yes. I can't think of a better way to end today than with dinner with both of them.

"Are you sure?" she asks, still seeming doubtful we'd want her there.

"It's decided, you're coming," Mom says, looping her arm with Alondra's, and I flex my hand, fighting the urge to place my arm around her again. *Am I acting like she's my girlfriend if I do that?*

I shove the thought to the back of my mind, trying to focus instead on how everything tonight seems to be going right.

It doesn't take us long to get to the local diner I usually take Momma to when she's here. It reminds me of the diner back home she used to take me to after my games if we had the money to spare. I left my jacket and tie in the truck, but I was worried that if I stopped at my house to change, Al would change her mind about coming with us.

"Three hot chocolates coming right up," the waitress, Cindy, says, skillfully balancing all three mugs to set them carefully on the table. I reach to help her pass them, needing to feel useful. "Are you ready to order some dinner?" she asks, pulling a notepad out of her apron, and I shake my head.

"Can we have a few minutes?" Momma asks, and the older woman nods.

"Of course, sugar. I'll circle back," she says, walking off.

I take a sip of the hot chocolate, immediately burning my tongue, and I wince, swallowing it.

"I'm sorry, did you just drink your hot chocolate without even blowing on it?" Al asks, gaping at me in surprise from her seat next to me, and a quiet laugh rings from Momma across from us.

"He's never waited to drink his hot chocolate. You'd think Jack would learn after all the cups of hot chocolate we would drink after his games, but his skull is a little thick," she teases, giving me a warm smile.

"Okay, wait, let me explain," I say, laughing. "If you burn your tongue to start with, then it's already burnt so you can just keep drinking it."

Alondra's hazel eyes widen and she wraps her hands around her mug. "No. Just . . . no. That doesn't make *any* sense, Jack."

"I've tried to tell him that for years, but maybe he'll listen to you," Momma says, combing her light brown hair back into a bun. It's crazy to think that when she was the same age I am now, she was chasing around a three-year old.

"It works," I argue, trying to defend myself. I set my mug down, pushing up the sleeves of my button-up to try to get more comfortable.

"I don't want a burnt tongue," Alondra says, blowing on her mug to cool hers, but whatever, I think my way works just fine. "So what do you guys have planned to do tomorrow?"

"I promised Jack I'd make some cookies for his roommates this weekend, but I think we're going to go to the aquarium," Momma says, picking up her menu to look through it.

"I've heard a lot about your cookies. They sound legendary," Al says, and my stomach rumbles at the thought of them.

"I'll make sure to set some aside for you. I've heard about the fights that have broken out in their house over them, and there's no reason for you to get caught in the middle of grown men fighting over cookies," she says, shaking her head. "You'll have to send me the recipe for the face masks you guys did, and maybe we'll do that tomorrow night. I bet I could get all four of them to try it," Momma says, and Al giggles, taking a small sip of her hot chocolate.

"If anyone could convince them, I think it'd be you, but you'll probably want to use the cookies as leverage."

"You might be a genius," she says, but my mind is stuck on how she found out about the face masks in the first place because I don't remember telling her. What exactly did they talk about during the game?

"Did you show her the pictures?" I ask, looking at Alondra, and she bites her lower lip, trying to hide her smile as she shakes her head.

"Wasn't me, but now I wish it was," Al says, giving me a smile before turning back to my mom. "Did Jack tell you how he got me to go to his games last weekend?"

Momma shakes her head, looking at me curiously. "No, he didn't say anything other than you went, and he thinks you're his new good luck charm."

"Oh really?" Al asks, and I feel my face flush because I did tell Momma that, but I wasn't planning on letting Al know she's my new superstition, even if the way I played tonight confirmed it.

"Momma," I complain, rubbing the back of my neck.

"Oh hush, you're fine," she says, waving me off. I definitely underestimated the trouble they could get into together. "So how did he get you to go?"

"He cheated at rock paper scissors."

"How do you even cheat at rock paper scissors?" Momma asks, her blue eyes lighting up with amusement.

Al opens her mouth to explain, but I scramble to answer before she can throw me under the bus any further. "I'm friends with Alondra's cousin, Macy, and she might have shared with me that Al's default when there's a disagreement is to play rock paper scissors, but she always picks rock," I explain, and Momma shakes her head.

"Just don't play cards with him. Jack has sticky fingers. He's not as innocent as he pretends to be," she warns Alondra. I hide my smile by taking a sip of my hot chocolate as I drape my arm over the back of the booth. She then tells Alondra about the time I hustled her out of a whole bowl of candy while playing Go Fish because she didn't realize there was a mirror behind her showing me all her cards.

I've told Momma a lot of stories about Alondra, and I didn't have any doubt they'd like each other.

What I didn't expect was how happy I would feel seeing them get along.

I wait for Momma to shut her door before I get back in my truck, but when I glance over at Al in the passenger seat, her eyes are shut as she leans against the headrest. "Hey, darlin'?" I ask, and her lashes flutter as they open for a brief moment to look at me before closing again as she hums an unintelligible response. "Thanks for coming tonight. Momma was excited to meet you."

"Aw, pretty boy. I think it's sweet you talk about me to your mom," she says, yawning while I reverse and pull out of the parking lot.

I clear my throat, trying to sort through the storm swirling in my head. "I'm really glad you came tonight, Al. I hope you had fun," I say, taking another peek at her after stopping at a red light, unable to hide my smile at the sight of Alondra wearing my jersey.

She blinks her eyes, catching me staring at her, but instead of saying something sassy with her smart mouth that haunts my dreams, Al smiles back at me. "Everyone was right, your mom is pretty great."

I tap my fingers against the steering wheel, looking back at the stoplight. This red light is taking forever.

"She is," I agree.

"You look just like her."

Thankfully. "I know. I'd rather look like her, though," I say, feeling restless. I bet everyone's still at Twin City. I could drop Al off at her place, and lock everything up myself before going to meet everyone and then backtrack to crash on the couch again. "Back to your place?" I ask, and this time her eyes are shut again when I look.

"Can we go back to yours?" she mumbles, and I'm surprised.

"You sure?"

She nods, shivering a little, and I turn up the heat, directing the vent toward Alondra. It doesn't work as well as it used to, and it's colder than it should be for this time of year.

Al's asleep by the time I'm parking in the driveway, and I feel bad waking her up. "Sleep," she moans, and I huff a quiet laugh.

"You can sleep, but you have to get inside first."

She sighs, reaching to undo her seatbelt as I get out. I help Al open her door, and she looks so tired. "Ellie said she was staying at Sara's tonight, but I don't have to crash here tonight if you don't want me to," Alondra says, blinking slowly at me.

"It's okay. I don't mind," I reassure her, offering a hand to help her out of the truck.

"I'm sorry, I don't know how I got so tired," she says, accepting the help.

"Why are you apologizing for being tired?"

Alondra shrugs, rubbing her eyes. "Because you played a whole ass game, and I only watched, but you seem perfectly fine."

I unlock the front door, opening it so she can step through in front of me. "I am tired, but I don't know. I usually go out after games to work off the rest of my adrenaline. I wouldn't trade having my momma here for that, though." *Or being here with you, but I can't say that.*

Al stumbles while walking into the house, and I'm afraid she's going to hurt herself if I let her try to walk all the way to the stairs. After locking the door, Alondra turns to face me after kicking off her shoes, and I take the opportunity to bend down and lift her over my shoulder. She squeaks, and I hold her legs as she kicks them, trying not to laugh. "I thought I told you to not throw me over your shoulder like a caveman."

"You're a walking disaster waiting to happen right now because you can't keep your eyes open long enough to get to the bed," I say, causing her to snort as I slip out of my shoes, making my way toward my room upstairs.

"I am *not* a walking disaster, and you barely even gave me a chance to walk. How would you like it if I slung you over my shoulder out of nowhere!"

"All I hear is complaining when you should be thanking me for carrying your ass up the stairs," I reply sarcastically.

Alondra smacks my ass in response, and a sharp laugh bursts from my throat. Maybe I should have let her struggle instead of carrying her.

I lightly spank her in return, causing her to yelp.

"Hey!"

"Hey!" I mock, opening my bedroom door to drop Al on my bed, and she crosses her arms staring at me.

"You're the one who threw me over your shoulder. I get to spank you, not the other way around," she says, glaring at me, but she's having the opposite effect on me instead. Arguing with Alondra might be my new favorite form of foreplay.

"I could be into spanking if it's something you're interested in," I say, and her sharp intake of breath echoes in the room.

"What about a little ass play? I've heard the prostate is a man's G-spot," Al says, and my dick stiffens in response.

I shake my head, moving to unfasten the buttons at my collar. "What the hell am I supposed to do with you?" I ask, chuckling under my breath. I need to play it safe instead of pushing to see how far I can take this before one of us caves.

"For starters, you can get me a shirt to sleep in, then I'm

going to bed," she says, pulling off my jersey, and I turn away, knowing we're wading into dangerous territory. I grab an old Wolves shirt, tossing it in her direction as my heart squeezes in my chest.

"Pretty sure that's my bed," I say, taking off my belt and pants to put on a pair of shorts to sleep in.

"Nope, not anymore," she says, and when I turn around, she's further up on the bed, hugging one of my pillows.

I look away, heading into the bathroom to finish getting ready for bed, fully intending to sleep on the couch downstairs.

Alondra's quiet when I step out, and I'm really not sure what I'm going to do with her. Does Al know she has me wrapped around her finger like one of her curls?

She could ask me to crawl to her from across the room, and I'd do it in a heartbeat.

Hell, I'm letting her sleep in my bed, and I've never let anyone stay the night with me before. As much as I don't want to admit it, Alondra's different for me, but I don't know how to be different for her.

I flip the light off, but when I open the door, the sheets rustle behind me. "Where are you going?" Al asks, her voice laced with sleep.

"Downstairs. Go back to sleep."

"Jack, just get in the bed. It's not like we haven't already slept together before," she says, and I try not to laugh, because it doesn't sound innocent when she puts it that way. It also ended up with both of us rocking bruises on our faces, so not exactly a shining example to use. "Okay, you know what I meant, but it's not like I'm going to jump you in your sleep, and I thought you'd be sick of sleeping on a couch after the last week and a half."

"It's okay if you jump me, I wouldn't mind," I tease, but honestly, I would love to sleep in a bed tonight. If she says it's fine, then I'm not going to argue with her.

"Be careful what you wish for," Al warns, and I smile, shutting the door. I plug in my phone and climb into the other side of the bed.

"I did tell Momma you were my good luck charm," I whisper after a few minutes, and she rolls toward me. "No pressure, but it'd be pretty awesome if you came to the rest of my games, so I could keep playing the way I did last weekend and tonight."

"Hockey players and their superstitions," Alondra says, and I know I shouldn't because this isn't what we are, but I don't fight the urge to reach and pull her against my chest. I've never craved physical touch from another person as much as I do with Al.

She relaxes against me, resting her head on my bicep, and I press a chaste kiss to the side of her head, holding my breath to see if Al protests. She doesn't say anything, but she does rest her arm on top of the one I have wrapped around her stomach.

If I really wanted to be an ass, I could ask her what she'd rate it, but now that I'm lying down, I can already feel my eyes falling shut.

All I can hear in my head is Dylan warning me to be careful.

I'm in so much fucking trouble.

CHAPTER 21

Alondra

I CAN'T BELIEVE how fast the semester is going by. We only have a couple of weeks before Thanksgiving, and then it's a race to finals week.

I take a moment to watch him from the side, practically seeing the gears turning in his brain as Jack focuses on a practice test I printed out for one of his other classes. I'm reading through the rough draft of his persuasive essay, but somewhere along the line, I started helping him with his other classes if he needed it. The least I can do is make it easier for Jack to succeed, especially after meeting his mother.

She cut his hair last weekend, and it looks good. It's shorter on the sides, and she left it a little longer on top. My fingers are itching to run through the soft locks, but I'm doing my best to keep my hands to myself.

Then my attention goes to his very kissable lips. I think about kissing him a little too much for being just friends, but it's not like he needs to know. His bottom lip is slightly more full than the top one, but they're proportional to his face. His cheekbones are high, his jaw sharp with a dusting of stubble across it.

Shit. I need to stop checking him out. All I can hear in my head right now is Ellie encouraging me to go for it with Jack because *You're hot. He's hot. You'd make hot babies.*

I appreciate her support, but aside from Jack kissing the side of my head when I stayed the night last weekend, nothing has changed between us. Actually, one thing has changed. Jack has finally let the other guys take their turns sleeping on our couch, and I try not to think about it because I don't know what it means.

"Done," Jack says, stretching, and I force myself to look anywhere other than where his shirt has ridden up, but I hate the uncertainty I find in his expression.

Jack's so confident and carefree in every other aspect of his life but classwork, especially when he tries so hard to be good at it.

It's not his fault. Dyslexia isn't something he asked for, and I want to scream at everyone who has made him feel like he should be embarrassed for having a brain that works differently than what people have decided is normal.

"How do you feel about it?" I ask, trying to focus on more than the score because it's just a practice exam. There's still time, and this will give Jack an idea of what to study moving forward.

"I don't know. I think I passed?"

He passes it to me and starts telling me about the freshman who showed up late to practice this morning while I compare the answers to the rubric I made. I'm not surprised when Jack says it's not the first time it's happened.

Jack was right about passing the test, but his score was in the seventies. Thankfully, he didn't seem too upset by it since it was what he was expecting, but he couldn't completely hide his disappointment.

"Do you want to keep studying, or should we call it a night?" I ask, and Jack groans.

"Do we have to?" he asks, but he's saved by a knock on Jack's door. "It's open!"

Nate pokes his head in. "Hey, Coach sent a message he's giving us tomorrow off, so we're inviting some people over. You guys done studying?"

"Please say you're done studying," Ellie says, popping up behind him, and I blink, trying to figure out when she got here.

Jack looks at me with a cheeky smile. "I think my brain has absorbed as much as it's going to tonight."

It *does* sound like fun. "Okay, we can be done," I agree, but I won't be having anything other than water the rest of the night. Jack and I are supposed to skate in the morning, and there's nothing worse than waking up hungover.

"Thank god."

Ellie bounces, making me wonder how much sugar she's had tonight. "It's gonna be really fun. Sara's already out at the bars, but I'm gonna text her to see if she'll come over."

Jack pauses, crossing his arms over his chest. "Wait, have you told Coop yet? He almost killed you and Dylan for how crazy Halloween was."

Nate laughs, shaking his head. "See, I was kind of hoping you would tell him?"

"Nope, this was your idea. You get to tell him," Jack says, and I can't help but laugh.

"You guys are afraid of Coop?" I ask, and Nate's face pales.

"You don't understand. He has this stare that just cuts right through you, and it's even worse when he's disappointed instead of mad," Nate says, and Jack nods.

"Can't say it's my favorite look to be on the receiving end of, so yeah, I don't want to be the one to tell him we're having another party a little over a week after the last one," Jack says, and Ellie rolls her eyes, giving me a look that resembles something along the lines of, *Can you believe this?*

"Oh my god, you guys are wusses. I'll tell him," she says, disappearing down the hall as fast as she appeared.

I agree with her—this is hilarious. Coop has been nothing but nice since I met him a couple of months ago, and sure, his height and size are a little intimidating at first, but he's a good guy.

"For the record, I'm not afraid of Coop," Jack says, and Nate scoffs.

"Okay, then why didn't you want to tell Coop we're having people over?" he asks, acting more smug than he should be considering he didn't want to tell him either.

"Not we, you and Dylan are having people over," Jack corrects, and Nate mumbles something under his breath as he walks out of the room.

"Coop isn't scary," I tease him, but he gives himself away when his ears turn bright red.

"Come on, let's go downstairs," Jack says, getting up from his chair, but instead of hopping off the bed, I stand up on the mattress. He gives me a weird look, tilting his head. "What are you doing?"

I motion for him to come closer, and Jack listens, moving toward me. Once he's within reach, I rest my hands on his shoulders, turning him around.

"You're being weird," he says, and I climb onto his back. Jack being Jack, he immediately hooks his arms underneath my thighs to support me, and I smile widely.

"Carry me."

"Really? Not even a please?"

If Jack can kiss me on the head right before I fall asleep after initiating cuddling with me, then maybe I'm allowed to bend the rules too. I drop my mouth until it's right next to his ear. "Do I need to ask, pretty boy?" I whisper, knowing exactly what I'm doing.

His grip on me tightens, and I take it a step further by

planting my own kiss on his cheek. Jack grumbles but wordlessly carries me down the stairs.

Dylan cracks a smile when he sees me. "What's up, Al?"

"Nothing much. Just wondering if you're as afraid of telling Coop you're inviting people over as Nate and Jack are?" I say, and Jack sighs.

"I told you I'm not afraid of him."

Coop walks down the stairs a few moments later, with a beaming Ellie behind him. "I'm not on babysitter duty tonight," he says, scowling. "Who'd you invite?"

"I sent word out to a few guys on the team. Guess we'll find out when they get here, but it's BYOB," Dylan answers.

"Al, you sure you want to stay? I can take you home if you don't want to," Jack offers, and I rest my chin on Jack's shoulder, content right where I am.

"Staying. Giddy up, cowboy."

His chuckle causes my smile to grow.

The guys from the team start showing up a few minutes later, but then a second group I don't recognize follows them in. Jack's grip tightens as we walk towards the tallest in the bunch.

"Schultz!"

"Seth, been a while," Jack greets, his tone warm.

His friend peers at me curiously before focusing on Jack again. "You know how it gets during season," he says, and I think I recognize him, but from where?

"I do. Surprised you're out. I thought your coach put you guys on a party ban this season?"

Jack's friend shrugs, cracking a smile. "What he doesn't know won't kill him. Besides, it's our bye week, and this isn't a party. Just a lil get together. Coach isn't an idiot, but as long as none of us get in deep shit then he'll let it slide this week."

"Whatever, man, it's your funeral."

I tap Jack's shoulder just as he laughs again. "I'm gonna grab a beer from the fridge. You can let me down."

Jack hesitates, before letting me slide down his back. "I'll come with you," he says, and I cross my arms over my chest, swimming in his sweatshirt.

"The kitchen is like ten feet away? You can watch from here."

"I know you," he says, and I raise my eyebrows, giving him a once-over.

"From where?" I ask, doubt creeping in.

He smiles, and even though he's not my type, he's cute. "You're the cowgirl from Halloween."

"Al," I say, offering my hand to him.

"Nice to meet you *officially*, Al. I'm Seth Kane," he says, winking at me, and it shouldn't surprise me that Jack's friends with the quarterback of Wilder's football team. "Are you Schultz's girl?" Seth asks, and Jack chuckles.

"No, but she's off-limits," Jack continues, a firmness to his voice I haven't heard before. "I'm going with you, Al."

"I can get it myself. I don't need an escort. I think Coop's in the kitchen anyway. I'll be fine," I say, causing Seth's smile to grow.

"You've got some sass, I see why he likes you."

"Just friends," I correct, and Jack nods after a moment in agreement.

"Friends, but she's too good for you, Kane."

"Ignore him, Jack's a bit overprotective," I joke, shooting Jack a questioning look before leaving them behind to go to the fridge I'd raided earlier. Now there are coolers that have appeared out of nowhere on the floors in front of the cabinets, but I don't know who they belong to, so I stick to the pack in the fridge.

Jeez, I guess if the hockey team says there's going to be a get-together, people come running.

I'm on my way back to Jack when Ellie pulls me aside to introduce me to some of her and Sara's friends.

I'm glad I stayed. I try to scan for Jack every few minutes, but now there are too many people I can only hope to see his tall head at some point over everyone else's. No wonder Nate and Dylan didn't want to tell Coop.

The only problem is all of these hockey players and whoever else is here are so freaking tall.

My anxiety is starting to creep into the back of my mind that maybe I should've stayed with Jack because how do I know Bradley hasn't just walked in and made himself feel right at home? *No, that'd be ridiculous.* Bradley's a lot of things, but he isn't stupid enough to show up here.

An arm slides around my waist and I smile, knowing it's Jack's way of getting me back for earlier. I know we're just friends, but maybe it's okay we're blurring the line a little. It doesn't mean anything.

Ellie swivels toward me, but her eyebrows knit as she looks above me, and her smile dims.

"How do you know Al?" she asks, and I turn my head to look up at Jack.

"We're old friends," Bradley says, giving her his most charming smile, and the beer I'm holding slips from my hand, crashing to hit the floor. The girl next to me shrieks as the beer splashes her, but I'm paralyzed.

Bradley.

Bradley.

Bradley.

Bradley's arm around me.

Not Jack.

Move, Al. Don't just fucking stand here.

Before I can even try to move, his hand on my waist tightens, holding me in place.

Alarms are going off in my head, but it's too little, too late.

"Let me go," I say, wishing I could shout the words, but it doesn't come out louder than a whisper. Oh my god, I should have told Ellie everything. Jack was right.

His grip becomes painfully tight, and the warning in his

eyes could not be more clear. "Angel, I can't believe you didn't tell your friends about me." He turns to Ellie who is putting her phone back in her pocket, and I'm horrified I let my guard down. "She's probably had too much to drink. Maybe I should just get her home," Bradley says, but if he drags me out of here, I don't know what's going to happen. I don't know how to put it into words how fucking terrified I am right now.

Bradley's fingers have slipped underneath my sweatshirt, digging into my skin. I feel like I've gone back a year in time. I bite my lip hard, trying to keep this from escalating from bad to worse. Ellie's smile is tense because we both know I'm not drunk.

"Actually, I'll catch up with you guys later if that's okay. I wanna hear more about Al's guy," Ellie says, without taking her eyes off him, but her friends who don't understand are quick to make their getaway, one of them grumbling about the beer I spilled on her shoe.

"Oh, why don't you tell the story?" he says, and I wince when his grip somehow tightens in warning. I'm not doing this. I got out before. I'm not trapped anymore.

"Freshman year," I mumble, clearing my throat. I can do this. "We met freshman year, but we've been broken up for eleven months," I say, finding my voice, and if we weren't in a crowd of potential witnesses, I'm positive Bradley would've already knocked the air from my lungs.

Why is he here?

His eyes are murderous, but to my relief, I hear Dylan. "What's going on here?" Ellie must have texted him.

"Al asked her ex to let her go, and he hasn't," Ellie explains, and Bradley's quick to pull me against his front.

Dylan's calm smile is misleading as he sizes up Bradley. "Dude, there's no reason to make a scene. Just let her go, okay?"

"No," Bradley says, his low laugh vibrating through my

whole body. "Why don't you go find your buddy and tell him I want to talk? Seems like Jack didn't understand the first time I told him to stay away from my girl."

"I'm not your girl," I say, trying to push his hands off me, and Dylan steps forward, causing Bradley's grip to waver enough for me to throw my head back, connecting with his chin. It's enough of a surprise I'm able to slip away as a few people turn toward us, and Dylan automatically steps in front of me.

"Leave now," Dylan says, and there's no room for argument in his tone. The music is still playing around us as the party continues, and I hear Ellie ask if I'm okay.

Bradley grimaces, rubbing the red mark forming on his jaw. "I know you didn't mean that, so let's go."

"No," I say, standing my ground, but it's a lot easier to do with Dylan standing between us.

"How well did that answer work for you last time?"

My stomach plummets, and I feel like I'm gasping for air, stuck at the bottom of his stairs in the negative degree weather again, trying to stay awake long enough to get a call through to Macy.

I don't have a chance to see the way Ellie's looking at me because Jack appears out of nowhere.

"Get the fuck out of my house," Jack says, not bothering with subtleties. Bradley's gaze bounces between Dylan and Jack, probably assessing whether it's worth taking on both of them to get to me. One on one, maybe. Two on one, no fucking way.

"I told you to stay away from her," Bradley says, his mask slipping to show his true, hateful nature for a moment. "*Alondra*," he snaps, and I flinch. I fucking flinch, and I hate giving him the reaction.

"I don't give a flying fuck what you told me. I don't answer to you, and neither does she. Get the hell out of my house before I call the police," Jack threatens, and a few people near us back up at the edge his voice has taken, paying close attention to the scene now that Jack's involved.

Bradley looks past Jack, staring directly at me, and I know I was a fool for thinking he loved me. Maybe at some point he did, but eventually, I became his favorite punching bag. He doesn't miss me—he just misses having someone to push around.

I'm not that person anymore.

He put his hands up in surrender, backing off at the mention of the police, probably realizing if I were to lift my shirt up, there'd be marks from how tightly he grabbed me. He's out of moves right now, and if he keeps pushing, he's risking football. It's the only thing he was ever terrified to lose.

After he walks away, pushing through bystanders toward the front door, I feel like I can breathe again.

Dylan grabs Jack's arm, pulling him toward the back door, and I'm quick to follow, shaking off Ellie's questions of whether I'm okay or not. Oh my god, everyone's staring at us. This is a nightmare.

"—you good?" I catch the last of Dylan's question after slipping through the open door before it shuts, sealing us out in the cold.

"No, I'm not fucking good. Did he touch Al?" Jack asks, not realizing I've followed them out.

Dylan doesn't say anything, and he swears under his breath, bracing his hands behind his head.

"I'm okay," I say, announcing myself as I move closer.

"Did he hurt you?" Jack repeats, and the fear lurking in the shadows of his features surprises me.

"No," I say, because telling Jack he had his hands on me would only pour fuel on the blaze of his fury.

"He *threatened* you. I heard him."

I cross my arms over my chest, pinching my eyes shut for a moment as if I can pretend to turn back time before tonight turned into a disaster. "It doesn't matter," I say, exhaling a long breath.

"What the hell do you mean it doesn't matter?" Jack questions, his tone biting.

I falter, instinctively taking a step back, bumping into Dylan, who helps steady me. I know Jack's anger isn't directed at me, but it's a reflex.

"Schultz, cool it or walk away," Dylan warns, and Jack looks stricken, his hand covering his mouth.

"Al . . ." he trails off, turning away to walk further into the yard.

"It's okay," I say, turning to reassure Dylan I'm fine. "Thank you," I add, catching us both by surprise when I hug him briefly.

"I'm gonna check on Ellie," he says, casting a worried glance in Jack's direction after I step away. "Are you okay? You should probably get an ice pack for your head. You got him good," Dylan continues, looking me over.

"I'm fine," I say, looking at where Jack is pacing. "I've got him."

He nods, heading back inside, and I shake out my hands, trying to stop them from trembling. Tonight could've been so much worse.

I keep my arms wrapped around myself, trying to conserve my body heat as I walk closer to Jack. "Hey," I say softly, unsure of where to start. *Thanks for the assist inside?* "It's okay, he's gone," I decide upon, trying to play it safe.

"How can you say it's okay?" he asks, each word sounding like it takes extreme effort to say.

"Because saying it's not okay doesn't change anything."

"*Alondra.*"

My brain hurts trying to dissect the way Jack says my

name. "What?" I ask, clenching Jack's sweatshirt in my fists to steady myself.

"Did Bradley hurt you tonight?" he asks, repeating the question again.

"What would you do if I said yes? Go after him and get yourself kicked off the team, blowing your future to pieces? Or, better yet, you'd probably find yourself thrown in a cell because he's smart enough to know what to say to get you to hit him first."

Honestly? I'm not okay. I should have been more careful tonight.

"I don't know what I'd do, but I know it's not okay. None of this is okay, and it fucking matters," Jack says, turning around to face me, his chest heaving.

"Except it doesn't! He isn't going to stop, Jack. The best thing we can do is ignore him because I'm done letting him control me, and living in fear of the next time he'll show up is just another form of the fucking mind games he used to play with me." The mental abuse was almost worse than the physical kind, making me doubt everything about myself.

"*You matter.* You matter to me, Alondra," Jack says, dragging his hands through his hair, and I fight the instinct to reach for him. "What did he mean after you said no to him?"

I snap my mouth shut, knowing the truth would be the tipping point for what little restraint Jack is holding onto. I shake my head, glancing away. Why do I matter to him? Why couldn't he have just left me alone after realizing I was his coach's daughter?

"Jack, don't . . . don't ask me about that. Please," I say, somehow managing to keep my voice from breaking. I press my tongue to the roof of my mouth, trying to keep the tears at bay.

"Al, I saw the look on your face."

I don't know how to tell Jack about it without bursting into tears.

"I promise you it can't be any worse than what I'm already thinking," Jack says, stepping closer to me, and I want him to wrap me in his arms because I think it's where I feel safest, but I need to find a way to make myself feel safe. "You went to get a drink and never came back. I shouldn't have let you walk off by yourself after realizing Kane and some of the football players we know showed up."

I scoff, reminding myself I can't always rely on Jack and his friends to be there to step between Bradley and me. I have to learn to stand on my own at some point. "I'm not someone for you to babysit. You should be able to talk to your friends without worrying about me."

"I can't help unless you talk to me."

Does he not realize I've already said more about this to him than I have with anyone besides Macy?

"What do you want to talk about? He was here. It happened. I can't change it, but he left."

"Bradley isn't going to stop," Jack points out as if it's something I don't know already. It's the only reason I've continued letting the guys sleep on our couch longer than a week.

"You think I don't know that?" I ask, a cruel laugh sounding from me.

"What happened the last time you told him no?" Jack insists, and this time, tears well up in my eyes before I can stop them.

"He pushed me down the stairs outside his house in subzero temperatures last January, leaving me to pass out in a pile of snow with broken bones and a nasty concussion. He didn't even bother opening the door when Macy showed up because I told him I was done. That's what happened last time I told him no." I stare at him, hating how his handsome face drains of color, but he wanted to know. After everything else he already knew about my relationship with Bradley, he had to know it wouldn't be pretty. "Are you happy now?" I ask, the crack in my voice echoing the way I've broken myself wide open.

"Darlin' . . ."

The tears are streaming down my face, and I wipe them away, angry they're falling. "Don't, Jack. I'm not your girl-friend, and I'm sure as hell not a problem for you to try and fix. Just leave me alone."

CHAPTER 22

Alondra

DYLAN TOOK Ellie and me home, and I didn't show up the next morning for skating.

I skipped class on Friday.

And avoided all of Jack's calls and texts, asking if we could talk.

I've never been more grateful for it to be a set of away games, and we had our couch back for the first time in two weeks. Ellie and Sara tried to get me to go out with them, but I didn't feel like going anywhere. Instead, they came over Saturday night, and we all stayed in watching some of my favorite movies from the eighties and nineties.

Thankfully, no one pushed me to talk about Jack, but the time away from him has done nothing to help me clear my head.

Coop crashed on the couch last night, and I hid in my room like a coward until he left this morning. I'm embarrassed Bradley made a scene at their house, but I'm more afraid of how they'll look at me once they know the truth.

I debated all morning if I was going to go to class, knowing I'd see Jack there, but I still feel like curling up in a ball after walking into the lecture hall. A quick glance to where he's usually waiting for me with a cup of coffee in hand causes me to deflate a little when I realize Jack's sitting where he spent the first two months of the semester, surrounded by his groupies. It's almost like he never left them in the first place.

We make eye contact, but he looks away first, down at his paper.

What did you think was going to happen after ignoring him all weekend, Al? He'd get down on his knees in front of everyone and beg you to talk to him?

I force myself to head up the stairs toward Keri playing on her phone.

"Hey, girl. Um, is everything okay?" she asks, her eyes wide, and I shrug, glancing down at my outfit.

My sweatpants and sweatshirt under my winter coat aren't as subtle as I thought.

"All good," I answer, swallowing the lump forming in my throat.

"Did something happen between you and Jack? He's sitting over there—"

I plop into the seat next to Keri, cutting her off. "We're fine."

"Okay then," she says, getting the hint, and I try to sink low into my seat.

The lecture feels longer than usual, but it's probably because I'm putting more effort into trying not to look at Jack than I am on the actual class. I'm so mentally drained by the time we're released that I'm ready to crawl under the covers and never come out.

I only feel more defeated watching Jack walk out the doors without any hesitation, and I think I've finally done it. I've finally pushed Jack away, and I only have myself to blame.

I've only replayed Thursday night in my head a hundred times, wondering what would have happened if I hadn't followed Jack and Dylan out back, or if Jack had listened instead of pushing me to give him an answer I knew he didn't want to hear. I never wanted to tell Jack the specifics of how things ended with Bradley, much less ask him afterward if he was happy to know what had happened.

Maybe I shouldn't have kept insisting it didn't matter, but I'm also aware that the more attention Bradley's given, the more he's going to act out. He's never slipped like that in public before. My best guess is he was drinking, and it caused his temper to flare.

The little bruises his fingertips left on my hip are fading proof. Just another picture to add to the collection.

I just want them gone.

I pull my winter coat tighter around myself, shoving my hands in my pockets. It's weird being by myself since I've grown used to Jack's constant presence, but I did tell him to leave me alone. I didn't think he'd really listen because he never had before, yet this time he did.

Maybe it's for the best.

The lines are starting to become blurred with us. I've been acting like I'm his girlfriend, and he's been acting like my boyfriend, but that's not what we are.

I've had a lot of time to think the past couple of days, and a part of me can't help wondering what everything would be like if I'd never gotten to know him.

When I make it back to the apartment, I'm struck with déjà vu by the tall figure pacing in front of the door. My first reaction is to pull the pepper spray from my pocket, until I focus enough on his face to realize it's just Dylan.

His gaze lands on my hand, and I shove it back in my pocket, trading it for my keys. "I think Ellie's still at class if you're looking for her," I say as he steps aside.

"Good to know, but I'm actually here to talk to you if you have a second."

"You could've given me a heads-up text you'd be waiting outside my door," I say, unlocking the door.

"I did, but you didn't respond," he says, and I unzip my coat, setting it on one of the barstools with my backpack as I reach for my phone to see he did send me a message. I just didn't check it before walking back from class.

"Sorry," I mumble, twisting my hair back and securing it into a low, messy bun. "So what's up?" I ask, and Dylan takes a seat on the couch, making himself right at home.

"You okay?" he asks, and I shrug, because what does he want me to say?

"Yeah. Fine."

He barks out a short laugh. "That is the least convincing '*yeah, fine*' I've ever heard after asking someone if they're okay."

"Well, I guess you have your answer then," I say, stepping into the kitchen to make myself a cup of coffee.

Dylan's scrolling on his phone when I walk back into the living room with my steaming cup and sit on the other end of the couch from him.

"Jack doesn't know I'm here. He said you wanted space, and we were supposed to give it to you, but he's not doing so hot. I probably shouldn't tell you this, but he's scared. Whatever your situation with your ex is, it scares the fucking shit out of him, and I've never known Jack to be afraid of anything."

I blink at him, trying to figure out what I'm supposed to say. Jack seemed perfectly fine in class. "What do you mean?" I ask, setting my mug down to grab my purple fuzzy blanket. It still smells like cinnamon and Jack from when he slept with it.

Dylan clears his throat, scratching the back of his neck. "The day you needed help because Bradley showed up here, Jack pulled me out of the middle of my class without saying anything other than you needed us. He ran the whole way here. I could barely keep up with him."

What? My mind spins with the new information as I reach for my coffee again, blowing on the top to help it cool down faster. For a brief moment, I think about how Jack drank his hot chocolate without hesitation, even though it meant burning his tongue.

Well shit. Now I feel kind of bad for not being more open with him about my history with Bradley. "I didn't know he did that. I'm sorry."

Dylan shrugs it off. "Don't worry about it. You're one of us now, and my professor believed me when I lied and told him it was for hockey. He's a huge fan of the team and didn't even question it, but my point is, Jack's different with you. I can't even pretend I understand whatever the hell's going on between you guys, but I know you care about him too. I can't tell you why it scares him, but he's afraid, and I think you should know that."

I groan, staring at my coffee to avoid looking at him. "There's nothing to understand because there's nothing going on."

"Sure," he muses, and if I didn't think I'd spill my coffee, I'd probably try to chuck a throw pillow at him.

"Dude, I don't have enough brainpower to figure out whatever riddle you're trying to give me right now. Can you just use actual words to tell me what you mean?" I ask, hoping he'll throw me a bone, because all he's doing is making my head hurt.

"You should ask Jack about his dad, and maybe more of this will make sense."

"Dylan," I complain, rubbing my temples.

"I'm sorry, it's not my story to tell. Just try to cut him some slack because Jack's blaming himself. He said something this weekend about your ex telling him to stay away from you, but he didn't listen," he says, and now it's making a lot more sense why Jack didn't even acknowledge me in class today.

"It's not his fault," I insist, my head snapping up to look at him. I might've thrown myself a pity party all weekend, but I never considered the possibility Jack would blame himself for what happened.

Bradley would have done something sooner or later whether Jack was in the picture or not.

"I know that, but I'm simply telling you he's blaming himself for what happened at the party. What you decide to do with the information is up to you," Dylan says, giving me a reassuring smile.

"Thank you," I say after a few moments, trying to wrap my mind around everything he said.

He stretches, grabbing the television remote and settles into the cushions. "Don't mention it. Now, what should we watch?" Dylan asks, and a quiet but genuine laugh sputters from me.

Maybe I was wrong all along, holding hockey players accountable for my father's shortcomings.

I sent Jack a voice memo before I left, but I wasn't going to blow off our tutoring session. Doesn't matter how confused I am right now, I need to be a big girl and talk to him instead of continuing to hide. He has that test next week in his business ethics class, and I'm not going to leave him high and dry.

Jack's truck is the only one in the driveway, but when he doesn't answer after I knock, I try the handle and find it unlocked. I walk in like I have a dozen times before, and everything looks normal. You'd never know there was a party here a few days ago.

"Jack?" I call out, slipping off my shoes, suddenly feeling unsure about this. "Are you here?"

I sigh, moving toward the stairs to check his room. He could be gaming with headphones on for all I know. If he's not here, he's not here, but then at least I'm not the one who bailed on tutoring.

I'm a few feet away from his door when I hear a low moan, and my curiosity gets the better of me.

I push his cracked door open, finding him sitting at his desk, but I'm frozen in place when I realize his hand is moving in his lap, stroking his cock. Jack's head tips back, and I'm relieved to see his eyes are shut as he slows his hand down, twisting as he fucks his hand.

Oh my god, I should leave. I should really just go and forget all about this.

Except I can't stop watching.

"*Alondra,*" Jack says, the sound of his moan muffled by the way he bites down on his lower lip. I cover my mouth, trying to keep from making a sound as I watch him drag his thumb over the tip, lost in the fantasy playing inside his head.

Is this really happening, or am I imagining it?

I'm what Jack thinks about when he gets himself off?

Real or not, I can't look away despite the fact that this is a major invasion of Jack's privacy. His hips buck, thrusting against his palm, and I remember what it was like to be touched by him.

Jack is shirtless, his corded muscles fully exposed but his sweatpants look as if the waistband has been pulled down just enough to free his hard length.

Pure want builds in me, and I try to ignore the ache for his hands to be on me as the harsh sound of Jack's ragged breathing increases along with the speed of his hand. "Fuck, darlin'," he mutters, and the use of my nickname snaps me back to reality.

I can't shut the door without risking making a noise, so I take a step back, but the floor creaks under the shift of my weight. *No.* Maybe he didn't hear it?

Jack's head snaps in my direction, his eyes wide as they meet mine, and any hope he didn't hear the sound disappears. I stumble back, turning around to flee down the stairs because I have zero intention of sticking around to explain how I ended up watching him.

Oh my god, please tell me this isn't happening.

I bounce off a firm chest, and large hands land on my shoulders to help steady me. "Al? You okay?" Coop asks, staring down at me, a confused expression forming on his face.

"Where's the fire?" Dylan asks, and I force a nervous laugh as the sound of heavy footsteps sound from above. *Fuck, why didn't I leave the second I realized what Jack was doing?*

"Um, I was just leaving. Bye!" I blurt, shoving my way through them as Jack thunders down the first few steps, trying to catch me.

"Al, wait," Jack calls, and I shake my head, shoving my shoes half on, desperate to make a quick getaway, flying out the front door to get to my car. It's fucking freezing, and this has to be an awful dream I'm going to wake up from any second.

I fumble for my keys in my coat pocket while I trip, cutting through the lawn on my way to my car parked behind Jack's truck when the front door opens again behind me.

"Alondra, just wait a fucking second!"

A quick glance over my shoulder has my jaw on the floor again because why did he follow me out here wearing only sweatpants?

"Are you crazy? Put some damn clothes on!" I ask, my tone rising in pitch, and Jack moves quickly to stand in front of me. Don't check him out. It doesn't matter how good he looks without a shirt on, it's inappropriate.

Now I decide to have morals? I draw the line at admiring Jack shirtless, but not when his dick is in his hand?

"Maybe I would if you stopped running away from me. What are you doing here?" he asks, his cheeks flushed.

"It's Tuesday," I stammer, crossing my arms over my chest, but I'm the one in the wrong here. "Your test is next week, and I sent you a message, but you didn't answer. I didn't mean to . . ." I trail off, grimacing.

"Watch?" Jack asks, his voice lowering as his nipples pebble due to the cold air. I shiver, forcing my eyes to stay trained on his face, but it's not easy. I was watching, and I got caught. He laughs, shaking his head at me. "Obviously I didn't see your text. I didn't think we were studying today since you asked me to leave you alone," he says, throwing my words back at me.

"I wouldn't bail on tutoring," I protest, my face burning.

"Fuck, Al," he swears, and I try really hard not to think about how my name sounded like honey on his lips.

"I'm sorry. I should have waited to hear from you before showing up unannounced. Um, I guess feel free to go back to whatever you were doing before I interrupted," I say, cringing the second I hear the words leave my mouth.

Jack stares at me in what I think is disbelief. "Can we just go inside and talk? It's cold as fuck out here," he says, and I shuffle my feet.

"No," I say, hating the way his face falls before I can finish. "Tomorrow morning at the rink?" I continue, extending the olive branch I came here intending to offer.

"Of course," he answers without a moment's hesitation. "Please, just . . . show up, okay?"

I nod, not trusting myself to speak because clearly I'm making awful decisions today. What the fuck am I doing? I just need to leave, and maybe drink a whole bottle of wine to cope with the level of embarrassment I feel.

It's only after I climb into the safety of my car, watching Jack glance back at me before he disappears inside the house that I realize the only person I've been fooling is myself.

Holy shit.
I think I might like Jack.
Fuck.

CHAPTER 23

Jack

ALONDRA'S already on the ice by the time I arrive at the rink, and I'm not sure I want to know what time she got up. It's four thirty in the morning, and I'm early after a night of tossing and turning before I finally gave up.

It was Nate's night to sleep on their couch, and I've learned over the last few nights I don't sleep very well when I'm not able to put myself between Alondra and her front door.

I shake out my hands, trying not to let my nerves get the better of me, but I'm scared shitless to talk to her.

Al walking in on me yesterday was awful timing, but I won't know how bad it really is until I find out how long she stood there. I swear the door was shut, so it was quite the surprise to see her standing there watching me.

In my defense, how was I supposed to know she'd come over for tutoring when Al hasn't spoken to me once since Thursday night? I also haven't been able to forget the comment she made about how she's not my girlfriend or my problem to fix either.

I'm not a mind reader, and those are the most mixed messages I've ever heard.

I lace up my skates, making sure they're tight, waiting to step onto the ice until Alondra comes around. Matching the pace she sets, we skate a few laps together as I figure out where to start: Bradley, yesterday, or me and Al? Is there even a me and Al still? Was there ever a me and Al to begin with?

Do I tell her it makes me sick to think about how Bradley treated her? How there's a part of me that wants to hurt him the same way he hurt her, especially after how he tried to intimidate her in my house—the one place I should have been able to ensure her safety?

He's a coward—a fucking coward for needing to hit someone half his size to feel good about himself.

I shouldn't have left her side, but the logical part of my brain keeps reminding me that I can't be with her every single minute.

Dylan told me about her headbutt to Bradley's jaw getting him to loosen his grip on her, and once I stopped losing my mind over the fact he put his hands on her, I was proud of her for getting away from him.

"I'm sorry for bailing. It wasn't cool of me," Alondra starts, pulling me from my thoughts.

"You don't need to apologize," I say, trying not to lose my balance after turning my head too fast to look at her.

Alondra looks different with her hair pulled back into a tight bun. "No, I do owe you one. I ignored you for four and a half days, and you didn't deserve it," she says, her resolve firm. "I was embarrassed, and I'm sorry."

"You shouldn't be embarrassed. I wish you would've just talked to me, but I never meant to make you feel like you're a problem I'm trying to fix. I spend time with you because I like being around you. I'm sorry I didn't make that clear."

The only time I didn't think about Alondra the past few days was during our games because I didn't let myself. The rest of the time, though? I couldn't get her out of my head.

Somehow she's become the first person I want to tell everything to, and I want to help keep her safe.

Alondra's skates scrape against the ice as she drags one behind her, and I follow her lead, coming to a short stop in front of her. "You can't be there for me every second of every day. I need a friend, not a bodyguard," she says, and I take the opportunity to look at Alondra, memorizing everything about her in case she disappears again.

"I want to be your friend, but I'm also going to worry. You mean . . ." I falter because I don't know what Al means to me. The immediate answer is she means everything, and trying to say anything less feels like a lie. I couldn't protect Momma because I was a child, but I can help keep Al safe. "I'm not sorry for wanting to protect you, but I'll make more of an effort to make you feel like I'm your friend and not a bodyguard."

I had just walked away from Seth at the party to find Alondra when I noticed there was something going on across the room. My heart stopped when I realized it was Bradley, but my vision went red after seeing the look of pure panic on Al's face after hearing what he said to her.

"I'm sorry," she says again, but the last thing I want to hear right now is Alondra apologize.

"God, please stop apologizing, Al. It's not your fault he can't take no for an answer. It's really not, and you shouldn't apologize for it."

Her beautiful eyes blink rapidly, but my chest hurts when tears pool in them. I hate seeing Al cry. I'd rather she yell and scream at me than cry.

Moving closer to her feels like the easiest decision in the world, and I lift my hand just in time to catch the first one that falls, brushing it away with the pad of my thumb.

Al's hand catches mine after I let it fall, and I'm surprised by how cold it is. "It's not your fault either," she says, squeezing my hand.

How does she know exactly what I need to hear right now?

I'd be lying if I said I hadn't wondered over the last few days whether Alondra would've been better off had I left her alone after learning who she was? But then I think about Ellie telling me just last week how much happier Al seems, and how I've changed since getting to know her.

I have never met someone like Alondra in my life, and I love being one of the people she trusts with the pieces of herself that Bradley tried to destroy.

She matters to me. It's the most honest and accurate way I can describe her.

"I'm sorry for what he did to you—I shouldn't have pushed you to tell me about it," I say after a moment.

Alondra was right. If she had told me right away that Bradley had hurt her, I probably would have ruined everything good I have going for myself. I want to believe I'm a bigger person who wouldn't beat the shit out of her ex if given the chance, but I know I wouldn't regret it if it happened.

She musters a smile. "I think he had too much to drink, and it's why he didn't care there were other people watching and listening. I doubt it'll happen again—there's too much on the line now."

"Alcohol is *not* an excuse," I insist, and Alondra takes in a shallow breath, slipping away from me once more by skating backward from me.

Message received. I guess she's done talking about this, but at least she didn't tell me it doesn't matter again.

"I promise I'll wait to hear from you before coming over next time," she says, a scarlet hue crawling up her neck to tint her cheeks.

"That's bullshit. You're welcome any time," I insist, but I also feel my face heat. "Maybe just, like, knock on my door first?"

"In my defense, I did call out to ask if you were there," Alondra says, and I force an awkward chuckle, rubbing the back of my neck.

"Sorry, I was a little preoccupied." More like I got caught with my dick in my hand, fantasizing about Alondra riding my thigh, but I don't think adding the details will make it sound any better.

"You know, you might be a little less preoccupied if you went out with one of the girls I picked out for you," she says, and I scoff because going out with another girl is the furthest thing from my mind.

"*Pass.*"

To my relief, Alondra laughs. "What? Are you afraid they'll find out you kiss like a two?"

"Good thing I fuck like a ten to make up for it," I say, winking at her, desperate to make her laugh again. I miss her laughter, her smiles, and I just miss Al.

Fuck, maybe I am whipped like Seth accused me of at the party before everything with Bradley.

Alondra shakes her head at me, and I feel some of the weight on my chest lift. "You talk a pretty big game, Jack," she jokes, and I skate closer to her, flashing a slanted smile.

"Do you need me to prove it to you?" I ask, loving how her cheeks somehow flush a brighter shade of red. This feels easy and normal. Al makes it all too easy to push her buttons, and right now, I want to know how far she'll let me take this before pushing back. "I told you I don't always mind an audience, but if you ever want to do more than watch, you know where to find me."

What the hell am I doing?

"I wasn't trying to watch," Alondra says, tipping her head up in defiance.

"Doesn't matter. You still were, and then you ran before I could finish," I tease.

She sputters, her pink lips parting, and she tugs at the

sleeves of her sweatshirt. "I didn't tell you to chase after me! But no, you ran out of your house half-naked to stop me from getting in my car," Alondra says, sarcasm and sass bleeding into her tone while she tugs at the sleeves of her sweatshirt before skating away from me, leaving me no choice but to follow after her.

"I'm not saying you told me to go after you, but if it were anyone else who walked in, I probably wouldn't have gone after them," I say, catching up to Al in no time.

"I didn't walk in. You didn't make sure your door was shut and locked," Al's quick to retort.

"Okay, fine. All I'm saying is that if it were someone else, I would have probably, you know . . . finished."

Oh hell. Did that really come out of my mouth?

Alondra raises a dark eyebrow, looking over her shoulder, telling me it did.

"Glad to hear I'm so important you put off *finishing* to catch me."

Her blades scrape against the ice when she takes off, and I snort, picking up my pace. "That's not what I meant," I call after her.

"Just stop before you dig yourself a deeper hole," Al suggests, laughing, and she's not wrong. At this point I should just hit myself over the head with the shovel to finish the job.

I recognize the concentration on her face as Alondra turns, holding my breath to see her jump. She pivots, picking up speed with a backward crossover only to propel herself upward into the air, rotating before landing on one skate, and I'm in fucking awe of her. I don't think I'll ever get used to seeing her skate.

I'm great at hockey, having spent more than half of my life on skates, but I don't have the grace it takes to figure skate like Al does.

The smile on her face glows, and my chest feels warm and

fuzzy at the sight of Alondra's quiet joy. She's getting stronger, and it's helping her confidence grow.

"Al?" I call out, running a hand through the shorter strands of my hair.

"How'd your games go last weekend?" she asks, changing the conversation, and it's tempting to take the distraction. Maybe it's a sign to follow, considering I don't even know what's left to be said. I'm doing an awesome job of saying the wrong thing, so Alondra's probably doing me a favor.

"Shitty—didn't have my new good luck charm there," I say, but logically, I know Al won't be attending any away series. I can only hope she continues coming to the home games.

For the first time in my life, I was more focused on a girl than the game I was playing Friday night, and I didn't get a single shot past their goalie. I played better Saturday afternoon, but I was off my game. Thankfully, my team had my back, and helped pick up my slack. I'm normally an expert at checking my personal shit at the door, always able to give hockey a thousand percent of my focus, but nothing could have prepared me for how much my shit was rocked by Alondra asking me to leave her alone.

I tried sitting in my old seat on Monday, and I spent the entire class trying not to turn around to stare at Al. It was fucking awful, and I couldn't have escaped the room fast enough, trying to give her the space she asked for.

"You're lucky I'm free for the next one," she says, and superstitious or not, it's a relief to hear.

"You better be."

Al's lips curve into a full-blown smile, and I don't hesitate to return it. "Catch me if you can," she says, surprising me.

I have no intention of pretending to let her get away, going after Alondra without a second's hesitation. I'm doing enough pretending these days, and for the moment, I'm sick of it. I want to hold her and feel the weight of her head against my chest.

Alondra slows just before I reach her, and I come to a sharp stop, folding the curves of her body into mine. We're a perfect fit, and I try not to focus on how right it feels to rest my head on top of hers.

"I missed you," I whisper, my voice wobbling, but I don't even care because her arms hold me tightly in return. There's a lot I don't seem to care about anymore when it comes to Al.

"I missed you too."

"Don't shut me out like that again, okay?"

Her head nods against my chest, but I don't let go, losing track of how long we stand on the ice holding each other.

The only thing I know is that it wasn't long enough.

CHAPTER 24

Alondra

WHY DID I think it would be okay to break my rule about the hockey team for the fucking captain? I should have sent Jack and his stupid dimples packing the second he asked for a kiss.

Instead, I took pity on him, and now I'm the moron falling for the guy who's quickly become one of my best friends.

I never should have made an exception for him.

This is only going to end badly with someone getting hurt, and I would rather it be me because I hate the idea of being the one to cause Jack pain.

I shove my gloves into the pockets of my parka as I move to unzip the front now that I've made it into the tunnels. I didn't like the cold before Bradley left me at the bottom of his stairs, but now I hate it, and unfortunately for me, winter's shown its face early this year with a record-breaking snowstorm in November. I'm so over it already. Not only do I like to torture myself by spending more time with Jack than without him, I also like to look at the weather in Fort Worth where it's sunny and in the sixties.

My fur-lined hood helped to block out some of the swirling snow, but classes should have been cancelled today.

The underground tunnels only reach a few parking garages on campus, and the worst part of having an eleven a.m. class is that the garages fill up by eight, making it impossible to snag a spot.

The sour mood I'm in only worsens when I walk into class, hoping Jack brought coffee, only to learn he isn't even here yet. I record a quick voice memo asking where he is because if I can be in class with a blizzard outside, then he can show up too.

Keri was smart to not brave the cold, but Jack doesn't even respond until class is already over, claiming to be sick.

He was fine when I saw him last night, and I'm not sure I believe him. A simple cold seems to knock out even the toughest men, but I had the flu during my freshman year for three days before Macy begged me to go to the doctor. Without sitting by Jack and Keri, I was bored out of my mind in Comp II.

I know Coop has a class in the building next to ours that gets out a little later, so I catch a ride with him back to their house where I learn Jack really is sick.

"I wouldn't go up there," Dylan warns after I walk past him toward the stairs.

"I tried to tell her," Coop says, and I roll my eyes.

"He was literally fine when he left my apartment twelve hours ago," I say, ignoring them to stomp up the stairs.

Jack's door is shut, but I've learned my lesson when it comes to showing up unannounced, knocking first. I cover my eyes with one hand, opening the door with the other. "Are you decent?" I ask, taking a step in as he coughs.

"Yeah," he says, groaning, and I can hear how congested Jack is, even with only one word spoken.

"Oh my god, are you okay?" I ask, after dropping my hand, spotting Jack wrapped in blankets on the bed, but it looks like he's still shivering.

"Fine. Just a little cold. I'll be fine by tomorrow."

"Jack! You have a game Friday night," I point out, and he pulls the blankets tighter around himself.

"I'm aware. I went to practice, but Coach B sent me home claiming I looked like shit. I'm hoping it's just a twenty-four-hour thing."

Definitely not a twenty-four-hour bug, but if he actually takes care of himself, he might be well enough to play.

"You do look like shit." I move closer, pressing the inside of my wrist against his forehead, and there's no doubt he's running a fever. Jack rolls, trying to shift away from me.

"Go away," he protests, and I scoff, shaking my head because there's no way I'm going to leave him lying in bed all day, miserable. I march into his bathroom, picking up the towel on the floor to toss it in his laundry hamper before running the water, letting it reach a lukewarm temperature before putting the stopper in the drain.

"Al, what are you doing?" he croaks, staggering behind me as I stand to grab his cinnamon body wash off the shelf, squirting some underneath the spout to create bubbles as the tub fills.

"Running you a bath. It'll help you feel better, but you also need to drink fluids to stay hydrated."

He runs a hand through his already disheveled hair, and my stomach flutters. Even when he's sick, he looks good. "I'm not lying in filthy water. I'm fine."

"Do you want to play this weekend or not?" I ask, putting my hands on my hips.

Jack's crystal eyes are heavy, laden with exhaustion, and he slumps against the doorframe. "Fine," he mumbles, admitting defeat.

He shivers after pulling his shirt off, dropping it on the floor, and if I weren't too busy staring at his body, I'd probably say something. *Pull yourself together*, I scold myself, tearing my gaze away to the still-filling tub. It's rude to stare, especially when he's too sick to even make a joke about it.

Jack drops his sweatpants next, his black briefs clinging to his thick thighs, leaving little to the imagination. He doesn't need to keep them on since I've already seen everything, but this feels like a bad time to bring that up. Jack grimaces when he steps into the tub, slowly lowering himself in the water. It's a tight fit, and I try not to laugh because I think if I do, he'll get out immediately. Jack's knees stick out of the water, and only half of his chest is submerged. Jack sighs, closing his eyes to lean against the tile. "You should go. I don't want to get you sick."

I grab his clothes from the floor, throwing them in the hamper as well, to take a seat on the lid of the toilet. "I have a strong immune system. I rarely get sick, even when I lived in the dorms, so I think you're stuck with me. I'd hate for you to fall asleep in the water and drown."

"If I didn't know you better, I'd say you might be wishing for that to happen."

"What? And then deprive myself of your friendship?" I ask, and Jack opens his eyes to smile, but it's faint.

"You were pretty insistent on us not being friends in the first place," he argues, closing them again.

"Well, *yeah*. You're a hockey player, and literally the only rule I had for myself was no hockey players—even as friends. Besides, I feel like we're on borrowed time until my dad finds out I'm not just your tutor."

"If you're not just my tutor, then what are you?" Jack asks, and it feels like a loaded question. I don't know what I am anymore. I know I'm his friend, but I like kissing him too much to only be Jack's friend. It's comical considering how hard I fought against becoming his friend, but now I don't want to risk ruining our friendship because I caught feelings. I wish it weren't so damn confusing and complicated.

I wish I wasn't afraid to let myself feel more than friendship toward him.

"I'm your friend," I say, because there's nothing else to

say. "And he's going to lose his shit," I say, knowing we're on a clock, running out of time.

Hockey has always been my dad's thing, and it was something I desperately wanted to be a part of until I realized it was hopeless to try.

Now with Jack, I'm knee deep in it, and somehow, Dad has no fucking clue.

"Do you really think Coach'll be that upset about it?" Jack asks, sniffling as he crosses his arms over his chest, bringing my attention once again to the delicate silver hanging around his neck.

"I've honestly tried to not think about it, but I don't think Dad would be as mad if it were anyone else on the team. But you're you, so I'd put money on it."

"What does it matter that it's me?"

I exhale a quiet laugh, tapping my fingers on my thigh. "Come on, pretty boy. Do you really need me to stroke your ego by pointing out you were the third overall draft pick two years ago, and you're his star player *and* team captain? I shouldn't be anywhere near you."

He coughs into his elbow, sniffling a few times before responding, struggling to keep his blue eyes open. "There's nothing wrong with our friendship."

I can't ignore the tightening in my chest at the word *friendship*. That's all we'll ever be.

"Maybe I'm wrong," I say, but I don't think I am.

"Sometimes I wish it was just about the game. No money, no draft—just skating and playing hockey. It's all I thought I wanted," Jack mumbles, and I'm not sure what he means by it. Has what he wanted changed?

I want to ask, but I'm pretty sure Jack's fallen asleep.

I'm in so far over my fucking head.

He's wormed his way into my life like a parasite, and now I don't know what to do without him. He's gone above and beyond to prove he isn't anything like Bradley, and whether

Jack knows it or not, he's helping to mend the pieces of myself I thought couldn't be put together again.

I step out of the bathroom for a moment, listening to hear if he moves, but now I'm noticing what a disaster his normally clean room is.

Jack's clothes from practice are on the floor by the bed, the dresser drawers are half-open, and his blankets are strewn everywhere from tossing and turning. I try my best to straighten things up, wishing I knew where his spare sheets were so I could change them. I'm sure his bed is exactly where he'll head once he's awake and out of the tub.

When I check on Jack, I'm relieved but a little concerned he hasn't moved, so I hover for a moment, waiting until I see his chest rise and fall again. Jack looks so peaceful, and he probably needed the rest, especially with the season in full swing.

If I were smart, I'd start distancing myself before this all ends in disaster, but maybe I just like playing with fire.

If he stays in the tub too long, it'll end up hurting more than it could help. I'm about to nudge Jack when Dylan walks into the room without knocking, typing on his phone. "Schultz, are you still one of the living dead, or can I tell Coach you're feeling better? He just called to remind us to keep all our sink cabinets open to keep the pipes from freezing and asked."

Ouch, Dad called them before me? *Why don't you just stab me next time, Dylan?* "He's sleeping," I answer, and he looks confused.

"Um, where?"

"The tub," I say, and Dylan walks closer to peer around me, finding Jack asleep surrounded by a mountain of bubbles.

"He's not actually asleep like that, is he?" Dylan asks, looking at me in disbelief.

"Yep."

He scratches the back of his neck. "Shit, we were hoping after sleeping all morning, he'd start to feeling better."

"I was just about to wake him up if you want to ask how he's feeling after?" I ask, and Dylan's dark eyes teem with what I can only assume is mischief, smirking.

"If you pass up the opportunity to draw a penis on his face, I'll be extremely disappointed," he jokes, and my jaw drops.

"He's sick!"

Dylan rolls his eyes, crossing his arms over his chest. "So? Jack once put pink hair dye in Coop's shampoo bottles, and he had to bleach his hair to try and dye it back to his normal color. Ended up turning orange, so then he buzzed it. Coop was more pissed off than usual for weeks."

"Jack wouldn't do that," I argue, but I'm not sure why Dylan would lie about this.

"Oh, he totally did. This is harmless in the grand scheme of things."

I look at him skeptically, but if he's going to do it, then he needs to hurry up. "So do it. Why are you waiting for my permission?"

"Because you'll be stuck here until further notice with his pissy mood once he's coherent enough to realize it's there. They just shut down campus. Coop just got back a few minutes ago from picking up Sara and Ellie, so they can crash here too. We're officially snowed in, but at least we can have some fun."

"I had nothing to do with this if he asks," I say, and he frowns.

"Where's the fun in that?"

"I'd like to think I can plan a prank more mature than, *Har har, let's draw a penis on his face.* What are we? Seven?" I ask, chuckling under my breath. I cast another look at Jack, feeling a little bad for him since he's sleeping peacefully, but it sounds like he's had it coming.

"Actually, I'm a five-year-old at heart. But if you want to step out for a moment to leave me alone at the scene of the crime, it'd give you plausible deniability."

"Good luck," I say, patting his shoulder to refill Jack's water. When I come back a few minutes later, Dylan's laughing so hard he can barely breathe, clutching his side.

I shake my head, shoving him out of the bathroom to check on Jack, who is still passed out, except now there's a graphic drawing on his forehead. I nudge his shoulder, trying to be gentle. "Jack, c'mon, you gotta get up. The water is starting to get cold, and you'll end up worse if you stay in here longer."

His eyes blink open lazily at me. "Did I fall asleep?"

I can't help smiling at him. "Yeah. You did."

"Thanks for not letting me drown," he murmurs, still sounding congested, but hopefully he starts feeling better soon.

"You won't be thanking me later."

"Huh?" Jack asks, and I shake my head.

"Never mind. Here's a towel," I say, grabbing a clean one from under the sink for him. Pretty sure Jack might be the only college guy I know who has clean *and* folded towels. "And a tissue, you might want to blow your nose."

I give Jack some privacy to get out because I honestly don't think I'm capable of watching him without staring to the point of crossing a boundary. I like Jack much better with clothes on. Just kidding, but it's certainly a lot easier to pretend we're friends when I'm not distracted by his lack of clothes.

I sit on his bed, checking my phone to fire off a quick text to Macy, asking if she's okay. She was hanging out with a friend from one of her classes when we spoke earlier, but she'll probably have to crash there tonight if she hasn't made it home by now.

It's hard to not feel disappointed when the only notifications on my lock screen are from Ellie asking if I got stuck on my way back from class. Jack walks out in only a towel a moment later, and it takes a lot of effort to not laugh at Dylan's handiwork. "I didn't have any clean clothes in there," he explains.

"No worries. How are you feeling?" I ask, trying to appear casual while he grabs some clothes out of his drawers I shut a little bit ago.

"Better, I think? I can kinda breathe now, which is better than earlier, but I'm still freezing," he says, tugging on his clothes.

"You sound a little better. I told you it would help. Have you eaten?"

"No, but I'm not hungry, though. I think I just want to sleep."

I nod because I expected he'd want to go back to sleep. I just wanted to check. I'm acting like a hovering girlfriend except I'm *not* his girlfriend. My phone vibrates in my hand, and I have mixed feelings when I see my dad's name. I wanted him to call me, but not as an afterthought.

I don't know how to make our relationship better, especially when I'm never his first priority. Still, I answer it reluctantly because ignoring it will only make me feel worse. He hardly ever calls without a reason. "Hello?" I answer, holding the phone up to my ear as Jack climbs into the bed next to me.

"Do you still have power?" he asks, cutting straight to the point.

"I think so, but I'm not home. I'm at a friend's," I lie, because it's not like I can say where I really am.

"If you want to come stay at the house tonight, I can come get all of you. It's been a while since we've seen you, and it'd make your mother feel better if you were home in this storm," Dad says, and I suppose I should be glad he hasn't seen me at the stadium, but I'd rather stay here.

"Dad, I'm okay, but thanks. We'll do dinner soon, or something?"

There's an awkward silence, and I can feel Jack staring at me. "How are your classes going?" Dad asks, continuing the conversation.

I reach for the end of my braid, twisting it between my fingers. "They're good. All A's."

"Good." This conversation feels like pulling on teeth.

"So, um, I'm assuming you still have power?" I ask, trying not to choke on the awkwardness I feel.

"Yeah, I've got the generator hooked up just in case. The damn news said it was only supposed to be a couple of inches, not a foot of snow with blizzard conditions."

"Well, I hope you guys stay warm, but Macy is trying to show me something, so . . ." I trail off.

Dad coughs, clearing his throat. "You guys too. We'll schedule dinner soon."

"Sure. Bye, Dad," I say, and he hangs up, but I feel beyond drained from that short interaction.

I drop my head against the headboard, and Jack reaches for my hand, squeezing it to offer his quiet reassurance. "You okay?"

I can't help smiling when I look at him because there's nothing like seeing a dick drawn on the forehead of the guy looking at you like he wishes he could fix all your problems. "Yeah," I say, squeezing back his hand dwarfing mine.

"This might be a dumb question, but why wouldn't they have power?" Jack asks, yawning.

"The snowstorm turned into a blizzard, and we're officially snowed in. You're stuck with me for the night."

"I don't mind. I like having you around, even if I'm shitty company at the moment."

My heart turns to mush at those words. "I enjoyed watching you get in a bubble bath."

He chuckles, his eyes drifting shut again as he relaxes into the pillows. "I knew you had an ulterior motive. If I find out you sent pictures of me lounging in bubbles to the group chat, I'll . . ."

"You'll what?" I taunt, and Jack shivers.

"I'll figure it out later. I'm too tired."

I pull my hand from his, still holding mine, to brush his hair from his face. Jack's full lips quirk upward into the ghost of a smile as I help pull the blankets further up to cover him.

I'm in deep shit.

CHAPTER 25

Jack

MY FOREHEAD BURNS from how long I spent trying to scrub the permanent marker off my face, but all it did was make it more noticeable.

I'm going to kill Dylan. What the fuck was he thinking pulling this shit when I fell asleep in the bathtub?

What makes it worse is he got Al to go along with it, and she didn't even say anything while we were talking afterward. I give her a side-eye, wondering what else he could've talked her into since they've become such good friends.

I couldn't even begin to explain how pissed off I was to see it in the mirror, waking up from the haze of a fever dream alone.

"I can't believe you let him draw on my face," I say, and Alondra sputters, much to the delight of my *former* friends.

"Woah, it wasn't my fault you fell asleep in the tub. I even tried to stop Dylan," she says, trying to defend herself, but as someone who's been on the other end of an argument with her, I don't think she tried very hard.

"She did," Dylan adds, and I flip him off.

"Count your days, Jones," I warn, and Ellie giggles at the counter, working on her homework.

I know I started this shit with what I did to Coop's hair, but in my defense, how was I supposed to know a gloss meant it would be semi-permanent?

"You know, normally I'd agree with you, Jack, but you did start this shit with Coop's hair."

Coop tugs a hand through his blond waves. "Do you remember how long it took for this to grow back? Too fucking long considering I never would have had to buzz it in the first place, asshole."

He's being dramatic. He should have noticed the color difference when he put the shampoo in his hands. I was sick and defenseless.

"But I'm sick," I argue, and Dylan mimics a crying baby. He has no idea what kind of hell he's just opened himself up to. I have a feeling it'd be really easy to get Al involved, and she seems to be an evil mastermind.

I wince, the pressure in my face somehow less than it was earlier, but it still feels like my head has its own heartbeat.

"Guys, I'm bored," Sara whines from her spot on the floor, and it's tempting to go upstairs because her worst ideas seem to stem from moments of boredom. With Al here, there's no telling what kind of unhinged shit she could come up with.

"What do you want us to do about it?" Nate snorts without looking away from the video game he and Dylan are playing.

"Suck a dick, Nate," Sara says, and I chuckle, pulling more of the blanket I'm sharing with Al, hoping she'll somehow get the hint to come closer.

It sounds dumb, but everything feels a little better when she's near.

"What do you want to do?" I ask, and Al doesn't get the hint, yanking some of the blanket back onto her. "Just move closer, Al, I'm cold," I grumble, and Alondra sighs, moving closer to me.

It's not close enough, so I wrap my arm around her shoulders, pulling her into my side. Al tenses for a second, relaxing into me, and I wonder if she's second guessing whether she'll end up sick now.

Odds are she's probably going to end up with whatever plague I have, given how often we're together—unless, by some miracle, she really does have the world's best immune system.

Still, I'm grateful Alondra stayed to take care of me. It's nice to have someone *want* to take care of me.

With Alondra tucked against me, it'd be easy to fall asleep again, but as if Sara can tell how peaceful I am at the moment, even sicker than a dog, she has to throw out the most unhinged option.

"Strip poker. First person naked has to run out in the cold," she suggests, and I have zero desire to see anyone except Alondra naked. But, at the same time, if I'm seeing Al naked during strip poker, then so is everyone else, and that sounds like my version of hell.

Dylan shrugs, and I bet the fucker hasn't thought it totally through, blinded by the idea of getting to see Ellie naked. "I'm game. You can all help me decide which cheek I'm getting Jack and Coach Brown's names on."

"Since when is your name a contender?" Alondra asks, tipping her head up to see me.

"Because I'm his best friend and a hockey god," I say, winking.

"Literally anything else please," Nate begs, thankfully being the voice of reason since I'm out of commission, setting his gaming controller down. "I see enough of Dylan's ass in the locker room."

"It sounds like more fun than homework, so I'm game," Ellie says, coming alive, and Coop shakes his head.

"Nope, I'm not playing strip poker with my sister," he says, and I relax, glad this has been settled.

"What about truth or dare? If you pass on something, you

can take a shot or take a piece of clothing off to make it interesting," Nate suggests, and Sara sighs, nodding her head.

Why does it have to involve taking clothes off at all? If you pass on something, why can't the other option be presented, and then you pick the lesser of two evils at that point?

"Sounds better than whatever we're doing now," Sara says.

Great.

The game starts out innocent enough, everyone taking little jabs at each other. Sara dares Dylan to try and fit his fist in his mouth—it doesn't work, but I think he deserves an A for effort. Coop spends five minutes trying to lick his elbow while Ellie has to tell us about the time she got caught skinny dipping back home in her neighbor's pool.

I've spent most of the game laughing, having recovered from my heavy dose of embarrassment earlier, but Dylan better watch his back. Al seems to be having a good time, even after Ellie dared her to eat a spoonful of hot sauce.

I didn't know it was possible for that combination of cuss words to come out of someone's mouth, and I think Ellie and Alondra are the perfect match for each other.

Dylan decided he'd be the first one to skip a dare tonight, pulling off his shirt instead of licking the inside of a toilet. I'm not sure I can fault him there, but I barely have enough energy to stay awake right now.

"Sara, truth or dare?" I ask, after settling back into my place on the couch while Al puts on the sweatshirt I just took off. I chose to shed an item of clothing to avoid answering Dylan's truth when he asked who gave me the hickey on Halloween. None of them would understand the significance for Alondra, but I do, and I was happy to be the person she trusted in that moment.

I slide my arm around Alondra's side after she curls back into me, and damn if it doesn't make my heart spin around and around in my chest seeing Al in my sweatshirt.

"Dare," Sara answers without missing a beat.

Al rests her head against my chest, and I'm stupefied by how lucky I am to be trusted by this girl when she has every reason not to trust another guy again. "I dare you to jump in the snow," I say, and she stands without a single complaint.

"It's way too cold for that," Ellie protests, shooting me a look, but if Sara doesn't care, then what does it matter?

It's hard to think of anything better when all I can think about is Alondra.

"Nope, I'm not a chicken like Dylan," Sara says, throwing a jab at Dylan who scoffs.

"Jumping in the snow is very different from licking the inside of a toilet, and I stand by my decision."

Nate stands, walking toward the kitchen. "She's crazy. I'd just take a sock off," he says, chuckling, but Sara doesn't even hear him because she's already stepped outside.

She runs back in a moment later, her teeth chattering. "Not a chicken, but it's really fucking cold outside," she says, plopping on the couch next to Ellie, grabbing her blanket to wrap up in. "Al, truth or dare?"

"Dare?" Al answers, sounding uncertain, and I can't blame her after the last dare she got.

"I dare you to kiss . . ." Sara grins, and her gaze jumps around the room, landing on Coop, who is staring at his phone. "Coop. Ten seconds, and with tongue."

Did I hear her right?

"Really, Sara?" Coop asks, looking up, but I'm too busy trying to let it sink in.

The last thing I want to happen tonight is to see my girl kiss one of my roommates, and Sara fucking knows it.

Ellie groans, and I'm glad I'm not the only one against this. "Maybe don't dare my roommate to kiss my brother?"

Nate chooses this moment to step back in the room, taking his seat again.

"Fine. I dare you to kiss Nate then—*same rules,*" Sara says, and I clamp my jaw shut.

"Who am I kissing?" he asks, taking a drink of his beer.

I know she's not really mine, but I hate this. I've denied that anything is happening between us, and if I protest, it'll only make them ask why.

Al still hasn't said anything, and it makes me hopeful she'll take off the sweatshirt she borrowed from me instead, but she shrugs, sliding out from next to me as the voice of reason in my head begs me to say literally anything.

"Fine," Alondra says, and I have never hated a word more than I do right now.

I've been doing my best not to act like things are different between us since Halloween, but I can't get her out of my fucking head. It's bad enough she walked in on me fucking my hand thinking about her grinding against my thigh, but I've just gotten her to stop running from me.

Sara has no idea what she's just set into motion.

Nate looks at me, but I'm caught between the lie of friendship and the fear of Alondra meaning more to me, making it impossible for me to say anything.

Alondra pulls her braid over her shoulder and lands in his lap. I think I'm going to be sick, but I can't look away, hating every second she's not next to me.

Al rests her hands on the back of Nate's neck, leaning forward to kiss him, and I've never felt blinding jealousy like this before. He reaches to cup her cheek, kissing her back while I clench the blanket in my fists. Dylan actually looks a little worried when he glances at me, and I need a fucking break.

She pulls away first, standing up, but everything feels wrong right now.

"Nine seconds, but it looked like you were swallowing each other, so I'll let it slide," Sara teases, and Al's cheeks are a rosy color as she walks toward the other end of the couch without looking at me.

"Ellie, truth or dare?" Alondra asks, tucking her arms around her knees pulled up to her chest, and I'm not sure I can sit here and wait for someone else to try using Al against me.

I'm aware my views of love are fucked up, but if I could be different, don't they think I would be?

"Truth," Ellie replies, and I can feel the weight of her stare on me. The energy in the room has shifted, and Sara has the damn nerve to look apologetic now that the dare is complete.

"I'm tired. I'll see y'all in the morning," I blurt out, standing up to walk away. I need to get my shit together before I say or do something I'll regret.

Nate is one of my best friends, but I'm not going to high five him for kissing Alondra when it should have been me.

I know it's not fair, but all I have to offer are pieces of a defective heart. After the hell it's been through, I'm not sure they can fit back together.

The only thing I know for certain is Alondra deserves better than my heart as cold as ice.

CHAPTER 26

Alondra

ONCE THE BLIZZARD LET UP, and it was possible for the city to start clearing the snow from the roads, the guys spent the next two days at the rink practicing. Thankfully, Jack was feeling better by this morning, and able to play tonight.

He's been in a great mood all night, though, and rightfully so, after the Wolves pulled off an incredible win in the last period. We're at Twin City celebrating with everyone as one last hurrah before they head out on the road for a quick away series while the rest of us go home for Thanksgiving.

Jack's been acting like nothing is different between us because technically, it's not. I only kissed one of his best friends on a dare, then Jack claimed he was tired right after and stormed off. I crashed in the living room with Ellie and Sara, but when he came down the stairs the next morning while I was making breakfast, he seemed fine.

I'm struggling to keep up with the whiplash, but I'm assuming Jack's perception of love is based on whatever happened between his parents, yet I've been too afraid to ask him about his dad like Dylan suggested.

It hurts to think, but the reality of this is that I can't change his mind about relationships, so friends are all we'll ever be.

The sooner my heart realizes the minor detail, the better off I'll be.

Still, here I am wearing Jack's away jersey again, but only because he insisted on it. It was more of a fight with him to not wear it, so I agreed. The guys have all shed their jackets, and look overdressed in their ties and button-downs, but I'm not complaining. Jack looks hot, and I'm not the only one who's noticed.

I've been sipping on the same beer for so long, it's now lukewarm. Coop looks like he'd rather be anywhere else than at the dartboard he can't use because of the girl standing in front of him, talking his ear off. Sara's flirting with a pretty girl up at the bar, grabbing us shots, and I've been chatting with Macy, Ellie, and Dylan most of the night, trying to avoid acknowledging Chad in the corner of the booth as he continues to try to speak over Macy.

Jack is talking to a girl who caught him on his way back from the jukebox, and I've looked over at them a suspicious amount of times that Macy hasn't stopped eyeing me. She has no room to talk, though. Chad's sitting next to her because Macy caved when he begged her to take him back, but I'm staying out of it.

I swear, she has no backbone when it comes to him.

Okay, fine. Now I'm staying out of it.

"You played one hell of a game," I say to Dylan who is sitting across from me next to Macy. Ellie is to my left, but she's too busy giving Chad a dirty look to notice.

"Thanks, Al. I'm just glad you were able to make it tonight. I think Jack plays better when you're there because he's trying to impress you," Dylan teases, and I roll my eyes.

"Whatever. He plays just fine without me there."

"And I'm chopped liver, I guess," Ellie says sarcastically to herself, and I take a sip of my warm beer, grimacing.

"You are not. I wouldn't go if you didn't, so that makes

you Jack's other lucky charm," I say, just as Jack slides into the booth next to me.

"Jesus, I didn't think she'd ever get the hint," he grumbles, fanning the spark of hope in my chest, but just because Jack didn't want to talk to her, doesn't mean he wants to talk to me.

Dylan snorts. "Well, it was a big night for you. Don't worry, Al was just telling me how great I played."

I sip from my beer again as Jack's thigh presses against mine. "And what about me? I scored the winning goal."

"If you're going to toot your own horn, then I don't need to," I tease, and Jack's eyes shimmer with amusement.

"You can toot my horn any day," he says, and it sounds so dirty, I can't help laughing.

"I think she wanted to toot your horn," I say, despite hating every word. I feel better when Jack rolls his eyes.

"The offer is only for you," he says, taking a sip of his water as Macy asks Ellie what her family does for Thanksgiving.

"Congratulations on tonight's game," I say, playing it safe while an old country song starts through the speakers, and he smiles, his dimple appearing.

"C'mon, darlin'. Dance with me," Jack says, pulling me along with him out of the booth before I can say anything.

I get a few dirty looks as Jack holds onto my hand, and we claim the small space in front of the jukebox. "Since when do you dance?" I ask, looking at him curiously, and his other hand slides around my lower back, tugging me closer.

"I'm from Texas. Everyone there knows how to swing dance. It's a rite of passage," he says, his eyes twinkling as he smiles down at me.

Despite being graceful on skates, I trip over my feet every other step while trying to follow along. There's a reason I skate solo instead of in a pair. Jack laughs every time I mess up, or squeal, forcing me to hold tight to him when he dips me dramatically out of nowhere. It doesn't feel like Jack's laughing at me, but more like he's laughing with me.

I laugh as he spins me out and back into him, his arms closing around me, swaying us back and forth to the pop song playing through the speakers after his ended.

"Al, you have to let me lead," he says, and I like the feeling of being in his arms a little too much.

"I'm trying."

"Do you trust me?" Jack's voice drops an octave, and the question is an easy one to answer.

"Yes," I say, and I catch a glimpse of his radiant smile when he spins me out, and I'm slowly starting to recognize the steps in a pattern as I let go of my need to control everything by letting Jack twirl and move me in whatever direction he desires.

It feels incredible to let loose, even in the middle of a crowded bar, because I know Jack won't let anything happen to me. He makes every reason why I shouldn't feel this way for him slip away as we dance together.

At one point I rest my head on his chest, feeling it shake with laughter. It's so easy to be with him. "What's my number?" I ask, trying to catch my breath.

"Solid six."

I look up at him, beaming. "A shining endorsement coming from you."

"I have no problem giving you the rating you deserve, despite you continuing to lower the rating you gave our first kiss," Jack teases and I roll my eyes. At least he didn't ask me to rate Halloween, because it would have broken the scale, and I couldn't have pretended otherwise.

"I'm telling you, it just wasn't very memorable, pretty boy."

Lies lies lies.

"Is that a challenge?"

I shrug, trying to seem indifferent until Jack tilts my chin up, his crystal eyes scanning over my face as if trying to see inside my mind. "What are you doing?" I ask after they land on my mouth, his pupils dilating with visible desire.

His fingers move under my chin to cup my jaw, and my breathing catches when Jack leans down, skimming his soft lips over mine to test the waters.

I lift myself up on my toes at the same time my fingers curl around the front of his shirt, pulling his mouth flush to mine. Jack's hand slides into my curls, demanding more from me as our kiss turns desperate.

It feels like I've been struck by lightning, every fiber of my being electrified by his touch. I want to bottle the feeling to savor it forever.

Holy fucking shit, I'm kissing Jack again, and I'm content to take whatever I can get of him.

He nips at my lower lip, not even bothering to ask nicely for me to open for him. I moan when his tongue caresses mine, leading this completely. I tug at his shirt again, impatient for his hands to be on me, forgetting where we are.

Jack pulls away, the pad of his thumb stroking my cheek with the softest touch I've ever been held with. He rests his forehead against mine, and I feel less self-conscious about how lightheaded I am when his chest is rising and falling underneath my hand as dramatically as mine is.

I'm afraid to move, hoping he'll kiss me again, but why did he kiss me?

Do I even care to know why, or should I just be glad it happened?

"What's my number?" he asks a few moments later, still breathless, and the question sobers me from the intoxicating moment.

This was just for a number. I guess it's better to know the truth now.

It's laughable he even has to ask, though. Ten. Fucking ten out of ten. "Five," I answer, wondering if this is what it's like to be caught in a riptide. Would it be better to let myself drown in Jack, or should I try to keep my heart from suffering any further blows?

Despite every part of me wanting to stay in his arms, I pull away to look at him, immediately wishing I hadn't. Jack's lips are swollen from kissing me, and there's a glint in his eyes I'd need a code to decipher.

"Really?" Jack raises his eyebrows, seeming doubtful, and his thumb drags over my bottom lip, pulling it down. *What is he doing? What am I doing?*

"I'm gonna go . . . um, freshen up," I stammer, stepping out of reach because I need space, but I regret it once I see his face fall.

"Al—"

I shake my head, moving fast in the direction of the bathroom, feeling my heart struggle to keep up with what my head already knows. This isn't going anywhere. He's my friend, and that's all he wants to be. It's all I should want him to be, and kissing him back was a terrible fucking idea, no matter how much I wanted it.

I splash some water on my face, glad I didn't wear any makeup because it'd be smeared all over my face now. How am I going to climb out of this sinkhole I've fallen in?

It was just a number to him. *I know that*, but it doesn't make it sting any less. It's not just a number to me, even if it's the game we're playing. This isn't a game I want to play anymore.

When I get back to the table, Sara's in the booth next to Dylan, and she passes me a shot with a knowing look, telling me she saw us. Jack has taken my seat next to Ellie and is asking Macy something without giving Chad a second look.

I tip the shot back, grimacing at the burn it leaves down my throat before washing the taste away with my lukewarm beer.

This sucks.

Jack bumps my leg under the table, and I will my smile not to fall while reminding myself that we're just friends. It doesn't matter how great that kiss was.

I once made fun of Jack for not having any friends who were girls, but now I understand why. He's just so damn likable, it doesn't matter how hard you try to fight it. Jack makes it way too easy to fall for him.

"Can we talk?" he asks, lowering his voice, and I shake my head.

"We don't need to talk about anything. It was just a kiss to help your bruised ego," I try to joke, making light of the situation.

His jaw tics, and he runs a hand through his hair, tugging on the chestnut strands. "My ego is fine. I think we should talk."

"We're here to celebrate your win. What just happened was no different than me kissing Nate for a dare, so let's not make a big deal out of it," I say, grabbing my beer.

"Got it," he says, turning away from me, but it feels a hell of a lot more like Jack's pulling away from me. Maybe distancing myself is a good idea.

It'll make it hurt a lot less when the game is over.

CHAPTER 27

Jack

"STOP IT! *Stop it right now, please!" I watch as Momma tries to push Dad away. I hold onto the trim of the doorway as he backhands her, and she falls to the ground.*

Why is he doing this? He shouldn't be hurting her. Momma says we don't ever hit people.

"You don't talk to me that way, got it?" he yells at her, the sound of his voice echoing like thunder throughout the house.

"I'm sorry, baby. I love you, just not in front of Jack. Please, baby. He's just a boy," Momma pleads, getting up to try and hold his face in her hands.

He laughs, and I don't understand why he's laughing. "Why not? He should know what love looks like. What being a man is like." Dad turns to me with a smile on his face. This . . . isn't what love is? Love is when Momma makes cookies and lets me lick the spoon, or when she tucks me in at night. Cheering for me at hockey practice and my games. "Son, this is what love is—pathetic and useless," he says, casting a look at Momma. "You're better off without it at all."

I look at Momma to see her nose bleeding. She mouths at me 'I love you.'

"Don't look at her, Jack. She's nothing." He pulls a gun out of

*his pants that looks really similar to the one I was playing with
outside earlier, but his doesn't have the orange tip on it. He holds it
up to Momma's head and she cries harder.*

I don't like this.

*I feel the tears starting to fall because I don't want to see
Momma cry again. It makes me sad. I wipe my nose on my sleeve.*
"But I love you?"

"You shouldn't."

I jolt out of sleep with a start, the smiling expression on my
dad's face as he held a gun to Momma's head still haunting
me thirteen years later. I wipe my hands over my face, noting
my shirt is sticking to the cold sweat lingering on my skin.

I get up, kicking off the blanket I'm tangled in on Al's
couch. I use their kitchen sink to splash water on my face, but
it does nothing to ease the chill haunting my bones. I feel . . .
empty.

That night was five months before he tried to kill her and I
had to call the police.

I've never forgotten what he said to me that night, but
what hurts the most looking back is knowing I could have
done more to try stopping him, and I didn't.

How am I supposed to know how to be in a relationship
when their relationship was my example of love while
growing up? Constantly watching my dad beat down
my mom?

I'm terrified to be like him—to be *his* version of a man.

And Al? Knowing she was hurt by someone who she
thought loved her just kills me. *It fucking kills me.*

She deserves someone who can love her without hesitation, because it's as easy as breathing for them, and I don't
know if I can give that to her. I want to, but I don't
know how.

The way Alondra looked at me earlier was like I hung the moon in the sky just for her while we were dancing, and I needed to kiss her. She said she trusted me, and the warm, fuzzy feeling I had in my chest exploded. Being around Al makes me feel like the best version of myself, where I want to be everything for her.

So I kissed her, and she kissed me back.

Al makes me happy, but I can't go there with her. It's only a matter of time until I do something to hurt her, whether I want to or not.

After I kissed her, she wouldn't even talk to me. She ran away when all I wanted to do was keep kissing her.

I move slowly around the living room, pulling on my hoodie before grabbing my phone from where it's plugged in. I step out onto their patio, calling the one person who might be able to help me make sense of where my head is at.

The chill in the air feels good, helping to ground me from the chaos.

"Jack? Is everything okay?" Momma asks, answering on the third ring, and I drag my hand over my face.

"I just really needed to talk to you," I admit, exhaling a long sigh that crystallizes right before my eyes.

"At four in the morning?"

I blink, pulling my phone away from my ear, surprised by the time. "I'm sorry."

"I thought you'd be wiped from your game. Your coach texted me and said you played great."

"I had a nightmare," I admit, wishing it were something I'd concocted from my imagination instead of the darkest corner of my memories.

"About your father?" she asks, but I've never had them about anything else. They started shortly after he went to prison, and while they've become less frequent, I don't think I'll ever hit a point where they won't happen.

I let out a short huff, irritated he gets to hold the title when he was everything but a father figure. "He's not my father."

"Jack, we can't change who our parents are. We can only control our own actions," she says, and I know Momma's right, but it still doesn't change the fact I wish I weren't biologically related to him. "Which one was it?"

I feel terrible for calling at this time. I should have checked the time before I did. "Does it matter?"

"He can't hurt us anymore, sweetie."

"I know, but it doesn't mean I've forgotten," I say, looking up at the clear night sky, and she sighs.

"No, you don't forget going through something like that," Momma says, her quiet tone reflecting the melancholy suffocating me.

I blink away the tears forming at the sound of her voice. "I miss you a lot."

"I'll see you in a few days," she reminds me, and I'm relieved it's so close. I just have to make it through these two away games tomorrow and Monday before I get to be home.

"Just a couple more sleeps," I say, but the heaviness hasn't lifted from my chest. "Do you believe in love?"

"Jack . . . " she trails off, and I sniffle, wiping my nose on my sleeve while I wait for her answer. "I do. I hoped that if I gave you more time without pressuring you to talk about it with me, you'd realize it on your own, but I think it'd be wrong to close your heart off from someone who cares about you. Don't let my mistakes affect your decisions with Alondra. You have such a big heart, and so much love to give."

"How do you know this has to do with Al?" I ask, swallowing the lump in my throat.

"I know I'm your mother, and you probably think I'm oblivious, but I saw how you were with her. You look at Alondra like she's more precious to you than anything else in the world. Tell me what happened," she says, and it's nice to finally talk to her about how confused I feel.

"I don't think you're oblivious, but it's kind of a long story," I admit, the soreness in my body finally catching up to me from our game last night, paired with sleeping on the girls' couch again.

"Good thing it's the middle of the night. All I have is time."

I tell Momma everything from learning about how Bradley treated Al, to her kissing Nate during fucking truth or dare, and how it made me want to punch one of my best friends in the face. I explain everything about last night at Twin City, and how I kissed her, but then she ran. It feels really good to talk to her about it.

And that's how I find myself knocking on Al's bedroom door before I can second guess myself.

She answers it, rubbing her eyes as I'm blinded by the contrast of the light cast by the lamp on Al's nightstand. Alondra's wearing the tiniest pair of sleep shorts I think I've ever seen, and my dick stiffens while my head is momentarily distracted by trying to figure out where she's been hiding them before now.

Great. Just what I need—a semi, while I try to get over one of my biggest fears.

"Jack? What's going on?" she asks, blinking at me in surprise.

"I need to talk to you, and you were ignoring me earlier." Somehow, I manage to say it without my nerves getting the better of me.

Her dark, long curls are falling over her shoulders, tempting me to tangle my fingers in them while I kiss her. I couldn't earlier because she ran, but maybe if I can be honest with her, Al will know she can be honest with me.

She blinks at me in shock and opens the door to let me in. "I didn't ignore you earlier," Alondra says, trying to defend herself, but she moves to lie back in her bed again, patting the spot next to her.

I realize this probably could have waited till morning, but I'm not going to be an idiot anymore.

"If this is about the kiss, it really didn't matter. It was for a number in whatever game we're playing with the whole rating system, or we can pretend it was like Halloween and never happened. Regardless, it really isn't worth waking me up at this time for. Seriously, I'm not going to let things become weird between us."

Okay, not off to a great start so far.

I didn't kiss her to play games, nor do I want to keep pretending Halloween didn't happen.

"It is about that, and it *does* matter, darlin'. It was a great kiss, even if you only rated it a five. I . . ." *Like kissing you, like being around you, falling asleep and waking up next to you.* My words fail me, and Al stares at me in shock while I sit in the spot next to her.

"What the hell are you talking about?"

I lean forward, pressing my lips roughly against hers. Al is slow to react, and I tangle my hand in her hair, coaxing more from her. Then she responds, matching my intensity by meeting my every move without hesitation.

I wasn't imagining it earlier—the connection between us only seems to burn brighter with every kiss.

And then Al turns her head away, breaking our mouths apart.

I drop my forehead to rest it on the crook of her neck, breathing in the dizzying smell of strawberries clinging to her.

"Jack, what is going on with you?" she asks, but now I can't think about anything but strawberries.

"Did you know you always smell like strawberries?"

"Um, my shampoo is strawberry scented?"

I smile, craving another kiss from her. "I want . . ."

"You want what?"

I try to get the words out of my mouth. *I want to try and be in a relationship with you.*

Except it's not what comes out of my mouth as fear gets the better of me again. "I want to try to be . . . friends with benefits with you."

Alondra stills underneath me, and I close my eyes, wishing I could take it back and tell her what I really want.

I'm just . . .

Afraid.

I'm terrified of this, actually.

I'm terrified of opening myself up to feel the type of hurt you can only experience through the people you love because, in my experience, they're the ones with the greatest power to inflict pain.

"Al, I know you deserve better than what I'm suggesting. I think you're beautiful, and I like spending time with you. Honestly, it wouldn't be much different than what we're already doing, except we'd actually be able to follow through on the tension between us. I don't want our friendship to change," I say softly, and I start to feel her pull back from me—mentally and physically. "Just think about it. We can still be us because I know you have to find me at least somewhat attractive, or you never would have kissed me the night we met."

She leans back, forcing me to meet her guarded expression. I continue my nervous rambling because I've really fucked this up. "Please don't feel like you have to say yes. I can leave your room, and we'll pretend this never happened."

Why can't I tell Alondra I want to be with her?

Momma helped. She really did.

But that doesn't change the fact that I don't know anything other than sex with no strings attached.

I'll get there. I need a little more time, but I really am trying.

It's just not as easy as it seemed on the phone.

"I'm not sure what to say," she admits, crossing her arms over her chest. "I'm exhausted, and I-I don't know, Jack."

I run my hand through my hair, pissed at myself for thinking I could make a good decision this early in the morning.

"I'm sorry. I'll go. Please forget I said anything," I say, each word feeling like a sucker punch, and I move to get up.

"Wait a second. It's too late, just stay in here. It's more comfortable than the couch."

"The couch is fine."

"I'm too tired to argue with you, and considering you were knocking at my door at god knows what fucking time, you're going to have to listen to me," Al says, leaving no room for argument.

"Are you sure?" I ask, and she gives me an annoyed look before leaning over to turn off her lamp, plunging the room into darkness.

"Either get in the bed or lie on the floor. Up to you."

Al climbs under the covers, and I shed my hoodie, following her lead to slip under the covers next to her. Al rolls to rest her head on my shoulder, draping her arm over my chest. I wrap my arm around her, breathing a short sigh of relief.

We lie there in silence, and I pray to God this isn't the last time I get to hold Alondra like this.

"Jack? Are you awake?" she whispers after a while.

"Yeah."

Alondra sucks in a shaky breath, the sound resonating through me. "I'm scared."

"I'm sorry," I say, pressing my lips to the top of her head.

"If I agree, do you promise that things won't change? I don't want to lose you."

"Al, you're stuck with me for a long time, no matter what we are to each other. We'll always be friends, first and foremost. I promise."

She shifts to lie more on top of me, her legs tangling with mine. "Okay. We can try it, but I'm only going to do this exclusively. No other girls."

I want to laugh because I haven't laid a finger on another girl since meeting Alondra.

"Not a problem, but the same goes for you." It really bothered me seeing her kiss Nate. I don't want to share her. "I'm all yours."

Al doesn't say anything, and I hold my breath until she does.

"Goodnight, pretty boy."

"Goodnight," I whisper back, wishing I'd been able to tell her the truth. I close my eyes, willing all thoughts of my dad to the furthest corner of my mind.

CHAPTER 28

Alondra

"WE'RE SUPPOSED TO BE STUDYING," I protest in between kisses.

Jack chuckles against my mouth, and it makes me smile. "Nope, I thought about this all Thanksgiving break," he says, and now it's my turn to laugh because Jack sent me a number of messages about things he saw that reminded him of me, and they were usually followed up with an *I miss you* and an *I can't wait to kiss you* message.

I can't even pretend I didn't spend all of last week thinking about Jack. It was better to disappear into my thoughts about him than to exist in my house for the chaotic holiday.

"How will you make it through winter break?" I ask, and Jack frowns, sitting back.

"Well I hadn't considered it before now, but I guess it means you'll have to come visit Texas with me," Jack says it so casually whereas my heart is ready to burst into fireworks at his suggestion he won't survive break without me. "I've been dying to get you alone, so I'm willing to sacrifice a little tutoring," he continues, pressing his lips against mine before I have a chance to respond.

My willpower is slowly waning, and he shouldn't be allowed to be this good at kissing. It makes it really hard to tell him no, when I actually want to say hell yes.

I run my fingers through his hair, and Jack's mouth is hot and heavy against mine, the papers I printed earlier in the library crinkle beneath me. "Jack," I say, but instead of sounding like the scolding I intended it to be, it comes out like a plea for more.

"If it makes you feel better, we can call this a different kind of studying," he murmurs, leaning me back on his bed to position himself over me. I'm putty in his large hands. I know if I actually wanted him to stop, he would in a heartbeat, but all the tension building between us has finally boiled over, making it impossible to separate from him.

I know friends with benefits is an awful idea I should have said no to when he knocked on my door a week and a half ago, but dammit. Saying no to Jack is something I'm not sure I'm capable of.

I wasn't going to say yes, but lying there in his arms? I felt safe, and it feels delusional to ask if this is his way of trying to see if he's able to be in a relationship. All I know is the little spark of hope has bloomed into a small flame, waiting to burn me alive.

Jack trails his lips down my neck, sucking and biting at the sensitive skin. My hand sweeps over his broad shoulders, feeling the strength and power in him. "Seriously, we should be . . . studying."

"Don't want to," he mumbles against my skin. Jack reaches for my hand to slip it under his shirt, and I trace the hardened planes. I don't like Jack for his body, but fuck, I sure am happy to appreciate the efforts of his work.

I tug his shirt up, relenting to the fact we're not going to get any studying done. He pulls away with a grin to yank his shirt off in one fluid motion.

Wow.

I smile up at him and his chestnut hair, tousled from my hands in it.

We're having fun so I should just enjoy this.

I sit up, pulling my own shirt off, willing my nerves to disappear as Jack's eyes fall straight to my chest. "Al, fuck. You have a *great* body."

"You don't have to say that," I say, but truthfully, it makes my heart glow.

"No, I do. Fuck, you have no idea what you do to me. You're beautiful," he says, meeting my eyes again. It's the genuine sincerity in his voice that gets me, and I don't know how to respond, so I lean forward and kiss him again.

Jack pulls me closer to him, and this time, he's the one on his back as I straddle his waist and he guides my pelvis to move over his, the outline of his erection pressing against me in all the right ways. *What the fuck have I gotten myself into?*

I rest my hands on his chest, feeling the warmth of his skin seep into the chill, and Jack cups my ass with both his hands, squeezing them as I yelp in surprise.

Jack laughs, his eyes shining while he smiles. "You have to be quiet, or they're going to figure out we're not really studying in here."

"How was I supposed to know you were going to grab my ass?" I ask, but all they'll have to do is try to open his door, which Jack made sure to lock after we came in here. I should have known right then we wouldn't be studying at all, but instead, he waited until I had pulled everything out of my bag to kiss me.

"Because it's a great ass."

I roll my eyes, shaking my head at him. "You're only saying that because I'm letting you touch it."

"Or because it's a fantastic ass," he says, a throaty laugh leaving him. Jack smiles at me, and the sight of his damn dimples causes the edges of my heart to soften. I like him. *Fuck, I really like him.*

Jack leans up to kiss me, my curls falling like a curtain around us, but this time, it's soft and tender—more teasing than anything else.

My hands explore his chest as Jack bites down on my lower lip, my short gasp giving him full access to my mouth.

His hard length isn't as on board with our leisurely pace as we are, and I roll my hips to create more friction, testing to see how far Jack will let me take this, considering last time he wouldn't even let me touch him. The low moan that slips from the back of his throat vibrates through me, and I smile, repeating the movement, pressing harder against him as shockwaves of pleasure spark through me. Jack's grip on my hip tightens, and I like the idea of him being at my mercy.

"Al, if you keep doing that I'm going to be really embarrassed by the mess I'll make in my pants," he says, pulling away to kiss my collarbone.

"Who knew it was that easy?" I ask, grinding against him again, and he laughs against my skin.

"Let's see how you like it," Jack taunts, slipping his hand underneath my bra, palming my breast. I arch into his touch, wishing I'd already taken off the damn torture device. "Can I take it off?" Jack asks, reading my mind, and I'm having a hard time thinking straight while he looks at me for permission. "Alondra?"

"Hell yes," I say, and he's quick to remove it, tossing it somewhere in his room as I kiss him again. Jack rolls us back into our original position, and the feeling of his bare chest pressed against mine is fleeting as his hand resumes kneading the peak of my breast, kissing his way down my jaw and throat, stopping on the swell of my breast.

He gives me a wicked smile before taking my other nipple in his mouth, and I drag my nails over his shoulders at the same time I arch into Jack's touch. I bite my lip, trying to soften the sound escaping my throat while I hook my leg around his waist.

It's so different from everything I've experienced before now. Bradley got off on controlling me, focusing only on himself by using me any way he pleased, whenever he wanted. Sometimes it even meant causing me pain for his own pleasure, but that's not how I feel right now.

Jack is treating me like I'm the only thing that matters to him right now, switching back and forth, his hand always picking up right where his mouth left off.

I twist underneath him, aching for more as Jack proves exactly how right I was to say yes to this crazy scheme.

Jack isn't Bradley.

Still, doubt begins to cloud my mind as memories threaten to pull me from the moment.

"Al, you with me?" Jack pulls me out of my head before I can spiral further.

"Yeah," I murmur after a moment, but my hesitation is enough for Jack to stop, reading me in an instant.

"What's wrong?" he asks, sitting up, concern warping his face, and I hate how quickly I've killed the vibe.

"I'm okay," I say, pushing myself up into a sitting position, shivering from the loss of his hot skin on mine. I swear, he sees everything, even when I don't want him to.

"Talk to me, please?" Jack asks, worry radiating from him.

"I got in my head," I admit, pulling my hair over my shoulders to help cover me. "I'm sorry. I want to keep going," I say, trying to smile at him.

Instead of kissing me, Jack wraps his arms around me, pulling my back flush against his chest. "I don't want you to apologize. It's okay. We have time, darlin'," he says, pressing a kiss to the side of my head.

"I know, but I do want to," I try to argue, but I think a part of me is relieved he doesn't say yes right away.

"Al, there's no expectations here. It's not a big deal—we're having fun."

Fun. I've never hated a word as much as I do now.

Jack presses a sweet kiss to my shoulder, and some of the anxiety swirling in my stomach starts to fade. "Thank you," I say, and he holds me fast while my mind settles.

"Is it cocky of me to assume my rating is climbing?" he jokes, trying to relax me further.

"Not at all."

We're still us, and knowing that calms me more than anything.

"You happy to be back at school?" Macy asks, sitting across from me at the table where we're camped out between classes.

"So happy," I say, resisting the temptation to scowl while replaying the family dinner I had to attend before going back to our apartment. It was worse than I imagined it would be because Dad asked all the questions he's supposed to ask as a parent, fulfilling his duty, then the conversation shifted to hockey like always. Jack was brought up quite a few times, along with Coop, and it took everything in me to not scream.

She gives me a sympathetic smile, and I hate how little I see her these days, despite living in the same apartment. She's always with Chad, but I have no room to talk because I'm with Jack more often than not.

I'm always here for her, but I wish Macy knew how much better she could do than Chad. He doesn't deserve her, but I don't know how to make her believe me.

"I'm sorry, Al."

I shrug because I can't change it. "It is what it is."

"Have you told your dad about being friends with Jack?"

she asks, but Macy already knows the answer, so I'm not quite sure why she's asking.

I raise my eyebrows for a moment, taking a drink of my water bottle. "Do you think I want him to lock me in my room and never let me leave? Of course I haven't told him I'm friends with Jack."

Macy chuckles, leaning back in her seat, a smug look forming. "Then what's your plan when he finds out you aren't just friends?"

"Again with this, Mace?" I say, letting her comment roll off my shoulders. She doesn't know. How could she know?

"Your hair is up."

My hand flies to cover the hickey I found this morning. Jack must have left it on my neck during yesterday's *fun*. I thought it was hidden by my hair and the mock neck sweater I'm wearing, but I forgot when I pulled my hair up into a clip.

"So? Am I going to have to pry details out of you, or do you want to share what it's like breaking your rule to be worshipped by the captain of the hockey team?" she asks, pushing aside her laptop to give me her full attention.

"I think my rule was broken a while ago, but how do you know it was Jack? Could have been someone else," I argue, and Macy rolls her eyes.

"Because yesterday was Tuesday, and you were tutoring at Jack's, but maybe he's the one tutoring you now," she teases, and there's no mistaking how hot my face feels.

"It's nothing, Macy."

My cousin laughs at me, and it only makes me wish I could hide under the table. "You don't get to hook up with Jack and expect me to take 'nothing' for an answer."

"There's nothing to tell! We're just having fun, or whatever. I don't know," I say, looking away to see if anyone is listening to us. I don't know why they would, but talking about this out in the open has me on edge.

I don't think I'm ready to tell her how great yesterday

was, even after I froze. Jack could have made me feel like shit about leaving him high and dry, again, but instead, he just held me and told me about some of the people he and his mom met while volunteering on Thanksgiving.

He didn't pressure me. Jack let it be my choice, and it meant the fucking world to me. I don't think I realized what it would feel like to have someone else put me and my needs above their own.

Jack is . . . Jack.

I don't know.

"Seriously? That's it?"

I roll my eyes, crossing my arms over my chest. "Seriously. I think it's what I need after Bradley. I'm not . . . I'm just trying to figure out who I am now after all that. I don't know if I'm ready for anything more than fun." I really don't. I love my friendship with Jack, and I really don't want to lose him, but I have feelings I wish would go away.

Her face softens, and I look down at my lap, because I know it's a bad idea to do this with Jack. I can't stop myself, though. "And how's that going?"

"I'm skating again," I admit, daring to take a quick glance up at Macy. Her jaw is wide open in shock.

"You're skating?"

I nod slowly, watching as tears well up in her eyes. I guess maybe I waited to tell her until I knew it wasn't a fluke, because Macy was there for all of it. She didn't know why I quit, but she tried talking me out of the decision for weeks, even if I refused to change my mind in the process. It got to the point where I refused to talk to Macy because she brought it up every time I saw her.

"That's incredible, Al. I'm so happy for you." Her voice breaks, and I feel my own tears well up.

There was no changing my mind then because I didn't want to hurt Bradley, even though it was hurting me. It was one of the many ways I put his wants above my needs.

After the night she took me to the hospital, I told her everything. She was horrified, but when I explained why I quit skating, Macy broke down and cried with me.

"I'm happy, Macy. I really am, and I know this thing with Jack could end badly, but I'm finding my way back."

Nothing worth having is ever easy.

CHAPTER 29

Alondra

"YOU DO KNOW you don't have to come with me every time I skate, right?" I ask, turning to look at Jack as he skates next to me. I'm trying to be more conscious of his sleep schedule since he's still crashing at our place most nights, rarely swapping with Dylan or Coop, but now he's spending them in my bed instead of the couch. I don't want Jack to get sick again, but he's also a grown adult. I can't tell him what to do, especially when I don't want him to tell me what to do.

"I know I don't have to," Jack says, the corner of his mouth curving into a smile. "Maybe I like skating with you."

"You're the one who has morning skate in thirty minutes and off-ice training again this afternoon," I remind him, but I like that he comes with me. Some days we don't even talk. I'll put in my headphones and build my endurance back up, and Jack will work on his shots, skating through solo drills. We've even ended up at the gym a few times, but Jack spends the entire time staring at my ass, so skating is far more productive.

Then there are the mornings like now where he skates with me, and we just talk.

Jack flips around to skate backward with ease, his hands shoved into the pockets of his sweats. "I'm aware, but I'd spend my whole day out here if I could."

"You wouldn't get sick of it?" I ask, curious to know more about how Jack got into skating in the first place. I feel like I still have major gaps in what I know about him.

"Never. When I was a kid, it was the one place my dad wouldn't go. It was safe for Momma and me, and I could just be a kid. Didn't take long to realize I was good at it," he says, winking at me, as if needing to offset what he shared.

Now I'm even more curious to know the story with his dad. His mom and I talked a little during the game about what Jack was like while growing up, but his dad was never mentioned. It feels like wishful thinking to hope the necklace Jack wears once belonged to his mom, instead of the alternative being a girl who broke his heart.

"Why wouldn't he go to the rink?" I ask, curiosity getting the better of me.

"Texas is football country. I could throw and catch a ball, but I didn't care for it. I didn't want to because it was something he wanted for me, but I've loved skating from the first time Momma took me. He didn't like that I was into something she showed me, and it became our sanctuary," he says, and it sounds familiar, but I think I'm just projecting my experience, trying to fit it into the blank puzzle of Jack's past.

"I'm sorry."

"I don't want you to ever apologize for him. He wasn't a good guy," Jack says, his tone firm, but leaving so much unsaid.

"You're nothing like him. I know I don't know him, but you're one of the best people I know," I say, hoping he knows how much I mean it.

He smiles at me, but it doesn't meet his eyes, feeling more like he's just appeasing me. "Thanks, Al."

I drag my skate behind the other, coming to a short stop, placing my hands on my hips. "No, I mean it, Jack. You've been a great friend to me." Jack moves to stop in front of me, close enough for me to reach out and touch him. I tilt my head up at him, meeting his gaze directly because there's no hesitation. "You're someone I trust and genuinely enjoy spending time with."

Jack makes the first move, reaching to tuck a few stray curls that have escaped from my bun behind my ear. "I feel safe around you," I continue, watching as Jack's blue eyes glisten, and he leans to press his lips to my forehead, lingering there for a moment before pulling away.

"I'm glad," Jack says softly. He clears his throat a moment later, dropping his hands from me when the only thing I want him to do is kiss me senselessly. "We probably have time for a few more laps before you should get going."

I push off, gliding fast around the corner, and Jack keeps pace with me, staying at my side.

I know I should be getting ready to leave, but I'm not ready yet. I love being out here. When I look at Jack again, he's smiling at me. "What?" I ask, raising an eyebrow at him, and he shrugs, his dimple winking at me.

"You just look happy."

"Because I am. There's nothing like being on the ice. I think you're right about wanting to stay out here forever," I reply, redoing the bun my curls are tamed into in an attempt to keep them off my shoulders.

Jack frowns, despite the fact I just told him he was right, skating closer to invade my personal space. I can't even pretend to mind. Being near him has become second nature, and I crave any moment I can spend with him. "You should leave your hair down. You always have it up."

I raise an eyebrow at him as he reaches to unravel it, and I let him because I'm curious to see what he'll do next. My chest hitches when his rough fingertips dance along the back of my neck, and of course he notices, his sinful lips quirking upward into a slanted smirk.

"You okay there, darlin'?" Jack asks, and I nod.

"Perfectly fine. Why do you like my hair down?" I ask, playing dumb. I know why he likes it down, but I want to hear him say it. *I also want him to kiss me.*

Jack combs his fingers through my loose curls, taking advantage of the opportunity to touch me. "Because I like tangling my hand in it when I kiss you."

I lift my head up, doing my best to frown so I don't show him how much his words and touch affect me. Jack's attention drops to my mouth, a hunger flickering in his handsome features as my desperation for him to kiss me grows. The air around us is buzzing with electricity, waiting for one of us to make the first move. I can't get enough of him. "Who says I want you to kiss me?" I ask, resting my hand onto his solid chest, the soft material of his sweatshirt begging me to steal it from him later.

"Everything about you says it," he says, his voice smooth like silk, gently tugging the ends of my hair back to tilt my head up as his other hand slides around my lower back, pulling me flush to him. I hold my breath for a moment, taking my time to drape my other arm around his shoulders, dragging my fingers through the short strands of his chestnut hair at the back of his neck.

What is Jack waiting for?

"Are you going to kiss me or not?" I finally ask, fed up with this particular game, and after what feels like an eternity, Jack grazes his lips over mine.

"Thought I'd see how long it took for you to ask," he teases, pulling away, and a sigh of disappointment sounds from me.

"That wasn't a kiss."

Jack's chest shakes with silent laughter underneath my hand before pressing his lips against mine in a manner so different from before, the only thing I can do is hold him close and hope he doesn't let me fall flat on my ass.

Our lips move in tandem, and I wrap my arm around his neck, holding Jack close as he deepens the kiss, understanding exactly how I wanted him to kiss me before.

Jack tugs at the end of my hair, tilting my head further as he kisses his way down my jaw, finding the same spot he left a mark on earlier in the week. "No more hickeys. You left one after our tutoring session," I say, trying to focus on my words.

His lips capture mine again for a fleeting moment before pulling away. "Sorry."

"You don't look very sorry." And Jack doesn't. Not a single bit, from what I can tell based on the smug expression forming.

"Because I'm not. What about hickeys where people can't see?" Jack teases, twirling a curl around his finger before tucking it behind my ear.

I choke on my laugh. "I think it's time for me to leave before you start something we don't have time to finish."

He raises an eyebrow. "Last time I checked, you were the one practically begging me to kiss you."

"Was not!" I protest, skating toward the exit. "I asked if you were going to."

"Same thing," he says, chuckling, and I stick my tongue out at him.

"Whatever." I grab my hard guards from the boards to put them on before walking off the ice to sit on the bleachers and setting my phone next to me so I can take off my skates. "Did you sharpen my skates again?" I ask, and Jack steps off the ice.

"Yeah, I had to drop mine off with Frank yesterday, so I snagged yours as well."

"Thanks, you didn't have to," I say, but Jack's saving me the time and money by having them done here instead of the small shop in town I'd have to take them to.

"It's not a big deal, Al. Sharp blades are safer to skate on," he says, stuffing his hands into his pockets again, and I roll my eyes.

"Just say you're welcome?"

He's too nice for his own good. "You're welcome. Are you going to come over later? I think everyone is planning to go to Twin City."

I slip into my winter coat, tugging my hat on my head. "Yeah, I think so. We're still on for tutoring, right?" I ask, feeling my cheeks heat at the reminder of our last session where we got no studying done. Maybe I can figure out some sort of reward system to entice Jack to study before play.

"Could we study this afternoon? Cause I was kind of thinking we could go with them. Sara and Ellie will be there, so I thought you could invite Macy if you want. It won't be for long, but it might be fun," he suggests, taking a seat on the bench next to me. And it does sound fun, but I'm not sure I'll be able to resist keeping my hands to myself if I get a little alcohol in me.

"Depends on how much actual studying we get done," I say, getting up, leaning down to peck Jack's lips, simply because I want to. "See ya later, pretty boy." I wink playfully at him, turning away just as I feel a slap on my ass. I glare at Jack over my shoulder, while he bats his eyes at me, feigning innocence.

"I didn't do anything."

Right, so a ghost totally just slapped my ass? "Whatever you say."

"I'm more of a boob guy than an ass guy," he says with a grin, and this I do know. He's not been very sneaky about looking for a while, and before the other night, I would've said I was imagining it.

My smile is wide as I readjust my hat to cover more of my forehead from the biting cold waiting for me outside, but as I step through the doors, I'm stopped right in my tracks, coming face to face with Jack's coach, and my father.

Oh shit.

He blinks, and my smile drops in an instant. I'm probably staring at him the same way he's staring at me, especially after how I doubled down during Thanksgiving to insist I was done skating when he broached the topic again.

"Alondra? What are you doing here?"

I panic, running all the possible scenarios through my head to explain, but I don't think saying, *Oh, I'm hooking up with one of your players, who's now a really good friend of mine, and we skate here a couple times a week?* is going to work. "I, um . . ."

Jack picks the perfect fucking moment to open the doors behind me. "Al, wait! You forgot your . . . phone," he trails off, barely finishing his sentence. "Hey, Coach. Uh, Al—*your daughter*—was here, um, giving me my notes for class, and must've just set her phone down."

The excuse is pathetic, and the exact same one he gave Johnny. Jack passes me the phone quickly. "I didn't realize you two were friends," Dad says, his eyes darting back and forth between us, evaluating the situation.

"Dad . . . I'm his tutor. Remember?"

Oh fuck, this is bad.

"Schultz, get ready for morning skate." Dad leaves no room for argument, and Jack nods once. He gives me an apologetic look, but I know he's in a shitty position here.

"Yes, sir."

Dad doesn't say anything until Jack leaves us alone, and for a moment, it's tempting to bolt out the front doors and run far away from here. "I want the truth. Are you and my *captain* friends?" Dad asks, placing heavy emphasis on exactly who Jack is to him. Always the coach first, and a parent second, and I can't forget it.

"I can be friends with whoever I want."

"That young man has a lot going for him. He's going places, and I don't want you distracting him from what's important." He pinches the top of his nose in frustration, and I'm not even sure why I'm surprised to hear him say everything I thought he would. I knew he would be upset. Jack is his star fucking player—*his captain.*

But telling me I'm a distraction when Jack is playing his best season yet? It's bullshit.

"Right. Cause hockey is always more important, how could I forget?" The sarcasm in my voice is unmistakable, and maybe this is it. Maybe this is where I finally tell him how tired I am of him putting hockey over me.

"For Jack, it is. You'll understand someday if you find something to love the way he loves being on the ice."

My jaw falls open before I can stop it, his words landing exactly the way he meant them to, and I take a step backward. I love ice skating. I love hockey. I love my friends. I love plenty of things. "No, I understand perfectly well. I'm not distracting Jack."

"Alondra, if I walk through those doors, will I find whatever notes Jack said you brought him? And if I check the security cameras in there, what am I going to see?"

I'm all out of moves here, and there's nothing I can do to stop the tears burning in my eyes. I forgot about the cameras. They never even crossed my mind.

"He doesn't need you messing with his head, Al. You can keep tutoring him, but past that, I don't want you spending time with him."

"I think he's perfectly fine to make the decision for himself."

Shut your mouth, Al. Don't dig yourself a deeper hole.

"Alondra, go home," Dad says, his jaw clenching as more players start to shuffle in through the front doors.

"Dad—"

"*Go home.* I don't want to see you here again."

I turn away from him without another word said while trying to keep the tears at bay. I pass Coop and Dylan who heard the last part, and I shake my head. It'll just be worse if they say something.

CHAPTER 30

Jack

"Do you want to talk about it?" I ask, glancing over my shoulder at Alondra. She hasn't been herself since this morning, and based on the mood Coach was in for practice, the interaction didn't get better after he dismissed me.

"Not really," Al says, pulling her knees up to her chest, leaning against my headboard. She seemed like she was on another planet the entire night, and all I want is to be there with her.

"You barely said more than five words all night," I say, but I think Alondra disappears into her head again because she doesn't react at all.

I step into the bathroom, brushing my teeth to give her a few minutes alone.

I want to know what Coach said to her, and if she won't tell me, I'm half-tempted to march into his office tomorrow to set the record straight. Alondra's been trying to tell me since I learned her true identity how her dad would receive the news of us being friends, and I hoped she was wrong.

Hell, even if she does tell me, I should still defend her to him. It's what I should have done this morning instead of being the dutiful captain, following Coach's directions.

She hasn't moved a muscle since I stepped into the bathroom, and I hate seeing Al like this. My loud, grumpy bundle of chaos has disappeared into herself, and I don't know how to fix this, but I'm desperate to.

"Al, I would never force you to talk about it with me, but it might make you feel better," I say, trying to tread lightly as I move to sit next to her.

Pain flickers across her pretty face, and Al shifts away from me. "I don't know what there is to talk about. Don't you know I'm a distraction for you?" she says, her voice dripping in sarcasm.

"No, you're not."

"How else would you describe your performance during your games in Wisconsin?"

I wasn't the only one who was off my game that weekend, but I was upset about where I stood with Alondra after the party. It wasn't her fault, though. I've always been able to check my personal life at the door when it comes to hockey, but I did a shitty job in Wisconsin.

"I'm allowed to have a bad weekend without it being your fault. I'm only one person, I don't dictate whether the team wins or loses," I say, but Alondra's mouth flattens.

"No, but you're the captain of the team. You play a pretty big role, whether you want to admit it or not."

She's throwing up walls, trying to block me out, but I won't let her.

I owe a lot to Coach, but he doesn't get to decide this for me.

I roll my eyes, dragging a hand over the stubble lining my jaw. "You're right. I am the captain, and your dad is my coach. I can't change that, but I'm not going to let it affect our friendship. Church and state, remember?" I can't get a read on her, but I refuse to let her pull further away from me. I know I'm lucky as hell she's even here with me tonight, considering I spent most of the day wondering if Al was going to run as far as she could in the opposite direction from me.

Was telling her she's a distraction the only thing Coach said?

Alondra shuts her eyes, pulling her knees closer to her chest, and I need her to believe me. "You didn't see how disappointed he was," she whispers, and the sadness in her voice stabs me straight through the heart. "He said I would understand why he's asking me to leave you alone if I ever loved something as much as you love hockey."

My inhale is sharp, and her reaction makes a lot more sense. *Fuck, why would he say that to her?* All anyone has to do is watch Al skate to see how she leaves everything on the ice. If anything, I'd even argue that Alondra might love skating more than I love hockey, and I hate how he's made her question herself.

"Shit, Al. You have to know how wrong he is. You love skating. I could tell from the first time I watched you just how much you love it. I'm sorry, Coach never should've said that to you," I insist, wishing I could grab him by the shoulders to force him to see his daughter for the wonderful person she is.

Alondra has more heart than most of the guys I've been on the ice with, and I'm disappointed in him. I want to respect Al's wishes, but he's wrong for this. I know it.

"What if he's right?" she asks, her eyes slowly opening to look at me, and it devastates me how empty they are. "I quit skating. If I could do that, did I really ever love it?"

I want to scream for her. From everything I've learned about her relationship with Bradley, quitting was the safest option, even if I hate him for taking it away from her. It reminds me too much of Momma.

Hearing the doubt in her voice as she questions everything is painful.

My hand drifts up to reach for her necklace, borrowing a fraction of her strength. "He's not right. He doesn't know what happened during your relationship with Bradley, or how you did it to protect yourself. And Coach certainly doesn't know you were fucking strong enough to leave him, because I know how hard it can be to make that decision," I say, my throat threatening to close up as my own nightmares surface.

A lone tear slips down her cheek, scarring my heart. "Thanks, but it's easy for you to say . . ." Al trails off, wiping her cheek with the back of her hand.

"My momma used to figure skate before she met my dad," I say, my voice catching. It's hard for me to talk about because I choose to focus on when it was only the two of us, instead of everything before. But I think Al might need to hear some of the before, because I hate hearing her diminish her choices. "She was good, but Momma skated because it made her happy, and he didn't like that she had something to love other than him. Her parents cut her off when she refused to give me up for adoption, so she didn't have anyone but him. When I fell in love with hockey, the rink became our safe haven from him, and just because she had to quit, it didn't take away the love she had for skating."

I think that even as a kid, I could see the difference in my mom when we would go skating compared to when we were at home, and I loved seeing her happy. Some of my best memories are of when we would go skating.

Alondra's face pales, her glistening eyes widening.

"Is the necklace hers?" she blurts out, and I'm shocked it's taken her this long to ask about it. I've caught her staring at it more than a few times.

I pull it out from beneath my shirt, twisting the skate pendant between my fingers, nodding. "She gave it to me when I started having nightmares after he went to prison. I wear it as a reminder that she's always with me, and we are free to live our dreams."

I can count on one hand how many times I've taken it off

since then. It's become a good luck charm in some ways, because Momma has a way of making me believe everything will be okay.

"What did he do?" she asks, her voice barely above a whisper.

Flashbacks of the night I woke to the sound of him screaming at her have haunted me for years. The nightmares still happen, though, not as often as they used to.

Putting it into words is more than I'm capable of.

I look away, dropping my hands to the comforter, gripping the soft material in my hands to ground myself. "Al, I . . . can't. I'm sorry, I just can't."

"It's okay," she says, and I'm caught in the torrent of comparing how similar Momma's and Al's stories are. What would have happened to Alondra if she'd never left him? I know better than to drift into what-ifs—

Her hand rests on mine, pulling me from my thoughts before I can spiral. Alondra's fingers curl around mine, and she settles next to me.

I clear my throat, turning toward Al. "I just want you to know quitting doesn't mean you can't still love it."

I wish I had the code to decipher the way she's looking at me. It makes me want to question everything I thought I knew, and my head can't make sense of it.

"Thank you," she says, her lips curving into a genuine smile for the first time all night. The relief I feel is overwhelming because I want Alondra to be okay. I want her to be happy. "This morning sucked, but I'm not sorry we're friends."

"I'm not sorry either," I say, leaning over to press a gentle kiss to her lips. It feels right being here with Alondra—more right than anything else. She makes me feel steady.

Alondra makes me dream of wanting more for myself.

She pulls back, squeezing my hand. "I love skating," she

says, and I cup her face, holding Al with the tenderness and care she deserves. I can't take away any of the hurt she's felt, but I can do my best to be a safe place for her to land.

"Damn right you do."

I slide my hand into her hair, grasping the clip holding her curls back to let them tumble over her shoulders and down her back. Alondra stares at me, pulling her lower lip in between her teeth, and I smooth my hand over them.

"Beautiful," I whisper, twisting one of her curls around my finger, and I wish she could see herself the way I see her.

"It's messy," she protests, but I don't care.

"I like messy. Real life is messy, darlin'," I say, because I'm aware of how imperfect I am, but I think she might be perfect for me.

She leans in, pressing her hand to my chest, right over where my heart is hammering against my ribcage. Alondra pauses just before our lips can meet. "So make a mess with me," she whispers, curling her fingers in the fabric of my shirt.

I close the gap between us, slanting my mouth over hers, and Al tugs me closer as she leans back, pulling me with her. She might as well have branded her name on my chest because the idea of being with anyone else is unbearable. I settle over her, and Al slides her hand under my shirt. I press my mouth harder against hers, a groan slipping from the back of my throat when she drags her nails over my abdomen.

It feels about as honest as we're both willing to be right now, moving in tandem, pushing when the other pulls, and Alondra takes everything I have to give her. I lose my shirt, and Al pulls hers off a few moments later before we're fused together again, and my hands are worshipping her.

She's soft and warm beneath me, driving every part of me crazy for her.

I tangle my hand in her hair, trying not to push things too

far tonight. I could lose myself in Al, and never regret a single second of it, but I don't want her to have regrets. Alondra shifts her hips up, rocking against me, and it takes everything I have to pull away. "We're not having sex tonight," I say, out of breath.

"Why not?" Alondra has the nerve to pout, driving me crazy when I'm already fighting to keep my hands to myself. I roll off her, shifting away before she can tempt me into changing my mind.

"Because I care too much about you to have sex, or do anything other than kiss you while you're upset. Al, I want to, but not tonight."

"Jack, I'm fine," she insists, and I smile, leaning to kiss her, making sure to keep our bodies firmly away from each other.

"Even if you are, trust me. I want the feeling of how fucking great it will feel when I'm sliding into you over *and over* to be the only thing you're focused on when we do have sex. Not distracted by whatever bullshit your dad said to you this morning, or remembering whatever your piece of shit ex did to you before. I want to have your sole attention, and I promise, it'll be worth the wait."

Alondra's mouth falls open, and I smirk when she nods, dumbfounded. "Okay."

She's never this agreeable.

"Just okay? You're not going to fight me on it?" I tease, and Al sits up, pushing the covers to the side to climb under them.

"Nope. It's bedtime. Goodnight."

I laugh, reaching to turn off the lamp to lie down next to her.

"Goodnight, Alondra," I say, and she nudges me with her foot.

"Don't say my name like that."

"Like what, *Alondra*?" I ask, taking care to drawl out her

name this time, causing her to grumble under her breath. I wrap an arm around her waist, pulling my girl against my chest as I bury my nose in her soft curls, perfectly content to hold Alondra for however long I'm lucky enough to have her.

CHAPTER 31

Alondra

I DECIDED I don't give a flying fuck what my dad said. He can't ban me from the skating rink because I'm friends with one of his players. Jack reminded me this morning I'm his good luck charm, and how my presence is highly encouraged at as many games as possible.

So here I am.

Jack's playing like someone's lit a fire under his ass, and I'm happy to take credit for it as his good luck charm. We just started the third period, and two of the four goals belong to Jack. Coop hasn't let anything past him, and all of the line changes tonight have been seamless. Nate has kept most of his hits clean tonight, staying out of the penalty box long enough to have Jack's back on the ice.

The energy in the building is unmatchable.

My dad hasn't spotted me yet, and quite frankly, I don't care if he does. Macy is bundled up next to me along with Ellie.

There's a burst of excitement when Jack gets a breakaway with the puck, sending a sick wrist flick into the net, just under the goalie's mitt. I jump to my feet, cheering loudly along with the rest of the crowd as they lose their minds. No way did he just score a fucking hat trick.

He scans his eyes through the wave of people as hats are thrown over the glass onto the ice, but I catch the smile on his face when he spots me before the team surrounds him.

Ellie nudges my shoulder, and I'm still beaming when I turn. "Think he'll score three for three with you tonight?" she asks, winking at me. I ended up telling Ellie about my arrangement with Jack this morning, swearing her to secrecy.

"I can dream," I joke and Macy's eyes widen, her jaw dropping.

"You still haven't slept together?" she asks, and Ellie snorts.

"Obviously they've slept in the same bed together, but they have yet to fuck," she clarifies, and my cheeks burn.

"He promised it'd be worth the wait," I say, pulling my curls over one shoulder, and Macy laughs.

"I'm sure he did, but I hope Jack can put his money where his mouth is to back it up," she says, and Ellie laughs, grabbing her side.

"I've heard the stories, and I think she'll be plenty happy," she says, and the guys in front of us turn around to look at us, annoyance written heavily across their features. I'm sure they're sick of hearing us talk about everything but the game. "Sorry, my brother's the goalie," Ellie says, giving them an apologetic shrug.

"Watch the game," I scold, but my face might be permanently scorched. My god, I shouldn't have ever told either of them anything. At least Sara isn't here to join in on ganging up on me.

The game finishes not long after, and I cannot believe I'm standing in the freezing cold, waiting to talk to Jack. But it's worth it to see his face light up when he sees me.

My smile is immediate as Jack walks toward me, his sparkling gaze fixated on me. With confidence in his gait,

Jack's pulling me into his arms, causing my heart to flip flop, and I laugh at his forwardness.

"Congratulations, Captain," I say, and he only squeezes me tighter. "It's not every day you get to see a hat trick in the wild."

"Al, you have no idea what seeing you in my jersey does to me." His voice is low and rumbling, sending shockwaves through me. "It's taking everything in me to not kiss you in front of everybody."

"Do it," I say, not giving a single shit. At this point, what do I have to lose? "I'm done living in fear of what other people think."

Jack sets me down on my feet, and without hesitation, he slides his hands into my hair, slanting his mouth over mine to steal my breath away. There's a loud whoop behind him, and a few moments later, Jack pulls away, our breath mingling in the faint space between us.

"I knew it!" Nate says, and I laugh, smiling at Jack.

"Shut up, Baxter," Coop says, as Jack goes back for seconds, and the promise of more makes my toes curl.

"You guys coming out tonight?" Dylan asks, and Jack groans, lifting his head to look at me for an answer. Going out with everyone and tiptoeing around how badly I want to be alone with Jack feels like the last thing I want to do, especially when I can't stop thinking about him throwing me over his shoulder like a caveman to have his way with me.

I bite my lip, shaking my head, and his smile widens.

"You guys go ahead," Jack says, without looking away from me, and my god, it feels like a crime to hope he never does.

We stumble through the front door, mouths clashing, noses bumping, and I can't think of a time I was this desperate to have someone's hands on me. Jack's arm tightens around my lower back as I trip over a stray shoe behind me. "You okay?" he asks, and I huff, pulling him closer again, slipping out of my sneakers, kicking them to join the others by the overflowing shoe rack.

"I'm perfect," I say, stepping back for a moment because I'm afraid if he kisses me again, I'll jump him right here without waiting to see if we'll make it up to his room. "Think you have it in you to score again tonight?" I ask, and he smirks, tugging a hand through his hair, making my mouth water.

"I bet I have a couple more left in me," Jack says, and I take my winter coat off, hanging it on their coat rack.

"I'd like to know now if you're planning on teasing me before I get my hopes up," I say, walking backward, but there's nothing teasing about the look on his face as he kicks his shoes off.

"Not unless you want to stop," Jack says, and the idea of me telling him to stop right now is laughable. I know he's a great guy, and I appreciate him making sure I'm aware I'm in charge, but I don't want him to treat me like glass.

The air is humming with electricity, and I have no problem being the one to throw caution to the wind.

"I want to be here, and dammit, I *want* you to fuck me."

He doesn't hesitate this time, closing the gap between us. Jack kisses me deeply, commanding control over me that I willingly give, and without breaking us apart, he lifts me into his arms with ease. I'm internally swooning at his confidence, wrapping my legs around his torso to hold on, feeling his erection press against me in all the right ways.

It's a miracle we make it up the stairs without falling because I can barely think straight, let alone have enough coordination to hold up another person. As we reach the top, I pull open the collar of his shirt, trailing kisses along the hollow of his neck.

We falter for a moment in the hallway as Jack presses my back against the wall outside his room, his mouth finding mine again as he grips my ass tightly. I comb my nails over his scalp as Jack groans, thrusting his hips against mine through the layers of our clothes, and I whimper with desperation.

God, I want him.

Jack fumbles for the door, kicking it shut behind us, and I feel the mattress dip below me as he sets me down, leaning over me. "You're going to wreck me, aren't you?" he asks, his voice low, and I open my eyes to look into Jack's.

"Do you want to stop?" I ask, trying to give him the same courtesy he's given me.

"Alondra baby, stopping is the last thing I want. Wreck me, ruin me, do whatever the fuck you want to me as long as it's with me," Jack says, and the only thing I'm certain of is that neither of us seems to have an ounce of self-preservation. If we did, maybe we wouldn't continue down this collision course that promises to end in disaster.

I pull him back down to crash his lips to mine, because if he's going down, then I'm going with him. I tug at his clothes, feral to feel his skin pressed against mine, and Jack chuckles against my mouth. "You're a needy girl," he murmurs, the weight of his body lifting off me and his fingers are quick to undo the buttons of his shirt.

"I want to touch you," I say, drunk on the desire coursing through my veins, and Jack's eyes widen for a moment, faltering.

"Okay," he agrees, and I love his lack of argument.

I get up, shimmying out of my leggings, but when I move to take off his jersey, he catches me off guard, blurting out, "No." I raise my eyebrows in silent question, and his cheeks flush. "I mean, can you please keep it on?" he asks, slipping out of the button-down, displaying his carved upper body for me.

"You want me to wear your jersey while giving you head?" I ask, lowering to my knees, reaching for his belt at the same time he does. I push his hands away, giving him a smile.

I forgot what it felt like to want to be intimate with someone instead of feeling like I have to, and I want him to enjoy this.

Jack's eyes are dancing with delight as he nods, his throat bobbing as I undo the buckle, making quick work of the button and zipper. "I told you I like seeing you in it," he says, and I tug the pants down over his thick thighs, my eyes widening at the prominent bulge in his briefs. Jack steps out of them, kicking them out of the way as I hook my thumbs under the waistband of his briefs, my confidence waning for a moment at the sheer size of his cock now that it's right in front of me.

"Sit down, pretty boy," I instruct, and he plants himself on the edge of his bed while I move between his open thighs. Jack curses when I wrap my hand around the base of his length, pumping.

"Al, you don't have to," he stammers, and if I weren't so damn turned on, I'd roll my eyes, especially by the way his hands clench at his sides.

"I know, but I want to," I say, winking at Jack. I take the tip in my mouth, sweeping my tongue over the sensitive head, tasting the saltiness of his pre-cum, and it's more effective at shutting up his protests than if I were to tell him to. My thighs shift together, trying to ease the ache between them as Jack's low moan fills the room, boosting my ego. I like having Jack at my mercy.

He's hot and heavy in my hand, and I lift my head, looking up at him as he watches me through half-lidded eyes. "This okay?" I ask, remembering how he twisted his hand when he stroked himself, but I don't have enough lubrication.

I spit into my hand, finding it much easier after, and Jack's mouth parts.

"Holy fuck," he swears, his core rippling, and I laugh softly.

"I want you to think about this moment every time you see me in the stands for you, wearing your jersey," I say, wrapping my lips around his cock, bobbing my head, succeeding at taking more of him in my mouth as his hips jerk up. I drag my nails, painted a sparkly purple, over his thick thighs, and I try not to smile when Jack inhales a sharp breath.

"Alondra," he moans my name when I hollow my cheeks, and it sounds like music to my ears. "Fuck, you're beautiful," Jack swears, pulling me up a moment later, a hungry look in his eyes, and I jut my bottom lip in a pout, disappointed he stopped me. "Don't look at me like that. If you kept going, I wasn't gonna last," he says, his voice strained as he cups my face. Jack's pretty blue eyes land on my mouth, and he brushes his thumb over my cheek, pulling on my lower lip.

"And what if I wanted you to come in my mouth?" I ask, playing with fire.

Jack tips his head back, his throat bobbing. "You're gonna be the death of me."

"You wanna let me finish now?" I ask, and he shakes his head.

"Later. I need to touch you first." Jack kisses me in a way to make me forget my own name, and his hands skirt along the bottom of the jersey.

My mouth parts, giving way to his demanding mouth as his fingers loop underneath the waistband of my underwear, sliding it down the sides of my thighs. I shiver when I feel the damp fabric brush against my skin, and Jack smiles.

Goddamn, I need him to touch me before I lose my mind.

"You're evil. I'm never going to be able to think of anything except how fucking beautiful you looked wearing my name on your back with my cock in your mouth," he says, this time lifting the jersey up over my head, getting rid of my bra next, flipping us back into our original position with him braced over me. Jack drops his mouth to the swell of my breast, his hand teasing over my lower stomach, my thighs parting in anticipation.

"You want me to apologize?" I ask, a short laugh escaping me.

"Never. You're a dream come true, darlin'."

Jack renders me speechless when he takes my peak in his mouth, sucking hard while his hand teases along the insides of my thighs.

I thread my fingers through his short hair, gasping when he drags a finger down my center, slick with my arousal. Jack's kissing everywhere but where I want his mouth to be. I feel alive right now, arching into him as he pushes a finger into me. "All this for me?" he asks, moving his finger in and out a few times before adding another, but I'm past the point of being able to give him a coherent response.

His thumb swirls over my clit as he curls his fingers in me, and without skipping a beat, Jack kisses me again, swallowing my moan. I grind against his hand, shamelessly chasing my high, and his cock rests against my thigh. He sweeps his tongue through my mouth as I turn into a puddle of mush, my body focused on one thing only.

He's making me feel safe and sexy—a prize to be won with the way he's worshipping me.

A third finger stretches me in the best way, and I clutch Jack's broad shoulders, breaking our contact as I tip my head back, crying out when his thumb applies more pressure, pushing me over the deep end, pleasure coursing through my body.

"One," he says, and my eyes flutter open, wondering what the hell he means by it. His smirk makes me want to strangle and kiss him at the same time.

"One?"

"I think I can get a second hat trick tonight," he says, kissing my bruised lips again.

"I'd like to see you try," I say when he moves to reach for his nightstand, pulling a condom out of the drawer.

Jack laughs, his dimples making an appearance as he smiles at me. He rips the foil open with his teeth, rolling the condom on, and I take full advantage of the opportunity to stare. He's beautiful.

"You with me?" he asks, his gaze meeting mine as he braces over me.

"I'm with you," I whisper, and Jack pushes in, his thumb finding my clit again a moment later as my body tenses, helping me relax as I try to adjust to the stretch of his size. I knew he was big, but my god, I'm not going to be able to walk tomorrow.

"Relax," he says, keeping his eyes on me the entire time, the eye contact only making the moment more intense.

"Jack, please don't stop," I say, my breath catching as Jack continues to push in, and I've never felt so full.

"I've got you. *Fuck, Al.* You're a perfect fit, taking me so well." He kisses me sweetly, and my heart swells at the praise. I can feel him tremble above me with the effort it's taking to stay still, and I rock my hips up, causing sparks to fly from the living flame I've been consumed by.

"You feel so good," I say, the words sounding more like a whimper, and I hook my leg over his, encouraging Jack to move.

He sighs in relief, shifting his hips back before thrusting into me. I gasp, my eyes shutting as he holds onto my hip, helping to guide us together. The sheets tangle below us as our bodies collide, the sound of his headboard hitting the wall.

Jack moans against my skin, kissing my collarbone. His necklace feels warm against my chest, and our movements become more fluid as stars fill my vision, the pressure coiling in my body again. "Fuck me," I beg, twisting under Jack as his movements pick up in urgency.

"Your pussy was made for me," he says through gritted teeth, and I hold on tight, taking everything he's giving me, doing my best to give it back as I time my thrusts with his. I drag my hands along his back and shoulders, and if anyone's being wrecked, it's me.

Jack's mouth is messy against mine, capturing the sound of my moan as it rolls off my tongue while my body thrums with pleasure, tipping over the edge again. His hips jerk at the same time as his body tenses underneath my touch, and a groan rips from his throat.

My heart is beating erratically in my chest, as he takes a few deep breaths before pulling out, getting up to discard the condom. I give myself a moment to catch my breath, watching Jack's powerful body walk across the room again. His upper back has faint red lines, and I feel my cheeks flush because holy shit, I didn't mean to leave those there.

"What's the look for?" he asks, as I sit up, covering my mouth.

"I'm so sorry," I apologize, laughing, and his handsome face twists in confusion. "Your back. You look like you were attacked by a cat," I say, sputtering, and Jack relaxes, dragging a hand through his hair.

"If you think about it, I kind of was," he says, chuckling. "Death by pussy. I can't think of a better way to go out."

I pull myself out of the bed, shaking my head at Jack as his hand skims over my hip when I pass him on my way to the bathroom. Just the simple touch from him already has me tempted to jump him again.

He's reclining on his bed when I'm done in the bathroom, his eyes quick to find mine before drifting down to my body, a smile tugging at his lips. "What's my rating?" he asks, and I climb onto the bed next to him, mimicking his position by lying flat on my back.

"Ten out of fucking ten," I reply, laughing as I look at Jack next to me.

"Thank you for finally giving me the rating I deserve," he says, snorting. "It's only two out of three, though."

"You're serious about that?" I ask, and he rolls toward me, his hand reaching to tweak my nipple.

"I never joke about orgasms," he says, and I think my brain might explode. "You think I can't do it?" Jack asks, a smug smirk forming, and I have zero doubt that if anyone were capable of scoring a second hat trick in one night, it'd be him.

"Give it your best shot," I say, and Jack kisses my mouth for a moment before trailing his mouth down my body, my toes curling at the sight of his head between my legs.

CHAPTER 32

Jack

I'D NORMALLY BE EXCITED about spending nearly a whole month at home with Momma, but for the first time, it feels bittersweet because being in Texas means leaving Alondra.

The thought of not being in the same room as her for that long makes my stomach twist into knots that only Alondra's capable of untangling.

"So guess what?" I ask Alondra as we walk out of the library.

"What?" she asks, taking a sip of her coffee, shivering when the wind hits us. "It's too fucking cold," Al hisses under her breath.

"So we went to Twin City last night while you were with Macy, and I'm playing darts with Coop when this girl comes up to me. She's waving her arms around, spouting some shit about how I told her she was stunning and some angel from heaven, but then I ghosted her. I'm trying to figure out what the hell is going on because I've never spoken to her before. Then I hear Ellie laughing from the other side of her brother," I say, laughing for a moment, and the look Al gives me says Ellie hasn't told her what happened yet. "Then, I connected the dots that she was one of the poor girls you were messaging from your brilliant idea to sign me up for a dating app."

Al gasps, covering her mouth to hide her laughter, but the twinkle in her hazel eyes makes me want to do anything to keep it there. "You never did go on any dates. We picked out some really nice girls," she muses, struggling to compose herself.

I shake my head because it doesn't matter how nice they are—none of them are the girl next to me.

"I'm sure you did, but I won rock paper scissors, which is why I never went on any. You deleted the profile, right?" I ask, and she nods.

"Your girls were blowing up my phone once I stopped responding."

I shake my head, chuckling under my breath as I wrap an arm over Al's shoulder. "They're not my girls."

What I want to say is *you're my girl*, but I don't. Why can I say stupid shit so easily, but anything meaningful is so hard?

She bumps me with her hip. "*Right.* How could I forget you don't want *any* girls?" Alondra says, her voice laced with sarcasm. I want to correct her, but I don't. I'm still not where I want to be, but Al already has everything I have to offer her, even if she doesn't know it. "So what happened next?"

"I told her she must've mistaken me for someone else until she showed me screenshots of my profile. Then, I had to explain how one of my friends thought I needed a girlfriend, so she signed me up and pretended to be me."

Alondra turns her head to look up at me, her nose and cheeks bright red from the wind. "Must be a pretty great friend you have."

"The best," I reply, smiling at her. I know Al did the whole dating app thing because she wanted me to be happy, but I am happy. *She* makes me happy.

"Well, that best friend has another class to get to, so she can get her degree," she says, slipping out from under my arm, but I catch her hand, pulling her back into me, careful of the coffee in her hand. Al laughs, the corners of her eyes crinkling. "Jack, I really do have to go."

I tug at her hat, pulling it further down onto her head. "I know, I just wanted to get another look at you."

Her face softens and she smiles at me. "Fine, you got another look, but I have to go."

I don't want her to go. I like seeing Al smile, especially when it's at me. I like making her laugh. I like being with her. She tries to pull away from me, but I'm not ready yet. "Wait, just . . . wait."

"What?" she asks, tilting her head.

"Do you have any plans for winter break?"

"Huh?"

I lick my lips quickly, trying to decide if this is the right decision. I've already been going back and forth about asking her since we got back from Thanksgiving, but if I think about it anymore, then I'll chicken out. Truthfully, I don't think I can make it a whole month without seeing her.

"Come to Texas with me."

She blinks, staring at me for a moment, her jaw dropping. *"What?"*

"I want you to come to Texas. Momma would love to see you again, and I could take you to see the ranch I work at in the summers. I'll show you anything you want, but I just want you there . . . with me," I say, rambling because I'm so fucking nervous. I can't believe I actually said it. "Please think about it?"

I take it a step further, leaning down to kiss her cheek.

Alondra's still staring at me when I step back, and I think I might've broken her. She exhales a deep breath, her eyes scanning over my face. "Okay," she says.

My heart leaps to my throat, and I try not to think about what it means. "Okay, as in you'll come, or okay, you heard what I said?"

"You're crazy," she says, her curls twirling around her with the subtle shake of her head.

"Never said I wasn't."

"If I can find something reasonably priced, I'll *consider* going, but are you sure you even want me there? I know how much you look forward to time with your mom."

If anything, the fact Al's taking my time with Momma into consideration, makes me more certain I want her there.

"I want you there," I say without hesitation, but this time, I don't kiss her cheek. I lean down, kissing Alondra deeply because I don't give a flying fuck who sees.

I've honestly never enjoyed kissing someone as much as I enjoy kissing Alondra. And sex? My god, I can't keep my hands off her. My back is scratched to hell, but it's a small price to pay to have Al moaning underneath me.

I can't get enough of everything with Alondra.

She smiles against my lips, pulling away before rising up on her tiptoes to kiss me briefly once more. "I really do have to go now, but we'll talk more about this later."

This time I let her walk away, but I really prefer to see Al walk toward me.

I shake my head, trying to shake my nerves because I already asked her, and at least Alondra didn't immediately say no. I pivot, turning toward the end of campus the barn is at. I left my truck in the parking lot of the rink this morning, knowing I'd be back to meet up with Johnny and Coop.

Coach talked to me this morning about potentially moving Johnny onto a different line to give him more playing time, and I want to see him use the skills we've been working on against Coop, who is arguably one of the best goalies in college hockey.

I might not like who the kid associates with, but I can't deny he has the potential to be a good player.

After changing into my gear, I grab all the shit I think

we'll need and head out to the ice, but I catch a glimpse of Al's bag, unable to keep from smiling.

Johnny's already out on the ice with another bulky figure, looking as unsteady as a baby deer taking their first steps. I don't bother hiding my laugh when I glide onto the ice, getting ready to go through my usual warm up routine as Johnny's buddy falls flat on his ass. "Richards, c'mon, man. Stop fucking around, you need to warm up before Coop gets here," I call out, moving closer to them.

My smile fades as I realize who his friend is, and Johnny's wise to look uneasy. "I will in a second, I just have to get Bradley off the ice."

"What the hell is he doing here?" I ask, refusing to take my eyes off Alondra's ex.

He has the nerve to smile at me, and I clench my jaw. God, I want to hit him, but it'd make me no better than him. I won't let Bradley bait me, but this place is my sanctuary. He doesn't get to be here.

"I thought it was fine since you've had people out here. He just wanted to learn to impress his girlfriend who likes to skate," Johnny stammers, and the fact that Bradley's now here, when he's the reason Alondra quit skating, makes my vision turn red.

"Get him out of here, and don't bring him back," I scold, struggling to maintain my grip on my temper, and Bradley puts his hands up, feigning innocence.

"Sorry, Jack, I didn't mean to cause any problems for Johnny. I just wanted to show Alondra how much she means to me by learning to skate."

"Dude, let's just go," Johnny says, trying to pull him along.

Hearing him say her name after *everything* he's put her through nearly sends me over the edge. Al can't know he was here. I know she's doing her best to keep him from controlling her life, but this is her safe place too.

"You ever go near Al again, and I'll make sure everyone knows what a fucking piece of shit you are." My voice is shaking with anger. I need to walk away before I do something I'll regret.

Bradley shakes his head, a twisted smile forming. "Actually, you can't. There's no proof of anything she told you because nothing happened. Alondra must be afraid to tell you how she really likes it in bed. A little roughness never hurt anyone, but she couldn't get enough of it," he says, winking at me, and Johnny's jaw drops, as if finally understanding what a piece of shit his friend is.

The thread of patience I'm clinging to snaps as I connect the dots. I lunge forward, but I'm knocked to the side by Coop, who comes flying out of nowhere, preventing me from making contact with Bradley.

"Jack, you can't throw the first punch. He's not worth it," Coop warns, blocking my path as I rip my gloves off, dropping them on the ice.

"Did you hear what he just fucking said about her?"

Coop grips my shoulders tightly while I struggle against him. "I know. I heard him, but she wouldn't want you to get in trouble over him."

But then Bradley opens his mouth one last time. "You might think you're better than me, but I know who you really are, Schultz, and the apple doesn't fall far from the tree."

I freeze, and Johnny drags his pathetic ass off the ice. I see Coop in front of me, and I know he's talking because his mouth is moving, but my ears are ringing, an icy chill seeping into my bones.

"911, what's your emergency?"

"He's hurting Momma," I whisper into the line, afraid he'll hear me because I can hear them. The breaking glass woke me up, and

they were fighting again. I grabbed the phone out of the hallway when I heard Momma scream. "Please, help her. I think Dad's going to kill her this time."

"Can you tell me your address?" her steady voice asks, and I say it slowly, making sure to get everything right. "We'll have officers there in two minutes. Can you tell me your name?"

I close my eyes tightly, hearing Momma cry out as I start to cry. "Jack. My name is Jack."

"Okay, Jack, can you tell me if your dad has a weapon?"

"He has a gun."

Everything unfolds quickly. From around the corner, I watch Dad point the gun at Momma, the policemen telling him to drop it, Dad getting handcuffed. Momma runs for me, and he stares at me from where the cops have him pinned to the floor, finally spotting me from my hiding place.

"The apple doesn't fall far from the tree, Jack! You're going to be just like me," he yells as Momma pulls me into her shaking body, hiding me from view.

"Thank you. You did so good, my boy. I love you so much," she whispers in my ear, kissing the side of my head.

"What the fuck did you just say to me?" I ask, shoving against Coop, who's still trying to hold me back. "Let me go," I say, shaking.

"I can't, Jack. *I can't.*"

How does Bradley know? The list of people who know here is so small I can count on one hand here. It's a public record in Texas, but the amount of work required to find the information is more than I thought anyone would try, especially without a reason to look.

"Cooper, get your fucking hands off me," I yell, shoving my best friend back from me as he watches me with sympathy I've never wanted.

A slamming door echoes through the rink, and I see Coach jogging down the steps a moment later. "Hey! What the hell is going on?"

Coop backs out of my way, and I inhale ragged breaths. I need to get out of here.

I tear across the ice, memories I've tried so hard to suppress threatening to break past the wall I've hidden them behind. I walk off, quickly unlacing my skates, fully intent on ignoring Coach standing next to me, waiting for answers I don't have. If I talk to him right now, I'm going to shatter the boundary in my mind separating him from my coach and Al's dad.

"Schultz, I'm talking to you," Coach says, and I look up at him, seething from the uncontrollable anger consuming me.

"What?" I snap, struggling to keep myself under control.

If I've surprised him, Coach doesn't show it on his face. "Jack, what happened?"

I tug a hand through my hair as Coop skates over, holding my stick and gloves in one hand. "Coach, it's fine—" Coop starts to say while I slip on my shoes, taking the opportunity to get away from here.

I drop my things in my stall, snagging my truck keys to drive back to the house, trying to ignore the pounding in my head begging to be let out. Dylan's watching the recap from our game last weekend on the couch when I storm through the door, turning to look at me.

"Shit, you scared me. I thought you were meeting Coop at the rink?"

I ignore Dylan, making a beeline up the stairs to my room.

Bradley thinks I'm like him. I would never hurt Al. I wouldn't ever hit a woman because I'm not like him or my dad.

"Hey, what's wrong?" Dylan calls after me, and I close my eyes, bracing my hands behind my head, seeing flashes of the worst night of my life.

I'm nothing like them.

Bradley is a sick fuck who got off on hurting Al. *My Alondra*, who is kind, feisty, and the best part of my day.

"Just forget it," I say, feeling sick to my stomach. I might actually vomit.

He fucking smiled after saying he'd hurt her during sex and . . . I don't know.

I shut the door in Dylan's face, needing to be alone with my thoughts.

Have I taken things too far with Al before in the heat of the moment, and not even realized it?

Taking a seat on the edge of my bed, I replay every moment with Alondra, no matter how insignificant I might have thought it was. Just because it was insignificant to me, doesn't mean it was for her.

Would she have told me if I was too rough?

The door opens, and I look up through blurry vision, ready to tell Dylan to get the fuck out when I see Al standing there. I don't know how, but I'm so damn glad to have her in front of me, there's zero hesitation as I take three quick steps to close the distance between us. "Jack," she says my name, and I bury my face in her curls, inhaling the scent of strawberries. The tension leaves my body in an instant, and her arms tighten around me.

"You're nothing like him," she whispers, and a sob catches in my throat.

She's okay. My girl is okay, and she's here with me.

"I'm sorry," I mumble. "I'm so sorry."

"Listen to me, you are nothing like him. You're warm, and sweet, and you make me feel like a version of myself I thought was gone. He is a terrible, shitty person who can't let go. Don't apologize. You have done *nothing* wrong."

"Darlin', it kills me to know he—" I choke up, cutting myself off because I cannot say the words out loud.

She rubs my back, offering her silent reassurance, and I cling to Al, letting her guide me toward the bed.

Alondra pulls back after we're seated, wiping at my cheeks to force me to look at her. "Jack, I can't erase my history with Bradley, no matter how much I might want to, but please don't focus on this," she says, watching me closely.

"Did he hurt you during sex?" I force the words out, feeling my stomach churn.

Tears glisten in her eyes, and she nods, cracking my chest wide open to absorb all of the pain the beautiful girl in front of me has been through more than she should've had to. I don't even realize I'm crying until my vision blurs the image of her, and Al is quick to wipe them away.

"You give me a choice in everything. I want to erase every terrible memory with him, and I want to replace them with you," she says, and I swallow the lump in my throat. I can do that. I can be the person she rewrites her story with, while I learn how to believe in happily-ever-afters.

"Promise me you'll always tell me if you want to stop," I beg, my voice a low rasp.

She nods, blinking back her tears. "Only if you promise to never compare yourself to Bradley again."

I press my lips to hers, tasting the saltiness of my tears in the process, because even if I don't believe in love, I do believe in Alondra.

CHAPTER 33

Alondra

THE SOUND of silverware clinking against porcelain plates fills the awkward silence as I slump in the chair of my parents' dining room I've been summoned to for dinner tonight. This is the last place I wanted to be tonight, especially because I'm on the second day of my period, and my cramps are barely being held at bay by the Motrin I took earlier. It's also finals week, but I haven't had too much to do, whereas Jack has been a bundle of stress, pushing himself to do well on all his exams. He's looking at having his highest GPA this semester since starting college, but I think it's putting more pressure than necessary on his shoulders. Regardless of how his tests go, I couldn't be more proud of him.

"It's delicious," Dad says, cutting through the tension to smile at my mom sitting next to him.

"Thanks, hun," she says, smiling back at him. "Do you have many finals left?" Mom asks, and I shrug my shoulders.

"One, but it's not a formal exam, just an essay I have to turn in later tonight," I say, taking another bite of the roasted chicken she prepared. I told Jack I would finish reading through his after I'm done here.

"Have you seen Bradley around?" she asks, and my entire

body stills, the chicken tasting like rubber as I finish chewing it. "He was such a nice boy. I don't know why you won't give him another chance," Mom continues before I'm able to swallow the food in my mouth.

Yeah, Mom. He was so nice, he liked to hurt me, and made me believe it was my fault.

"We're not getting back together," I say, because what's the point of saying anything else? I could show them the whole hidden folder on my phone of the marks and bruises that Bradley left behind, but I'm not certain they'd believe he gave them to me.

Dad takes a sip of his water, making eye contact with me, but he doesn't say anything. He hasn't said anything to me since our run-in at the rink after Thanksgiving, but I'm wondering if this dinner is an elaborate scheme to ask me about what happened with Jack last week. That would require Dad talking to me, though, and since we're clearly not doing that, I say nothing either.

"Are you seeing anyone else?" she asks, and Dad huffs.

I set my fork down, and now is not the right time to tell them I bought a ticket to visit Jack the day after Christmas because I'm incapable of telling him no. Lucky for me, I'm frugal with my savings account, but I got a good deal on an early flight, and now all I can do is hope the weather cooperates.

"Kind of," I say, smoothing the napkin in my lap.

"I thought we agreed you were done seeing Jack outside of tutoring," Dad says, and Mom's eyebrows knit, her gaze bouncing between us.

"Who is Jack?"

Only the best person I've ever met.

"My captain," he says, and her eyes widen.

"We didn't agree. You dictated, and I decided to let Jack make the choice for himself. He thinks he can have hockey and be my friend," I say, and Dad scoffs, setting his utensils down.

"You're a prime example of why I want you to stay away from him. You had everything going for you, and you still quit for a boy who broke up with you four months later," he says, but that's not what happened.

"Keith," Mom says, and I'm surprised, because normally she's the first person on his side. She's not a bad mom, she's just very averse to conflict, but maybe she's finally getting there's more to this than the assumptions that've been thrown in my face for the last year. "Alondra, maybe you should listen to your father," she says, proving me wrong in the same breath.

"Are you serious?" I ask, my pitch climbing in disbelief. "I'm sorry, but being friends with Jack doesn't mean he's going to quit hockey. Why can't you just stay out of it?"

Mom sighs, taking a breath. "And why do you feel the need to fight your father on everything he asks of you?"

"Maybe I should bite my tongue more, but if you ever considered there might be more to the story than whatever it is you think you know, I wouldn't have to. I've been helping Jack with all of his classes this semester to make sure he keeps his eligibility to play hockey, and I haven't missed a single game he's asked me to go to. I love skating the same way Jack loves hockey, and I'm sorry you don't believe me," I say, swallowing the lump in my throat, and pushing my chair back from the table as my parents stare at me in surprise. "Thank you for dinner, but I have to go help your captain with his final, Dad."

I grab my things by the front door, slipping into my boots to make my great escape before another lecture can start. I'm calling Jack by the time I get to my car.

"Hey, darlin'," Jack greets, and as much as it drove me nuts in the beginning when he called me that, I've come to cherish it. "You on your way over?" he asks, already under-standing my next move.

"Is it okay if I am?" I ask, starting my car, blasting the heat since my teeth are already chattering from the cold. I definitely think I would've lasted longer through dinner if I weren't on my period, but unfortunately, my hormones are out of wack.

"You never have to ask," he says, and I already feel better after that shitshow of a dinner. I hear the guys whooping in the background, and Jack groans. "Sorry, we're playing Irish Poker."

I chuckle, shaking my head because I can only imagine the chaos. "Is it Dylan's turn?"

"Yep, Coop is the dealer," Jack says, and I can hear the smile in his voice.

"Is Nate helping him?" I ask, and tiny snowflakes start to hit my windshield.

"If you mean by helping him, he's telling him all the wrong answers, yes," he says, laughing again. "Oh, I meant to tell you I picked up some of those things from the store for you."

Could he be any less specific about what those things are? "I don't know what you're talking about, pretty boy," I say, trying to figure out if there was something I asked him for, but I don't think there is?

"I didn't know what kind you like, and there were a lot of options, so I got a few different types. If I got it wrong, then I can just take them back, or donate them, or something," he rambles, but I'm still not following.

"What did you buy?"

"Well, I know you're on your period, and since it's supposed to happen every month, I didn't want you to feel like you have to worry about having stuff here, so I bought some tampons and pads to keep in the bathrooms," Jack says, and I blink, sputtering as I try to think of how to respond to that.

It's moments like this I have to remind myself he's not actually my boyfriend, because I find myself falling for Jack a little more every day, finding a new part of him to love.

"You didn't have to do that," I say, trying to play it off, and Jack laughs.

"Why wouldn't I if it makes you more comfortable? Besides, they're here for Ellie and Sara too, and I guess if any of these buffoons get girlfriends, they can use them too," Jack says, and I think I'm in some real trouble.

How am I supposed to pretend I'm not falling head over fucking heels for Jack?

"Al?"

I clear my throat, glad he gave me a heads up about this so I have a chance to compose myself before I see him, because I'm ready to burst into tears. *Stupid hormones.*

"Sorry, I was focusing on the road. It just started snowing," I say, buying myself a moment.

"I'll let you go then. Drive safe."

"See you in a few," I say, trying to calm the butterflies fluttering in my chest.

It's not just a little crush.

Leave it to me to fall for the most unavailable guy on campus I have no chance with.

I park on the street in front of their house, dragging my hands over my face. What am I doing here? Maybe I should go to my apartment instead, and ask Jack for forgiveness for ditching. On the other hand, there's nowhere else I'd rather be than with him, even if it causes me more pain in the end.

Is it really that far-fetched of an idea to hope Jack might return my feelings, even if he's not ready to admit it?

I climb out, tucking my arms tight around myself while I run to the door, flurries kissing my cheeks. I knock once before opening the door, and Jack's entire face lights up when he turns my way, hopping over the back of the couch to greet me at the door, helping me out of my coat.

Jack kisses my cheek, and the damn butterflies are back. He scans over my face, and I give him a smile, hoping he can't read too far between the lines to see how I feel about him. "I'm sorry it didn't go well," he says, keeping his voice soft while he tucks my hair behind my ear.

"How do you know it didn't go well?" I ask, as Nate laughs from the other room.

"Because you were supposed to be there for another hour. I might not be a genius, but even I can connect the dots that you and your dad got into it," he says, and I don't love the dig he makes at himself.

"Hey, you are smart," I say, and Jack shrugs, leaning down to distract me with a kiss.

"Wanna play with them?"

"Sure, but I have to work on our essays at some point," I say, sliding my arm around his lower back. Dylan's walking down the hall, looking confused by the plastic wrapper in his hand, which I immediately recognize as a tampon. I guess Jack didn't wait to let me look through the boxes.

"Hey, what are these in the bathroom?" he asks, and his timing couldn't be better because my lower stomach cramps serve as a reminder I'm in hell for the next few days, and I grimace.

Jack and I stop, waiting to see how this plays out.

Coop snorts, taking a drink of his beer as Nate flips another card over for him. "Why are you holding a tampon?"

Dylan looks at it, his eyes widening. "This is a tampon? What the hell does the *S* stand for?"

"I think it's the size or something," Coop says, and Ellie trained him well, but Dylan's making it painfully obvious he doesn't have any sisters.

Dylan tears it open as Jack sighs next to me, but I'm curious to see how this will play out. His mouth drops, and he holds the plastic applicator up. "And they do what with these?"

I cough, causing all of their eyes to dart to mine. "Um, you don't know how a tampon works?" I ask, and Coop shrugs. I look up at Jack who also is looking at the tampon like it has claws and teeth, and I giggle, covering my mouth. "Do you want a demonstration?"

Jack's eyes widen, he looks down at my stomach before looking at his friends. "Um, Al—"

I hit his chest with the back of my hand as his face turns crimson. "Oh my god, I'm not going to show you with my vagina!"

Nate laughs, shaking his head. "Wow, you really need to be more specific."

"I hate living here," Coop says, rubbing his temples.

"You know what, sure, why not?" Dylan says, plopping down on the couch, and I chuckle, slipping away from Jack to find an unopened water bottle.

I move their game of Irish Poker out of the way on the coffee table, holding out my hand for Dylan to hand me the tampon he opened, and I wish Ellie was here to witness this. "Okay, so first, you obviously take off the wrapper which Dylan already did, and if it had an S, it means it's a super for when your period is heavier, and you're trying not to bleed through it."

"I'm sorry, you can bleed through your tampons?" Nate asks, and I'm wondering what else they don't know about female anatomy, because they all should have had to pass a health class to graduate high school.

"If you don't change them so often, yeah," I say, cracking the lid on the water. "So basically the lid is the vagina, and you'd insert the applicator." I demonstrate, not pushing the plunger in yet, trying to take this seriously, when all I really want to do is laugh at their ridiculousness. "Once it's far enough in, you push the plunger, and the tampon is inserted," I say, watching the cotton expand as a visual. "Then you take out the applicator, throw it away, and go about your day. Any questions?"

The room is silent as all four of them stare at me, and I purse my lips, trying not to crack.

"I'm sorry, you walk around with that just in you?" Nate asks, and Coop grimaces.

"No wonder Ellie gets so pissed off on her period."

I scoff, nodding. "And then in addition to having to use these, you're also constantly checking when you get up from sitting to make sure you didn't bleed through onto the chair. Then there are cramps, mood swings, and the hormones that can cause your face to break out. Some people get them twice a month, and they can last anywhere from three to seven days. It's straight up, not a good time."

"How do you get it out?" Dylan asks.

I hold up the string I left hanging out of the bottle, and his face pales. "You pull it out, wrap it in toilet paper, throw it away, and replace it with another."

"I am so sorry," Jack says, shaking his head as he stares at the water bottle.

I can't hold my laughter back anymore, and I double over, laughing until I can't breathe. "Oh my god, I can't believe you guys," I squeak out, gasping for air. "This is amazing."

"That is horrible," Dylan asks, taking a long drink of his beer.

"Maybe you should spend more time familiarizing yourselves with female anatomy," I say, getting up from the floor, still laughing.

How the hell am I supposed to focus on our essays now?

CHAPTER 34

Jack

I HAVEN'T BEEN able to keep my hands off Alondra since the moment she arrived.

Whether it's having my hand on her thigh while I drove her back from the airport, or having my hand on her lower back as we walk. It's like Al isn't really here if I don't have my hands on her.

It was cute Alondra was worried what Momma would think when I put her bags in my room, but Momma told me she's not oblivious about what's happening at school, and it saves me from having to sneak into the guest room later.

I might've accidentally eaten the cookies Momma made for Al, and I found the secret stash she hid, so I'm doing my best to replicate the recipe. Self-control has never been one of my strengths, especially when it comes to these cookies.

I think I've followed the recipe, and it looks the way it's supposed to, but Al looks skeptical from where she sits on the counter next to me.

"Come on, Al, just try it please."

"Pretty sure there's a reason Coop warned me not to ever eat anything you try to make. Something about food poisoning?" she teases, and of course she brings up the one time

Coop asked me to make dinner, and I didn't check to see if the chicken had expired first.

I roll my eyes, crossing my arms over my chest. She's been sitting on the counter next to me the whole time. "It was one time, and he's never let me forget it. I followed Momma's recipe exactly, and you've been watching me make it," I say, handing Al the recipe, and the little checkmarks I made in pencil next to each step and ingredient.

Al chews on her lower lip, before nodding. "Fine, but if it's bad, never again," she says, and before she can change her mind, I grab a spoon from the drawer, scooping cookie dough on it to hand to her. Al's cheeks are rosy, and her curls are falling over her shoulders.

She takes a small bite, but it's the cringe she tries to hide from me that gives away the fact I messed up somewhere along the way. I reach for her water bottle, handing it to her while also reaching for the recipe card to see where I could have gone wrong.

"I followed the recipe, and it looks fine?" I stare at the bowl, and it looks the exact same as when Momma makes it, but no one makes that face when they eat hers. "I don't know what I got wrong?"

I dip my spoon in, trying it, and the amount of salt I put in this is criminal. I swallow it, grabbing my water immediately to wash away the taste. Holy shit, I must've mixed up the letters.

Alondra coughs, clearing her throat. "I think next time, you should try it before you ask me to," she croaks, and I feel my cheeks heat as I rub the back of my neck. This is beyond embarrassing.

"I'm sorry," I mumble, taking another drink of water while Al plucks the recipe card from my hand.

She scans over it before smiling, shaking her head. "Thank you for trying to make more, but next time, just save me one of your mom's, okay?" she asks, reaching for me.

Alondra never ceases to amaze me. Not once in all of our tutoring sessions did she make me feel like shit for messing up, or taking forever to read through something. She's been patient and kind.

Right now would be the perfect opportunity for her to give me shit for reading the amount of salt wrong, but I've noticed that when it comes to my dyslexia, she never does. Al gives me crap for other shit without hesitation, but this? Never, and aside from Momma and my friends at Wilder, I've never met someone more understanding.

I move closer to Al, unable to fight the urge to have my hands on her. She licks her thumb, wiping away something on my forehead, and I smile at her.

"It's the thought that counts," she says, and if I didn't think I was falling for her before, I think I can admit to myself I am now.

"Thanks for understanding."

"I don't think your mom will be so understanding when she sees the mess you've turned her kitchen into," Alondra points out, and Momma's definitely not going to be happy, but I think she'll be more annoyed I ate the cookies she made for Al.

I nudge Alondra's legs apart, stepping between them to cup her face. "I'll clean it in a little bit," I say, because cleaning everything up is the last thing on my list of priorities right now. Her hazel eyes stand out prominently against her pale skin, but my body thrums with electricity when Al reaches to pull her dark hair over one shoulder.

Sliding my hand down the exposed slope of her neck, I brush my thumb back and forth over the smooth skin, relishing in how Alondra shivers from my touch.

"And what's your plan until then?" she asks, her voice low.

God, she's perfect. "This," I whisper, leaning in to kiss her sweetly.

Her hands cup my face when I sweep my tongue over the seam of her mouth, and she opens to me, giving me the chance to increase the depth of the kiss. My hand holds her hip, pulling Al closer to the edge of the counter while my other rests on the back of her neck. I can taste the salty sweet combination from the dough, but I'm distracted when she bites my lower lip.

Here, I can exist in the delusion she's mine and I'm hers.

A soft groan rises from my throat when Alondra drags her nails over my scalp, and I want her so badly.

I always do.

I tear my mouth from hers, quick to land on her jaw while my fingers slide into her hair, tipping her head back to kiss my way down the curve of her neck to where her pulse is beating fast.

Having Alondra here is better than I could have hoped for.

"Jack," she whimpers, tugging at my hair as she hooks her legs around my waist, pulling me closer.

"Beautiful," I whisper, scraping my teeth teasingly over the spot on her neck I know Al likes. I'm rewarded with a quiet moan, followed by a laugh.

"What are you? A vampire?"

This time I actually bite her, and her legs tighten around me, pressing against my dick, begging for more. I laugh at the same time Alondra does. "I'm going to suck your blood," I mumble against her skin, lifting my head to smile at her.

She's so relaxed, and I dip my hand in the bowl of cookie dough next to her, wiping it on Al's cheek. Alondra gasps in surprise, and she stares widely at me.

"You did not just do that."

I'm too busy smiling at her to notice her reaching for the bag of flour, flicking the white powder on my face and clothes. She pushes me back, leaving a full handprint on my shirt when I look down, sputtering in disbelief while Alondra slides off the counter.

"Then I'll get you back," she threatens, grabbing the spoon she bit off. I catch Al's wrist as she moves to get my face, laughing.

"I don't think so, darlin'," I say, leaning down to kiss her briefly at the same time I reach for the bag of flour myself, grabbing Alondra's ass with the same hand.

She yelps, jumping back from me, twisting to see the large handprint clear as day against the black fabric of her leggings. I laugh harder when Al glares at me, still holding her wrist in the air. "Let me get you back."

Oh? Normally she likes to earn her wins instead of being handed them.

"I should let you wipe cookie dough on my face? I thought you hated it when I let you win?"

"No, I hate it when you cheat."

"And am I cheating now?" I smirk down at her, loving how she's pretending to be mad at me by avoiding my question. "Alondra."

Her hazel eyes narrow. "Don't say my name like that."

"And how am I saying your name?" I ask, flashing Al with an innocent smile. I'm distracted by her pink lips, especially when she wets them.

I'm too late realizing it's a decoy when Alondra catches the side of my nose and jaw with cookie dough.

She is evil, teasing me like that.

I let go of her wrist to pick her up by the waist, lifting Al onto the counter, resuming the same position we were in a few minutes ago. I slant my mouth over hers, and Alondra hooks her arms behind my neck, holding me close, even when I lift my head to look at her.

She looks beautiful—her mouth swollen, cookie dough smeared on her cheek, curls messy, and her eyes fluttering open to meet mine. "You're something else," I whisper, and the way my heart is trying to beat out of my chest should scare me, but it doesn't.

"Good or bad?" Alondra asks, watching me closely.

I inhale a sharp breath, doing my best to memorize everything about her right now. "Good—too good."

She softens, as if somehow understanding entirely what I'm saying between the lines.

I wish I could find the words to explain how Alondra makes me feel, but instead, I kiss her again, leaving them unspoken.

CHAPTER 35

Alondra

JACK WAS SENT on a last-minute errand to the grocery store while I helped his mom make everything else for dinner. He asked if I was okay with staying, but I adore his mom. I even feel a little guilty for wishing my mom were more like her.

"Thanks for helping me with dinner." His mom smiles at me from where she's standing next to me, seasoning the celery and onions in the pan on the stove.

"It's no problem. I'm happy to help." I return the smile as I pinch the crust together in the pie pan.

"I was excited when Jack said you were coming to visit. He talks about you all the time, and he's been so happy to have you here. I'm not sure I've ever seen him care about cleaning as much as he did the day you flew in," she continues, her laughter soft as she pours milk into the pan, turning down the heat while stirring.

"He's not terribly messy, but I have noticed he struggles to shut his dresser drawers," I say, trying not to linger on the part where he talks about me all the time. "Thank you for having me."

"Do you want to take over stirring this for me so I can cut up the chicken?" Ms. Schultz asks, and I take the spoon from her, stirring slowly to mimic her movements from before. "Has Jack taken you skating here yet?"

"Yeah, we went this afternoon," I say, trying not to laugh at the reminder of how Jack challenged me to a race, but then another skater lost their balance right in front of him. He had to swerve to avoid them, making it easy for me to beat him. "Jack said you used to skate? Do you still?" I ask, watching a wistful look appear in her expression.

"I did, but I quit once I found out I was pregnant with Jack. It was a little after my eighteenth birthday. His father wanted me to quit long before that, though," she says, and it's something I already knew, but it doesn't make it any easier to hear the similarities between us.

"My ex didn't like that skating took time away from him," I admit softly, but I don't regret saying them. "It was a mistake to quit, but I've recently started getting back into it."

Her eyes meet mine, and my shoulders relax after seeing the understanding I've never gotten from anyone else. It feels better than the horror and pity I get from everyone else, even though I wish more than anything that she didn't understand.

"I'm glad to hear you're skating again."

"Does all of it ever get easier?" I ask, the words scraping against my throat like sandpaper.

She smiles, nodding as she turns toward the freezer, pulling out a bag of mixed vegetables to set on the counter. "It does. You've already done the hardest thing anyone in that situation can do by leaving."

"Then why does it feel like I'm always waiting for the shoe to drop?"

"It might not seem like it yet, but you'll stop letting moments of fear and panic control your decisions," she says, reaching over to squeeze my hand reassuringly. "Is there something else going on?"

I chew the inside of my cheek, nodding. "Bradley is

having a hard time letting things go—letting me go," I say, correcting myself.

She sets down the knife, reaching to open a cabinet, grabbing two wine glasses and then a bottle of wine out of the fridge. "First of all, please call me Penny—Ms. Schultz makes me feel old. Secondly, this feels like a conversation requiring something stronger than water." Penny pours two hefty glasses of white wine, sliding one toward me.

I take the glass and her kindness, smiling at her. "Thank you."

"The sauce looks thick enough, so let's fold the chicken and vegetables in," she says, holding up the cutting board to push the cubed chicken into the pan, followed by the mixed vegetables. She helps me pour the sauce into the pie pan over the crust, and we work to lay the second layer of crust over the top. I set the pan on the oven rack while Penny sets a timer, before grabbing the wine bottle, motioning for me to follow her to the kitchen table.

"It smells really good."

"It's one of Jack's favorite meals," she says, taking a sip of her wine, a quiet, nervous laugh escaping her a moment later. Penny twists the end of her ponytail around her finger. "Sorry, I'm not trying to make you upset with Jack, but he mentioned what you might be going through. He wasn't trying to break your confidence, and it was only when he needed someone to talk to."

"No, it's okay. I'm not upset with him at all. Honestly, I kind of assumed he talked to you," I say, taking a drink of my wine, the sweetness softening the topic of this conversation. "You were right to get the wine."

"Definitely makes it easier to talk about this," she says, her smile faint as she takes another drink. "I'm not sure how much he's told you about his father, but he wasn't a good man. He liked to cause pain—internally and externally."

"Jack doesn't talk about his dad at all. I know he's in prison, but Jack didn't want to talk about it, so I didn't push."

A faraway look forms in her eyes. "There's a lot of things Jack saw because I was afraid to leave, and I'll never forgive myself for it. He internalized everything David said, and his scars run deep. I wish I'd been able to protect him more."

God, I thought things with Bradley were bad, but at least I didn't have a kid with him. I can't even imagine what I would have done then. "Did he ever touch Jack?" I ask, careful with how I word the question, and she sighs in relief, shaking her head.

"No, he didn't. I was always able to distract him before it could get that far, but the things he saw . . . Jack was the one who called the police. He was nine, and I thought he was asleep, but David's yelling must have woken him up. He had a gun to my head when the police showed up," Penny says, rendering me speechless. I knew whatever happened with his dad was bad, but I didn't imagine this.

God, no wonder he doesn't believe in love. How could he?

"You did protect him. You did the best you could, and you raised a wonderful, kind person," I say, the words getting caught as I force them out. "I can't imagine what it would have been like going through that."

Penny stares at me with a look similar to the one I get from Jack sometimes. "Sadly, I think you do understand, whether you had a child or not in the relationship. When was the first time?"

I take a drink of the wine, washing away the lump in my throat. "Two months in. I thought I loved him, and he loved me, so I told myself I imagined it. I tried to convince myself I'd stumbled instead of facing the fact my boyfriend had shoved me into a wall. Until it happened again, and the shoves turned into fists and a broken cycle of apologies. The mind games he'd play would twist my head so far around, I couldn't even figure out what the truth was by then," I admit, and her smile is grim.

"If I had a dollar for every time I heard, *I'm sorry, it'll never happen again,* I'd be a very rich woman."

I tell Penny everything from the beginning of the relationship to current times, trying to leave out any part regarding my non-relationship with Jack. She is, after all, still his mother.

She listens and doesn't pass judgment, or look at me a certain way. It's the kind of conversation I wish I could have with my mom, but I'm not sure she'd react the same way.

"Have you thought about a restraining order?" she asks once I finish explaining how Bradley has been popping up around campus, Jack's house, and my apartment. I know the guys can't sleep on our couch forever, and eventually, this friends with benefits thing will end with Jack, ending our sleepovers.

"Would it even matter? I feel like all a restraining order would accomplish is making Bradley angry, causing him to lash out," I say, pouring more wine into both of our glasses.

"If he does lash out, the restraining order will protect you. It might be what he needs to know you're serious about being done."

Bradley's warning that we're not over until he says we are echoes through my head.

"Al, you do get a say in when it's over. Consider the restraining order," Penny continues, her tone gentle.

"I'll think about it," I agree, twisting my fingers together. I can see the glimmering lights from their Christmas tree reflecting around their living room from here. I used to love this time of year when I was a kid, but being here with Jack and his mom is making some of the magic return.

"One of my biggest regrets is letting Jack go on like this for as long as I have. I was so busy trying to make myself okay again to be there for Jack after David went to prison, I didn't realize the depth of how it affected Jack until he was in high school."

"Like how he doesn't believe in love?" I ask, turning back toward her, eying his mom with curiosity. They're so similar. I know his mom was young when she had Jack, but all of his best features he got from her. They have the same light brown hair and piercing blue eyes, framed by the longest lashes I've ever seen. His heart is incredibly warm and giving, and there's no doubt where it came from, even if Jack thinks he doesn't believe in love.

"That among other things, but I hope you won't give up on him."

"What do you mean?" I ask, trying to understand if Penny's saying what I think she is.

She chuckles, and I think she sees right through my bull-shit. "Alondra, I know my son, and you make him light up in a way I've never seen. Just give Jack some time to come around on the whole love thing." Penny gives me a quick wink, causing my cheeks to erupt into flames, and I haven't had enough wine for this. Did I say something to give away whatever the hell is going on between us?

"I don't feel that way about Jack," I protest, taking a long drink.

"I never said you did."

Yeah, she's saying one thing, but implying another. I don't have a chance to ask more because the front door opens, and Jack steps into the kitchen a few moments later, grocery bags in hand. "Next time, I vote we don't have dessert. I had to go to three different stores because everywhere was still out of everything after the holidays," he says, setting the bags on the counters, just as the timer on the stove goes off.

"Perfect timing. Thanks for going and letting me borrow Al. She's wonderful," Penny says, patting Jack on the cheek.

His eyebrows raise at the empty bottle of wine sitting on the table, and our two glasses. "I was out running around so you two could drink?" Jack mocks, his eyes shining as he smiles at me.

"If you stopped eating all of the cookies, you wouldn't have had to go out for dessert," I remind him, and Jack scoffs, rolling his eyes.

"I have not eaten all of the cookies," he argues, but his mom laughs, pulling the chicken pot pie out of the oven.

"Sure, sweetie. We must have a monster who stuffs them all into his mouth when no one is looking," she teases, and Jack nods.

"Totally must be it," he says, and I laugh, drinking my wine. "So what were y'all talking about?" Jack asks, and Penny grins, winking at me.

"Wouldn't you like to know?"

"Well, yeah, Momma. It's why I asked."

She waves him off, ignoring his question as he walks behind me, his hand drifting across my back. "Dinner just needs to cool off for a bit, so why don't y'all go hang out, and I'll call for you when it's ready. After the mess yesterday, I'd rather handle the rest on my own."

I can't really blame her for that. We got a little distracted before we could clean up, and Penny definitely got home as we were still trying to clean up all the flour we splashed everywhere.

"Are you sure you don't need help? I can . . ." He wisely stops talking after the look his mom gives him, and he laughs. "Got it. Going to go hang with Alondra."

Penny smiles at me, and I'm really glad we had a chance to talk about everything. She's given me a lot to think about. "Thanks for the help, Al. I can see why he likes you."

Jack stumbles over literally nothing as his cheeks turn bright pink. He grumbles something under his breath I can't hear, and I follow Jack into his room where he flops onto the bed, kicking off his shoes in the process.

"Since when have you started calling me by my full

name?" I ask, sitting on the edge of the bed. I'm trying not to think about everything his mom told me about his dad, but Jack makes more sense to me now.

"Since you told me how much it bothers you," he replies, smirking at me. His fingers wrap around my wrist, gently pulling me to settle into the spot next to him.

"It doesn't bother me," I insist, even though the way he says it totally does.

He rolls his eyes, his chest shaking with quiet laughter. "Sure. Whatever you say."

I stick my tongue out at him, pulling my phone out of my pocket to respond to a few texts from earlier, before setting my phone down and rolling to face him. "Is it bad I don't want to go back to Minnesota?"

"No, I don't want you to go back either. I'm enjoying having you all to myself," he admits, and I wish he could see himself how I see him—how everyone sees him.

So the game continues. "I'm glad you and Momma are getting along."

"Does she not get along with many people?" I ask, doubting it from everything I know about her.

Jack's eyes widen for a moment, and he shakes his head. "No, Momma does. It's just nice to see you two get along. She seems to really like you."

"She's great, and I know I keep saying it, but your mom really loves you, Jack."

"I know," he says, his eyes trailing over my face. "She was right about you, though. You are wonderful."

I smile at him, leaning forward to press my lips against his for a moment. "Thanks."

"Will you tell me what you and Momma talked about?"

"Nope," I say, laughing as I cup the stubble lining his jaw.

Jack's protests about how it's not fair and he deserves to know send me into a fit of laughter. I'm glad I came here, but more importantly, I'm really glad I met Jack in the first place.

Maybe Penny's right. A restraining order might do me some good. The pictures from our relationship and the texts I have are more than enough proof to hopefully get it granted, at least temporarily.

How can I expect Jack to get over his demons when I'm still dealing with mine?

"Do you ever wonder what would have happened if you didn't find me in my father's office that morning?" I ask, gazing at him with wonder.

Jack groans, playing with the ends of my hair. "I think I'd be kicking myself for not pushing harder to get your phone number, and I probably would have failed Comp II again because of my stupid dyslexia. I think my life would be a fucking disaster if I hadn't found you in his office, Alex," Jack jokes, using the wrong name I let him believe was mine. His words should make me laugh or at the very least, happy, but all they do is cause my heart to ache.

I rest my head on his chest, unable to keep looking at him unless I want to word vomit my feelings all over the place. It'd be so easy to say how I feel, but I don't want to lose him. I can't, and if I tell him now how I feel, then I *will* lose Jack. "In my defense, you asked if my name was Alex, and I didn't correct you."

He doesn't respond for a moment. "But most of all, I'd be missing you." His arm tightens around my back, holding me in place. I close my eyes, feeling unshed tears burn in them as I fall deeper and deeper into my feelings for Jack.

I think I'm past the point of no return.

Fuck.

Why couldn't he just be an asshole?

CHAPTER 36

Jack

AFTER SPENDING ALMOST a week straight with Alondra in Texas, I was desperate to go back to Minnesota. I loved seeing her in all my favorite places, always being able to touch her or kiss her whenever I wanted.

Now since getting back, I've become a bit of a grouch as we try to line up our schedules with my hockey schedule, and I'm going through withdrawals. It's different from spending nearly every waking minute with her.

A part of me was surprised by how easy it was to spend that much time together, because even spending long amounts of time with Dylan requires breaks, but I never needed that with Al.

It feels like since we got back to Wilder, we're only alone for a few moments before someone needs something from either of us. Al was helping me look over an assignment the other night, and I was about to lean over and kiss her when her phone rang with a call from Macy because Chad broke up with her again. I know her best friend comes before me, but it's pathetic how jealous I am of Macy right now.

By the time Al came back that night, I was already dead

asleep when she crawled into my bed, and I had to get up before her the next morning for hockey.

We were studying the other day and I was just about to lean over and kiss her when Sara came in, claiming that she needed help on a paper for one of her classes.

Tonight, I'm at Twin City with Seth and Dylan, sipping my water as they drink their beers. Coop had a headache, and Nate had to meet with a group from one of his classes for a project, or he'd be here too.

Seth is complaining about how they lost their bowl game, and I feel bad for him because he's a damn good quarterback.

I'm only half listening to the conversation, though, distracted by checking my phone to see if Al is going to come over tonight.

Dylan kicks me under the table. "Just because you keep staring at your phone doesn't mean she's going to text back."

Seth snorts, and I flip him off, turning my phone over to prove a point that I don't care that much, but I do. "I was waiting to hear from your mom what time she wants me to come over," I say, my voice dripping with sarcasm, causing Dylan to frown.

"Dude, does she know how miserable you are without her?" he asks, and I roll my eyes, trying not to look at my phone again.

"Are you talking about the cowgirl? You're still with her?" Seth asks, grinning.

"She has a name, and no. We're just friends," I say, tapping my fingers against my glass.

"Right, you're totally just friends." Dylan snorts, takes a swig of his drink. "Jack gets a little protective of her," he warns Seth, giving him a quick side glance.

"I think I remember him jumping down my throat when I met her. If it's the same girl anyway. It's Al, right?" Seth asks, and Dylan nods in confirmation as I glance at my phone lying face down, my hands itching to check it to see if she messaged back. "What's it short for? Allie?"

I can't help chuckling because it was my initial guess too. "Alondra."

Fuck, I love saying her name. I'm about done calling her Al, because even thinking about the way she looks at me when I say her real name is enough to make me hard.

Seth blinks, doing a double take. "Wait, are you sure that's her name?"

"Um, yeah. We've been friends with her for over four months now, I think we know her name," Dylan says, answering so I don't have to.

He shakes his head, scratching the back of his neck. "There's this guy on O-line dating a girl named Alondra. Just odd you both are talking to a girl with the same name."

I suck in a sharp breath, but it's not like I didn't already know Bradley was telling people they're still together. "Same girl, but they've been broken up for about a year."

Seth doesn't look any less confused. "Wait, are you serious? Honestly, it makes sense they're not together since no one has seen her around. Good for her for breaking up with him, though. The way he talks about her is disgusting." He grimaces, taking a sip of his beer, and I try to keep my anger in check.

At least I know Johnny isn't friends with him anymore. He came to me a couple days after the day at the rink and apologized for bringing him there. Said he'd never seen Bradley like that, and he didn't want to be friends with someone who could talk about women that way.

Dylan casts a quick glance at me. "We've got a pretty good idea."

I'm positive Coop told him what happened because I refused to repeat it. Part of me wishes I'd hit him, but the other part of me is glad Coop held me back. I don't know if I would have been able to stop once I started.

"He's a fucking asshole," I say, taking a drink of water to try washing away the bitter taste lingering in my mouth.

"Can't say I'm a fan of the guy, but he's sure saved my ass from getting flattened a few times," Seth says, picking at the peeling label on his bottle. "What I don't get is why tell people they're still together? No one cares if you get dumped, but it's fucking weird to still claim her a year later."

I bite my tongue, not trusting myself to say anything without giving away what he would do to Al. I know how hard it is for her to talk to people about it, and I don't think she'd appreciate me telling Seth anything.

I look at my phone again as Dylan answers, "Who knows."

"Who do you guys play next?" Seth asks as the music playing in the background changes.

"We fly to Boston Friday morning, and get back Saturday night," I say, glad for a change in conversation.

"I hate away games. I mean traveling is fun and all, but it gets exhausting when it's every other week," Dylan says, and I roll my eyes.

"Flying is better than the bus," I remind him. I still wish it were a home game, though. Just means more time away from Al.

Goddamn, when did I start measuring time on whether it meant I got to see Al or not?

"Fair."

I'm a little worried about sitting next to Coach on the plane. He hasn't been acting differently toward me since Al's trip to Texas, but we also haven't had to sit next to each other for three hours yet. Still, I wouldn't trade the time with her for anything.

I finally cave, checking my phone again, but there's no notifications.

"Schultz, are you sure you guys are just friends, because

you're definitely acting like you're in a relationship," Seth muses, and Dylan laughs.

"No, they're just friends because Jack is still too much of a pussy to admit he has feelings and wants a relationship with her."

I scowl at him because he doesn't get it. *I'm trying.* I'm trying so fucking hard to get there with her, but I freeze up every time I think about putting that label on us. Relationships mean falling in love, and love leads to heartbreak. I don't want to hurt Alondra. It's the last thing I would ever want to do.

I'm trying to protect Al because I'm terrified of what I feel for her. She deserves someone who knows how to love her, but the idea of Alondra being with anyone else causes my stomach to twist in knots.

What can I offer her, though? All I know is the destruction from loving someone.

Momma was a ghost walking through life for months after Dad went to prison. She tried her best, and I was never neglected, but she was destroyed.

Al has been through the same hell, and I want her to only know happiness.

I'm trying to get there, but I can't promise her anything, especially when I don't even know if that's what she wants from me? For all I know, Al doesn't want to be anything more than my fuck buddy, even if it hasn't felt like that ever.

"Fuck off, Dylan," I snap, tugging a hand through my hair. I'm being a dick, but Dylan's pushing too hard about this. My phone vibrates on the table, and I feel a rush of relief at the sight of her name. *Thank god.*

ALONDRA

Can I sleep over?

JACK

always

I slip into my coat, ignoring the look Dylan gives me, while Seth is too busy eyeing a girl at the bar. "See y'all later," I say, getting up from the table.

"Tell Al I said hi," Seth says, shooting me a quick wink.

"Yeah, I'm not wasting my time with her talking about you," I say, waving at a couple people on my way out who call my name, trying to get my attention.

I've just pulled into the driveway when Al parks on the side of the road, and my smile is wide as I watch her climb out, her furry hood covering her face. She's cursing about the cold when I walk to meet her, too impatient to wait for her to get to me first.

"Shit, were you not home?" she asks, a slight frown marring her full lips I'm desperate to kiss.

"I was at the bar with Dylan and Seth," I answer, pressing a short kiss to her lips, trying to turn her frown upside down.

"You didn't have to leave. I could have hung out with Coop or Nate."

Now I'm the one frowning. "Seriously?"

Al giggles, tipping her head up at me. "Am I not allowed to hang out with your roommates?"

Honestly, I'm glad they're friends, but it doesn't mean I want to share her with them. I open the front door and hang my coat up on the rack Coop insisted we get, kicking my shoes off without putting them on the rack. Coop will have a coronary, but he'll get over it.

Al hangs hers next to mine, and then before she can spout any more shit about hanging out with them instead of me, I pull her toward the stairs.

"Jack," she says, laughing as she keeps up with me. "You can slow down."

"I've hardly seen you all week, and I want all the time I can get with you," I say, looking back at her, only to find her staring at my ass.

Alondra grins at me, shrugging her shoulders as she climbs the stairs. "What? You think you're the only one who gets to stare?"

"I'm glad you know what a great ass I have," I say, unashamed when I start taking the stairs two at a time as Al laughs again behind me.

"At least you know it," she says, following me into my room, and I shut the door, locking it in case we have any unexpected visitors.

The moment I turn around, Alondra is pulling me down to kiss her. I don't miss a beat, tugging her against me, and Al smiles against my mouth. "How's Macy?" I ask, moving us toward the bed.

"With Ellie."

I press another short kiss to her mouth. "Should you still be there?" I ask, straightening out of reach of her addicting lips. I can't help smiling when I realize she's wearing one of my sweatshirts. My god, Alondra is my ruin.

"They're probably going to be together again by tomorrow morning. I did the shots with her last night, and the wine the night before with the sappy movies, but holy fuck, Jack, I couldn't take it anymore. Even just thinking about drinking makes me want to vomit. I had to get out of that apartment, and I missed you a lot," she says, dropping her head against my chest, wrapping her arms around my torso.

I drag my fingers through her hair. "If it were a contest, I think I'd have you beat for missing you more," I say and Al sits on the bed, her face softening before she blinks, smiling mischievously at me.

"Well, isn't that good for my ego? Jack Schultz missed me."

I really did.

She unbuttons the front of my jeans without looking away from me while she pulls them down. Alondra's hand dips into my underwear, and I swallow my groan as her hand closes around me. "Nope, not how the rules work," I choke out when she swipes her thumb over the sensitive tip.

Al doesn't listen and moves her hand up and down anyway, and I don't stop her. "Didn't realize there were rules for orgasms," she says, giving me a sweet smile.

Oh fuck, I think she's trying to kill me.

"Unwritten rules for guys, darlin'—always give before receiving."

I love giving, and seeing Al come because of me is almost better than sex. The keyword: *almost*.

"Fuck the rules. Maybe I want to give before receiving," Alondra says, and it's her confidence that shuts down any logical argument for why I should say no. I don't want to take any power away from her in these moments, especially ones she initiates.

The last of my self-control slips away when Al pulls my briefs down around my thighs, and her fucking mouth is sucking and licking. I tangle my fingers in her hair, quiet groans leaving my mouth as she makes me delirious with want and need.

"Look at me, pretty boy," Alondra says, and I look down, watching as she pumps my cock in her hand.

She's a dream come true.

"Tell me what you want," she says, and my hips jerk, thrusting into her hand.

"You," I say, exhaling, and Al takes the tip in her mouth, flitting her tongue over it as I bite back a moan. She's perfect, but also an evil mastermind, bringing me to the edge before slowing down again, taking her time. I seriously think she's trying to torture me.

"*Alondra, please,*" I beg, panting when she hums around me. The sensation is fucking incredible, but I lose control when she decides to take pity on me, tightening the pressure of her mouth, and I come hard enough to see stars in my vision.

I'm out of breath when Alondra tucks me back into my pants after pulling them up for me, and I feel like I'm made of jelly.

"Goddamn, you're mean," I breathe out, collapsing on the bed next to her as she laughs.

"Consider that my apology for not being around much the past few days. I wanted to make it last for you." Al grins, and I shake my head at a loss of words.

"You didn't have to do that because you weren't around. I'm perfectly capable of taking care of myself. I'm just happy you're here," I finally manage to say, reaching for her hand, lacing our fingers together.

"Jack, did you ever consider I wanted to? I promise you, I wouldn't have done it if I didn't want to," she says, and a horrible thought crosses my mind I should have thought of when I first asked her this.

Does she want things to be purely physical? What if sex—*as great as it is with her*—is all this becomes? I love being Al's friend, and just sitting in the same room as her. I like going to the library and bringing her coffee. I think she likes all of those things too, or at least I hope she does.

"Okay," I say, squeezing her hand. I push the thought to the back of my mind because Al is the last person who would make this all about sex.

Al shifts up to lean against the headboard, and I move my head to rest it in her lap. She runs her fingers through my hair, and it feels good to be taken care of like this.

"How are Dylan and Seth?"

It feels like a cop-out to admit I have feelings for her by saying I spent the majority of the night waiting for Al to text me back. I also don't want to sour her mood now that I finally have Alondra alone by telling her about the piece of shit she dated. "They're good. It was mostly just catching up after the long break."

"Are you excited for the games this weekend?"

"Yeah, I think it'll be fun." It sounds like hell because I don't want to leave her again.

"C'mon, buddy, you have to give me more of an answer than *it'll be fun,*" she teases, laughing quietly, and I get stuck on the word buddy.

Fuck, why couldn't I just spit it out that night? Why did I have to ask to be friends with benefits with Alondra?

"I'm going to love kicking Boston's asses on the ice."

"That's better." Alondra smiles at me, and I wonder if this is what love is supposed to feel like?

I'm not sure how Coach could ever think she's a distraction when Alondra's actually the best damn thing to happen to me in a long time.

Shit, Dylan's right. I need to pull my head out of my ass before I lose Al because I'm too scared to admit that I've developed real feelings for her.

CHAPTER 37

Alondra

THE FIRST NIGHT Jack was in Boston, I received a text from Bradley asking if I'd finally decided to listen to him, and I had enough.

I'd spent a lot of time after my conversation with Penny thinking about filing a restraining order, and I can't always rely on Jack and his friends to help keep me safe. So the first thing I did Saturday morning was head to the police station to ask for help filing a restraining order until I could go to the courts on Monday.

The pictures I had saved of the abuse during our relationship, the threatening messages, and the fact that Bradley had shown up at my apartment were enough for the officer I spoke to at the station to contact a judge for an emergency protective order. For the first time in a while, I didn't feel like I had to look over my shoulder. It was easier to breathe.

Jack's mom was right. This is something I needed to do for myself to take some of the power back.

I deserve to feel safe in my apartment without the fear that Bradley could show up at any time. I should get to be free with my friends, and not have to worry he'll make a scene, or act like we're still together.

If Bradley contacts me or comes within a hundred feet of me, all I have to do is call the police and he'll be arrested.

I'm worried this could send him into a spiral, but I feel better knowing I've taken the first steps in making sure Bradley knows I'm serious about him leaving me alone.

Macy's getting lunch with her parents, and I'm honestly excited to tell her. She wanted me to do this a year ago, but I wasn't ready.

Seeing how Penny picked up the pieces to make a life for herself and Jack showed me I can take this first step. As she so eloquently said, *You'll stop letting those moments of fear and panic control your decisions.* I'm done letting Bradley scare me into submission.

I texted Macy and Ellie to ask if they want to get celebratory drinks tonight because I had big news, and they've been blowing up my phone for the last thirty minutes asking if it has to do with me and Jack. I rolled my eyes and ignored them because I want to keep it a surprise.

Nate asked Ellie to water his plants while they're out of town for their away game, but she said she'd be home soon. I think I'm ready to tell her everything.

It's crazy how much a person can change in a few months. If anyone had asked me at the beginning of the school year if I thought I'd have a new group of friends, consisting mainly of hockey players, hooking up with a guy I'm crazy for, or filing a restraining order against Bradley, I would have laughed in their faces.

Maybe I'm crazy, but I also feel more like myself than I have in a long time.

"Where the fuck did I leave my water bottle?" I ask, walking around my apartment for the third time, trying to find the stupid thing. I know I could just get a glass from the cupboard, but I'd rather just figure out what I did with my water bottle.

Did I leave it in the car earlier?

After another lap, I admit defeat, slipping into one of my jackets and slippers, grabbing my keys out of the bowl on the counter to run out to my car quick.

I'm zipping up the coat as I flip the lock, opening the door, so I don't realize Bradley's standing on the other side until it's too late, and my heart stops. I try to grab the door to shut it, but he shoves his way in, tossing a crumpled piece of paper on the ground.

Oh my god.

"A fucking restraining order?" His voice is deathly calm, shutting the door behind him.

The walls feel like they're shrinking in on me, caging me in place. "I'm going to call the police. You're violating the restraining order," I say, willing my voice to be strong, but when I feel for my phone in my pocket, it's not there. Fuck, where's my phone?

Why is today the day I'm forgetting everything?

"They served me at the fucking stadium!" Bradley bellows, his eyes glittering with rage. I flinch backward, tripping over my backpack next to the couch. "Do you know how embarrassing it was to get served in front of my coaches and teammates? You need to drop this shit right now. Tell them it was a mistake and you lied."

My hands are shaking as I try to look for where I could have left my phone, but I feel cold when I see it sitting on the counter behind Bradley. Oh my god, this is really bad.

"I loved you, or at least I thought I did. I made so many mistakes during our relationship, but this isn't a mistake. I'm not lying or hiding how you used to treat me like I was your personal punching bag. You have been threatening me for months, but if you go now, maybe I won't call the police," I say, my voice starting small, but I'm not letting him do this. I don't have to take it anymore.

His eyes widen as he stares at me, stunned, and I move to

dart around him, desperate to use the element of surprise to get past him to my phone, but Bradley's reflexes kick in.

Bradley's arm flies out, knocking me to the side, but he sends me sprawling into the barstools with a crash. The pain in my side is sharp, and tears immediately spring to my eyes. I try to blink them away, my breath stolen.

I'm slow to push myself up, and Bradley laughs, the sound a low warning. "What? You start fucking Jack, and you think you're worth something now? Daddy still doesn't love you, and you think getting with his player is going to fix that? Angel, you're never going to be enough."

"Fuck you," I spit out at him, feeling a tear drip down my cheek.

Bradley reaches out to grasp my chin tightly. "Does he let you act like this? Why the hell do you think it's okay with me? You used to know better."

"I do know better," I grit out through clenched teeth, "than to let someone like you tell me what I'm worth."

His grip tightens, causing a whimper to escape from my lips. "This fucking piece of paper doesn't mean shit. If you think it protects you, then good for you. Jack is fair game, and it'd be a shame if something were to happen." I jerk my chin out of his grasp.

Fear paralyzes me at the idea of Bradley hurting Jack. Convincing him this isn't worth a fight will be hard enough, but Bradley's left marks today, and Jack's patience only goes so far. "He's done nothing to you. Leave him alone."

He smiles at me as the pain in my side throbs. "Maybe if you ask nicely."

"Please leave Jack alone." I think I'm going to be sick.

"*No.* It's not very fun to hear, is it?" he taunts and I glare at him.

"At least I'm not going to push you down any stairs for saying it." I smart off before my head snaps back after his fist hits my eye. I gasp, covering my mouth to stop myself from saying anything more.

I can already feel my eye start to swell shut, and Bradley stands up, taking a few steps back.

"You tell the police I did this, and Jack's career is over before it starts," Bradley warns as the tears spill quickly down my cheeks. I'm unable to stop them now. He leaves right after, not bothering to give me a second look.

He's never hit me in the face before.

I pull myself up, scrambling for my phone. I can't believe how stupid I was. I know better.

My face is throbbing, and honestly, everything hurts when I try to fix the stools, but I think a leg must be broken because it falls to the ground again after I stand it up.

I should call the police, but will Bradley really hurt Jack? I wouldn't exactly put it past him, especially after this. A part of me had forgotten what it felt like to be so powerless.

The door swings open and I hate how I flinch, spinning to see out of my good eye who's there. "Sorry, Nate has so many plants, and you wouldn't believe the detailed instructions he left, but I'm ready for this surprise! Is Macy back yet?" Ellie asks, kicking her boots off, but her hand flies to cover her mouth when she turns, spotting me. "Oh my god, what the hell happened?" The coat in her hand falls to the floor, and she moves to look closer.

I inhale a ragged breath, wiping my nose on the back of my sleeve, but I wince, the pain in my face spiking. "Looks worse than it is," I say, wishing I'd never filed the restraining order in the first place.

I should have left things alone.

"Al, we need to call the police. This isn't okay," she says, her voice trembling.

"We can't," I whisper, my voice hoarse as more tears fall.

"They can help," Ellie argues, and I shake my head, but it causes my face to throb.

"I'm okay," I say, but it might be the most unconvincing lie I've ever told.

I hate myself for being weak enough to think Bradley ever loved me.

"Let's get some ice on your face, and you can tell me what happened," Ellie says, and I catch a glimpse of the front door.

"Did you lock the door?"

Ellie steps away, checking the door, but she looks wary when she turns around to face me. "Al, are we safe to stay here?"

"I don't know. I don't think he'll come back here," I say, but I've been wrong before. "I'm sorry."

"What are you apologizing for?" she asks, an incredulous look forming on her face. Ellie moves into the kitchen, grabbing an ice pack, and wraps it in a hand towel before offering it to me. "Do you want me to call Jack?"

"No," I blurt out, because the last thing that needs to happen right now is for one of us to tell Jack when there's nothing he can do about it. "His game is in a few hours, and they're flying back tonight. He'll find out then."

I've never been more glad Ellie wasn't home when Bradley showed up. I don't think having a witness would have changed anything.

"Should I take you to the hospital?" Ellie asks, but then she kneels down, picking up the piece of paper that ruined everything. "What is this?"

"A restraining order," I say, turning around to move toward the bathroom in my room with my phone in hand. "Be right back," I mumble, shutting the door behind me, giving myself a few moments to not be fine.

When I look in the mirror, I don't feel better seeing my reflection. My eye is completely swollen shut, and my cheekbone is bright red. I take a few pictures, trying to get this over with, but my side has a red mark, and I'm positive they're bruised, but hoping they're not broken.

The pictures are especially important now after filing the restraining order. I don't know if I'll use them because I don't want anything to happen to Jack, but it's comforting to know I have proof. I'm not crazy or imagining it.

Ellie knocks on my door a moment later, poking her head in. "Al, I know you said you didn't want to, but I think we should call the police," she says again, and I sigh, moving to lie on the bed, trying not to jostle my ribs or face too much.

"It'll make things worse, trust me," I say, and I don't need to look at Ellie to know she doesn't agree with me.

"Please tell me how this can get worse? Your ex gave you a black eye after you filed a restraining order."

I don't say anything about my ribs. It doesn't change anything.

Bradley's warning rings clear in my mind, and I can't be the reason Jack gets hurt. There's a lot I can't control, but I can control this. This isn't what Jack signed up for.

"Will you stay with me please? I really don't want to be alone right now," I say, avoiding her question, but she doesn't ask again.

"Whatever you need, Al."

This isn't how today was supposed to go.

But I guess that's life.

You hit a high point, and then the only way left to go is down.

CHAPTER 38

Jack

I'M LIVID, going out of my mind with worry. Once we got off the plane, I checked my phone to see if Al sent me anything since I hadn't heard from her all day, but instead, I had a series of messages from Seth that turned my blood cold.

Every single text and call I made to Al while we loaded into the shuttle back to Wilder went unanswered, and my brain immediately thought of the worst-case scenario.

The text Coop showed me from his sister made me feel a little better because at least I know where Al is, and she's not alone. Still, I haven't been able to catch my breath since I read Seth's text about Bradley being served at the stadium in front of everyone.

Why didn't Al tell me she was filing a restraining order? Did something happen she didn't tell me about?

I'm taking the stairs two at a time, desperate to make sure she's okay. I've been on autopilot, my anxiety radiating off me, but I know nothing will make it better. Not until I see Alondra for myself.

Why haven't I heard from her? The only possible reason is something must've happened, and she didn't want to be a fucking distraction from hockey. It's the only thing that makes sense to me, but it makes me angry because I'd prefer anything over the silence causing my mind to run rampant.

I knock on the door, the brutal chill in the air finally hitting me now that I've stopped moving, waiting for someone to answer.

The sound of the deadbolt makes me feel a little better, but I'm wishing the girls had said yes when Coop offered to install a chain lock for them last month. The way Macy looks at me after opening the door, tells me everything I need to know without her saying a goddamn thing.

Macy steps back to let me in, and my head is spinning. The adrenaline pumping through my veins isn't helping me see clearly, but I can't imagine it's good.

"What happened? Why didn't either of you call me?" I slip out of my shoes, dropping my keys on the counter as I wait for them to answer me.

"I wanted to, but Al asked us not to." Ellie's lower lip trembles, and she wipes her nose on the back of her sleeve.

"Jack, she's sleeping," Macy says, and I look around the apartment for any sign of what happened. I feel nauseous at the sight of the broken pieces of a barstool set inside a trash bag. *What the hell did he do to my girl?*

Why didn't Al let them call me?

"Where is she?" I ask, my voice cracking, and Macy glances at Alondra's door. I take a few steps, but Ellie darts in front of me, putting her hand up to stop me.

I'm trying not to take my fear and anger about the situation out on the tall blonde in front of me, but I need to see Al.

"Let Macy see if she's awake before you barge in, okay?"

My vision blurs, and the crushing weight on my chest presses harder on my lungs, making it difficult for me to draw in a breath to calm myself while I wait for the all-clear.

How fucking bad was today if they're stopping me from going in right away?

I know Al has been crystal clear about not wanting me to act like her bodyguard, but I didn't do enough to protect Momma from Dad, and I promised things would be different with Alondra.

I move closer, hearing Macy ask if she can let me in, and it takes every ounce of my self-control to wait for Al's answer.

"It's okay."

Thank fuck. I push the door open further, stepping past Macy to get in the room, and I nearly fall to my knees when the light from the hallway shows the damage done to her face. One of her eyes is a hideous shade of purple, swollen shut, and my stomach rolls. I shut the door, reaching for the light switch, on a one-track mindset to make sure she's okay and then I'm going to murder Bradley for laying even a finger on her.

"So how were the games?" Alondra asks, twisting her hands in her lap as she watches me.

Gentle. Be gentle with her. She's not the one you're upset with.

"I'm going to kill him," I promise, dragging a hand over my jaw, feeling my entire body tremble with hatred.

Al's shoulders sink, and I take a step forward to close the gap between us. Her cheekbone is an angry red beneath her eye, and I wish I'd been here. I know why I wasn't, and I'm aware of how important hockey is, but Al was hurt, and I wasn't here to stop it.

"Don't say that, Jack. You know better than to sink to his level because of me."

I look to the spot next to Alondra on the bed, and as if understanding the silent question, she nods.

She doesn't have to tell me twice, and I perch on the side of her mattress, reaching to gently brush a stray curl out of Al's face. How could he do this to her?

"He *hurt* you. I saw the broken stool, and they said you wouldn't let them call me. Al, what the hell happened?" I ask, struggling to keep my emotions in check. Losing my mind doesn't help Alondra.

Hesitation and skepticism fill her bruised features, and she glances down at her lap. "I filed a restraining order after he sent me a text last night, and Bradley was mad. I wasn't thinking, and I went to look for my water bottle in my car, but Bradley was standing on the other side of the door. I'm okay," she says, her words slurring together at a few parts from how quickly she's trying to explain. I want to wrap my arms around her, but instead I turn, putting my head in my hands. "I'm okay," Al repeats, but it only makes me feel worse.

She shouldn't be trying to make me feel better about this.

"Why didn't you call me?" I ask, and the bed dips behind me as Alondra moves closer. I should have known when I didn't hear from her all day that something was wrong.

I should have been here, and maybe this wouldn't have happened.

"There wasn't anything you could do. At some point, I have to stand on my own," she explains, pressing her lips to the back of my shoulder, yet it does little to ease me. "Jack, we've talked about this. I need a friend, not a bodyguard."

It's not fair for her to remind me when she's sitting here with a fucking black eye and who knows what else. "As your *friend*, I get to worry about you. It's my decision," I say, leaving no room for argument. "Is it just your face?" I ask, twisting to look at her.

She nods, and the weight on my chest loosens, relieved by her answer. I would've thought it was worse.

"I think my eye is a badge of honor," she tries to joke, cracking a smile.

"Don't try to make light of this," I say, guilt wreaking havoc on my internal war to stay right here with her. I should have been here to stop him. What good am I if I can't protect Al when she needs me the most? "I'm sorry I wasn't here."

"I don't want you to be sorry. It's going to be over soon."

"What did the police say? Did they arrest him for violating the restraining order?" I ask, and her entire body stiffens. *No.* I can tell by looking at Al she didn't, but I need to hear her say it. "Al, you called the police, right?"

"No," Alondra says, trying to straighten her shoulders, and my brain malfunctions.

"He showed up here after being served a restraining order, entered your apartment without being invited in, hit you in the face after spewing whatever bullshit I'm sure came out of his mouth, and you didn't call the police?"

"Jack—"

I shake my head, needing to move to get rid of the energy begging to be let out. I stand, trying to make sense of why she wouldn't have called. He hit her in the fucking face, and she didn't call?

"Did he threaten you?" I ask, turning toward her, and Al is sitting there like a statue. This is it. He threatened her, but with what? "What did he say to you?"

My mind is spinning out with possibilities as she clamps her jaw shut, refusing to say anything. I drag my fingers through my hair, shoving aside the tiredness and ache setting into my bones from my game earlier.

"Alondra, if he threatened you, that's all the more reason to call the police." I'm trying to soften my delivery, but I'm terrified it won't make a difference in what I say.

"I'm not calling them."

"Then I'm calling them," I argue, and the shrug she gives me makes my heart crack.

"Fine. I'll deny anything happened. I'm clumsy and I tripped over my own feet, hitting my face on the edge of the counter."

My jaw falls open, staring at her in disbelief. How can Al say that?

I move to kneel in front of my beautiful girl, taking both of her hands in mine. "Al, I'm begging you. Please report this. *Please*," I beg, hoping she'll change her mind.

There's more to this than Al's admitting, but she shakes her head, looking away.

"I'm sorry, but I can't."

CHAPTER 39

Alondra

I HADN'T HEARD from Bradley in over a week now, and I know Jack is upset with me for not calling the police, but I did follow through with going to the courthouse to file for a long-term protective order. I got a lot of looks because of my face, and the judge was quick to grant a continuance of the emergency protective order until a trial date is set where Bradley can argue against the protective order.

Jack has asked me a couple more times what Bradley is holding over my head, but I've refused to answer.

It was hard to explain to Ellie everything that transpired during my relationship with Bradley, but she's thankfully been really understanding about it and wasn't upset with me for not being able to tell her sooner. She should be mad because all I've been doing is running through the possibilities in my mind of what would have happened if Ellie had answered the door for Bradley instead.

I only made it two days—which was honestly longer than I expected—before Jack found out my ribs were bruised after I rolled the wrong way, and I didn't bite back the groan of pain. He saw right through me when I refused to take my shirt off in front of him, and by some miracle, I convinced

Jack to stay with me instead of getting himself in a world of trouble.

There's nothing good that will come from anyone confronting Bradley, especially Jack.

I've gotten used to waking up cocooned in Jack's embrace, and despite wishing it wasn't under false pretenses, there's nowhere else I'd rather wake up than in his bed with his arm slung over my hip.

Right now, I'm not sure I could get up even if I wanted to. My internal alarm always wakes me before my actual alarm, but from all the nights I've spent sleeping next to Jack, I've learned that he doesn't wake up before his alarm, but once he's up, there's no falling back asleep.

I enjoy the quiet moments in the morning before he's awake because it's even easier to pretend he's mine and I'm his. There's none of the additional shit involved with both of our pasts haunting us. If only it could be this way in real life.

My phone starts to vibrate next to my pillow, and Macy's right on time. I slip out of Jack's grip, careful not to wake him as I answer.

"Happy birthday, bitch!" she shrieks into the phone.

In all truthfulness, I hate my birthday. I don't like celebrating it. Dad was never there for it because it was in the middle of season, and the one day that was supposed to be my day, never was. It, along with everything else, still belonged to hockey.

Macy is obsessed with birthdays, though. It doesn't matter whose it is, she loves to celebrate them. It's the only time she willingly wakes up early. Macy's goal is to be the first person to tell someone, *Happy birthday*.

"Thanks, Macy," I whisper, kind of surprised that Chad is chill with her being so loud so early in the morning.

"We'll have to go all out for this one because your twenty-first was nowhere near the celebration it should've been," she says, and Macy isn't wrong. Bradley didn't want to go out, insisting we stay in, and it was part of the catalyst that pushed me to end our relationship.

I muffle my laugh with my hand, trying not to let the past affect me today. "I thought we were waiting until Friday night to go crazy?"

"Semantics. What are you and Jack going to do today? I am going to pull the best friend card to steal you away for lunch, but I figured you'd want to spend time with him."

"He doesn't know it's my birthday," I admit, peeking at him in the dark to see if I've woken him yet, but Jack is still motionless next to me.

She gasps, and it's too early for her to be this dramatic. "I'm going to pretend you didn't just break one of the birthday rules."

Where the fuck do people keep coming up with these rules? Orgasm rules, birthday rules—what's next?

"It's your birthday?" Jack mumbles, stretching, and I guess he wasn't as asleep as I thought he was. "Happy birthday."

"I gotta go, but I'll meet you for lunch wherever you want. Love you," I say, hanging up as she protests it's my birthday, and I should be the one picking. I don't care where we go, I just want to make her happy. I plug the phone back on the charger, lying down next to Jack, and he doesn't hesitate to pull me closer. "It's early, you should go back to bed."

"Why didn't you say your birthday is today?"

I shrug, wrapping my arm over his warm chest. "I don't like to make a fuss about it. It's just another day of the year, but Macy has this obsession with birthdays." I didn't want to bring it up either, with all the chaos surrounding my situation with Bradley. The swelling has gone down on my eye, but the discoloration stands out.

He yawns, resting his cheek against the top of my head. "Maybe I want to make a fuss about it. Happy birthday."

"You don't have to do that," I whisper, closing my eyes

again. I wish I could've pretended for a few more moments we were together. I know Jack isn't ready, but is it selfish to want him to at least talk to me about it? I want to know if I have a fighting chance or if I need to let go of the delusion we might become more.

"Of course I do, Alondra. You mean the world to me, and you deserve a great day."

I might mean the world to him, but I still don't mean enough.

"I'm really okay with staying in," I reassure Jack as we walk in his house with our Chinese takeout. Jack wanted to go out to dinner after his practice finished, but it felt like too much, especially with my black eye still attracting all kinds of unwanted attention. I was on the receiving end of a lot of stares during my lunch with Macy.

Sometimes I catch Jack looking at it, and then he gets this look in his eyes before turning away and saying nothing.

Jack rolls his eyes. "You shouldn't be okay with staying in, darlin'. It's against the birthday rules."

"Oh my god, what is it with you people and these stupid unspoken rules?" I ask while laughing. My laughter doesn't last long, because it causes a tightening in my chest.

Jack shoots me a weird look. "What are you talking about?"

"Orgasm and birthday rules—none of these are actual things! I swear you and Macy have been making these up."

"We're just on a more superior level than you. Deal with it." He ruffles my hair, and I bat his hand away. "Don't worry, I'm sure the celebration Macy and Ellie are planning for Friday is going to be a blast."

"I tried telling them I didn't want to celebrate, but they didn't listen," I say, and Jack opens the door for me.

I'm not surprised that no one else is home, but I didn't realize how frequently they hang out at Twin City. I finish eating long before Jack does, even though he insisted on making my plate for me and serving me first. He's gone out of his way to make me feel special today, and I wish I could enjoy it, yet instead it feels like we're circling the drain.

As much as I want to believe what Jack and I are doing right now can continue, it feels insincere to continue going along with it when I know I feel more for him.

So I use my time wisely while Jack inhales an absurdly large portion of food, committing all his features to memory in case there comes a day when I won't have the chance to.

His chestnut hair is cut shorter on the sides and a little longer on top. It highlights his cheekbones and strong jaw. I'll never get over how annoyingly long and dark Jack's eyelashes are, making his blue eyes pop even more. Hell, and then there's his full lips I love to kiss and be kissed by.

They turn upward into a smirk, and I know I've been caught, but I don't care.

"If you're done ogling me, we can go watch a movie upstairs. It's your birthday, so you get to pick."

"Why wouldn't we watch it down here? No one's home," I retort, grabbing our trash to throw it away.

Jack smiles, his dimples becoming apparent while he lifts his shoulders in a shrug. "Because I have something to show you."

"If it's your dick, I'm not going to be impressed."

He laughs, radiating pure joy. "Good one. We both know you're impressed with my dick, but it's not the surprise." Jack offers me his hand, leading me upstairs.

Jack stops me before his room and lets go of my hand. "Stay here for a moment."

"You're acting weird," I say, and he winks at me, disappearing into his room. He cracks the door a minute later, angling his body so I can't see past him, and if I wasn't sure he was up to something before, I definitely am now. "Jack, what are you doing?" I ask, because I'm terrified of the warmth in my chest spreading everywhere.

I'm not just lying to myself when I pretend to be only his friend. I'm lying to Jack too.

"Close your eyes, please?" he requests, and I sigh, choosing to listen without argument for once. Jack still covers them with his hands, and I allow him to walk me into his room, trying not to laugh when his breath tickles my ear. "Are you ready?"

"Yes, I'm ready."

He drops his hands, sliding them around my torso, taking care to be mindful of my ribs. "Happy birthday, Alondra."

I blink, taking in the flickering candles placed throughout the room, and despite Jack telling me I could pick, *When Harry Met Sally* is queued up. I'm not sure I've ever told him it's one of my favorites. There's a bag of chocolate-covered pretzels and a small white pastry box sitting on top of a new fuzzy blanket.

"I told you it wasn't my dick, but I'm sure we can arrange a showing later if you want," Jack teases, pressing a short kiss to my cheek, rendering me speechless.

Oh my god.

He didn't . . . *how* did Jack have this all ready? I was with him most of the day, and he didn't even know it was my birthday until this morning?

I clear my throat, turning back to look at him. "You did this?" I ask, my voice cracking as all of the emotions I've been trying to suppress when it comes to Jack, threaten to overcome me. I've tried not to fall in love with him, but he makes it so damn easy to love him.

"Do you like it?" he asks, the candlelight flickering in his eyes. "I know you haven't had the easiest couple of days, so I thought a low-key night would be perfect."

I can't believe he did this for me, but I also shouldn't be

surprised. This is exactly the type of person Jack has proven himself to be, time and time again.

I don't know how he can't believe in love, because this is exactly what love is. It's taking the time to see and accept all the parts of someone. Love is showing up over and over again. Love is helping them be the best version of themselves, but I can't make Jack believe in it if he isn't ready to.

But this isn't fun anymore, and I can't pretend that it is.

Every kind gesture Jack has done for me has only poured gasoline on the slow burning flame of hope inside my chest, igniting to encase my whole body, and that's when I know.

This hurts, in a visceral sort of way, and I hate to even consider the idea we've danced too close to the sun, burned too bright, and now the only thing left is a black hole, ready to destroy anything in its path.

I can't change Jack until he's ready to face his demons, and because I love him, I shouldn't force it.

Tears flood my vision, and I wipe them away in time to see Jack's beautiful smile fade. "Alondra?"

I rest my hand on his chest, pushing him away, and his arms fall to his sides. The loss of warmth is immediate.

"I can't do this," I whisper, knowing it's better to end us now than to continue down this path. *Is there even an "us" to end if we're not in a relationship?*

"What?" he asks, tilting his head at me.

I inhale a shaky breath. "I love you, and it's okay that you can't say it back. I'm not expecting you to, but I can't do this anymore. It's too confusing for me."

His face pales. "Al, just give me t—"

"I want to. God, Jack, I want to so badly, but I can't," I say, wrapping my arms around myself. "I wish you could see yourself the way I see you because you're an incredible person. I know your dad did some fucked up things you don't talk about, but I don't think all the time in the world will make a difference until you face it. I have to deal with what happened during my relationship with Bradley, and what comes next for me, but I hope you're a part of it."

"Please, I—"

I cut him off. "Don't. This is hard enough." I take a hesitant step closer to Jack, leaning up to kiss his cheek, and I hope it's not goodbye. "I'm going to go, but thank you for all of this. You don't know what it means to me."

"*Alondra.*" For once, the way Jack says my name doesn't cause my heart to swell. It causes it to break.

"Bye, Jack." I walk past him, covering my mouth with my hand to prevent the sob from escaping. I flee down the stairs, faster than I should because it causes my ribs to burn.

Yet, the pain in my ribs is nothing compared to the splintering of my heart as I walk out the door.

The game of pretend is over.

CHAPTER 40

Alondra

EVERYONE HAS ASKED me what the hell happened between me and Jack, but I couldn't find the right words to explain it to them in a way to help them understand why I pushed Jack away when I hate the idea of letting him go. As much as I hate my decision, I don't think I was wrong.

I meant what I said about hoping Jack can be a part of whatever comes next for me. At the end of the day, I like being his friend, and if that's all we're meant to be, I'll find a way to get over my feelings, but the lines have become too blurred. I don't regret agreeing to his idea of friends with benefits, but it wasn't a good idea for me or my heart anymore.

My goal for this year was to find myself again. I've learned how to find the colors in the world, and to let myself feel them instead of throwing up walls with the people who care about me.

Jack has been tiptoeing around me all night, and I'm not oblivious to all our friends' stares, trying to figure out our new dynamic. I don't know how to make it better, though.

I've been taking it easy tonight, still nursing my first beer, unlike Macy, Ellie, and Sara who are taking full advantage of the chance to go all out. I think between the four of them, they'll have no problem doing enough shots to add up to twenty-two without me participating.

Ellie throws her arm over my shoulder, leaning in to drunkenly kiss my cheek. "I'm so glad we're roommates," she says, giggling.

"Me too," I say, leaning into her hug. She's been a really good friend to me this year.

I don't miss how, out of the corner of my eye, Jack says something to Dylan before standing up, pulling his coat on. "I'm gonna call it a night, but y'all have fun," he says, his smile not quite meeting his eyes when he says it, and I feel awful.

Sara boos him, pointing her thumb down. "Lame, it's not even eleven, and you're already ditching us?"

"Sorry, but I played a whole game tonight, and I'm wiped," he says, his blue eyes flitting to me for a moment. "Happy birthday, Al," he says, and I smile back at him, but it feels so fucking awkward.

"Thanks, Jack," I say, reaching for my bottle.

After he walks away, everyone's eyes land on me, and I feel like I'm about to be scolded like a child.

Coop sighs, dragging his hands over his face. "Look, I am the last person who wants to be involved in whatever the fuck was going on with you two, but that was painful," he says, and I take a drink of my beer.

"We're still friends," I point out, and Dylan shakes his head.

"Bullshit," Macy says, waving her finger in the air. "You love him."

I sputter because I'd prefer if she didn't announce it in front of his roommates, but it's a little late now. "Mace," I scold.

"What? Does anyone think I'm wrong?" she asks, her

challenge hanging in the air, but no one looks surprised. Am I really that transparent?

"It doesn't matter," I say, shaking my head as Sara laughs.

"Except it does, because you both looked like lovesick fools trying not to stare at the other all night. For fuck's sake, I was ready to shove your heads together and yell, *Kiss!* because I think it would solve everything," she says, and Nate laughs. "Or maybe I'd dare you to kiss Nate again to spur him into action."

"I'm game if you think it'd work," he chimes in, and I glare at him.

It's funny now to think about how jealous Jack was after it. I think it's fair to say it was arguably the reason why Jack asked to be friends with benefits.

"Even if you dare me, I'm not kissing anyone."

"Dylan, any words of wisdom?" Ellie asks, and he shrugs.

"Don't look at me. I told him to pull his head out of his ass after Halloween, and now it's almost February," Dylan says, and this is news to me. "Al, if it makes you feel better, you're the closest anyone's come to Jack changing his mind about love. Hell, I think he's in love with you, but he's not ready to admit it."

If anything, it only causes my head to spin out further.

Maybe Jack had the right idea leaving early.

Like Ellie can tell it's too much for me to hear, she tries to salvage the night. "Al, we don't have to talk about it anymore," she offers, but I need to clear my head. It's too much.

"Don't hate me, but I'm kind of tired," I say, and I feel bad because Macy was so excited, but I'm just not in the mood to celebrate after the last couple of weeks.

"No, please stay," Macy says, flashing her best puppy dog eyes, but at the pace they've been doing shots tonight, I don't think they're going to make it past midnight.

Ellie shoots Coop a look, and he flinches, putting his

hands up. "Sorry, maybe I shouldn't have said anything," he mumbles, and this time he yelps. "Ellie, stop kicking me, I'm apologizing," Coop says, and she huffs, shaking her head.

"Don't be so dramatic, I didn't even kick you that hard," she says, and I chuckle at their sibling dynamic.

"What Coop is trying and failing to say, is we just want you both to be happy, and obviously neither of you are very happy right now," Nate says, and I know they're right, but it doesn't mean I can fix anything.

"I know, but I can't make Jack change his mind," I say, admitting my hands are tied. "I'll let you know when I get home." I stand up before any of them can argue with me. I reach into my bag and pull out two twenties, setting them on the table. "Next round's on me to make up for it," I say, and Dylan shoves it back at me.

"You're not buying us drinks. I've got it," he says, and Sara looks excited.

"Fuck yeah, breaking out the black card. Let's get Vegas Bombs," she says, and everyone seems to cheer up enough for me to slip away unnoticed, ordering an Uber.

It's only after I've stepped into my apartment, I realize my whole body is still wired despite my emotional state feeling absolutely brutalized.

The one place I think I could actually try to figure my shit out is on the ice, and at least it's almost the middle of the night so no one will be there. Before I can overthink and talk myself out of going, I've changed out of my jeans and sparkly top Macy begged me to wear into leggings and one of Jack's sweatshirts I've refused to give back, then I'm on my way to the rink.

The parking lot is empty, much to my relief, and once I use my key to unlock the front door, I take a second to make sure the doors have locked behind me before going into the locker room to snag my skates from the shelf on top of Jack's stall, holding my breath the whole time.

Ten minutes later, I have the lights turned on, and I'm stepping on the ice, gliding across the smooth surface.

Being out here has held so many memories for me, but I suppose it's only fitting that most of my recent ones all include Jack. It's been the place of so many happy moments in my life, but it's bittersweet at the same time knowing it's the source of some deep-rooted pain. I've spent years trying to be good enough at skating to win my dad's love, then I gave it up for a boy who never deserved me.

I lose myself in the mindlessness of my warmups, skating until everything hurts a little less. I pop my first jump, and I can't explain it, but it's warranted. It feels like a well-deserved punishment to not skate at the same level I used to, and I push myself again and again, demanding more of my body despite the screaming in my side until everything hurts.

My knees ache as I miss my landing again, and I give myself a moment to catch my breath despite my leggings soaking in the moisture from the ice, overcome with emotion.

I feel the joy of loving something so much it physically hurts to know I went so long without it, and the devastating reminder of how easily I let Bradley control me. *How could I have ever quit skating?*

I love this more than anything in the whole fucking world.

It's overwhelming and all-consuming, and I'm crying as my chest cracks wide open. Tears roll down my cheeks, and my whole body shakes as I sob. I've been free of Bradley for a year, but I haven't fully broken free from the shackles of fear until now.

"Alondra!"

I lift my head upon hearing my name, but my vision is too blurry to make out who it is. At the last moment, I realize it's Jack, just as he appears in front of me, dropping to his knees, his hands touching me everywhere. "Hey, talk to me. What happened? What hurts?"

I don't know how to explain that I'm feeling *everything* for the first time in a long time, mourning the girl I was and the one I am now.

"Did you fall?" he asks, cupping my face in his warm hands, the rough feeling of his fingertips touching me gently. Jack is always so careful with how he touches me. "*Alondra baby,* you gotta tell me what happened or I can't fix it."

"I-I—" I can't make the words come out.

I haven't been living. I'm ashamed of how long I spent merely existing, and it's not enough for me.

He smooths my hair out of my face, wiping away my tears. "How can I make it better?" he whispers, the words a soft plea.

"I-I'm okay," I choke out through quiet sobs, trying to smile at him because there's not anything to fix. This is me feeling every damn part of myself I thought was broken, but like bruised ribs, time was all my bruised and battered heart needed to heal.

"You're okay?" he asks, and I nod, countering the tears still falling.

Jack pulls me into his arms, pressing the sweetest kiss to the side of my head, and I give myself a moment of selfishness letting him hold me before using everything in me to move away.

"Sorry," I stammer out, wiping my cheeks.

"Don't be," Jack says, watching me, and I'm afraid of what he sees. The two of us haven't been alone since my birthday, and now it's like we're struggling to fit in the boundaries I put around us.

"How did you know I'd be here?" I ask, pushing up into a standing position, and Jack follows my lead, shoving his hands in his pockets.

"I didn't," he says, a sad smile forming when his eyes drop to my torso. Shit, I'm wearing his sweatshirt. "I came to clear my head. Guess we had the same idea."

If it weren't so damn ironic, I'd laugh, but instead, my

cheeks flush. How embarrassing is it to think that he came here to find me when he actually just happened to be in the right place at the right time?

I brush the ice off my pants, the cold sinking into my bones, and I put space between us because it's so tempting to apologize and take back the feelings I vomited all over the place in the heat of the moment, but I know better.

My love isn't something to apologize for.

I said it, and I'm not ashamed of my feelings for him.

"I'll leave you to it," I say, skating away from the man I love toward the exit.

"Alondra," Jack calls, and I look over my shoulder, hating the tortured expression I see. "I'm sorry."

My smile is real, even if it breaks my heart in the process. "You don't need to apologize. It's okay."

"It's not okay. I hurt you, and I never wanted to be like them."

"You're not like them, and I hate that you would ever make the comparison. I'm a big girl who knew what I was getting myself into. I was hurting myself, and that's not your fault," I say, and Jack shakes his head.

"I miss you so fucking much it hurts. Does that mean I'm hurting myself too?" he asks, but I say nothing because I'm right here. I've been right here, but I'm not going to beg him to love me. "Everyone keeps telling me what an idiot I am for losing you, as if I don't already fucking know," Jack admits, and the sound of his voice echoes through the arena he commanded only a few hours ago.

"You haven't lost me, Jack," I whisper, hating the distance between us.

"I'm sorry I messed us up." He's not the one to blame. We were messed up from the start. "I . . ." Jack trails off, and I shake my head.

"You don't have to say anything," I say, and even if Jack isn't ready to believe in love, I can believe for us.

I don't want to leave, but I know I have to.

No one ever said love was easy.

I hesitate before knocking on the frame of the door, and my dad looks up at me from behind his desk. "Al, come in."

When I woke to his text this morning asking me to swing by, I was certain he was going to bust me for tearing up the ice last night, but I've decided I'm not even sure I care. What's one more lecture?

I got a happy birthday text from him the morning of my birthday, but nothing else until now.

"Hi, Dad," I say, stepping into his office.

"I wanted to talk to you about a couple things," he says, setting his playbook down on the desk. "You can sit if you want." Dad motions toward the empty chairs in front of me.

I take a seat, and I'm wondering if the football coach has finally talked to him about Bradley. Probably, or maybe he saw me in the stands last night.

"I talked to Jack," he starts off, and I try to keep my face composed. When did Jack talk to him? Was it before I imploded everything, or after? "I'm sorry, Alondra. I should never have said what I did. I overreacted to the two of you being friends. You're welcome to skate whenever the team isn't using the rink."

Holy shit.

Is Dad really apologizing to me? Am I dreaming?

"He shouldn't have said anything to you about it. I asked Jack not to," I say, hoping he'll give me a little more information as to when this conversation would've taken place.

Dad clears his throat, and I'm stunned because even an apology after all our arguments about Jack is more than I ever expected. Sure, a little frustrating he was willing to hear out Jack and not me, but I feel like this is a win I should take, regardless of where it came from. "No, he was right to. I know I haven't been very . . . accepting of your friendship, but I'm okay with it. I never asked how your trip to Texas went? Did you have a good time?" Dad asks, trying to start a normal conversation.

"Dad, why am I here? I know it can't only be to talk about Jack," I say, cutting to the chase because I don't want to think about that trip. It was incredible, but after last night, it just hurts a little too much to think about it.

He sighs and leans forward to rest his forearms on the table, looking uncomfortable. "Did you file a restraining order against your ex-boyfriend Bradley Smith? The one on the football team here?"

This is it. I'm finally going to tell them what really went on during my relationship with Bradley. "I did. He used to physically assault me while we were together and is now refusing to leave me alone, even though we're broken up." I'm shocked by how easily it comes out. My voice is strong and never wavers. I'm done hiding.

A short giggle escapes my lips, and I'm sure it makes me sound crazy.

His jaw drops, closes and then clenches as he struggles to find the words. "He what?" he chokes out, and I feel my stomach flip when I reach into my coat pocket, pulling my phone out to find the hidden folder where I saved everything. I slide it across his desk to let him look through them, holding my breath. With each photo he looks at, his eyes grow cloudier, and he doesn't make it through all of them before sliding the phone back. He's seen enough to know the protection order is warranted, but I still feel bad because they're hard to see.

"Why didn't you come to us for help?"

I leave the phone where it sits. "I didn't feel like I could come to you. I didn't feel like anyone cared about me except

Bradley. We accept the love we think we deserve, and I thought I deserved to be treated like that."

Dad's jaw drops once more at my admission. "Why do you think you deserved to be . . ." he falters, unable to say the ugly truth.

"Because I've never felt good enough. It didn't matter what I did, Dad. I felt like I could never measure up to your players and hockey. I was great at skating because I loved it, but all I really wanted was for you to be proud of me, and to love me." I pull my ponytail over my shoulder, playing with the ends. "I'm not saying it's your fault. I know I should have ended the relationship long before I did, but it felt like he loved me."

His eyebrows furrow, and he rubs his jaw, finally connecting the dots. "But you quit skating?"

"You weren't at that competition, but I wouldn't stop looking for you after you promised you'd show up. Bradley was there, and he wanted to know why it wasn't enough that I had him there. He told me it didn't matter how high I placed because you were never going to put me over hockey. I argued because you *promised*, Dad, then he hit me in the ribs so hard I couldn't breathe. I never would've been able to finish the long program, so I dropped out. He apologized so many times, and somehow managed to make me believe he hurt me because he loved me. Then came the threats that if I left, he'd hurt himself, and I didn't want to lose Bradley, but instead I lost the one thing that ever really mattered to me. You were so quick to believe it meant I didn't love skating."

He looks like he's going to be sick. I feel robotic telling him everything, and it's so different from all the other times I've had to explain, but I think maybe I needed to fall apart in order to put myself back together again.

"I'm so sorry, Alondra. I should have been there. I should have noticed," Dad says, and I twist my hands in my lap.

"I'm okay now. Jack's mom helped me realize maybe a

restraining order was the answer to getting Bradley to leave me alone." Except all it did was weaponize my love for Jack, giving Bradley something to lord over my head. Even after escaping him, he still found a way to control me.

"Jack knows?" he asks, and I'm slow to nod.

"He tried to be there for me when he could, and if it makes you feel better, he wanted to tell you. I wouldn't let him because I thought you'd be mad at me for staying as long as I did."

"No, I'm not mad at you at all, honey. It's not your fault," he says, reaching across the desk to offer me his hand, and it feels like a lifeline. I rest my hand in his, taking the path for forgiveness because I don't want to hold on to this anger anymore. It's exhausting, and I'd rather just let him be my dad. "I'm so sorry I ever made you feel like hockey was more important than you, but you're my daughter. You've always been the most important thing in my life, but I should have made sure you knew it. I should have been listening before, but I'm listening now."

It's kind of all I've ever wanted to hear from him.

CHAPTER 41

Jack

I'VE REPLAYED NEARLY every moment with Alondra since I met her, and I've come to the conclusion that the memory of her is not something I'm capable of living with when I can do something to fix what I've broken between us. At least, it's something I hope to fix if Coach B doesn't kill me for knocking on his hotel door first.

"Goddamnit, I'm coming," he swears as the chain rattles when he unhooks it. His hazel eyes, so similar to hers, widen when he sees me standing here. "Schultz?"

"I'm sorry, sir. I wanted to talk to you about something, and it couldn't wait," I blurt out, feeling my insides twist because I have such mixed feelings about this. He's my coach, and Al's his daughter, so as much as I don't want to have to explain why I'm asking for his okay, I still need to.

Coach is silent for a moment, crossing his arms over his chest. "Okay."

"I know it's a big ask, and I'll understand if you say no, but when we go to the airport in the morning, I want to fly to Texas to visit my father in prison. I have some unfinished business with him to clear up, and I'd like to take care of it sooner rather than later," I say, and his eyebrows knit together, causing my palms to sweat from how nervous I am. "I swear, I'll be on the first flight back to Minnesota, and at practice Monday morning."

"Does this have to do with my daughter at all?" he asks, and I hesitate before nodding.

"Respectfully, she's incredible, but Al dumped me because I can't admit I love her after everything I saw my father do to my mother growing up. She was right about everything she said, and I want to be the type of man she deserves. I promise my performance in games and practices won't change. Hockey is my entire life, but she means a lot to me."

Coach Brown sighs, and I hold my breath preparing for the worst. I just about shit my pants when I told him he was wrong banning Al from the skating rink. This might be worse, but it's worth it. *She's* worth it.

"You understand if you hurt her, there won't be a body for the police to find, right?"

My smile is from ear to ear. "The last thing I'd ever want to do is hurt her."

"Don't make me fucking regret this, Jack."

"You won't, I promise. Thank you, Coach," I say, feeling an immense wave of relief.

"Thank you for being there for her with Bradley. She told me everything, including how Bradley threatened to hurt you if she called the police to tell them he violated the restraining order."

He threatened her with me?

Holy shit.

It explains so much about why she refused to call them even after he violated the restraining order. Al was trying to protect me, and as much as it pisses me off, I understand where she was coming from because if the roles were reversed, I can't say I wouldn't do the same.

"Of course. She's my best friend. I'd do anything for her."

And I would, including facing deep scars that have haunted me for years.

"Son."

I flinch, even though he's on the other side of the glass, and I hate it. "I'm not your son," I say, my tone firm. He doesn't get to call me that when he's the reason I'm so fucked up.

My father's hair is almost completely gray, despite only being a year older than Momma, but the difference between them is stark. His skin appears more sunken in than I remember, but there's no mistaking his cold eyes that have haunted so many of my nightmares.

"Well, *Jack*, why are you here? It's been twelve years," he muses, staring at me with his dark eyes I'm so grateful I didn't inherit. I remember how they used to seem almost black when he'd get angry.

My heart is hammering fast in my chest, and I know it's been twelve years, but I never planned on seeing him again. I'm shocked Coach even approved this impromptu detour, but I don't have long before I need to be back at the airport for my flight to Minnesota. "I met a girl—the most incredible girl, but you fucked me up so badly I can't tell her I love her."

"Why are you blaming me for this?"

"Because I'm terrified to be like you. How could you treat Momma the way you did?" I ask, trying to rein my temper in.

His face shifts, and for a moment, he looks remorseful for what he's done. I guess he's had twelve years to repent for his crimes. "The fact you're afraid to be like me tells me you're nothing like me. I was a coward back then, and—"

I interrupt him, "And you're different now, right? I'm supposed to believe that after all this time you've changed."

"You don't have to believe me. I know you don't know

who I am. I've sent you some letters over the years, but I never heard back from you," Dad says, and all I can do is stare at his prison suit.

"Because the last time I saw you, you were threatening to kill the person I love most in the world. *'The apple doesn't fall far from the tree, Jack. You're going to be just like me.'* That's what you said to me before they took you away." My hands are shaking, and I hide them beneath the counter. "I ripped them all up. Every single one of them."

His nostrils flare, and it's satisfying to know I've gotten under his skin after the way he's been rotting underneath mine. "It's how it works—the cycle of abuse. My daddy hit me, and his hit him. Just be grateful I never struck you. Maybe you won't be like me, maybe you will."

"No, I just had to watch you beat my mom down and hold a gun to her head more times than I can count. How many black eyes and broken bones would've been enough for you, or was it really that big of a power trip for you to pick on someone half your size?" I ask, disgusted his excuse for how he treated us is the cycle of abuse. I know it's a real thing. It's why I've never wanted to tempt it.

Not until Alondra.

I'm here because I want to get past this instead of hiding from it.

"I'm a drunk, son. I didn't know what I was doing most of the time. But I guess knowing I held someone else's life in my hands was a power trip, as you put it," he admits, and it's in this moment I realize something.

I'm looking at my dad, and I don't see a single similarity between us.

I've been so afraid of turning into this person, but the only way it happens is if I let myself hide behind excuses like him. Momma made damn sure I learned to take accountability for my actions.

"I am not your son," I repeat, rising out of my chair to my

full height. "As far as I'm concerned, you died the day you went to prison. I'm nothing like you, and I'm never going to be."

The best part is, I actually believe it as I walk away from him for good.

I know the nightmares probably won't ever end, but facing the worst one is a really good first step.

When I get to the safety of the world outside, I feel like I can breathe again, but not entirely. I pull my phone out, ordering my Uber to the airport, and flip through a few pictures I have of me and Al together.

She makes me happy—even just the sight of her in a picture.

I want to talk to her and tell her what I just did. I want to tell Al how she's the best fucking part of my day and without her I feel like I've lost a part of myself.

I *want* to tell Alondra I love her. I think I've loved her for a while, but I was wrong to think I didn't believe in love. The truth I didn't want to admit was, I'm terrified of love, but if Alondra can get past her shit by admitting her feelings for me, then the least I can do is believe in myself by trusting my momma raised me right.

My Uber pulls up in the parking lot, and I climb in, feeling better than I have in weeks because I'm not running away anymore.

I'm running toward something.

I'm more tired than I think I've ever been, and of course, there's a fucking snowstorm threatening to ruin my chances of making it back to Alondra.

It's like the universe is betting against us before we can even start, and we sure as hell can't start anything if I can't make it to her to profess my love. I got the last flight in before the storm really kicked up, and I was glad to be leaving instead of one of the hundreds of people stranded in the airport waiting for their flight to be rescheduled.

Out of everything I've accomplished this weekend, I didn't think I'd get stuck in the home stretch.

"I'm glad you pulled your head out of your ass," Nate says, clapping my shoulder from the backseat.

"Me too. For fuck's sake, you both looked miserable without the other. It felt wrong to say Jack and Alondra instead of Jack *and* Alondra, ya know?" Dylan says, and Coop scoffs, leaning forward in his seat as he tries to see through the snow coming down.

"No, it sounds the same to me," Nate argues, and I chuckle at their ridiculousness.

"Y'all realize I only actually asked for one of you to come pick me up from the airport, right? I didn't need everyone to come," I say, but it's easier to focus on this than the fact I'm hopefully on my way to the girl of my dreams.

"No way were any of us missing this. It's like the end of an era—Jack Schultz is off the market and in love," Dylan says, and Coop shakes his head.

"Shut the fuck up before you scare him," Coop scolds, and I can't say I blame him for it.

"I'm good," I say, but I am worried about how this is going to go with Alondra. I already know how she feels, so it's not like I have to stress about whether she returns my feelings or not, but I wouldn't blame her if she slammed the door in my face before I have a chance to explain. I hope I'm not too late.

I've been careless with Alondra, and I shouldn't have been. It was stupid to ever suggest friends with benefits, but looking back, it seems silly to think the label mattered. Al and I were together more than we weren't, and it became natural to fall asleep next to her. I wash my sheets once a week, but I haven't washed the pillow she used when she slept at my place because it still held the faint scent of strawberry.

"Good," Coop says, and I'm on pins and needles the rest of the drive, mainly because I'm worried Coop might crash his truck trying to get me to Alondra, but we make it one piece.

I feel a little better after all of their encouragement, but I'm still shaking on my way up the stairs to the third floor, and it's not from the blowing whirls of snow.

I knock on the door, and Ellie opens it a few moments later, her face peeling into a wide smile. "Bout time," she says, jumping forward to hug me. "Oh shit, it's cold." She shivers, stepping back into the apartment. "Al, it's for you," Ellie calls out, and I shrug out of my coat and my sneakers.

Al steps into the hallway a moment later, freezing when she sees me. "Jack? What are you doing here?"

My heart skips a few beats, happy to be in the same room as her again, and I look her over, finally recognizing the quickening of my pulse for what it is: *love*.

I'm so fucking in love with her, I want to smack myself upside the head for not knowing sooner.

Her dark hair is piled on top of her head, and she's drowning in a giant sweater and sweatpants. I feel my smile grow when I spot her fuzzy penguin socks as Alondra stares at me, presumably waiting to hear why I'm here.

"Can we talk?" I ask, and she nods, motioning for me to follow her into her room.

"What was so important for you to show up in the middle of a snowstorm instead of calling?" she asks, taking a seat on her bed, while I shut her door behind me.

"I needed to see you," I say, trying to keep a short rein on my self-control because I don't want to just blurt, *I love you*.

"So you drove here in the snow?"

"Actually, Coop, Dylan, and Nate were picking me up from the airport. Almost didn't make it back because of the damn snow, but I was lucky enough to get on the last flight before they shut the airport down," I explain, dragging a hand through my hair. "The team flew back this morning, but I took a quick detour back home."

Alondra blinks, crossing her legs. "You flew to Texas for a few hours and then came back here? Why would you do that?"

"I saw my dad."

Her eyes widen as she inhales a short breath. "Jack—"

"Just let me finish, okay?" I ask, hoping I don't mess this up more than I already have, but I feel like it's pretty impossible to do at this point. She watches me, nodding slowly.

"Okay."

If only she agreed this easily all the time, but I think I'd hate that. I'm glad she knows she can argue with me.

"You were right. My dad fucked me up. I've been terrified of turning into him, and I thought the best way to prevent it from happening, meant doing everything possible to not put myself in a situation where I could. I thought if I didn't believe in love, it meant everything was fine—I wouldn't be in danger of being like him."

I sit on the bed, realizing now that I've started, I can't stop talking. "He tried to kill my momma, and it's why he's in prison. I called the police on him after watching him beat her for years. Sometimes he'd do it in front of me, claiming he was showing me what a real man was like. It wasn't that I didn't believe in love, but I was afraid of it."

Al moves closer to me, resting her hand on mine. I grip it tightly, grateful for her silent reassurance. "I realized if I was going to face my fear of love, I needed to look him in the eyes. I always believed in love, but I had to prove to myself I'm nothing like him, and now I know I'm not. He's a sorry excuse for a human, and Momma raised me better than that. I'm not his son, and I never will be. I'm a momma's boy through and through, and proud of it."

I drag a hand through my hair, and I'm sure it's sticking straight up by this point with how many times I've run my hands through it today alone. "I don't want to be afraid of love, and I wish it was this switch I could flick on, but I'm working on it because I *want* to be the type of man who deserves to be with you. Seeing you is the best part of my day —actually, *you* are the best part of my day every damn day.

"And I'm not saying this because I feel like I have to. Alondra, you make me want to be a better person. I want to open up to you like I never have with anyone else, and I want to find out what it means to be in a relationship with you. You're so strong and the most beautiful person." I smile at her as she sniffles and wipes her nose on the back of her sleeve. "I love you. I'm in love with you. I feel every type of love I could possibly have for you, and I want to know what it's like to be called yours."

"You love me?" she asks, her hazel eyes welling up with unshed tears. "Please don't say this if you don't mean it."

"How could I not mean it? Fuck, I've been trying to work up the courage to tell you how I've felt fo—" I'm cut off when Al presses her lips against mine.

She rests her forehead against mine, her thumb stroking back and forth where it rests on the back of my neck. "I love you too."

"Thank fucking god. I'm sorry I didn't pull my head out of my ass sooner."

Her smile is a ray of pure sunshine, bright enough to light up the darkest night, and I lean forward, unable to resist kissing her again.

"What do you say? Can I be yours?"

"Took you long enough, pretty boy."

CHAPTER 42

Alondra

I'M FLYING across the ice, all my worries far behind me.

Jack is practicing his wrist shot from all different angles around the goal, and I'm working on getting more speed and rotation in my layback spin. Jack is smiling at me the next time I glance in his direction.

"What are you looking at?" I call out, grinning at my boyfriend. God, it still feels insane to call him that.

Jack sweeps another quick shot into the back corner of the net. "My talented girlfriend."

Yeah, I could get used to hearing Jack call me his girlfriend.

I laugh, pushing my feet forward, stopping within reach of Jack. "Keep up the compliments, and I bet you'll make her really happy."

"Isn't it my goal to keep her happy? I'm pretty new at this whole relationship thing, but I'm positive that's how it works," he teases, winking at me after dropping his stick on the ice next to the pucks.

"Good thing you're a fast learner," I say as Jack slides his hands around my waist, pulling me close.

Things with Jack have been really great since he confessed his love last week. We were snowed in for a day with Ellie and Macy, but it gave us the perfect opportunity to clear all the space between us.

I came clean with Jack about Bradley's threat, only to learn my dad had already told him.

Since my conversation with my dad about Bradley, and how he's made me feel like I've had to earn his love, he's been making an effort with our relationship. It's slow going, but anything is better than the years we've spent holding each other at arm's length.

What Dad didn't tell his captain was how he went with me to the police station to tell the police the restraining order had been violated, and additional threats had been made against Jack.

Both my parents, Jack, and all of our friends have made sure I know that if Bradley comes near me, I'm supposed to call the police regardless of whatever threats he makes.

"She's worth it," Jack says, leaning to kiss me, and I feel light.

"I love you," I say after he pulls away, the words rolling off my tongue with ease.

"I love you too." He smiles, tugging on my ponytail, causing a laugh to rise from my chest. I can't help thinking how every moment leading to us being here was worth it. "Your spins are looking good," he compliments, and I'm overcome with happiness.

"They feel good. I've been toying with the idea of skating one of my old short programs just to see if I could even make it through half without falling flat on my ass," I say, but it sounds silly to admit out loud. "It's probably not even possible. I'm nowhere near where I was before quitting."

"Do it," Jack blurts out, and the spark in his eyes is the only reason I even consider it.

"Now? But I haven't—"

"No one is here but us. So what if you mess up in front of me? Falling on your ass will only leave a bruise I promise to kiss better later," Jack says, and if I didn't know better, I would guess part of him might be hoping I'll fall. "Please? I want to see it."

I hesitate, but then he flashes his goddamn puppy dog eyes at me, and I'm a goner. "You can't laugh if I fall."

"Promise," he says, darting away to gather his things from the ice, and I stretch more, trying to loosen up. I'm glad I wore a tight long sleeve today, shrugging out of the cropped black vest to drop it by our bags.

I queue up the song my program was set to, passing it to Jack, who's waiting eagerly on the side. I assume my starting position in the middle, letting muscle memory take over my movements.

I feel free, which is becoming a common theme these days, and I can't help the wide smile on my face after I land my double axel. I haven't let myself try for my triple, but my hope is that with more strength training and time, I'll land it again. My smile doesn't fade when I pop my triple toe, only rotating twice instead.

It's messier than it should be, and I'm glad my old coach can't see me skate now because he'd yell, *Again!* at me over and over.

I come to a stop, and I'm startled by the loud whistle that echoes off the walls as Dylan and Coop clap while Nate whistles again. Jack looks utterly fascinated, watching me with an expression I can only compare to awe.

"Where the fuck did you learn how to skate like that?" Dylan asks, as they all shuffle closer.

"Told you I knew how to skate," I say, skating toward them as Jack steps back on the ice. "You're early for morning skate," I say, grabbing Jack's sweatshirt from where he hung it over the boards, slipping it over my head.

Coop flashes me a quick smile. "We wanted to see what

you actually do while you're here," he explains, and Jack chuckles.

"And?" he asks as Nate starts lacing up his skates.

"Dylan bet you two would be making out on the ice."

Dylan's jaw drops, and he glares at Nate. "Dude, you're acting like you didn't agree with me. Way to throw me under the bus."

"Sorry to disappoint, but we actually skate out here," I say, as Jack wraps an arm around my back. If I thought he was bad about always having some point of physical contact with me before we were together, now that we're a couple, it's a soothing constant reminder he's there.

"Not everyone fucks in the living room with other people home," Jack retorts, planting a kiss on my cheek.

"Whatever," Dylan says, shrugging.

"I think I like seeing you in my clothes," Jack says, lowering his voice to whisper in my ear.

I smile, laughing as I twist to look at him. "Thought you liked me better out of them?"

"I feel like there's no right way to answer this, so I'm gonna plead the fifth," he says, mischief shining in his pretty blue eyes. "You were fantastic, Al."

I slip away from him, gliding backward. "It was hideous, but far more graceful than the way you all tear up the ice."

"I think I could figure skate if I really tried," Dylan chimes in, joining us on the ice, Coop and Nate following a moment later.

"I'd pay good money to see you fall flat on your face trying, Jones," Nate says, and I laugh, crossing my arms over my chest, smiling at my friends and my boyfriend.

"C'mon, are we going to stand around chit chatting, or are we going to skate?" I ask, and the sound of blades scraping across the glassy surface has never sounded more like music to my ears than now.

After everything it's taken to get to this point, I never would've thought I'd be calling these hockey players some of my closest friends, but I've never been more glad to be wrong.

Maybe some rules are meant to be broken after all.

Epilogue

MY CHEERS DROWN out with the rest of the crowd going wild after Jack sinks his second goal of the night in the upper corner of the net.

The energy here is electric with it being the North Regional Semi-Finals, and if they win tonight, they'll qualify for their second Frozen Four appearance in back-to-back years. The Wolves have worked hard this season, and many of them are having their best season yet, including Jack.

Sara is yelling, but I can't hear her over Macy, who is cupping her hands around her mouth to amplify the sound of her own yelling before she turns to look at me and Ellie. "Dude, I love hockey."

"Me too," I say, and Ellie hooks her arm with mine, wearing her brother's jersey, always his biggest supporter, no matter how boring she claims to find hockey. Sara's pink hair is a glowing beacon on the other side of her, making it easy for the guys to find us in the sea of purple and gray filling the seats.

Dad pulls Jack off the ice for a break, and I don't disagree with his decision considering we're up three to nothing. It doesn't make sense to leave Jack on the ice with hopefully their two biggest games of the season coming up in the following weeks.

Jack's been pushing himself hard getting ready for play-offs, desperate to prove to the team and coaching staff that they did the right thing putting their faith in him as team captain.

Meanwhile, I've been working my ass off in my classes and helping Jack study to help keep his GPA up.

Bradley tried to contest the protective order, not realizing I had been taking pictures of the abuse, and once the pictures were submitted as evidence, the judge granted the protective order to be upheld for five years. Dad encouraged me to notify Wilder University of the protective order, and Bradley ended up getting kicked off the football team.

Since then, he's laid low, and if we ever do cross paths on campus, the moment he sees me, he immediately turns in the other direction. It's a relief knowing he's obeying the restraining order, and I'm hopeful I'll never have to worry about him putting his hands on me again.

Jack is sitting on the bench, spraying water into his mouth, and I'm practically foaming at the mouth over how stupidly hot he is. Almost like he can feel me staring at him, he scans the crowd, smiling when his eyes find mine. I blow him a kiss, and his smile grows wider.

I'm so fucking in love with him.

The rest of the game flies by, and the second Jack appears after the game, I'm wrapping myself around him as he catches me without hesitation. "You played fucking amazing," I say, hugging him tight.

"Thanks, darlin'," he says, and the use of his favorite pet name for me causes me to shiver. I press my lips roughly against his, feeling Jack reciprocate a moment later.

"Do we have to go to Twin City to celebrate?" I mumble against his addictive mouth. I don't particularly want to put a pin in this until later.

"Fuck no."

I laugh as he kisses me again before setting me down on the ground after I unwind myself from around him. "I should probably say hi to my dad, he looked excited about the win," I say, as the rest of our friends walk up to us, unsurprised when we say we're skipping the celebration at the bars tonight.

My dad is busy with a post-game press conference with Coop, of all people, but I shoot him a quick text congratulating him on the win.

We started doing family dinners every other Wednesday, making an effort to mend the fractured relationship. My dad realized after a couple of weeks of Jack and I dating that we weren't something temporary, and he extended an ongoing invitation for Jack to join us.

A few weeks might not seem like much to some people, but for Jack, who had never committed to anyone before? It was an eternity, proving that he was serious about us being together.

After a little over two months, Macy and Ellie are planning our wedding.

I'm happy, Jack's happy, and he's still performing well in games. Actually scratch that—he's fucking amazing, but I don't think those are the same verbs my dad would use.

Ha, suck it, Dad. I'm *not* a distraction to him.

When we get to his truck, I'm tempted to pull Jack into the backseat, but it doesn't give us enough room to do everything I hope we're going to do tonight. I even sit on top of my hands while he drives because I don't trust myself to keep my hands off him.

It's never enough with him. I want his hands on me all the time, and I can't tell if I like to be under Jack's powerful body more than I like to be on top of him.

The minute we're at his house, all bets are off. Our mouths are clashing against each other, his tongue is in my mouth, and mine's in his. My hands are in his hair as Jack presses me against a wall, grinding against me.

Jack releases a soft moan, and it's music to my ears. "Jack," I breathe out, and he presses his mouth against mine again, silencing me.

Close, closer, *not close enough*.

Jack trails down, sucking on the soft skin at the base of my throat. "Jack, you've given Dylan too much shit for us to fuck in the living room." The idea is tempting, though.

"We could, and just not tell them." Jack pulls away, breathing heavily as he tucks some of my curls behind my ears. "Much better. I want to see your pretty face."

"Nope, it's a shared space, and I prefer your bed, or maybe even your shower?"

"Fuck, you're right. Upstairs it is."

He's like a man on a mission, lifting me up and causing me to giggle while he takes the stairs two at a time.

The second we cross the threshold into his room, I pull off his jersey, shedding the rest of my clothes as Jack does the same. My mouth waters at the sight of his muscular body, and Jack tilts his head at me, smirking. "Are you checking me out?"

There once was a time I would have rather died than admit I was checking him out, but now, I hold my head high. "One hundred percent, yes. If hockey doesn't work out for you, I think you should consider a career in modeling."

"Whatever. Business is my future if hockey doesn't work out." Yeah, right. Jack would suffocate in an office job. Hockey is most certainly in his future.

He moves closer to me, and I smile widely at him. "If that's what you want."

Jack leans down and kisses me sweetly, tangling his hand in my hair. He pulls on it, causing me to arch into him when I gasp, allowing Jack the opportunity to invade my mouth again.

I guide us back toward the bed, my hands holding onto his arms, feeling the corded muscles flex under my touch. Jack trails his hand down my body, and the rough pads of his fingertips scraping against my smooth skin is one of my favorite feelings.

"I love you, Alondra," Jack whispers against my lips. His beautiful ones are watching me with so much emotion I don't want to ever forget this moment.

I lift my hand up, cupping his cheek. "I love you too."

Jack smiles and curls his finger he's pushed inside me, inciting a short moan from me. "You are so beautiful."

His lips drop to my throat, and my eyes fall shut again, dragging my nails over his shoulders. "Are you really going to make me beg for it?" I ask, my breathing slowly growing heavier as Jack swirls his thumb over my clit. My hips jump up in reaction and Jack lets out a low laugh.

"Maybe."

"*Jack.*"

His fingers slip out of me, my desperation growing when he winks, sucking them clean. I lift myself up onto my elbows to watch Jack roll a condom on, fisting his hard length before settling between my thighs. "Fuck, I can't wait to make a mess out of you," he says, dragging the head of his cock over my core.

"Then stop talking and do it," I taunt, causing him to grin.

"Since you're asking so nicely."

Jack maintains eye contact the entire time he pushes himself into me before his mouth slants over mine, kissing me deeply. I arch into him, grabbing the sheets as he pulls back, keeping a controlled and steady pace.

A quiet groan leaves his lips, but he's not moving fast enough for my liking, and I lift my hips to meet his thrusts. He chuckles, slowing down even more. "You're impatient."

"Stop teasing me." I try to pull him closer, and Jack

presses his mouth to my throat. I hope it never stops feeling like this with him.

"You're so wet," he murmurs against my skin, thrusting again, harder this time.

"More, please," I beg, dragging my nails over his shoulders.

"Tell me what you want, Al."

"Faster, harder, I literally don't care as long as you please fuck me."

Except Jack does the exact opposite by pulling out, lying down next to me. I'm about to ask what the hell he's doing as he shoots a quick grin at me. "So ride me, and take what you want."

I move almost too quickly to kneel over his waist, and Jack laughs at my eagerness. "Fuck, yes," I say, aligning myself with him, moaning at the incredible full feeling in this position.

Jack keeps his hands on my hips to help me raise and lower myself repeatedly while I clutch his shoulders, over-whelmed by how right it feels to have his body pressed against mine as I work myself to the edge and him along with me.

My body shatters into a thousand stars when Jack's mouth takes my breast in his mouth while I rock my pelvis against his, the friction too much for me to handle, setting him off as well.

Jack grabs a water for me while I use the restroom, but we're quick to fall back in the bed. I lie on his chest as he wraps his arms around me, and I realize there's a new pendant added to his necklace I missed before.

"When did you add this?" I ask, tapping the second silver skate so he knows what I'm talking about.

"A few days ago, but I thought you would've noticed sooner," he says, and the sound of his heart beating under my ear threatens to lull me to sleep.

"What's it for?"

"Do you need to ask, darlin'? It's for you. To keep you close to my heart," Jack says, and a small gasp escapes me as I lift my head to look at him.

"I don't know what to say, Jack," I whisper, trying not to ruin the moment by crying.

"You don't have to say anything at all. Just you being here is enough for me," he says sweetly, and I press a short kiss to his chest before resting my cheek down again. Jack combs his fingers through the ends of my hair, and I hope I make him feel a fraction as happy as he makes me.

"I didn't ever think it could be like this—being in a relationship and with someone you love," Jack admits a minute later while I breathe in the intoxicating scent of cinnamon.

It's crazy to think that it's only been six months since I met him. Now I can't imagine what everything would be like without him. I close my eyes, relishing how close I feel to Jack right now. "I didn't think it was possible to let myself feel safe with another person like I do with you. I trust you."

Without a doubt, this is what love is supposed to feel like.

Jack's arms tighten around me before he kisses the top of my head with so much tenderness, and I feel like I'm home.

Acknowledgments

First and foremost, if you or a loved one are experiencing abuse in any form, please visit https://www.thehotline.org/ or reach out to the national hotline for help: *1-800-799-7233*.

When I initially wrote *Cold As Ice* in 2022, all I knew was I wanted these characters to be different from anything I'd written before, and of course, a happy ending. When I went back to rewrite the story this year, I knew I wanted it to still hold pieces of the original work, but I wanted the focus to be a healing journey for two lost souls who deserved to believe in themselves, to learn how to trust another person with the fragile pieces of their heart, and to find their beautiful (and well-deserved) happy ending.

Jack and Alondra are imperfect characters who've both experienced trauma at the hands of people they believed loved them, and struggled with finding the path to move forward. Out of all of my books published so far, their story is the one I might be most proud of because I think everyone deserves to find their happy ending, and I especially believe in Jack and Alondra's.

If you can relate to any of the themes in this story, I hope you know how strong you are. Love can be complicated and messy, but like Alondra, I believe the right person is out there for everyone. If you haven't found them already, please know they're out there somewhere waiting to love you too.

This isn't the last time you've seen Jack and Alondra, but it won't be until November 2026 when Book 2 in the *Wilder Wolves* series will be out. I can say it will focus on a grumpy goalie and a girl whose sunshine has been dimmed by her on-again-off-again boyfriend that doesn't deserve her.

The first time I proposed the idea of writing and releasing three books in a year, my friends looked at me like I was insane. Now, nearly a year later, they're still looking at me like I'm insane, and begging me to never do it to myself again while I'm also working full time as a teacher.

I significantly underestimated how much work it would be, but if you're reading this, then I somehow pulled it off.

However, despite their insistence on never doing three releases in a year again, this book wouldn't exist without my friends and all of their love and support.

Nicole, thank you for being the best friend I could've asked for. I'll forever be grateful to know you, and have such a wonderful person in my life.

Brianna, I can't thank you enough for all of the late night calls and messages you've answered, and for giving me a place to rest my brain when I needed it the most. I'm so lucky to have a friend worth flying across the country for.

Natalie, thank you for being the biggest cheerleader for Jack and Alondra's story, and for loving every version of them. I'll never be able to thank you enough for all of the support you've shown me. You're an actual fairy godmother doing your very best to help my dreams come true.

Amanda, I can't believe this is our FIFTH book together! You are such an incredible friend, and have been such a huge supporter of my writing since *Little Do You Know*. Thank you for taking a chance on me, and sticking with me every step of the way.

I'm so lucky to work with a wonderful editor, Hannah, whose suggestions helped make *Cold As Ice* look as pretty on the inside as it does on the outside!!! I am so grateful for your kindness and everything I've learned from you to help better myself as a writer. I can't wait for many more books together!!!

Bruna, I know I'm always professing my love for you and the incredible art you create, but you are a DREAM to work with! Thank you for helping me bring Jack and Alondra to life for this cover. I have been in awe from the first draft.

Thank you to the amazing team at Books and Moods for taking Bruna's art and making it the most beautiful cover I've ever seen. Somehow, you always manage to outdo yourselves.

The biggest thank you to Ellie at Lovenotes PR for handling the ARC distribution of *Cold As Ice* for me! It was such a weight off my shoulders, and I know I'm in the best hands with you!

Carley and Jess, my favorite smut peddlers at *Under The Cover*, thank you for everything! The kindness you've shown me means more than you could ever know. I absolutely love the safe space you have created for the romance community, and I will never forget seeing my books on your shelves for the first time. Thank you for all that you do!

Lastly, from the bottom of my heart, the biggest thank you to all of the readers who have taken a chance on me and my books. None of this would be possible without your support.